THE PRINCIPAL

BENJAMIN SIEGEL

THE PRINCIPAL

HARCOURT, BRACE & WORLD, INC., NEW YORK

To William R. Honest

THE PRINCIPAL

CHAPTER ONE

The Superintendent of Schools, Eberly, a big man who must once have been bigger the way his jacket hung loosely, a bald man with a square-tipped nose, introduced Robert Evans to the members of the School Board of Central District Number One of Pine Hills, New York. Robert then sat down at the end of the long table, forcing his hands to remain still in his lap although his chin had begun to itch, making himself look relaxed and confident while remembering not to seem too confident, or too relaxed.

Farmer, the Chairman of the Board, who was elderly, spare, in an out-of-fashion double-breasted suit, opened the folder in front of him as the others did the same with theirs. "I assume we're all familiar with Mr. Evans' résumé—"

The one woman present, whose name was Lobrige, stared at Robert. She had large teeth and kept forgetting to cover them with her upper lip, to which clung an abortive mustache. She wore the kind of overlarge, heavy glasses that on some television actresses look piquant. They kept sliding down her nose and did not look piquant. He was a man, Robert thought, at whom beautiful women never stared. It hit him then: Why was he bothering, this new opportunity. For whom?

Farmer said without looking up, "For the past five years you have been Principal of the high school in New Canniston?"

"Yes."

Vincent, a small man with the peppery manner of some small men, said, "New Canniston. That's what they call a depressed area, isn't it?"

"Yes."

He watched as they studied his professional life. The minutiae

3

of schools and degrees and positions. Background. Except that the important things could not be in there.

There had been a railroad terminal in New Canniston but the trains had stopped running long ago. The more men who were out of work, the more dingy the bars that erupted for their solace. These were bars that never heard a request for a martini. But even a shot of bar rye costs more than a loaf of bread. These were the fathers, hands in pockets, coat collars up, faces averted as he passed. The fathers of the students to whom he was committed to reveal the glories of plane geometry, balanced sentences, the life cycle of the fruit fly, the conquests of Caesar. The pall over the town reached into the suburbs, into the homes of the professional and business people, none of whom had ever worked on a train in his life.

It reached into his home, and his wife never complained. A protesting wife might have induced defensive self-justification. A wife always sweetly resigned leaves no way out for a man but self-torture. He wanted her to understand and so forgive, but she would recognize no fault. He wanted to explain, but she took for granted the correctness of his decisions.

They subscribed to the New York Sunday *Times* and she always turned first to the theater section. And next, to the fashions. So on vacations they would go to New York and see three, four plays in a row, and she would wear the clothes that were out of place in New Canniston, and there would be a honeymoon feeling for a while, but the city was not, for her, a place only to visit. When he took her home she went meekly, uncomplaining, with a dullness as if a tap had been closed on vital juices.

She had always been frail, with a luminous attractiveness; before they were married she had been a model. She could bear no children, a deficiency she regarded with the culpability of an Oriental wife. And there was no way to reach her with the assurance that this made her no less valuable to him. She died without fuss, almost apologetically, when he was away from home, of what was called a heart attack but which he knew to be a simple case of exile.

4

For three days he was aware of a vast emptiness that exhausted him of all feeling. Then guilt burst. Not having been able to get her to listen, alive, he pleaded to her now that she was dead. At night, alone in his house, he told his wife how it was.

He was a product of the depression era in the United States, leaving high school at a time when graduates of universities vied for jobs as dishwashers. His father was able to keep the family in food and the roof repaired; but Robert was an extra mouth and could find no work, so it seemed logical that he leave. He went to New York City and watched men sell apples in the streets. He found work, degrading and poorly paid. In some impossible way he got together enough money for the first semester at college and alternated study and work and lived through it, as had others. And then, so many years later, in the midst of prosperity in the rest of the country, a vacuum at the bottom of a whirlpool, there was New Canniston.

These kids, he told his wife, had to be shown that the apathy of their town could be counteracted for them by books and formulas and ideas. And he, who had been through this, was the one to show them; he knew from remembrance the heavy dull resentment these students bore.

Not that there was anything dedicated, or inspired, or noble about what he did. He liked working in New Canniston. He had all the weaknesses of any man, and more than some, and he cashed his checks thankfully and spent the money and waited for the next payment. It was not, he told her, a mission with him.

His wife, now dead, was not more vocal than in life about her bitterness that her husband chose to make their home in a miserable town immoderately far from the theaters and auditoriums and department stores and museums of the city.

Lobrige, her voice sounding faintly accusing, said, "You're rather young, aren't you?"

"I'm forty-one."

"I leave to the other members of this Board questions concerning your professional qualifications for the opening we need to fill, the replacement for our retiring high-school principal, John Loomis. But I think you should know that he leaves a rather large pair of shoes."

"Shoes?"

"For somebody to fill," she said with asperity. "For thirty years Johnny has been a credit to this community. He is a revered person—" Her voice began to rise in hostility, as if Robert were contradicting her.

Vaguely alarmed, he said, "I don't know him. I am sure—"

"He was loved! By everyone!" She had half risen. Now she sat back and said in an exhausted voice, "I doubt that we shall ever find anyone to take his place."

They were looking at their folders again. All except Casella, a sardonic-looking man interested in his fingernails.

The Chairman, Farmer, said, "Perhaps we might start with a fill-in in your own words, Mr. Evans."

Whose words, Robert thought, does he think he's been reading?

Lobrige was watching him and frowning.

"Where would you like me to start?" Robert asked.

"Suppose," said Farmer, "you tell us how you got to New Canniston in the first place."

"All right. I'll go back a bit before that. I had my Master's and was teaching, when the army indicated an interest in me—" The Superintendent in New Canniston had once taken his wife to a baseball game because she had, as he said, "indicated an interest."

"What did you do in the service?" the Superintendent, Eberly, asked.

Combat backgrounds always impressed boards. Eberly and he had talked about the army on his first, private interview. Eberly was bringing it up now because he wanted to sell Robert. Why him? There were three or four good men looking for this job.

"I was in the Tenth Mountain Division in Italy. I was an infantry lieutenant."

"You don't look old enough," said Lobrige, pushing back her glasses.

Robert began to tell her his age, and remembered he already had.

"After the war I was working at Columbia toward a doctorate in intergroup relations. In order for me to do that, my wife had to work. She wasn't very well and had to stop. So I accepted an offer from New Canniston to teach at the junior high there and interne for the junior high principalship. I was principal of the junior high for two years when the opening came at the high school."

"Is that when the school started its evaluation program?" Eberly asked.

"I can't take the credit for that. The evaluation had been in progress under the former principal. We did, however, become accredited while I was principal."

Farmer turned a sheet and checked back. "Let's see now. To get it real clear. For the past five years you have been principal of the high school in New Canniston, New York?"

"Yes."

Eberly said, "And during that period the school was evaluated and subsequently accredited by the Middle States Association?"

"Yes."

That was it, then. His one big asset. The reason he was being considered when there were good solid men with large families looking for this job. Eberly wanted his high school accredited. Robert, having been through the process, was an expert.

Vincent, the little man who even seated seemed to bustle, pushed his papers together and took off his glasses and looked at Robert like a district attorney at last ready for the cross-examination. Robert cleared his throat.

"Why do you want this position, Mr. Evans? Why do you want to leave New Canniston?"

"We can be honest here," Farmer said. "We're most of us businessmen. And Vince, he understands the technical end, used to be in education himself. What I mean to say is, we're offering something good for a good man. We're prepared to pay our new principal two thousand a year more than what New Canniston pays. Plus a real bright future."

"The way I see it," Vincent said, "Mr. Evans had a pretty bright future where he was. Would have been in line for super-intendent of schools, wouldn't you, Mr. Evans, given a few more years?"

"I might have had a chance at it."

Farmer said, "Let's not talk ourselves down, Vince. We're the fastest growing county within a radius of fifty miles of New York City. We've got this one big new high school in our district and a projection of three more needed by 1964. There's opportunity here, let's not play that down."

Casella, lines on his thin face as if he were perpetually suck-ing on something at once sweet and sour, spoke for the first time. "I'd like to hear from Mr. Evans. I don't believe a man makes a big change just for a couple of thousand more a year."

Why. All the wisps of unrecognized pressures to send you here instead of there, the pain-prodding that sends a lab-oratory animal into this path instead of that . . .

Robert said, "You have to know the kind of place New Can-niston is. The district draws from a wide area. Farm country, as well as what was the railroad-centered community. A number of terminal students, cases where everyone in the family has to scratch for a dollar for food on the table. Some of the men there have been out of work for years—"

"But the school was accredited," Eberly said.

"As you know, accreditation takes into account the phi-losophy and objectives of the school. Although we increased the academic program considerably, there is a theory held there that a boy hanging around until he's legally old enough to milk cows for his father should not, necessarily, be crammed full of advanced math—"

"Dr. Thorndike," Eberly said modestly before his school board. "His theory of identical elements."

"Sure," Vincent said. "Johnny Loomis believed in that, didn't he, Bill?" As Farmer nodded absently, Vincent went on, "Johnny used to say that the job of the school was to teach

8

those subjects related to the work kids would be doing after they were out of school. Otherwise, you're just wasting their time."

"I'm going to miss Johnny Loomis," Farmer said. "I sure know the students will."

"He was a great principal," Vincent said.

"Fine man," said Eberly.

"The best," said Lobrige, staring at Robert.

"We should have had Johnny in at this meeting," Vincent said. "He could have had some things to ask Evans here."

"He's retired," Farmer said. "Thirty years is enough. I didn't want to bother him."

Casella said, "Mr. Evans, you believe in that? You don't teach a kid anything he can't use in his work?"

These were honest citizens, elected by their peers and serving without pay, concerned with providing for their own and their neighbors' children the best schooling they could. Their position was one of great authority and responsibility. They had the power to decide what was taught, and by whom, and how. They were buried under mountains of new materials and were tickled by leached ideas from which they extracted the phrases that stood for nothing. They were no worse than the professionals. The trick was to give them back their own, to use the jargon trippingly, to make the series of secrct signs that passed for knowledge and committed one to nothing.

But Robert said, "No. I don't believe in that."

"Oh?" said Casella, interested.

"Oh?" said Vincent, half affronted.

"Oh," Farmer said, confused. "Johnny Loomis—"

"Perhaps," Eberly said, "Mr. Evans could explain what he means."

"Yes," Robert said. "I have a number of reasons why I do not feel we should teach only 'useful' subjects. Certainly the expenditure of time impressing algebraic concepts into the mind of a boy who is going to spend the rest of his life selling shirts and ties seems pretty silly. Except, who is to say where and at what he shall spend the rest of his life? This notion of identical ele-

9

ments has always seemed to me to presuppose a kind of rigidity of caste, 'your father is a shoemaker, you're going to be a shoemaker' kind of thinking. Shall we not teach foreign languages unless we have some guarantee that those learning them intend to go into foreign trade, or foreign service? Except, didn't I read lately about certain of our ambassadors not being able to speak the language of the country they're assigned to? The point is, I think learning is something like showering a child with sparks, without our knowing where or when or if at all one of them might not set something afire. Students have to be exposed to as much knowledge as we can give them without our even presuming to understand the physiology or the motivation of the learning process."

"That doesn't sound very practical to me," Farmer said. "You have to have objectives. You have to have a sound curriculum."

"I don't disagree with that."

He sensed a wariness of him now that was not quite disapproval. Except for Casella, who, surprisingly, was grinning. He had square, tobacco-stained teeth.

Vincent straightened his papers nervously. "Getting back to your reasons for wanting to leave New Canniston. From what you say of the place, it sounds as if it would be an area for a good administrator to grab hold and take some pride."

"You're right, Mr. Vincent. I took some pride."

He considered telling Vincent of Joey Brewster, the boy who was borderline retardation—the way they had built a program around him, filling in the reading gaps, the breakfasts he never got at home, the talent buried so deep beneath arbitrary IQ testing it would never have been discovered except for the concern of Mr. Evans, the Principal, and a couple of teachers whose intuition had withstood the prescribed education courses.

"Did you ever hear of a student with an initial seventy-five Stanford-Binet getting a scholarship to New York University? I think I grabbed hold, Mr. Vincent."

"What was it then, Mr. Evans? You became unhappy there, didn't you?"

"There comes a time, Mr. Vincent, when you feel you've gone so far at something, and you're never going to get any further. That's what I feel about New Canniston. For me. I can maintain what I have done, and maybe improve it a little, but not significantly. It's time for another man. And since Mr. Farmer mentions business frankness, there isn't any more to be squeezed out of the district in the way of financial support. There just isn't the money for new programming, for expansion, for experimentation. You can't change a textbook because the old ones are still in pretty good condition, even though the content has become useless. For me, professionally, Mr. Vincent, it's just time to move."

"You take Johnny Loomis," Farmer said. "I mean, we're not hoping to find another Loomis, things don't work out that way, and I guess there are things Johnny did we wouldn't necessarily want to go on with, but the kids loved him and so did their parents, he had students whose fathers and mothers went through the school under him, he was kind of an institution in this town."

"Yes?" Robert said.

"Take one of his activities, for example. Just to get your opinion. Many's the time you'd see Johnny in the cafeteria with his sleeves rolled up, dishing out lunches to the kids. Now you tell me, Mr. Evans, would you ever do a thing like that?"

Only one possible answer. Why sure, Mr. Farmer, if it wasn't beneath good old Johnny Loomis to help out like that, why of course I would, too.

He made a pretense of thought. Eberly was looking at him with hope and Lobrige with disdain and Casella with amusement. Vincent was looking down, framing his next question. Robert thought: All they're really worried about is how popular will their choice be, carrying the burden of following the great Loomis. If they select someone people will dislike, the onus will be theirs. So tell them how eagerly you will dish out the soup and sandwiches, reassure them. And don't be petulant, Evans, because your views on education, so painfully and manfully conceived, are not the main issue here.

11

Casella said, prodding him with a smile, "I suppose you'd hand out a muffin if you had to, wouldn't you, Mr. Evans?"

And Robert answered shortly, feeling he had already blown the interview, too "young" for Lobrige and not humble enough for Farmer and at odds with Vincent's secondhand impressions of educational philosophy, "I doubt that I would. I wouldn't consider handing out lunches the function of the Principal unless, of course, there were some emergency."

"Good for you," Casella said, ignoring Lobrige's glare. "Twelve five is a little high for a cafeteria worker."

"When Johnny did that," Lobrige said coldly, "he was just showing what a warm human being he was, close to the kids and—"

"Could we get back to this interview?" said the Chairman. "Vincent—"

Vincent nodded. "There are other educational areas in which I would like Mr. Evans' opinion. Do you believe in a comprehensive high school, and what are your notions about programming for gifted children?"

"Enrichment," said Farmer. "What about enrichment?"

What a nasty word. Robert kept himself from grimacing. Cloying, sticky, sickening.

"What's your opinion?" Vincent asked.

If you really would like to know, Robert said grimly to himself, the first thing I would do in my school is outlaw all the words, all these facile, staling, substitutes-for-thinking words.

He said aloud, "Yes, a comprehensive high school because I think this suits us, suits Americans. A school to take in the bright and the less bright, and the less than less bright. A widening of the gap between the most and least able, while at the same time increasing the accomplishments of the least able. And, frankly, I'm not terribly concerned about techniques. The ones that work in the classroom are the ones I favor."

"Go on, Vince," said Casella. "Ask him another. Like, you know, about Rickover, something like that."

Vincent said, almost apologetically, "What we're trying to find out is your educational beliefs—"

"Of course. You have to know that. Well, I do not agree with the Admiral that a school should be run like a race with the Russians—"

"What about the Russians?" Farmer said. "You think they're ahead of us?"

"In what?"

"That's what I'm asking you."

"I think their attitude toward their teachers might be superior to ours."

"They've got better teachers?"

"They respect teachers."

"Our pay scale's—"

"I meant that our best students go into law, engineering, medicine. Not teaching. It's not really an honored profession. A curriculum is meaningless, no administrator can get anywhere, without decent people in the classroom."

"That's true enough," Eberly said smoothly, having been anxiously awaiting an opinion of Robert's he could support.

Lobrige said, "How long is it since your wife died, Mr. Evans?"

He wanted to grin at her to show how unaffected he was. He wanted to say something sick and shocking. He wanted to say that it was none of her damn business.

She said, "You have no children?"

There were more questions coming at once so he did not have to answer. Casella rapped on the table with his ring. Farmer scowled at him, but there was silence.

Casella said, "There's one thing I want to know. If you were principal and you wanted to fire a teacher because you thought he was a lousy teacher, and the Board here wanted to keep that teacher on because maybe they knew his family or something and they asked you to reconsider, what would you do?"

Robert suddenly felt tired. He knew how to phrase an answer to this that would take no single strong position and offend no one. Then he thought to hell with it because he was sick of his own profession, which seemed no longer a way of directing the educating of children but had become an infinitely complicated

13

game of public relations, the juggling of nonsense syllables in magic ritual, the pandering to (well-meaning) stupidity.

He said that he would fire that teacher. Then, to underscore it, like a man who, accidentally breaking one of his wife's treasured dishes, continues in a fury of guilt to smash another, "I believe a principal must be in complete charge of his school."

CHAPTER TWO

After the meeting they were all cordial, shaking Robert's hand and thanking him for coming down, even Lobrige who pushed her glasses back to look at him squarely and say his views had been most interesting. Eberly said Robert could expect to hear from him within two weeks—that would make it around the seventeenth of July; by then the Board would have decided. As Robert knew, there were two men still to be interviewed. Robert said good-by and left, keeping his shoulders straight to show that the beating had not affected him at all.

He had intended to spend the night at a motel—this was Friday—and have the weekend in New York City before returning to New Canniston. Instead, he decided now to take the three-hour drive back to his home. He walked down to the parking lot at the foot of the hill below the building in which the Board of Education maintained its offices. The three-year-old Plymouth gave off a familiar smell as he opened the door, the steering wheel under his fingers had no unexpected contour; with his right hand he felt for the section of seat where the cover was wearing thin. Because this automobile was uniquely and comfortably his, it fed his desire to leave this place of his interrogation, to be among his own, to forget what in retrospect was the humiliation of examination. He felt he had answered questions like one of his own students attempting to conceal unsureness with arrogance. He had given offense when it would have been so simple to mollify. He had disagreed when disagreement was not only imprudent but not even truly felt. The Principal dishing out food. So what? They were mistaken in thinking Loomis had not been present at the interview.

He drove into a gas station and had the tank filled and the oil checked and asked the attendant to examine the right front tire, which Robert suspected of having a slow leak. He drove onto the Thruway and settled back for the long ride. There was little traffic, and he moved into the right-hand lane and watched the needle climb to sixty-five and kept it there. There was a sort of suspended animation in this kind of driving, and for a while loneliness was a near memory like opiated pain. He was driving from nothing to nowhere, and if, as the philosophers said, the journey was more important than the point of departure or the destination, where now were your insights, Evans, your truths, your understanding? He drove like an infant, swaddling clothes around his spirit.

After an hour he stopped at a service area for coffee. There were a few truck drivers at the counter, and a young couple with a child, and two middle-aged women. Robert envied them all. They had purpose. Robert was a hamster on an exercise wheel. He drank his coffee and continued his journey.

He reached his house and went to bed. He slept for ten hours —for Robert a long, self-indulgent time. He got up without liking himself and, unwilling to face the emptiness of his house, went out to a diner for breakfast. There was a time when Saturdays had been bright days in New Canniston, for home owners to run down to the store for a can of paint, for kids to line up at the movies, for housewives to linger over breakfast, and for young people to plan the evening to come. But the town around him moved on rag-swathed feet.

It was an atmosphere from which each day, secretly and without remorse, a little oxygen was removed, so small an amount that no one noticed his neighbor's increasing shortness of breath and dullness of eye. Some died sooner than others, as Robert's wife had died.

Pine Hills had been the only opening Robert had applied for—a feeler, a toss of a coin. But now he was choking. He examined the listing of placement opportunities that had been sent to him from Albany, and he wrote letters. He was asked to come for an interview to a school district in Massachusetts. By now the seventeenth had come and gone. Before writing for an appointment, he called Eberly.

16

The Superintendent said, "Evans? Good to hear from you."

"I wanted to check, not having heard from you. There's another opening, I have to decide."

"We haven't come to a decision yet. Give us another week, can you?"

"I thought it was dead."

"It's close. One other applicant. One more week? Don't do anything."

Robert roamed the school restlessly to see what he had wrought. Would this youngster be as bright and informed without Mr. Evans, would he have found the books anyway, would he have withstood inept teaching? Would this dull-normal have been no worse off, and this average student no less than the mean? I have nothing, he thought, to balance her loss. I leave no mark here. He examined the follow-up charts on the latest graduating class. He had a boy at Dartmouth, and four others in Eastern schools. (The sign of accomplishment: how many did you get into the ivy league?) Seven at colleges in the Midwest, one of whom had made the Dean's List. Fourteen at State Teachers. Joey Brewster had a B-minus average at New York University. One boy was managing a quartet that had a best-selling record. None in the Reformatory. The one discovered pregnant senior was married.

Be proud, he thought.

There was a passion in him to walk. One afternoon when he arrived home, he found a message from the woman who came in to clean. Mr. Ebby had called and said he had good news.

For a time there was a flurry in New Canniston, a gratifying effort to hold on to their principal. At least there was an editorial in the local paper listing his accomplishments and wanting to know why his salary could not be raised to match the out-of-town offer. It did not last very long, no longer than the edition of the paper. No one seriously considered offering Robert more money. He was glad.

He walked the corridors of the school and the streets of the town. You can live in a house for a long time and be away only for a day or two to come back and see it as if for the first time. The comfortable chair with the tear in the upholstery that never seemed important and suddenly it's a disgrace. The windowsill in the bathroom that had flaked itself free of paint—how could you live that way?

He walked along the river. Every town ought to have a river. Even if it did not have stretches of well-tended lawn down to the banks with a punt on the water. Here were the backs of garages with small mountains of punctured oilcans and pieces of discarded transmissions. Beneath the gummy surface the water flowed. Having been someplace better, going someplace better. He had delivered five commencement speeches of exhortation and hope and promise. Now he delivered one to himself.

It was time to meet Eberly. Robert parked in the lot in Pine Hills and walked up the hill to the offices of the Board.

The last time, he had been just one more visitor to see the Superintendent. Now, waiting as a secretary notified Eberly on the intercom, Robert was aware of a this-is-he appraisal. This main office had a no-nonsense functionalism, the same atmosphere apparent in the school buildings of the district. Metal files, metal desks, metal lamps, crowded together with the minimum of aisle space, an air of activity that could have been the result of understaffing or underproductiveness as much as work load.

Eberly came to the door of his office. "Robert! Come in, come in."

He stood until Robert was seated, and then the Superintendent sat behind his desk, beaming, making obvious and delightful the difference between applicant and addition to his staff. Robert, while wryly apart, still felt the warmth pleasurably.

"May I say at once how pleased I am to have you here. I hope our association proves, as I am sure it will, of great benefit to Central One and to yourself. Above all, Robert, remember I am here to help. Not to dictate, you understand, but to give you the benefit of whatever experience I have. You're carrying the ball, I'm in the backfield—"

"Thank you, Doctor—"

"Fenton. My first name, Fenton. Mother's maiden name, you know. I like the way some of the old families carry that tradition on, don't you, but sometimes I wish I were named Joe or Al, I certainly felt that way all through my school days. I hope you don't mind if I call you Robert, that is, among ourselves of course."

"I'd be pleased, Fenton. You know, I was somewhat surprised to find out I had the job. That interview—"

"Yes. Oh, everyone was for you. In the end, that is. Of course, I don't wish to give you the roll call, bad administrative technique, wouldn't you say. You expressed some strong opinions—"

"Badly, I'm afraid."

"Well, you couldn't be expected to know your people, what their prejudices are, and so on." Eberly put his fingertips together and sat back. His fingers were unusually wide at the ends. He tapped them together with a sound like tiny bongo drums. "In the end, as I say, there was unanimity. Casella was quite violent—"

"Casella?"

"—for you. He said he didn't envy you, following Johnny Loomis, but better a man with opinions than another Loomis. He and Johnny never got on, I'm afraid."

"I didn't think there was anyone who didn't get along with Mr. Loomis."

"I'll tell you, Robert. I've been here only for three years. John Loomis was a principal in this town for thirty. Actually, I had to prove myself to John. In a sense. Or to the community through him, if you know what I mean. I am proud to say we became good friends, sharing a number of educational views. John was always concerned with the well-being of his students, and of course so am I. But speaking frankly, Robert, some of his methods—well, you know how policy has changed. He was just a little—permissive. The school finally grew too large for him. You just can't treat the individual problems of a thousand students. Not personally. And speaking of problems—"

"Yes?"

19

"Student control, I think that's number one. I'm afraid they've become accustomed to roaming about. Passes to leave the building are rather common."

"During school hours?" Robert heard himself say foolishly.

"Lunchtime, mostly, but early dismissals for not very sound reasons, I'm afraid. But the real problem is the lunch period. They go wandering off. And often there are students congregating in the halls—even during class hours. John was rather lenient, I'm afraid."

"I'll do something about that."

"A tight ship, Captain, right?"

"Do I have suspension power?"

Eberly looked vague. It was his way of shying away from a subject, an almost fastidious withdrawal indicated by a blinking of the eye and sudden attention to those oddly powerful fingers. The Superintendent, thought Robert, watching him rub his fingertips, would have been in his natural environment on a city pier, hoisting cargo. It seemed a waste of breadth of shoulder, height, long arms, to keep them behind a desk lifting nothing heavier than a pencil.

"You bring up a problem area, Robert. Of course, it is not possible to run a school effectively without resort on occasion to certain punitive measures. After all, the prerequisite of supervision is discipline. You yourself would judge a teacher first with his ability to control a class before considering his teaching skills, isn't that so?"

Robert nodded without commitment.

"Teen-agers. Puberty. Although, I must say, we were never as conscious of the condition as the children of today. Wouldn't you say? They are so aware that we are so aware of their problems. They read about themselves. We've made them self-conscious of their peculiar condition, so is it any wonder they have to behave, they feel, in some expected manner? Have you made any arrangements yet about where you're going to live, Robert?"

Bewildered at the *non sequitur,* Robert took a breath to help his reply, when the buzzer sounded; Eberly excused himself and took the phone.

20

When he was finished, the Superintendent swiveled back to Robert, smiling. "So. Where were we?"

"We were talking about the suspension right," Robert said stubbornly. "State law, of course, does not give a principal the right to suspend. It is in the jurisdiction of the Superintendent of Schools. However, I feel you ought to grant me control. I functioned that way in New Canniston. How has it been done here?"

"Ticklish," Eberly said, looking at his hands. "Sensitive area, a very sensitive area. Do you feel it would hamstring you, Robert, to bring me each case for discussion?"

"Yes, it would. Certainly I would take no major step without consulting you, I would not want to. But for the sake of the discipline you mentioned, I need the power of immediate, temporary suspension of students if I think it necessary."

Eberly sighed, and for a moment Robert felt sympathy. Eberly worked for the community, was hired by the community, could be fired as a result of its displeasure. How much of his energy, how many of his decisions, were diverted by the need to placate, to maintain his "image," to explain and coddle—and what was left for the problems of administering this wildly growing school system?

"All right, Robert. One to five days over sixteen, maximum of three days under that. I need hardly add that this should not be abused. I think John himself never had to suspend anyone, at least not since I've been here. I understand that when a student broke a rule he would take him into his office and feed him."

"What?"

Eberly shrugged. "Loomis had a theory that a student who was acting up was usually hungry."

"I see," Robert said carefully. "Keeping students after hours and so on—my jurisdiction?"

"I want you to have a free hand."

"Good. Any other immediate problems?"

"Student control—that's the largest. You're on salary, incidentally, as of the first of August. You can take your time about settling in, of course. What are your personal plans?"

"I'll look for a room, apartment, something. I've got some clothes, books, a few odds and ends in the car. I won't be bringing any furniture down. The house in New Canniston is up for sale with everything in it."

"There are some real-estate agents up near the plaza, that's up to the corner to Main Street and a block to your left. Near the bus stop. You'll see some store fronts—insurance, real estate. I think that's your best bet. I wish I could help more actively—"

"That's all right. It shouldn't be difficult to find a place."

The buzzer sounded again, and Eberly raised his hands apologetically.

Robert stood up. "I'll get out of your way."

"You're not—" Eberly reached for the phone. "Look around, take your time, then we'll talk again."

"Fine."

He went out through the main office, aware again of the curious glances. The door to the street was an oven opening after the air-conditioned office. He walked up to the corner, to Main Street. Here the old was relentlessly being concealed or pushed out by the new. Store fronts in aluminum and glass covered frame buildings that had stood for seventy-five years. There was a great deal of automobile traffic along a street that had never been designed for it. Women, a few men, walked along wearing shorts. The women in shorts did not seem to have good figures. Robert wondered if this were a law of nature. Across the street was the shining façade of a movie theater, while, above the marquee, was more of the ancient brick. Above the store fronts seemed an unusually large number of dental offices. Compared to New Canniston, even in the summer heat the town had an air of movement.

A beautiful girl came toward him. She wore a tennis dress, she walked with a contained and exciting grace, her hair was gamin-cut, her legs and arms brown from the sun. As she came close he saw that she was not beautiful at all, her features were coarse and sullen. When she passed he looked after her, and from the back the illusion returned like some

22

trick of light. He thought of two faceless parents discussing their high-school children: "You can do what you like, but I'm not sending my boy to the high school, not with a principal like that new Mr. Evans. How can he be trusted to take care of teen-agers, he's no better than an adolescent himself." Robert added, murmuring aloud, "And as everyone knows, a forty-year-old adolescent is the worst kind." He breathed in the smell of summer and was grateful he could feel the ache and the longing.

Beyond the railroad tracks intersecting Main Street was a police booth; around it the plaza contained police station, village hall, a bar, bus terminal, a taxi stand, a liquor store, and on the corner, recently refurbished, a diner-restaurant. Across the street he saw a sign advertising the practice of law, insurance, real estate. He went in. An enormously fat woman looked up from a typewriter.

"I was looking," Robert said, "to rent a furnished room or two."

"Yourself and wife? Children?"

"I'm alone."

"I have a number of desirable places. Won't you sit down?"

Robert sat on the worn plastic of what seemed to be a kitchen chair while the woman drew a rolling file case toward her. She pulled open a drawer, humming, her thick fingers flicking at the cards. Robert noted that she was humming a theme from a Beethoven quartet and then berated himself for the snobbishness of his surprise. Her eyes were a serene blue.

"May I have your name?"

"Robert Evans."

"Is this to be temporary, permanent?"

"I hope to live here for a while."

"Evans—you wouldn't be the new principal?"

"I would."

"Well," she said, "welcome."

"Thank you."

She looked at him with open curiosity. Robert found his separate qualities being totaled. He waited for the sum.

"You look sturdy enough. You'll have to be to keep all those monsters in line. Are you as fierce as you look with that broken nose? How'd that happen?"

"Walked into a swinging bat." She was inoffensive. He smiled.

"That's it, that makes the difference. You know the one thing we can't ever see is our own smile? You try it in front of a mirror, and it just isn't the same, not the way others see it. Some people can smile and the face is just the same anyway. Yours is a real changer. Remember to use it when you talk to the PTA."

"Sure."

"My name is Rose Pink. I mean, it really is, I always have to say that to people the first time. You can call me Rose, if you care to."

"All right, Rose."

"You won't have it easy."

"Why is that?"

"Some people are going to blame you because Johnny Loomis is leaving."

"I'm afraid there isn't much I can do for those people."

"They say you're a widower."

"Yes."

She looked him over, top to bottom, like an analyst. But not, he thought a little sadly, like a woman. "Some of the kids are worried, they hear you're going to be very strict."

"How does this get around so fast?"

"My kid sister had a ninety average in Latin two years running and couldn't pass the state regents. Failed it twice."

"Whose fault was that?"

"I'd say it was the school's."

"If it is, I would try to do something about it."

"I think you just might. It'll be worth watching, anyway. Well—this doesn't get you a place to live. You'll be getting twelve five, and you're single, so I guess you can afford whatever I come up with."

"One request."

"What's that, Robert?"

He tried not to wince. "Evidently I can't keep many secrets

from Pine Hills. But I'd like some privacy at least when it comes to where I live. I don't know about sharing a house, or anything like that."

"We don't have apartment houses. Not yet. They're working on a change in zoning however. The way new people are streaming in, you'd think there was a plague in New York City. It's coming. Apartment houses, subways, traffic. This used to be a small town. A kind of nice small town."

"It still looks like a nice town. And I'm sure I saw some grass and some trees."

"Not for long. I make my living, mainly, from the sale of real estate, although I have a law degree and sometimes I practice a little, but we're joining the rest of boxcar America. The architecture of the future. A couple of living cells and a shrub in front. Instead of tenements, we're building suburban slums. You think these gimcrack development houses can last?"

"Are there any old enough to tell yet?"

"A man used to build a house there was pride in it, so it lasted. A builder puts up a row of houses to cut his costs as fine as he can get away with. How can his product last?"

"Well, if you can find me a pleasant place to live, in a building good for another year or so anyway—"

"I've got it," Rose Pink said. "I should have thought of it before. Ballard. If she still wants to rent it out. It'd be perfect for you."

CHAPTER THREE

Following the directions Rose Pink had given him, Robert drove north on the main road and at precisely three miles on the indicator looked on his left for the marker. He saw it, the name Ballard painted in Old English script on a flat rock. There was a private dirt road just wide enough for one car; it wound for a few hundred feet through untended woods to come into a clearing. A kind-of-colonial house, small and two-storied, stood beside where the road became a gravel turnaround. Next to the house was a row of peony bushes past bloom. A woman, legs apart and straight, her back to Robert, was digging in the ground with a trowel. She did not turn around at the sound of the car. Her shorts were tight and very white against tanned legs. Robert noted the gluteal definition and was suddenly responsive.

He stretched the moment for the pleasure of watching her, then with a feeling of guilt got out of the car.

"Hello," he said loudly.

"Yes," she said, without turning. "Just a second."

Now there was justification in watching her, excused as he was from voyeurism. When she turns around, Robert thought, she will be plain. The woman straightened up with a mock groan and she was not plain at all.

"I'm sorry. I get involved and I forget my manners." She smiled and held out her hand. "Mr. Evans? I'm Kathy Ballard."

"How do you do." Her hand was good to hold. He released the pressure before he wanted to and before she did.

"Isn't it deliciously hot," Kathy Ballard said.

She had a smooth, broad forehead. Her nose was high-bridged, the nostrils defined. Her mouth was alive with a promise of excitement.

"It's lovely here," Robert said.

"Isn't it nice? We moved out ten years ago, and it's just continually delightful. The cottage is in back. We can't maintain the place as well as we would wish—"

She waved toward the house, and Robert saw the need for paint, a break in the gutters, bricks loose on the chimney.

"Let me show you the cottage."

Robert followed her along a brick walk behind the house. Fifty feet away stood a bungalow, painted white with black trim like the main building; attached to it was a garage now filled with lawn mowers, gardening tools, furniture in the process of being repaired and refinished. The grass needed cutting. Behind the cottage was a wood. To his question she said they had five acres of woodland.

"We're actually close to town, a supermarket's ten minutes away, but we have the illusion here of complete isolation. Having your cake nearby and eating it."

There was a tiny porch, just large enough for a pair of chairs. Mrs. Ballard tried the door. "Damn. Forgot I had locked it. Key's in the house, be right back."

He watched her run to the house and back. Robert wondered about her age. She had the lightness of a girl. She came to the porch holding up the key and laughing. He had an impulse to pat her on the head and say, "Well done." As she put the key in the lock, she brushed close to him. It did not seem consciously provocative but almost a settled intimacy, as if they had been together for a long time. Robert stepped back a little, and then wondered why he had, since the contact had been pleasant. There were people who were not bound by the frozen norm, who greeted strangers without suspicion, who at first meeting telescoped the stiff period of searching out one another into immediate closeness. Like a dream sequence: introduction, recognition, lovers. And laughter. Constant bubbling laughter in place of the sourness that is called proper reserve.

It is not, Robert told himself sternly, that way at all. Wish fantasies are fashioned out of need. This is an emotional mirage.

"It won't," said Mrs. Ballard, opening the door, "be very clean, I'm afraid. There's been no one here for months."

27

At first sight Robert wanted to live there. Stone fireplace, planked floor painted a Chinese red, soft chairs, coffee table, bookshelves.

Mrs. Ballard went to open a window. She turned back to Robert. "Rose Pink didn't say. About your family, I mean. There's just the one bedroom—"

"I'm alone."

"Oh?"

"My wife died a year ago. I have no children."

"I see. Well, I'm sure this would be— We were going to live here ourselves, my husband and I, and rent out the main house. There are just the two of us. We wound up renting neither the main house nor the cottage through not being able to decide what to do. Not being able to decide something is what the Ballards do often."

"But you've decided now, haven't you? I mean, the cottage is for rent, isn't it?"

"Yes. Of course. Beyond there is the kitchen and off to this side is the bedroom. You want to see them?"

"There's time for that. I like it. How much is the rent?"

"Well—would you like to come back to the house and let me make some tea and we could talk about it?"

"Fine."

The tea was iced, and they sat in an enclosed flagstone patio, on wrought-iron furniture. Robert would have wanted to see the rest of the house, always interested in the signs of individuality—the books and pictures. He sat and sipped his tea and was glad to be stirred by the sight of her crossed bare legs, the tip of sandal moving up and down. He thought of the long period when he had functioned only with the memory of reaction.

"We had been renting it to a young couple, honeymooners practically, and then he was transferred out to Arizona someplace. That was a couple of months ago, after which we went into our typical indecisive period. First when we thought of living there ourselves, and then when Fred thought he might want to use it for a studio—"

"Is your husband an artist?"

"Commercial. He works for an agency in New York. He's an anomaly, really, he works in advertising and doesn't make much money. It's because he fights it, I think. He wanted to be a serious artist and didn't really have the drive, and now he does work he despises and I'm afraid it shows."

Robert nodded uncomfortably, his interest not extending to personal revelation.

"We did nothing about the studio notion, of course, and then I mentioned to Rose Pink—isn't that a delightful name?—that I might want to rent it again, and now here you are."

"Yes."

"And you're the new Principal of the high school."

"Yes."

"Is that what you always wanted to do, be in education?"

"Careers are things you find yourself drifting into as often as something you actively pursue."

"But do you like it?"

"Yes."

"Here I am," said Mrs. Ballard, "trying to open you up and all I get are monosyllables. Can't you use a big ear?"

"They don't look that big." He wagered with himself to see if she would touch one. He won, she did, the feminine gesture exploratory and reassuring.

"The big question," she said, "seems to me to be—what would a person do with his life if he didn't need the money. If a teacher earned as much as a principal, would you prefer to teach? Or is it the power, being in charge and all that."

"The power means I can get things done, make changes. A teacher is stuck; if the curriculum says teach it this way, then he has to. I think I'm pretty much where I want to be."

"You're one of the lucky ones."

"I tell myself that every day."

"Fred—" Whatever she was going to say, she thought better of it. "About the cottage. The honeymooners were paying a hundred and ten dollars a month. I guess you can have it for the same amount."

"That would do fine. If it's all right with you, I'd like to move right in."

"Why not?"

While Robert carried in his belongings from the car, Mrs. Ballard brought in fresh linens and made up the double bed. Robert saw with satisfaction the reading lamp attached to the headboard, the night table, the oval colorful rug. The kitchen, Mrs. Ballard said, flinging a sheet over the mattress, had a functioning gas stove and a small, serviceable refrigerator. Gas and electricity went on the main bill, and if Robert did not mind, he could then reimburse them for his share. Robert said he did not mind. What bothered him slightly was the amount of the rent, surely too little for all this. He did not want to take advantage of what might be Mrs. Ballard's ignorance, but on the other hand rents in this area might be less than in New Canniston.

He hung his clothes in the closet, Kathy Ballard made his bed, the domesticity was disturbing.

"We have a woman comes in to clean, I could have her come in here, too, if you like."

"Thanks."

She gave the bed a final pat and put her hands on her hips and pulled her shoulders back, sighing. "Old bones," she said, smiling. Her breasts jutting, she was like the figurehead of a ship bearing down with him resigned to and even inviting collision.

"I haven't been to the bank yet. I will sometime today and give you a check. Will that be all right?"

"Of course."

"Then I'll be going."

"Come back to the house first."

His impression, this time seeing more than the patio, was of color and warmth. The way, he thought, a home should appear at first glance. There were a number of fashion magazines about, Kathy explaining that they contained some of Fred's work. Over the fireplace was a large painting of Kathy Ballard. It had been done with desperate flair, as if the skills for likeness-portraiture were there but were stretched into a semiabstraction that, for Robert's taste, added nothing but diffusion. The artist had given his model a look of bemused searching.

"That was done ten years ago," Kathy said, looking at the painting with the rueful half pride with which we regard old photographs of ourselves. "To Fred I must have looked like an adolescent. I was twenty-nine. What an age for a woman. Old enough, and young enough."

"Everybody seems worried about numbers. We do things if we're old enough, or we do things if we're young enough. Today I'm thirty-seven, hang up the handball gloves. Although it was all right to play yesterday when you were thirty-six and eleven months and twenty-nine days."

"You have to go along with guideposts, don't you? Nobody wants to be responsible for anything, not even for himself."

"As if a friend stops you in the street and asks how you are, and you say, I don't know, I haven't been to my doctor lately."

"What *are* we talking about?" Kathy said.

"That's an unfair question."

"I'll ask a fairer one. Scotch or bourbon? When you move into a new home, there has to be a toast."

"It's awfully early for me."

"A little one. It's important, it's an occasion."

"A few drops of anything, then."

She went to a sideboard and took out a bottle and glasses. She poured. Robert accepted his doubtfully; she raised her glass. "This is all that is left of the moving-into-a-new-house ceremony. Driving the pin and all that. Cheers." She drank in a smooth, practiced movement.

Robert took a sip. "I'll tell you, Mrs. Ballard. I have to stop by at the school in a little while. If you don't mind—"

"I understand." She took his glass. "Can't pour it back, not without a funnel. Besides, it'd be bad luck. I'll just have to force myself." She drank it.

"Well—" Robert got up and moved to the door.

She came with him. She touched his arm in a gesture oddly diffident. "I hope you'll be happy here."

"I'm sure I will be," he said.

He drove back toward the village. The cottage was more than he had hoped for; he had been willing to settle for a bed and a place to put his books. He thought of his new landlady, letting himself go for a moment in safe speculation. He was happy to know he cared again for these matters, that the period of grief-and-guilt-brought emasculation was over.

He drove past stretches of woodland with low mountains visible through breaks in the trees. He came to a cleared area with one proud new model house, banners streaming, a sign proclaiming the many advantages of the houses soon to follow. He thought of Rose Pink, making her living from the sale of these development houses while decrying their encroachment. He stopped at her office to notify her he had rented the cottage.

She seemed not to have moved from her chair behind the desk. "Hello, Robert." Said with the ease of long acquaintance.

"Hello, Rose," Robert said, relinquishing, for her, his right of personal stiffness.

It was very hot outside and the office was not much cooler, but Rose Pink, despite her bulk, showed no signs of discomfort.

"You took it?"

"Yes."

"Good. This calls for a drink."

"This *is* a drinking neighborhood, isn't it."

"Kathy Ballard, I suppose, took care of that?"

"From an old custom, something about installing the lintel."

"Don't misunderstand an old fat woman who watches her body temperature." Rose reached into a drawer and brought out a bottle of Coke. She set it on the desk top, reached in again for opener and two paper cups. Robert considered the likelihood of her passing her life without moving from that chair, reaching in drawers and pressing buttons to take care of all her needs: ablutions, food, dress. The chair probably converted into a bed. He gravely accepted the cup.

Rose said, "Good luck."

"Thanks for the drink." Robert stood up. "Where's the bank?"

"Out, turn left, two blocks. You come and see me once in a while."

"I will. Thanks, Rose."

In the bank he arranged an account with the checks he had brought from New Canniston. The bank building was fairly new, and he went reluctantly to the door, loath to leave the air-conditioned coolness. A hand clapped him on the shoulder. "Evans!"

He disliked that, and turned around coldly. It was Casella, in half-sleeved sport shirt and cotton trousers.

"Hello, Mr. Casella."

"I'm glad to see you, Evans. Why aren't you glad to see me?"

"That greeting of yours. I seem to remember some kind of commando training—'Hello, Joe!' and as he turns, your knife goes neatly upward behind the rib arch."

"Commando? That's the way we do it in Central One. But I'll be careful from now on. You had your lunch? Join me. You have the time?"

"I was going to look at the school. I guess I have the time."

They went across the street into another of the new-façaded buildings. The sign said "Tucci's Restaurant," a bar on one side of a partition and tables on the other. Very little light came in from the street, the room grudgingly illuminated by some cove lights. At one end, above the cashier's desk, fish swam lazily in a lighted aquarium. There was the faint, agreeable smell of cooking and wine. It was a natural cavern against the sun, more pleasant than the aggressive mechanical chilling of the bank lobby. Robert sat back and realized that he was hungry.

"What do you like to eat?" Casella said. "The spaghetti is just fair. They make a good prosciutto sandwich, I'm having one."

"I'll have the same."

"Bottle of beer?"

"Fine."

Casella signaled a young girl in white-nylon uniform, who took their order.

"So," Casella said. "You settled in yet?"

"I just rented a place this morning."

"Good. Now tell me—Robert. Can I call you Robert?"

"Please do."

"Call me Sal. Salvatore. I'm interested, I'm very interested in the kind of high school we're going to have under you. I don't like what it was. I mean, it just wasn't as good as it should have been. That is, I think that. I'm no expert. I've served on the Board—this will be my second year. Not really time enough to be experienced. I haven't had much formal education myself. High school. But I care, and I've been trying to learn. You think there's a chance we can educate our kids properly?"

"I suppose it depends on what you mean by 'educate.' "

"Oh, no." Casella shook his head disgustedly. "And I was sure you weren't going to turn out to be one of those. You didn't sound cautious during your interview."

"I'm not being cautious. It's just that the trickiest thing there is, is trying to find out what the words mean. Democracy. Education. Security. Peace. Definitions vary from place to place and time to time and person to person."

Casella looked dubious.

"What's your definition, Mr. Casella? What do you mean by 'education'?"

"Sal."

"Sal."

Their beer had been brought and Casella took a sip. "I'd say that a kid coming out of high school ought to know something about his country and his world, his relationship to them as an individual, his—well, he ought to be equipped mentally for—"

Robert poured some beer for himself.

Casella said, "All right. So I can't really define it."

"I think you did very well, as far as you went. I also think that few people, in or out of the field, could do much better."

"Are you trying to tell me that you can't define the thing in which you're supposed to be an authority?"

"Sorry you hired me? Already?"

"Godammit, I'm in the feed business. Grass seed and fertilizer and kitty clean—"

"Kitty clean?"

"It's for cats."

The waitress brought their sandwiches, placing them on the table as if they were votive offerings, and glided away.

"Good," said Robert, chewing. "You were right."

Casella impatiently waved away the question of food. "How could I be in business if I didn't know what my business was about?"

"I know what my business is about. I was talking about terms, words. What happens is they take a problem and invent a word for it, and the problem remains, although the idea seems to be that the coining of the word should have taken care of it. Like that monstrous thing—'life adjustment.' As if all kids are the same, as if first come the niches, all measured, and the kids are shaped to fit. Education—the rearing of the young, the training and instruction and schooling, as the dictionary says—can be applied only to individuals. Maybe every bag of kitty clean you put out has the same specifications. Not kids. Here's an educational truth—a very important one: children are not bags of kitty clean."

"Don't tell me you can run your school without specifications. You're turning out a product, just as I am. Every parent has the right to feel that his kid, graduating from high school, is filled with certain information—"

"Information. Sure. I thought we were talking about education."

"I see." Casella took a gigantic bite of sandwich and rinsed it in beer. When he was able to, he said, "We're talking about something that I can't define, and you say nobody else can do much better. That's great. You're getting twelve five to do something nobody knows what it is."

"It's not really that bad." Robert smiled. "We can do a lot. Not miracles, but a lot."

"Let's start all over. Say you're running a private school, and there's no compulsion to send my kid. So sell me. What have you got to offer? What can I expect if my kid studies in your place three, four years?"

"I would hope that our teachers would be able to increase

35

the efficiency with which your child is able to educate himself. Along with that, he would get the information you speak of, and would know where to find more. He should be able to speak, read, and write reasonably well. He would be 'informed' in specific areas—science, languages, history. With a little luck he should be ready for some education by the time we get through with him."

"I don't know whether you would sell me."

"Don't forget a good salesman would know something about the desires of his prospect. The chances are a number of the things you would want for your child, the unexpressed things, couldn't be accomplished in the school at all. These 'aims of education' that we talk about. They're usually community aims, which vary from place to place."

"You're beginning to worry me."

"What made you hire me in the first place?"

"Instinct. I like hardheads."

"Mr. Casella, let me buy you another beer."

"My pleasure, Mr. Evans."

"Sal, you want to tell me about the other Board members?"

"All right. Lobrige. Her husband was a member for years. He died and she's filling out his term. They were friends and admirers of Johnny Loomis."

"I gathered."

"Farmer's been chairman for three years. He's a retired car dealer. Vincent used to teach in New Paltz, but he got married to a girl whose father was in insurance and now Vince is in insurance. There are two other members, they're not what you'd call extremely active. Arnie Miller is a lawyer, and there's Ralph Lund, he has an apple orchard."

"Do you have any advice for me, Sal?"

"Would you follow it?"

Robert smiled.

"You'll go your own way, I know that. Which is just as well. You can't please them all. There are people haven't even seen you and they hate you already. Some of the kids, too, they hope you fall on your face. They'll be watching everything you do waiting for that one big mistake."

"Thanks."

"On the other hand, you may be able to pick up a couple of friends."

"Thanks again."

"There's the big aims and the little aims. You could cram your citizens of tomorrow to the gills with special courses and enrichment, which all looks mighty fine and impressive in those thirty-page brochures Eberly is always having his office people turn out, which he sends to Albany for a pat on the back." Casella's voice became wistful. "Tell me, Robert, would it upset all your theories of education if the graduates of Pine Hills knew how to spell?"

"I haven't checked, yet, on whether the teachers can."

"I'm serious."

"I probably am, too. Have you children, Sal?"

"I've got a kid in your school now. Angelo. He'll be a junior, eleventh grade. I wasn't going to tell you about him, I wouldn't want any special favors. Two little girls still at home. I always expected Angelo to be the first Italian president."

"How's his spelling?"

"He spells by ear and he's tone deaf."

"Well, it shouldn't be a handicap. Presidents now have staffs made up of Harvard professors."

"You don't have any kids, do you, Robert."

"No."

"Well, I guess you can feel it, anyway, what goes on in a father's head—"

"Thanks for assuming I can. I think I can. Most of the fathers who ever talked to me were sure they invented fatherhood, and I couldn't really know how they felt. Maybe they had a point, I don't know."

"I have a special thing about that boy— There I go, proving what you just said. But ever since he was a little guy, I've watched him with that kind of pain you feel, the way you suck in your breath at a sunset—" Casella looked down in embarrassment.

"I know what you mean."

"He was always so eager. That—" Casella held his hands apart like sizing a football. "That wanting to know everything."

In the dim light Casella's face looked transformed.

"A little guy, always the bones showing, little face, big eyes. Excited over a book, an idea, something new he had discovered. Once he came to me and told me all about how birds fly, he had read about it in the encyclopedia. It was like he was the only one in the world had ever found this out, you know? He was shaking with the joy of it."

"Is he still making these discoveries?"

"No," Casella said flatly. "You know what he is now? He's a bum."

CHAPTER FOUR

T he high school sat back from the main highway in a land-scaped area of several acres. From the road you could not tell what it was unless you were familiar with suburban school architecture, and then you suspected it was a school building (although now they were putting up town halls that seemed to be done from the same plans); but there was no indication whether it had been designed for kindergarten or college-aimed students. It was cinderblock and brick, with some colored plastic panels, stripped and void of expression, the product of school boards worried about the reaction of a community worried about tax rates. Did not the function of a school building go beyond the enclosure of usable space? He was sure this building was light and clean inside, and obviously the equipment had to be new, but if he were a boy about to enter manhood—and those were the doors to it—would it not be fitting to have a structure to match the excitement he was bringing to it? He wondered if the Board thought not only of bringing in a building within the budget but also of having it look as if they were not wasting good taxpayers' money. Like—suppose the architect, who had to use the basic block, decided not to have the cinderblock use him. The obvious reticence on the part of the architect to lead. It didn't have to be a palace, but why did state minimums always have to be the guide? There should be something here to awaken respect—and even a little awe—in the student.

He thought with surprising nostalgia of the WPA-built high school in New Canniston—three stories because young legs can climb, and a principal had the school in his grasp instead of wandering over an acre to find out what was going on. Government marble and pillars—

But just a little stuffy, wouldn't you say, Evans? Imposing. But stuffy? Maybe. But it gave the kids a feeling of dignity and importance. They came up from the little farm schools, and by Aristotle the world of learning was opening up for them.

There were a half-dozen cars in the parking field, and Robert noted that all of them were newer or more expensive models than the one he drove. He hesitated at the outer door. The Principal enters his school for the First Time. Should there not be some symbolism, drum rolls, a flashing in the sky? A boy dashed out, flinging the door wide and nearly catching Robert in the head with it. The boy mumbled an apology without looking at Robert and ran off. Robert laughed. Old proverb. When you stop to examine an act for meaning, you stand to get your head knocked off. What he was, was a man going into a building.

The corridor went straight ahead, another one led off to the left with classrooms on either side. At the juncture a glass showcase held books and banners obtainable at the school store. Everything was decorated with PH in orange and black. The floor was corktiled and clean. Along the walls were exhibits from various classes. Robert examined a series of paintings in oils and noted the name of the teacher: Altman.

A man in custodian's uniform came down the hall, pail in one hand, mop in the other. Robert asked him where the office was.

The man had the face of an old, tired prize fighter. It was odd to hear his voice come out crisply, with the diction of an educated man: "Turn right at the next corridor, sir. You'll see it on your left."

"Thank you. By the way, my name is Evans, I'm the new principal."

"How do you do, sir. I'm Peters. Carl Peters." He looked down at the mop in his right hand as if considering shifting it should Robert offer his hand. Robert smiled and touched the custodian's elbow in acknowledgment.

Peters said, "You may want to make some changes in your office. Anything I can do to help."

40

"Thanks."

Across the hall from the offices was the cafeteria. Robert looked in. Stacked on tables were colored plastic chairs with black metal legs. The room was bright and clean. The serving section was stainless steel. He found it unattractive and wondered what was the matter with him. It was too pretty, too consciously sterile, he decided. It looked like any new lunchroom in a modern factory. He thought, Were he to sample the food, he would find it functional, pastel, neat, and tasteless. He cautioned himself against becoming old and crotchety. Since when had he become a proponent of sloppiness? His defense was weak, and so general as to avoid the issue. He hated packaging. Meats in cellophane wrappers. The despicable arts of freezing and dehydration. What had happened to the long wooden tables with initials cut in of students who had gone before? Tradition. Continuity. The factory process relentlessly rejecting the individual. To maintain efficiency you had to work from prepared molds. Out from the hopper they come at graduation, neat and shining and aseptic, two by two in perfect step, regurgitating information at the press of the proper button, lost in a new situation and programmed to be suspicious of a new idea.

Robert shook himself free and went across the hall. A door was marked "Office" and next to it a door marked "Principal." A triangular pane of glass in the office door permitted a glance inside. A high, long counter, and a woman at a desk in the area behind it. Robert went in.

He stood and waited. It was a large square room with files and two metal desks, at one of which the woman sat reading a pamphlet. To the left a door said "Assistant Principal," and to the right a door led to the principal's office.

Robert shuffled, leaned on the counter, and finally cleared his throat. The woman looked up, blinked, and went back to her reading.

Robert waited and listened to his own boiling. His plans for the time when he became ruler of the world had always included immediate execution for those clerks, receptionists, and minor executives in businesses and civil service whose notions of self-

41

importance were based on keeping people waiting unnecessarily.

The woman was in her fifties. She wore glasses; her face was long and her mouth pinched.

Robert said, "May I ask what you're doing?"

"Really," said the woman. "I'll be with you in a moment."

Robert went behind the counter and over to the woman's desk. She watched him in frozen disbelief. He took the pamphlet from her hand. It was from a vitamin house in New York proving the advantage of buying directly from them rather than a drugstore.

Robert said, "I don't know what your job here is, but since you're here, I assume it has something to do with finding out why people come into this office."

"What—"

"My name is Evans, I'm the principal here. May I ask who you are?"

"Mrs. Farrow."

"And your job?"

"I'm school secretary. I'm sorry, Mr. Evans, I didn't—"

From the office of the assistant principal, smiling, hand outstretched, came a round jovial man who seemed to bounce as he walked toward Robert. "Mr. Evans? I was just on the phone to Dr. Eberly. I'm Perry Dickinson."

Robert shook hands with him.

"Well," Dickinson said.

"Let's take a look at my office," Robert said.

He went to the door. Mrs. Farrow said, "It's locked. I wasn't expecting you today, Mr. Evans."

"I gathered that. Would you get the key, please."

"I don't have it. Mr. Loomis locked the door when he left."

"Who has a key?"

Mrs. Farrow looked resentfully vague.

Dickinson said, "Maybe the custodian, I'll get him."

He went out. Robert looked at Mrs. Farrow. She went to her desk and put a sheet of paper in her typewriter.

"Mrs. Farrow, how long have you been here?"

"Almost fifteen years."

"Did you function as Mr. Loomis's personal secretary, as well as school secretary?"

"I did."

"And Mr. Loomis always had the only key to his office?"

"The question never came up."

"Mrs. Farrow, what are your plans?"

"Regarding what?"

"Regarding your position here. Had you intended to remain?"

"There's never been any question of my competence, Mr. Evans. I have always done the best I could, and Mr. Loomis was always perfectly sat——"

"I am sure he was. But I will have to determine your qualifications for myself, will I not?"

"I suppose, but——"

"I could hardly have come to any decision before I even saw you, could I?"

"I suppose not, but I fail to see——"

"I was merely trying to establish, Mrs. Farrow, that it might have been—shall we say, fair?—for you to have exercised the same discrimination in judging me."

Dickinson came back with the custodian, Peters, who went to the door and opened it.

"Thanks," Robert said. He looked in the principal's office and at once came out. "Mrs. Farrow. How long is it since Mr. Loomis was here?"

"A few weeks. His retirement took effect at the end of June. He was in and out a few times since then."

"Do you know when he's coming by again?"

"He didn't say."

"I see. This is what I would like you to do, please. With Peters' help. Would you"—he turned to the custodian—"pick up a couple of cartons? Mrs. Farrow, go through this office and collect all of Mr. Loomis's personal belongings. Then send this letter to him, please."

"You want to dictate a letter now?"

"Please."

He waited while she found a pad, moving with exasperating slowness.

"Dear Mr. Loomis—"

Mrs. Farrow said, "You'll have to give it to me slowly, I don't take shorthand."

I will be, Robert said to himself, a model of calmness. I will not rant, I will breathe deeply and evenly, and think noble thoughts. "Did you not tell me, Mrs. Farrow, that you have been a secretary to a school principal for fifteen years?"

"Yes, but—"

"And you were never able to take dictation?"

"Mr. Loomis always gave his letters to me slowly enough for me to take in longhand."

"All right. Take your time. Dear Mr. Loomis: I hope, soon, to have the pleasure of meeting you. Meanwhile, I am taking the liberty of having Mrs. Farrow collect your personal effects to be picked up at your convenience. Or, if you prefer, I will have them sent on to you. Sincerely—"

He repeated it for her. Then he went in to take another look at the principal's office. It was a fairly large room with walls of painted cinderblock. There were windows at waist level along one side. On the wall adjacent to the windows was a bulletin board with notes pinned to it. On the wall across the room was a picture of Lincoln with a piece of bunting draped above it. There was a Millet print. In front of the windows was a large desk with two telephones. On the desk was an open bakery carton with a piece of pastry in it. A pair of storm boots stood in a corner. There was a box on the floor, the label addressed "John Loomis, Pine Hills High School." It was open, with excelsior sticking out the top. On a chair was a stack of books and periodicals. Robert, in mounting anger, stopped his inventory.

Peters had come back with two large empty cartons. Robert asked, "Were you not responsible for keeping this office clean?"

"Normally, yes." Again that voice, so out of keeping with the face. "But only when Mr. Loomis was present. He insisted on that."

44

"Mr. Dickinson," Robert said, "could we use your office?"

"Certainly."

In his assistant's office Robert accepted a cigarette and sat in a chair of molded plastic, somewhat larger than the ones in the cafeteria that had irritated him. At Robert's insistence, Dickinson had taken the desk chair. The niceties of who sits where in whose office.

Dickinson said, "Where do you want to start, Mr. Evans?"

He sat forward with just the right combination of deference and eagerness. He wore a natural-shoulder suit, with white shirt and narrow tie. His round guileless face belonged on a graduate student about to be briefed by a faculty adviser. The illusion stopped at his eyes, which were small, veined, and experienced.

"Let's begin with first names, Perry. How long have you been here?"

"Five years. I was administrative interne under Loomis, and I've been assistant for the last year and a half."

"Before that?"

"I taught at Great Neck."

"Did you put in for Loomis's job?"

"Yes."

"Are you going to be resentful of me?"

Dickinson calculated, then smiled broadly. "Yes, I was prepared to be resentful. But I knew, when I put in for it, that the Board was strong for someone from outside the district, so there was some face-saving in that."

"Would you like to see me make a mess of the job the way Mrs. Farrow would, I think?"

Dickinson said cheerfully, "I thought of that. The answer, actually, is no. If you did a poor job here, it might reflect on me, and not to my credit. If you made a name for yourself, the reflection would do me no harm at all."

"Good. Now tell me, what kind of school do I have, and what do I have to work with?"

"Nearly a thousand students, staff of seventy-seven. Marvelous public relations. It's got the name of a number-one school."

"And it isn't?"

"Not really. If you want to use scholarship standards, the number of state scholarships we get aren't anywhere near the potential of the students."

"Where are the weaknesses?"

"English and languages, I think. Math and social studies not bad."

"College admissions?"

"Fair. Ivy-league representation and all that. But what's happening is what I saw on the Island. People have money. There's a hell of a lot of private tutoring going on. Of course, the school gets the credit."

Robert looked at his cigarette tip, trying to decide if the ash was long enough to warrant flicking.

"I want to meet as many teachers as I can before school opens. Would you set up a list for me? Start with the department heads. Everybody who's available and can come in."

"Will do."

"What's the condition of the office?"

"Another clerk besides Mrs. Farrow. Betty Turner—on vacation now—handles teacher records and substitutions. You'll probably need someone in addition. Loomis hated to hire anybody. He was a man wanted to do everything himself. I don't think he ever got used even to my being here. Came in on his days off and so on. What else, Robert?"

"What about Mrs. Farrow?"

"What about her?"

"Look, Perry. Let me explain what your function here is. I expect you to be a rat. About everybody. If you're consistently wrong or if it gets personal, I'll fire you."

"Oh?"

"Do you think I can walk into a school of this size and have any notion of what's happening? It would take months. I haven't got the time. So to start with, I have to accept your opinions. Since you're one person and close to me, I can find out soon

46

enough if your opinions are any good. But I have to begin some-place. So you have to be a rat. Fair enough?"

"No." Dickinson looked down and played with the end of his tie. "How much time do I have to decide if I'm going to be your rat?"

"How about—mmm—three seconds?"

"I've decided. Who's first, Farrow?"

"Farrow."

"Loomis's aide-de-camp. She also makes judgments of her own. It goes back. When there were only a couple of hundred kids in the school, she and Loomis knew them all by name. It wasn't a question of a student being just a folder someplace. Loomis consulted with her. After a while, as I understand it, if you wanted something done, you saw Farrow. Often you didn't have to see Loomis at all. By the time I got here, it was a real entrenched thing, except that the school had become so big she couldn't control everything."

"In addition to that, what kind of person is she?"

"Mean."

"While the Power is cleaning out my office, let's take a walk."

They toured the school. In the gymnasium Robert was intro-duced to the head custodian, who was supervising the installa-tion of a trampoline. His name was Underwood, a burly man with a reddish, drooping mustache who almost blushed with pleasure when Robert complimented him on the condition of the building.

"They've been working through the summer getting the place ready for the fall madhouse," Dickinson said. "Under-wood has seven men under him, they work around the clock in shifts."

"Peters is one of his men, then. What kind of a fellow is he? His face and voice don't match."

"I don't know how he wound up in a job like that. I hear he's a pretty tough fellow."

"How, tough?"

"He was accosted on the way home one night last year. Two men. Peters sent them both to the hospital."

The floor of the gymnasium shone with layers of varnish over the cabalistic lines of the basketball markings. There was the smell of cleaning fluids, enclosed air, trace of the clean sweat of young bodies. "I suppose," Robert said, "basketball is important here."

"Is religion?"

"How is the team, any good?"

"They're willing. Pine Hills doesn't really have a top-notch team in any of the sports."

"Do you care, Perry?"

"What do you mean?" asked Dickinson cautiously.

"Something in your voice. Do you find our organized sport— boring?"

"Not me!" Perry said. "I'm a good American!"

"Sure."

Against the wall were spectator benches and Robert sat down, leaning back with one arm against the second tier. Perry sat beside him.

"You can be honest with me," Robert said, smiling.

Perry said, "When you ask me to be a rat for the good of the school and the perpetuation of my job, I defer to your position. When you ask me to rat on myself, I stand on personal privilege. Especially when the subject involves subversive thinking."

"So you don't believe in competitive sport."

"Thou sayest it."

"It's necessary for school spirit, isn't it? With it morale is good, and without morale a school isn't worth a darn. Isn't that so?"

"That is so."

"So what's wrong with competitive sport?"

Perry looked truly uncomfortable, and Robert frowned mock surprise.

"You're getting damned personal," Perry said.

"Yes."

"All right, I'll talk, get those lights out of my eyes. But I'll deny everything later. Yes, I hold to a basic un-American belief —I take a very dim view of our system of sports, professional *and* school, although I'm all for games and running about and all that sort of thing."

"Go on."

"I speak to you now as a father whose twelve-year-old son thinks his dad is queer. A few years ago he discovered baseball. So he lives it. A perfectly normal American pattern. He has in his head the most complicated series of averages and records, ask him what Babe Ruth hit in 1930, and it comes right out like a tape from IBM. But ask him for comparatively simpler information—say a rate/time equation, or considering the fantastic ability to memorize, a line or two of poetry, and you get a blank stare."

"And that's baseball's fault?"

"I'm just getting started. The justification for this sports emphasis is the basic one, that it makes for that elusive thing called 'sportsmanship'—the child will learn consideration for others, how to get along with his peers, and so on. Mind, now, I'm leaving out the physical advantages, I'm all for those. But sportsmanship! What actually happens? Back to my son. A nice kid. A really sweet, decent boy. He's out in team play every chance he gets. And what has he learned? First, he's learned to cheat. If you think this is exaggerated, watch any sand-lot game. Listen to them screaming he's out, he's safe. Not because the runner *is* out, or *is* safe, but the one who shouts the longest and loudest often gets the decision. And what is the point? You have to win. Everything geared to that one objective. You have to win."

Robert said mildly, "And the cliché, if you will, that this is a competitive world, and education is supposed to prepare a child for that world?"

"You're devil's-advocating me. But I'll go along. Life is a contest, to the victor the spoils and all the rest of the garbage. But we're not here just to train winners. Most of our kids are going to be losers. What do we do with those?"

"Are we supposed to turn out a citizenry of expert losers?"

"I wasn't talking about training them to *be* losers. I never expected to win this argument. I can't win it with my own son. Like asking him how he can feel any personal loyalty for a ball-player who's traded around like a slave and would be playing against his own team tomorrow if he got paid enough."

Perry wiped his forehead. He said, mocking himself, "I don't know why I get worked up over this silly thing—"

"You're a good man," Robert said. "Suppose you were in control. Would you really try to do away with baseball, football the works? No competition?"

"I'd look for something to substitute for that win drive. Laughter, knocking yourself out—impossible?"

"You'd have to get to them awfully early."

"I'm no expert. It's just that I say to hell with the all-American ideal of the all-American."

"Probably sour grapes around somewhere. Tell the truth, you're the kid who never made the team, right?"

"As a matter of fact," said Perry proudly, "I was a pretty fair athlete. Won my high-school letter in my second year. Cross-country track."

CHAPTER FIVE

Robert went back to his office, from which most of the apparent possessions of Mr. Loomis had been removed and stored, he noticed, protectively beside Mrs. Farrow's desk. She brought his letter in for signature, placing it on the desk and waiting.

"What are the two phones for, Mrs. Farrow?"

"The unmarked one is a private line to Dr. Eberly's office. The other has the button arrangement: two outgoing lines, hold, signal to my desk and one to Mr. Dickinson's. There's a difference in the rings. Dr. Eberly's is much lower."

"Thank you."

He read the letter. She had left out the *i* in "convenience." He pointed it out to her, wondering whether her typing or spelling was at fault. Without apology she took the letter back. He decided, watching her go, that she had the most unbending back he had ever seen. He wondered if it was worthwhile to do anything to palliate the animosity with which this woman was seething.

He began to open drawers and go through them. After the third he got up and looked out the window. He could feel, insidiously beginning at the back of his neck, the slow, pulling pain that would inevitably rise into the back of his head, and then come forward. He went to the door and asked Mrs. Farrow if she had any aspirins. She said she was sorry without looking as if she felt sorry.

Perry, hearing, came out of his office with a bottle and a paper cup. He filled the cup at the cooler and brought it to Robert. He said, as Robert shook out a couple of pills and washed them down, "You get headaches often?"

"Depending upon the provocation, Perry. Depending upon the provocation."

He massaged the back of his neck and looked at the bulletin board. He read a notice about the "bussing and debussing" of students. He made a small sibilant sound.

Perry said helpfully, "Maybe you're not emotionally suited for your profession. Like a medical student who can't stand the sight of blood."

"What's 'debussing'?"

"I beg your pardon?"

"It wouldn't do you any good."

"Are you all right, Robert?"

"Yes. No. 'Debussing'?"

Robert took his assistant's arm and brought him behind the desk. "Perry. Look here." He opened a drawer. From the conglomeration, which must have taken years to accumulate—you don't find a golf ball, earmuffs, a broken ruler, all in the same day—Robert picked out pieces of paper and placed them on the desk top. There were triangles as if torn from brown paper bags and crumpled memo sheets and sections of pocket notebooks. They shared in common the fact that they were unidentified.

Robert, demonstrating, said, "Every drawer has some of them, just in there loose. Going back maybe years. Perry—"

"Yes?"

"I'm afraid to think what they might be. You want to tell me?"

Perry looked at a piece of paper and picked up another and examined it.

Robert said, "I don't care if the man was a collector, and I don't care if he wasn't neat. But if these scraps are what they seem to be—"

"Names. Students. This one looks like a grade—"

"Would you say that this might be information that might belong in the school records?"

"I don't know."

"Perry, you've worked with Loomis for five years. Did he actually keep records in this manner, is it possible?"

"Well, he evidently made notes to himself this way. But as far as school records are concerned, we have the permanent cards here in the files and they're up to date, and Guidance has a separate folder on each student."

"If it develops that my predecessor played with the future of these kids by this sort of carelessness, if at any time we cannot supply accurate transcripts or there is a discrepancy between what the student thought he had achieved and what the records show—I don't care what kind of a mess he preferred to keep his own office in, but I can think of nothing more unfair and damaging to the students."

Mrs. Farrow, coming in with the redone letter, was in time for the end of Robert's tirade. Her face was unhealthily flushed. Robert said, "Mrs. Farrow, do you know anything about this?"

"If they come from the desk, I assume they belong to Mr. Loomis."

"That's clear thinking. If they are personal, please have them included with the rest of his belongings. If they pertain to the school, I would like you to classify them and see that the information is put where it belongs. In a day or so I want to go through the school records and student files."

Mrs. Farrow said, "I would like to say something."

"Go right ahead."

"For the fifteen years I worked with Mr. Loomis, I found him to be a fine man. A fine man, Mr. Evans. And a fine principal. He loved the students and they loved him. Many still write to him, from college, or working in other parts of the country. This community thinks very highly of him and was sorry to see him go. I feel that I have been privileged to have worked with him all these years."

"I admire your loyalty, Mrs. Farrow."

She nodded stiffly and went back to her desk. Perry stood looking down, rolling the end of his tie.

"The habits people get into," Robert said.

"What?"

"Nothing. Important, that is. What's your problem?"

"I owe Mr. Loomis a word, too."

"Say it."

"I liked working with him. I don't have any criticism of him."

"As I said to Mrs. Farrow, loyalty is admirable. I'm going to finish cleaning out this desk. Have you anything to do?"

Perry's eyebrows went up a few millimeters. He turned and went out.

Robert muttered, "Loomis never spoke to you like that, did he?"

He opened a drawer, looked inside, slammed it shut. He opened it again. He ran his hand through his hair and pinched the back of his neck. He got up and went through the main office into Dickinson's. Perry, busy over some material on his desk, looked up. Robert said, "No call for me to speak to you like that. I'm sorry."

"That's all right." Perry's voice was cool.

Robert returned to his office. His head was aching fiercely. The phone rang, a button lit. The ringing was interrupted and the buzzer sounded. He pressed intercom. "Yes?"

"Dr. Eberly for you, Mr. Evans."

He pressed the lighted button. "Hello."

"Robert?"

"Fenton?"

"I kind of figured you would be on the job, although, not being positive, I didn't use the private line. Mrs. Farrow explain that?"

"Yes."

"Take your time settling in, Robert. Don't feel you have to change everything overnight."

"I wasn't thinking of doing that."

"Good, good. Luckily you have two good people there to help you over the indoctrination period, steer you through the rocky waters."

"Two?"

"Both Dickinson and Mrs. Farrow are there, are they not?"

"Dickinson and Farrow. Yes."

"Mrs. Farrow has a lot of background. Anything you need to know, she should be able to come up with the answer."

"I've needed one or two answers already."

"Good. Robert, as long as you're there. If it's all right, I want to send someone over for you to interview. For your English department."

"This afternoon?"

"If you're not too pressed."

"I'm not too pressed."

"She's here with me now, that's why I called. She seems very good to me, Robert."

"Then she ought to seem the same to me. I haven't looked into personnel yet. I didn't know there was an opening."

"Yes. Check with Perry. Old Mrs. Herriman won't be coming back this year, she's going out to Arizona to live with her daughter. Actually she wanted to leave last year, but we persuaded her to stay on. I think you will like this applicant, Robert, good background, experience, comes extremely well recommended."

"All right, Fenton."

"Is everything satisfactory, Robert? You sound a little strained."

"Strained? I don't know why I should sound that way. What's this teacher's name?"

"Loomis. Elizabeth Loomis."

"The name isn't that common. A relation—?"

"His daughter. Johnny Loomis's only child. A bit of a surprise, her applying here. Johnny would never let her teach in his own school, said she ought to be out getting experience on her own."

"I'm not in favor of relatives in a school," Robert said. He was, he knew, babbling as he continued, "Anything that prevents or influences a teacher being judged on his own merit is, I believe, to be avoided."

"Yes, of course, that's what Loomis had in mind."

"I should think the situation might still apply."

"How's that, Robert? It's your school now."

"I know but—all right, I'll see her, Fenton."

"Fine. I'll send her right along."

Robert hung up the phone and shook his head. He leaned back and stared at the ceiling and shook his head some more. He picked up the phone and signaled Perry.

"Perry? You're not still mad at me, are you?"

"Well," said Dickinson, "no."

"I understand we have an opening in the English department."

"Yes. I'm drawing up now a list of the teachers I'm having in for you to meet, and along with that I'm indicating where we will need extra help."

"Good boy. What do you know about Elizabeth Loomis?"

"You skip around so, Robert."

"The story of my life. This is your ex-boss's daughter I'm asking about."

"I never met her. I hear she was a whiz at school, Loomis was always bringing in her prizes and citations and so on. Got her key at Smith, postgraduate study in Europe. What about her?"

"She's coming in for an interview. She wants to teach English here."

"I'd say we were in luck."

"Why?"

"The usual applicant here is fresh out of State Teachers filled with ed courses and not much else."

"I see. So we're in luck."

He cleaned his desk, and with each newly discovered scrap of paper his headache increased and the name Loomis was like sand rubbed on a sunburned back. After a while the buzzer went off, and Mrs. Farrow announced that Miss Loomis was here to see him. He told his secretary to send her in. He went back to his papers, scowling invisibly, not looking up when he heard the door open. Then because Robert hated the approved manner of doing anything, and this affecting not to notice some-

56

one through absorption in desk-top matters was a cliché, he stood up and held out his hand. "Miss Loomis?"

"How do you do." She gave him a firm handclasp, her palm through some marvel of metabolism in this heat cool and dry to his touch.

She looked very young, principally because she was small and her eyes were wide with curiosity and candor. She had long black hair pulled back and tied in a businesslike bun. She had a full mouth with secret shadowed corners that could be reserves of sweetness or scorn or laughter or sadness. She wore a blue-striped cotton dress with a stand-up collar and no sleeves. It looked as if she had spent a lot of time in the sun. When she took the chair Robert offered her, he noticed automatically that she had very good legs. She sat neither back and relaxed nor forward and tense. She waited with perfect composure for Robert to speak.

The packaging, he thought. The bright, appealing colors; the soft lovely contours. I will not be influenced. I am an irrational buyer. This is a Loomis.

"Why do you want to teach here?"

She thought about it, lips together, frown lines between her eyebrows. They were full, not plucked into nothingness.

"My father's decision to retire made me realize that he was getting old. I haven't seen much of him for several years. I thought I wanted to be with him for a while. Does that answer your question?"

"Partially."

"Also, I graduated from this school. I think I can remember how I felt, what I wanted, what I needed without knowing that it was a need. There's a chance that I can supply something of value."

"Where did you last teach?"

"Rumson, a junior college in Vermont. Three years. Before that, I studied in Switzerland."

"You've never taught secondary school, then," he said happily.

"Student teaching only. I've been certified however."

"How old are you, Miss Loomis?"

"Twenty-nine."

"May I ask a question that's not really my business?"

She made a gesture that neither gave permission nor denied it.

"You have never been married?"

"I was married. It was annulled."

He nodded, as if this confirmed the reason for his asking. He took out a pack of cigarettes and offered her one. She shook her head.

"Are you familiar with the English department here?" he asked.

"No."

"Nor am I."

Robert signaled for Mrs. Farrow and had her bring in a copy of the English curriculum. The period of waiting for Mrs. Farrow should have been a break in the formal interview; he should have been saying something innocuous and friendly. He could think of nothing to say. She volunteered nothing, looking down at her clasped hands, serenely contemplative as if she sat alone on a park bench or in a church.

If only, he thought, her name were Smith, or Kastrinski.

Mrs. Farrow brought in some stapled sheets, and Robert looked through them briefly, then handed them to Elizabeth. He watched her face as she scanned it. He decided that she was purposefully showing no reaction.

"Could you teach from that curriculum?"

"Certainly."

"Happily?"

"Perhaps not completely."

"What bothers you about it?"

"I'd have to study it before giving you an opinion."

"I don't want an opinion, I want a reaction. Somebody with your background ought to be able to get the feel of this, you don't have to eat the whole fish to know if it's bad, the judge at the cake fair doesn't eat all of the cakes."

"Well, I could not 'happily' teach literature and its appreciation if examples are to be taken from *Reader's Digest* condensations. I notice that this is recommended."

"If you were hired to teach from that, would you do it?"

"It's the teacher's job to use the school curriculum."

"You'd go along with it even if you thought the whole idea was bad?"

"I doubt that I would have a choice."

"Come now, Miss Loomis, would you teach untruths, bad grammar, a love for mediocrity?"

"Perhaps," she admitted, "I would make some modifications in the classroom."

"I see," he said, as if he had scored a point. "Do you think your father was a good principal?"

She looked at him to see behind the question.

"In intent, that is not a personal question. Suppose I were to disagree with this curriculum and have it changed. That would represent criticism, to some degree, of your father's administration, would it not?"

"I would expect any new person in charge to make changes."

"Suppose there were many areas that I thought needed improvement. If I were in your father's position—or close to him —I might be sensitive about this."

"I don't quite—"

"As your father's daughter, working here, might you not feel some pique, some resentment?"

"I might. I don't know. But should it affect my competence as a teacher?"

"What I'm concerned about is my competence as an administrator."

She gave her hand a quarter turn. That's your problem, it said.

He wondered what kind of man she had married, and why the marriage had been annulled.

He got up and took from the bulletin board the notice about "bussing and debussing." He handed it to her. "As a teacher of English, what do you think of this?"

She looked from the page to him and back.

"No opinion?"

"I've seen a number of such notices in schools."

"I want to know what you think of its English content."

"It's a not atypical educational memorandum."

"Is that an opinion?"

She looked at him gravely, and he returned her gaze with an expression equally solemn. He was doing what the Board had done to him. She had the same choice. She had to decide what opinion was required, and either give it or take a chance.

"Would you recommend this kind of syntax to your classes, Miss Loomis?"

She decided. "I'm afraid if a student came up with something like this, I'd have to fail him."

"Look at this." He passed her a copy he had noticed earlier of a directive to teachers.

PLEASE READ TO TWO CONSECUTIVE CLASSES:

This afternoon and hereafter pupils who ride on Bus N (that stops at Little Falls and Aston Place) are to take bus AA. Tomorrow morning and hereafter pupils that usually ride on Bus N will take Bus AA. In other words, Bus N is being replaced by Bus AA. Pupils concerned are to look for Bus AA when they are dismissed with the rest of the bus pupils, for it is expected that Bus AA will be waiting for them.

As she read, the corners of Elizabeth's mouth began to twitch. She controlled it. She handed the paper back.

Robert said, "Each teacher was required to read this, twice to each class. That includes English classes. It would have included you were you teaching here. What would you have done?"

"I always have difficulty with hypothetical questions. Surely you made up that notice just to interview English teachers with—"

"No, but it's not a bad idea. No, this is official. This is another executive notice. It will get immortalized in whatever

60

folder the flimsies of these notices are kept. Difficulty with hypothetical questions or no, how would you present this thing to your English students?"

"I would have little choice. I would have to show it as a horrible example of official redundancy."

"All right," he said, unsmiling. "You'll be notified through the office, Miss Loomis."

He stood up, the abruptness of action and final sentence at last catching her off guard.

CHAPTER SIX

That evening, having eaten without pleasure at a diner, and having determined for the future to cook his own dinners at home (how did it look for the Principal publicly to reveal his aloneness?), Robert drove to his new quarters. There was a car in the driveway, an old Mercedes coupé toward which he felt a moment of yearning; he carefully drove around it and left his car in front of the garage beside the cottage. Lights were on in the main house, and he considered knocking on the door with the excuse of the rent check to be handed over, but decided it would be wrong to establish a pattern of visiting that might interfere with his privacy as tenant.

His key worked in the lock, which gave him satisfaction. He then went prowling, picking things up and putting them down, opening drawers and cabinets and closing them, as if he needed to know this new place of his with his hands. He went into the bathroom and let the water run in the tub, sloshing it about before closing the drain, adjusting it to a tepid flow. He went out and took a while to decide where he wanted the radio, settling finally on a place in the bookshelves close enough to an outlet. He turned it on. Now he stood a moment and surveyed his home: water running, lamps lit, music.

Satisfied, he undressed, found a science-fiction magazine, and got into the tub. This was a self-renewing ritual he had discovered for himself. He stretched out, and with the big toe of his left foot let the water run hot for a while, turning off the faucet just short of discomfort. He began to read.

The warm wet cradle eased away the accumulated strain of the day. The choice of reading managed to divert without intruding identification or the need for critical appraisal. The actual suspension of concern lasted for only five minutes or so,

62

but it was enough, a catnap of the spirit, for rejuvenation. Then the world came back in.

Something was wrong. He had sought a thing, and achieved it, but was no happier than he had been. He reflected that a workable definition of happiness was a state of being the existence of which is unquestioned. Looked at, it had a tendency to vanish. But why? Was his dissatisfaction professional? The major question in the book of judgment had to be: what did you accomplish? What did you leave behind to justify your having used the air and the space that might have been occupied by a better man?

What does a man without positive religious beliefs, children, or the ability to produce an enduring work of art do for immortality? Tentatively he let his thoughts approach the edge of the teacher image (the Principal, in selecting, encouraging, helping to train, is entitled to share in this, is he not?), the kindly inspirer of the great deeds to come. Robert rejected the sentimentality, as pleasant as it was. The truth—or the fact, not necessarily the same thing—was that Mr. Chips was rarely found in the schools. Teachers—like most people—were generally irascible, dull, and incapable of passing on an inspiration that they had either never experienced or had forgotten. But Robert had once seen a collection of the crude woodworking tools used by eighteenth-century craftsmen, and contrasted this with the lovely, delicate work they had produced. So how could anyone of any sensibility blame the inadequacy of his equipment for the disappointment of the results? Any graduate of Pine Hills had the right to blame the Principal if the student's education had been deficient.

Could this be the cause of this wretched sneaky nibbling that would not stand still to be examined—that his position, at best, was necessary only for the mechanics of order? Like a lousy doctor, given just normal luck, who could practice successfully for a lifetime secure in the averages of the number of patients who would have recovered without exposure to his ministrations.

Robert got out of the tub and dried himself. He put on pajamas and a robe, and stretched out in a chair and studied his bare feet. They were long and narrow, and reminded him of the feet in those emaciated sculptures by Lembruck in the Museum of Modern Art. He curled his toes up and then down. "I feel," he said aloud, "just great. And you know what you can do, Evans, with your stupid negativism. For the truth, the whole, and the nothing but, is that I am where I want to be, doing what I want to do. All over America fathers of teen-agers are grousing about the quality of high-school education. And I, father of no one, can do something about it."

What, then, is it? he asked himself.

And slowly, and in trepidation, like a man called to the morgue for identification gingerly picking at the corner of the covering sheet, he said aloud the name of his wife. And waited.

Cautiously probing, he examined himself. The live grief was gone, and the cold sucking vacuum of her loss.

Someone was knocking on the door. At first the knock was tentative, and then it turned almost peremptory, as if impatience were being pump-primed. Robert, thankful for small favors, went to the door relieved that the interruption had not come while he was in the tub.

The man standing there at once announced that he was Fred Ballard, as if he did not, even for an instant, want there to be any doubt of this. Robert cordially invited him inside.

Ballard, average height, with quick, white, nervous hands and the face of a self-doubter, looked about the room uncertainly. Robert waited at ease for the obvious purpose of the visit: introduction, welcome. "I'm glad to meet you," Robert said.

Ballard said, "There's been a mistake."

Robert, perversely refusing to show reaction to this, said, "Come and sit down. There hasn't been time to stock anything, so if you'll take a rain check on a drink—"

"That's all right. Thanks." His eyes were anywhere but on Robert's; Ballard's gaze getting as far as the bridge of Robert's nose, then sliding back to his mouth and chin, and then vaguely to one side or another. Robert did not immediately consider this a sign of moral failing, having known too many candid eye-meeters quite capable of killing their mothers. He sensed in the man a gentleness, abraded by circumstances, that could not heal into the toughness required for adjustment and was left perpetually vulnerable. He was sympathetic, and wary, because weak people were always unpredictable.

"What mistake?" Robert said, sitting down and waving his visitor to a chair.

Ballard hesitated, then sat down as if giving up an advantage.

"I'm afraid my wife was too impetuous, Mr. Evans."

Robert found himself worrying guiltily as to whether he had done more than speculate about this man's wife. "You mean letting me move in without my handing over the advance rent? I explained that. I did manage to open an account this afternoon, and I can give you my check now if you like."

"It isn't that."

"You haven't changed your mind about renting out this place?"

"It's the amount," Ballard said quickly. "You must admit, Mr. Evans, that a hundred and ten dollars a month for a place like this is rather unusually low, wouldn't you say?"

"I found it attractive."

"I hope you'll understand that my wife is not a business-woman, and really she had no right to settle anything without consulting me. It is true that we had rented this place out for that amount before, but that was rather a special case, I knew the boy, they were just starting out and—"

"I understand."

"Then—"

Robert found it difficult to watch what tentative relief was doing to Ballard. What had to be so damned important about money that it could peel back a couple of layers from a man's person into areas that belonged to him alone. Or was it more than money?

"What did you have in mind?" Robert asked.

"Well, this cottage is worth at least a hundred and fifty—" At Robert's frown he went on hurriedly, "But, considering the arrangement Mrs. Ballard already made, I'd say a hundred and twenty-five—"

"Sure," Robert said.

It was too unexpectedly easy and Ballard's face was blank at first, then the blood moved into it, and he blinked and began to overflow at the mouth. "That's awfully nice of you, Mr. Evans, I know this was a rotten way to go about it, and after all you had a kind of verbal agreement with my wife and you had already taken occupancy, and I'm not sure what the legalities would be—"

"Can't we forget it?"

Robert went to the closet, where his checkbook was still in the pocket of his jacket. He made out a check for a hundred and twenty-five dollars, noting the purpose on the back and handing it to Ballard.

Ballard's hand trembled as he took it. "Thanks. And I apologize for—"

"Nothing."

"I wish you'd come back to the house for a drink." Then, looking at Robert's attire, "I suppose that wouldn't be convenient, but why don't I bring over something?"

Robert almost begged off at once. But when he was not giving up cigarettes, he was promising himself to do something about other bad habits, and one he particularly regretted was the tendency toward the quick and unthinking refusal. It had not started through conviction but as a safety measure to insure a congenital need for privacy. But it was not a way to make new friends, and a man could always use a friend or two, he told himself as Ballard waited.

"Why not?" Robert said, and waited half regretfully as his landlord went back to the main house.

To wave the check triumphantly in the face of his wife? To prove something?

While he was waiting, Robert went to the cupboard and was pleased to find some glasses there. Also dishes and pans and pots. He had not been looking forward to bachelor shopping for kitchen basics. The manifestly manifold advantages of mar-

66

riage. And stopped, almost shocked, for this was the first time he had thought of marrying again, and so crassly, without even a girl in mind. He shook his head in self-reproof.

Ballard came in bearing a tray with bottle, glasses, a dish of ice cubes, and a wicker bowl filled with pretzels.

"I asked Kathy, but she had gone to bed with a book."

This man, Robert realized suddenly, wants to talk, the way a deprived man wants a cigarette or a woman. So Robert sat down, accepted a drink, ate a pretzel, and gave Ballard his attention. Ballard tasted his own drink, then he took out a pipe and filled it, lighting it with the deliberate care of a personal rite. A man who smokes a pipe never gives an impression of frenzy: the cheerlessness, the near panic of Ballard's approach, was gone. Robert lit a cigarette and felt his presence and the companionability of the occasion acting on his host like water on a parched plant.

"Mr. Evans—"

"That doesn't seem to fit, does it?"

"I guess not. Bob?"

"No. My parents never called me anything but Robert. They weren't particularly formal people, it was just that that was the name they had given me, and the name they chose to use. It never did become Bob, not in school or among my friends growing up. I guess a conclusion about my character could be drawn from this."

"I was *named* Fred. It's spelled that way on my birth certificate. My mother was a simple woman, and when the nurse came in for the name of the new baby, she said, 'Why, Fred,' not Frederick or whatever else it might have been, and that was the way the nurse wrote it down."

Robert nodded gravely in tribute to all mothers, simple or sophisticated.

"I suppose I owe you an explanation," Fred Ballard said.

"I doubt that."

"Well, about my coming in all fluttery to raise your rent. I have to admit I was disturbed, because I always am where money is involved. I can't talk about it, think about it, hear about

67

it, without getting upset. I can't earn it, either, which is probably the reason for the way I feel."

"Mrs. Ballard tells me you're a painter."

"Yes. I've had a couple of one-man shows," Ballard said off-handedly, finishing his drink and pouring more whisky over the half-melted cubes.

"As a man with no creative talent, I envy you."

"Really? Why?"

"Because the satisfactions must be tremendous. I was thinking about that. Not about painting, as such, but what a man can leave behind to show he's spent some time on this earth."

Ballard drank some more and poured some more. He said, "You must make out as poorly as me, although you're in an admired position, but I've always noticed that the ones who begin to think about reasons for being and all that, why, they're seldom successful. When you're successful, you don't bother to rationalize your existence."

"Depends what you mean by 'success.' "

Ballard, giggling, said, "I thank you for sitting and drinking with me, for protecting my manliness by not arguing about the rent, and for the safe clichés with which you salve my lousy artist's conscience—"

"What clichés?" said Robert, bridling.

"Depends on what you mean by 'success.' Really, now. Did you ever hear of a Ballard painting? Canaday ever write about him? Anybody you ever heard of bought one? When's the last time anybody stopped Mrs. Ballard in the A & P to congratulate her upon her husband's achievements?" He took a long pull at his glass. "And let me add the most significant rhetorical question of all. When is the last time Ballard painted anything? Rhetorical, hell. I'll answer that one. Ten years. That's when. Ten stinking, empty years."

Robert wondered at how quickly the whisky had affected Ballard, and how thin the wall of his confessional was.

"I'll tell you what, since you didn't ask. A young man starts to paint, right?"

"Right."

68

"Now he can be good or bad. He can be a kind of genius or he can be a derivative nothing. It's, as they laughingly say, a free country, so a kid feels like painting, he paints. Let's say he takes himself seriously, he reads the lives of the artists and haunts the museums, and after a while he accepts the number-one lie, the one most harmful, sinful invention of the myth-makers—that the best artists starve in their lifetimes and are seldom appreciated until after they're dead—"

"Is that so much of a lie?"

"Yes. No matter to how many it applies, it's still a lie. Because what this does is shore up the bad painters. What it does is fill the world with stubborn miserable failures. But not me. You understand that. It's always the other fellow, not me. And the second lie is when the psych fellows say you must learn to face the truth about yourself. Are they kidding? That's what they call mental health? To take a good look at the filth and falsehood and crawly things inside and say, smiling, 'Hello, Me'? Know thyself. Shakespeare put that gem in the mouth of one of his prime fools, didn't he? Because what is it keeps a man away from the gas pipe? Only one thing, the ability, most of the time, to say to yourself that you are not a failure. Not. Not."

Robert, who didn't want another drink, made himself busy pouring and stirring and tasting to keep his eyes away from Ballard's face. When he did look up, he was surprised to see the painter serene and secretly smiling around the stem of his pipe.

"Thought you had a hysterical man there for a minute, didn't you?"

"It seems to me that survival alone is no mean accomplishment," Robert said.

"That's good. Now tell me this, just to see if you were listening. What is the most important fact about me I've given you so far?"

"I don't know. That you had two shows?"

"Sure. You know where? At some influential 57th Street gallery? In an art-supply store right here in town, that's where."

"I give up, then."

Ballard looked at him with scorn. "I told you. A man doesn't

69

paint for ten years, how is it he can still refer to himself as a painter?"

"Because it's something you are, and not based on what you do from day to day?"

"The point, as the blue-painted Britons used to say, is moot. If I think like a painter, use my eyes and mind and feelings like a painter, and I never pick up a brush, am I still a painter? The important thing is the woman you're married to, wouldn't you say?"

"You just lost me."

"Did you ever hear that failure has a smell? It has to Mrs. Ballard. But then, my wife is a very sensitive woman. An artist, naturally, would select a wife with sensitivity, wouldn't you say?"

"Naturally." Robert thought he had no business to be listening further; a man didn't talk about his marriage to another man who wasn't psychiatrist, counselor, priest.

"Take this little store in town," Ballard said. "It was a gourmet shop, cheeses from Europe and little delicacies and all that, it was a great success. It wasn't a fancy place, stacks of cans all over, huge cheeses, slabs of smoked fish, you walked in and it was great, just seeing the stuff made your mouth water, and you walked out having bought twice as much as you had intended to. The fellow who ran it made his, and he sold out. A family bought it, a youngish couple and an older woman, I think the man's mother. There was a child who wasn't quite well, retarded I suppose, about seven or eight. Well, in a couple of weeks business dropped off. It used to be you couldn't get in the place. What was it that had changed? The same cans were stacked up, there were the cheeses and the fish. The man and his wife were eager to wait on you. But there was just something there. Sometimes the door to the back room would be open and the kid would wander in and out, and the grandmother would be after the child with a roll or something he hadn't finished eating or with a cloth to wipe the kid's mouth, I don't know. But Kathy said the place had the smell of failure in it, and she stopped going in, it depressed her. And sure enough, in a month or two the new people sold out."

"That's a hell of a sad story," Robert said.

"Yes. Kathy has this feeling about certain people. There can be a guy who never made it, but he can be bright and fighting and talented, and with every slap down from a critic or a dealer he'd curse them cheerfully and go back to work, and it was all healthy and you knew that sooner or later the wave would go up and take this guy with it. Then with another fellow in the same position, you could see the sourness setting in, he'd be uncomfortable to be with, and you made sure the conversation never got around to his work. Imagine meeting a friend and never asking how he's doing. Before you know it, you never want to see this guy because his own continual lack of luck was too damned degrading. Kathy always said she could smell the failure in a person even before it was really apparent to anybody else."

"I guess I know what she means. It's in the eyes and around the mouth and in the voice. You're talking about people in your field, but I've seen it in mine, too. Of course it's more obvious and more deadly with free-lancers trying to sell their talent. But you can find it even in a field where there's tenure. The teacher who is always passed over when a new department head is selected, he gets ingrown and after a while he looks smaller, I mean physically smaller, it's a funny thing. And he becomes a lousy teacher."

Ballard had put his pipe down and was helping himself to Robert's cigarettes. He was blinking a lot. "Take a look at my eyes, at my mouth, listen to my voice. Tell me, Robert, you see those signs on me?"

"Hell, no," said Robert roughly.

"Thanks."

"You're not a man goes around feeling sorry for himself, are you?"

"Yes."

"The trick is to recognize it and give yourself a kick in the ass."

"Yes," Ballard whispered.

"Why don't you tell me how you became a painter?"

"I went to Syracuse, took a BFA. Lot of art history, anatomy, I had fun there. I came out eager, interested, and pretty generally a nice kid, I think. And then of course guilt set in."

"Guilt?"

"My family just about managed to see me through school. And what had I to show? What was I supposed to do with all this training? What was their money spent for? So I told myself an artist owes allegiance only to his art, and for two years after that I lived at home, painted, and earned nothing, thinking that when I'd be discovered, it would rub off on my folks, and they'd be happy. Meanwhile, my father was running out of excuses to the neighbors, and my mother believed that everything would work out if only I ate enough."

"What was your painting like, then?"

"I was impressed with a phrase I had picked up—'order in the universe.' I decided my paintings would represent my reflections on this order. I did complicated, compressed things, tight design. Then, within a couple of months of each other, my parents died. Pneumonia, both of them, an odd thing, and there weren't antibiotics then. They didn't live long enough to see me accomplish anything, and I stopped painting, that was the first time."

"I know how your own stubborn direction can hurt your family, and their dying too soon."

"There was a little insurance, so I continued to live on them even after their death. Then I met Kathy. I sold her a bill of goods, I was going to be a great painter. She loosened me up, and my painting changed. Then I sold something to an uncle of Kathy's because it was the right size for a hallway or someplace, but then a man bought something of mine in a fair where I was exhibiting. I heard that he was a collector, he owned a Matisse drawing. That was the high point, and Kathy and I got married. She went to work, I painted, it was great."

"Did she think your work was good?"

"I don't think she ever looked at what I was doing."

"And after a while you had to find a job."

"Yes, except I made sure to look for things that couldn't turn out to be permanent, the idea was I had to have time to paint. So I did the usual things for the untrained—I sold encyclopedias and took out a real-estate-salesman's license and I looked into insurance and we scratched along, and each year it was worse between Kathy and me. Like your schoolteacher, I was getting smaller. Then I got this job. Fancy title in a fancy industry. Art director. Advertising. Except that it's a fringe agency, and the art director is a layout handyman. And I haven't picked up a brush since."

For a while after that, they just sat and drank and didn't speak. Then Ballard got up. "I've talked too much and kept you up too late."

"I'm glad you came over."

"Good night."

Robert went to bed. In the early morning he was awakened, he thought, by a bird that sounded exactly like the last cycle of a washing machine, the dry whirring before it comes to a halt. Then he heard, perfectly clear in the stillness, the voice of Kathy Ballard coming from the main house. "Leave me alone. Just leave me alone."

CHAPTER SEVEN

Robert felt that a necessary decision unreached (even, and sometimes especially, the most minor) was an added thread to snag man's motility, and movement was life. This applied to an unmade bed, dishes not cleaned and put away immediately after eating, his car's change of oil after a thousand and within two thousand miles. It applied to the hiring of Elizabeth Loomis, and he found himself inexplicably in difficulty. Her answers had been forthright, her manner possessed (too much self-confidence?), she was not dependent upon safe jargon as a substitute for thinking, and she would probably make a good teacher. Why, then, have hesitated? Why not at once have agreed with Perry Dickinson that they were in luck to have had her apply in the first place? Because the image of her father stood in her way? Nonsense. He could not be that small of spirit. He told himself he would have to think about it. The thread spun out, dragging, and picked up all manner of things. Like a tremendous and unwarranted curiosity concerning her marriage and why it had failed. Like wondering how anyone in this sad world had picked up so much self-assurance in so short a time.

Perry began to send the teachers in to meet Robert. Robert was cordial, asked if they had problems for him to consider, asked if they had ideas for improving instruction in their subject. Perry functioned in the agreed role of rat, made somewhat more cheerful by his better knowledge of Robert and the conviction that what Perry had observed and reacted to would anyway in a short time be equally as apparent to Robert. After Robert had talked to a teacher and formed his own estimate, he spoke to Perry. The teachers came in all sizes, from a few who seemed extremely good to several who, Robert decided, one way or other had to be kept from the students. After a couple of days of this, Robert was depressed.

"So far, Perry, it's been one hell of an average. And why so many young, inexperienced ones?"

It was the end of the day, and he and Perry had filched some coffee from the cafeteria and were in Robert's office.

"I told you that," Perry said.

"But why?"

"Eberly likes them malleable, I suppose. And he especially doesn't like the ones with experience from New York. A number of teachers moved up here as part of the exodus. What they do, most of them, is continue to commute to their jobs in the city. Very few of those who have applied here have been hired."

"Why is that?"

"They may have been bitten by the union bug, for one. I'm sure that would worry our Superintendent. He likes the safe company practices of the State Teachers Association."

"I like the notion of teachers who have passed the city orals. That Spanish teacher—what's her name?—Coleman, she speaks with a whistle. Took me five minutes to learn to separate the words from the sibilance."

"She's been whistling Spanish verbs here for twenty-two years."

"A couple of weeks and school begins."

"I like it," Perry said. "What it gives me is a feeling of rebirth, or continuation, or whatever. This is a wonderful time for kids, and most of us get one lick at it and it's gone. Here I can get this vicarious bang over and over. Coming back after a summer, anxious, new things to learn, all the excitement of change—"

"Are you saying that you've gone in consciously for arrested development?"

"Sure."

"Don't you find that continual exposure to immature minds finally brings down your own mental level?"

"I've known teachers who were worried enough about that

possibility to take a sabbatical and do nothing but read the most abstruse philosophical works they could find."

"I've decided, Perry, that people come to teaching either forward or backward. I think I'll write a paper about it. Seems to me I can classify everyone I've seen so far."

"Forward or backward?"

"Yes. Forward—positive, aiming, what they want to do. So damned few like that. And backward—security, looking for a hole, escaping."

"That's unfair. I'm beginning to realize you're an unfair person, Robert. The only thing that saves you is you're not mean—at least not all the time."

"What's unfair about me?"

"Take this statement you've just made. This hole analogy, this escaping. What's wrong with a man wanting no part of the dog-eat-dog frenzy of the great world?"

"What about the refugee who eats her students like a mother fish? You notice I say 'her'—that absolves you and me. She's found a field where she doesn't have to compete against the secretary at the next desk. In her classroom she's Queen of the Sea. (Notice how I maintain the metaphor.) She hates the little girls because she knows they're going to grow up and be like that secretary she ran away from, the one with the blond hair and slim figure who always made her feel dowdy. And the boys? They're going to grow up into the men who take out the blond competitor."

"Boy," Perry said.

"Mind you, I haven't really worked this out yet."

"Send me a copy when you're done. Clare says I have to invite you for dinner tonight."

"I accept. What's she having?"

"Hamburgers. How should I know?"

"On the other hand, what happens to my image if I allow my assistants to feed me?"

"Your image gets a decent meal for a change, that's what. I don't see how you can live boy-scouting up in that cottage of yours. Don't you get sick of soup and spaghetti?"

76

"Made myself a stew the other night. Delicious."

"I bet."

"Talking of stew, I forgot to ask you about Wilson. He came in this afternoon. Math teacher."

"I know him. Why stew?"

"He's kind of like a rabbit, isn't he? He's an example of the backward entry into teaching, isn't he?"

"You're a rough man. As a matter of fact, you couldn't be wronger. He's an awfully good teacher."

"Tell me about him."

"Porter Wilson. He's got four little kids, I think he's around thirty-four. His wife is a shrew. A real nasty woman. I met her at a gathering one evening, and she buttonholed me and spent twenty minutes telling me what a spineless runt her husband was, with what he knew, why wasn't he out in private industry making a buck. And maybe she's right. He's a fine mathematician. Last year we were playing around with a special math course for picked students, and he was supposed to run it."

"What happened to the course?"

"Budget trouble."

"He looks a little shabby."

"Budget trouble."

"Can he control a class? He looks like somebody the kids would automatically take advantage of—skinny little man with those vague gestures."

"He has surprisingly little trouble. Maybe just because of that inoffensive quality, plus a real love for his work. The students sense this."

"Sold. Who's coming in tomorrow?"

"The Queen. Lucretia Pomeroy."

"Her name's not really Lucretia."

"It is. Miss Lucretia Pomeroy, head of the English department, Garden Club, Historical Society, etc., etc."

"I think I'll do some homework on that English curriculum before I talk to her."

They had stayed late, and Perry insisted Robert come right home with him. The Dickinsons lived in a modest house in a modest development. It was different from the other houses on the block, for in place of the pitiful little shrubs and against-the-house tulip arrangements was a giant oak tree in the middle of the lawn. Perry said that the tree was the reason he had picked the house. He'd be damned if he was going to stagger home drunk and peck at some neighbor's door with his key. You had to be awfully drunk not to make out that tree.

Clare Dickinson greeted Robert with warm attention not diminished by the fact that she was basting a roast in the oven; helping Marty, the twelve-year-old, with his flute practice in the next room by yelling each time he blew flat; and trying to memorize a poem from a book held open in her left hand. She was a plain woman with a tendency toward plumpness she did nothing to counter, and Robert fell in love with her as soon as they met. She was an example of a combination so rare that she might have been the only example of it in the world: a complete woman who was a complete mother and a complete wife.

After dinner she brought the coffee to the living room. Robert sipped at his. The coffee, like all the food that passed through Clare Dickinson's hands, was marvelous. Robert said, "I watched you. Tonight I watched you, and I didn't see you do anything I don't do, so why is the coffee I make myself so awful?"

"Witchcraft," Perry said. "I ever tell you Clare's maiden name was Strega?"

"It's not that good," said Clare, pleased.

"Life defeats me," Robert said. "No matter how often you say to yourself it's haphazard and unplanned and pointless, it's a human weakness, or strength, to look for a pattern. Rewards and punishments. So what I want to know is, how can an unprepossessing, undistinguished fellow like Perry Dickinson catch himself such a prize for a wife, while brilliant, handsome men are doomed either to bachelorhood or marriage to inferior women?"

"I deny I am undistinguished," said Perry, "although I admit to being very lucky."

"I shall invite you again and again," Clare said to Robert.

78

"An end result, I suspect, not completely unforeseen when that devious speech was made," Perry said.

They talked for a while without strain and without gossip, and then Robert said he had to leave in order to do his homework. He said good night, thinking how pleased he was to have a man like Dickinson as assistant. And how fortunate Perry was to have a wife like Clare. Yet, wasn't Perry's luck especially that he was capable of being drawn to a woman who was not a beauty? But then you had to consider the homely women who were slatterns and drabs, and the good-looking ones who were bright and delightful. And you had to consider men like Robert, doomed by personal fetishism to be interested only in women with good legs and a certain kind of mouth and forehead and the way the hair was drawn back, long hair tied simply, and there he was thinking of Elizabeth whose last name was Loomis. A pure example of *non sequitur,* he said to himself. Just because there she was, an untied thread. He would make up his mind; he would decide by tomorrow.

He took out the English material he had brought home, and he sat down with it.

Lucretia Pomeroy came into Robert's office with regal condescension and proceeded to interview him. He was not aware of this for the first several minutes, assuming that, as with the other teachers who had come to see him, it was obvious who was principal and who was teacher. Some people transcend subordinate roles by an excess of personal security or a blindness to the limits of their position. Miss Pomeroy was simply a steam roller with ribbons. She was a little woman, dressed vaguely like an ante-bellum character in a Southern novel. Her hair was blued, her mouth small and prim. After Robert had explained his background to her, and how he had come to apply for this job, and what his views were on women being permitted to walk around town in shorts, he shook himself mentally like a dog coming out of the water, and he sat back and made a production out of lighting a cigarette. From the slightly strained look around her eyes he decided that Miss Pomeroy was offended that he had not asked her permission, and he decided to leave it that way.

"I've been looking at the English curriculum for Grade Eleven, the one that was prepared under your direction, Miss Pomeroy, the one that is called 'A Course of Study in Language Arts'—" He thought a little desperately that something in this woman induced prattling, a throwing of unnecessary phrase on phrase, as if it was better that you talked than she talked, and if this happened in her classes she was contributing to English idiocy.

"I'm glad you approve of it, Mr. Evans. It was a great deal of effort but very worthwhile, a contribution, I felt, to the fine school system we have enjoyed here for so long."

"Did I say I approved of it?"

"I can't take full credit, you understand. There were some fine teachers assisting me."

"I want to discuss that course of study, Miss Pomeroy."

"They did a fine job on the physical side, didn't they? It was done all of it in Dr. Eberly's office. He sent a copy on to Albany. I must say he was quite laudatory to me. Although I did only what I felt was called for by the responsibilities of my position."

"I see. Was the copy proofread, Miss Pomeroy?"

"Naturally. I took care of that myself."

"I noticed some errors in grammar," he said meanly.

The tip of Miss Pomeroy's pink tongue came out, tested the texture of her bottom lip, and retired.

This can be an unflinching and quite deadly enemy, Robert thought. On the other hand, I can get so easily smothered in this powder-puff land that I will never get the dry female smell out of my nostrils. I will not be politic, pleasant, and safe. I will be crotchety, sharp, and disliked. If, eventually, they fire me, I will be able to live with the notion that, although stupid, I resisted hypnosis.

"I would like to discuss that curriculum," he said.

"By all means."

80

He took out the copy he had marked. "On page five, under 'Objectives in Teaching Literature,' number four reads: *To develop right attitudes and patterns of conduct through reading books that reveal the characteristics of the good life.*"

"Yes?"

"I'm not sure I know what that means, Miss Pomeroy."

"I should think it were obvious, Mr. Evans."

"Perhaps. You would have to define 'right attitude,' and toward what and when in which context and at which phase of your life. And what would you say are the 'characteristics of the good life'? Good for whom? And if you could define those 'characteristics,' how would a student determine these from reading a work of literature?"

"We have never had the slightest difficulty in putting this course of study into practice in this school, Mr. Evans. Right there under your hand you have the introduction written by Mr. Loomis himself. I'm sure he understood and approved of what we were attempting to do."

"Don't misunderstand, Miss Pomeroy. I am not attempting to discredit Mr. Loomis, or cast any doubts on the merits of your accomplishments. I am merely making a plea for clarity. There are statements here that I cannot understand, and I am asking you to help me."

"Well—"

"Like, a little further on, under 'Desired Skills': *development of mature reading taste and critical powers of evaluation.* I should think 'critical powers' assumes evaluation, wouldn't you say? No matter. The next line reads: *the ultimate preference for reading matter that uses adequate and appropriate literary forms of expression.*"

"And what is wrong with that?"

You'd best stop this now, he told himself. This is not only going to be fruitless, but it is beginning to show signs of the vindictive, and I must not hold this woman to account for the sins of the language destroyers.

"Perhaps we can take this up in detail at another time," Robert said.

"I think that, having begun your little critique, you ought to go on with it."

"Well," Robert said mildly, "I have, really, only one criticism. I am not sure literature ought to be *studied* instead of read. You talk here quite a bit about what is 'good,' and you give certain measurements using terms like 'local color,' 'realism,' 'humor,' 'character development.' And so on. So you show the student how to tear down the walls to examine the nature of the plumbing. But isn't something missing?"

"Really, Mr. Evans, I must take issue with you. An ability to analyze is extremely important in order to enhance appreciation. That is perfectly obvious. Have you, for example, seen the section on our treatment of *Silas Marner*? The newspaper procedure? Why, that has been our most successful approach to the study of George Eliot. We separate the students into groups, and they put together a newspaper. Individual students for each situation. For example, one does a report on the trial of Marner as if it is happening somewhere in the world today. Then we have a *Better Homes and Gardens* type of article by Nancy Cass in which she discusses preparing a dinner for her guests. An article on hand-loom weaving. And so on. You must be able to see how successful this approach is."

Robert swallowed. "Your objectives, as stated, had to do with the appreciation of literature, the development of taste— isn't that so?"

"Of course."

"Isn't there room, anywhere in this course of study of yours, to speak of this mysterious thing called empathy? The sense of wonder? Don't you admit anywhere that after all the writer's devices are examined and the structure scattered all over the dissecting table, something is left that is undefinable, not subject to analysis, something that just *is?* And there is one word I've missed in your entire treatment—has it gone out of fashion?— 'beauty.' "

Miss Pomeroy laughed condescendingly. "Really, Mr. Evans, who would have thought you to be old-fashioned. We have to keep up with the latest advances in pedagogical practice, don't we? Now I'm *very* proud of this newspaper approach, and Dr. Eberly has been ever so kind in letting me know what *he* thinks of it, and I'm sure you will understand its advantages after you are here for a while. I can understand this all being new to you, after all, we try to be as progressive as we possibly can here at Pine Hills."

"I can see that. But we can't allow ourselves to close our eyes to what is good in the past, just because it's not fashionable, now can we, Miss Pomeroy? After all, Shakespeare is rather dated, don't you think, and we do, I notice, still manage to include a slice of him in the course of study. Not, of course, a very big slice."

"Mr. Evans, I do think you're joshing me. I'm beginning to see that you are a complex man."

"I look forward to more chats with you," Robert said.

"Yes, I must be going. Oh, one more thing, Mr. Evans. I understand that Elizabeth Loomis has applied for a job here, and in my department."

"She has. I had intended to speak to you about that. What do you think?"

"Well—you know, I actually had Elizabeth here in some of my classes. How the time flies. Of course, I had a tremendous admiration for her father—"

"Yes?"

"Elizabeth was always—how shall I put it?—a rather fretful kind of girl. I wonder if she has changed."

"Fretful?"

"She never wanted to *accept* anything. You know how extremely annoying this can be to a teacher. I even spoke to Mr. Loomis about her once or twice, as I recall, although it was the last thing in the world I wanted to do."

"I never dreamed you had been teaching here so long, Miss Pomeroy."

"Almost as long as Johnny—Mr. Loomis. Of course, if *he* approves of Elizabeth teaching here, I certainly shall have no objection."

"Mr. Loomis," said Robert quietly, "is no longer in a position to approve a teacher's hiring."

"I meant as a father."

"Oh," said Robert, feeling she had scored.

"Elizabeth Loomis, coming back here to teach. My, my. As I say, *I* will have no objection. Of course, when it comes to engaging a teacher, we mustn't be influenced by personal considerations, wouldn't you say, Mr. Evans? I mean, even if she is Mr. Loomis's daughter, we would have to make sure she had the necessary qualifications, and if someone applied who was better qualified, we would not be justified in attaching undue weight to her relationships here, wouldn't you say?"

"I would indeed," Robert said.

As soon as Lucretia Pomeroy left, Robert signaled Perry with a sense of urgency that was like reaching for an aspirin bottle.

"Elizabeth Loomis. Do the necessary. Any slight doubt I may have had about taking her on has just been resolved."

"Will do. You all right?"

"You keep asking that. As if I just came out of the hospital and mustn't tax myself."

"Don't be sensitive. It's just my way. I say that to Clare when she calls during the day."

"I'm fine except for a vague feeling that little old ladies in crinoline skirts are flying around my head with their tongues stuck out at me."

"Paranoid already? Usually takes a new principal a couple of months."

"Not paranoid. Pomeroy'd."

CHAPTER EIGHT

School began.

Robert would have liked to experience some of Perry Dickinson's delight in this, but where is the pleasure in being pulled, harried, torn, dragged, pinched, pushed, and chivied. Parents (mothers) came to see him without appointments and in droves. Mrs. Farrow filled the main office with them. He called her and Perry into his office.

"How many of these people called for an appointment?"

Mrs. Farrow opened her book. "Mrs. Chullin at nine thirty, Mrs. Frank at nine forty-five, Mrs.—"

"And you didn't bother to tell me?"

"I'm sorry, Mr. Evans, you were so busy with the teachers that I didn't want to interrupt, especially since this is sort of routine. Mr. Loomis always had me arrange matters this way. He always made himself available—"

"Perry!" Robert said.

"I'm afraid it's so, Robert. I should have briefed you about it. I forgot."

"How many just dropped in?"

"Seven or eight. There'll be more."

"And Loomis just held open house?"

"He never refused to see anyone," Mrs. Farrow said.

"Nor shall I. Which does not mean I'm in favor of chaos. Mrs. Farrow, go out and have everyone who just 'dropped in' make appointments if they would like to see me. I'll see the others."

Perry drew him aside. "They're here, see them now. Believe me."

"Perry, you can't run a school that way, and you know it."

"I know it. I also know the most warranted toughness is still going to be hard for those parents to take right now. They're worried. They want reassurance."

"Image, right?"

"Yes, if you want to put it that way."

"There are two images, Perry, so far as I'm concerned. One is that of the school—for that I want the best public relations, the fullest community support, and that means we're going to be efficient, fair, and uncorrupted. My personal image is a beast of a different stripe. I keep it separate."

Perry's round face showed his concern. "You can't keep it separate."

"I can. *I* am not the school. I am not, for that matter, John Loomis. And unless I choose to run down Main Street without my pants on, my own identity is going to be uninvolved."

"I think you're overreacting. I think that rather than test your own likability against your predecessor's, you'd go out of your way to insure unpopularity."

"Very good, Doctor. But that's the way it is."

Perry shook his head. "If only I didn't like you. Oh, well, into the breach."

"You know what that means, Perry?"

Perry thought. "No."

"Neither do I. Have to ask Miss Pomeroy about that."

Robert got behind his desk and Mrs. Farrow showed in Mrs. Chullin, a breathless woman who wore braces on her teeth. Robert had never seen an adult with this mark of adolescence. He got up and shook hands.

"I'm glad to meet you, Mr. Evans. What I came for won't take a minute, it's just kind of routine, but I thought I ought to attend to it in person."

All the things around here, Robert thought, that are routine.

"It's about Albert. He's my son, in the tenth grade. In social studies he's been put in Mr. Dewey's class, and I want him in Mr. Noonan's class. Also, in English, I don't know about Miss Pomeroy, Albert didn't get along so well with her last year. Maybe he'd be better off with someone else. Would you make a note, Mr. Evans? I'd appreciate it."

86

"Are you asking to have your son changed from one grade level to another, or to a different teacher on the same level?"

"Why—the same. Sure, the same. That's why it wouldn't be a problem. It's just that I like Mr. Noonan better. Not to say Mr. Dewey is a bad teacher, I certainly am not complaining about him, but the way Mr. Noonan handles the subject I think Albert would benefit more from him."

"I see. I can't do it, Mrs. Chullin."

"You *can't?* Of course you can. Why, you're the Principal!"

"Thanks for the correction. I will not do it, Mrs. Chullin. Let me explain. Vertically—that is, from one level to another—a change can be made if it is for the student's benefit. But horizontally, as a matter of preference, this I'm afraid I will not do."

"But Mr. Loomis—"

"Of course. I know. But our classroom assignments are carefully made out and balanced, and we have no room for distinctions between teachers in the same subject and grade. Suppose the whole school wanted to be in Noonan's class and no one wanted to be in Mr. Dewey's. What then?"

"Oh, it wouldn't come up. After all, Mr. Evans, how many mothers have the interest?"

"That may be true. Well, I'm sorry, but I can't—excuse me —won't do anything for you."

She stared at him unbelievingly. "Every time I wanted a class changed for Albert, Mr. Loomis has helped me. The school is still standing, right? Nothing happened to make trouble for anybody, right? All that happened was Albert made out well, he got good marks, and who was unhappy? Now we're coming into the junior year—College Boards. College Boards, Mr. Evans. This is the important time. Isn't it my responsibility to see that Albert has the right teachers?"

"No. That is our responsibility, Mrs. Chullin. Not only toward Albert, but toward every student in the school."

"And you won't—"

"No. I'm sorry."

"Then I'm afraid I will have to see Dr. Eberly. You're just

being arbitrary, I must say it, Mr. Evans. I'll have to take this further."

"I'm sorry I can't do anything for you, Mrs. Chullin."

He did not let himself feel sorry for her or for her son. The water table of his sympathy was just below the surface, and if once he let it be scratched at, he would drown. He had a thousand Alberts. And one school. How the hell, he thought, did you do it, my popular Mr. Loomis?

Mrs. Frank brought in the coincidence that reduces the law of chance to a child's doodling; she wanted her tenth-grade daughter moved from Mr. Noonan's class to Mr. Dewey's, and Robert was shaken.

He almost rang for Mrs. Farrow to hasten after Mrs. Chullin and bring her back. What in the world could be the harm in an even swap? He asked Mrs. Frank why she wanted her daughter changed.

Mrs. Frank, an angular woman with a European background underlying a Midwestern accent, said, "I'll tell you, Mr. Evans, I've been with the PTA since my children entered the school system here. It's a long time. The others are all past school age now, Mary is the youngest. I've always taken an interest in the children's teachers. I know what a great leeway the individual teacher has so far as his methods are concerned, so long as he sticks to the state minimums in curriculums and so forth. I don't like Mr. Noonan's approach. He's date-oriented, if you know what I mean. Ten sixty-six, Battle of Hastings, never mind what was happening in Romania or Japan. I feel Mary should be getting the wide view. I think your Mr. Dewey looks at history that way. I'm sure you understand."

"I do. But I can't do anything. There are undoubtedly differences of ability as well as approaches between one teacher and another in the same subject, but I cannot discriminate, I can't steer a particular child to a particular teacher. I must be firm about that. I know that Mr. Loomis—"

"Did it all the time. But Mr. Loomis was a fool," Mrs. Frank said. "As it happens, I agree with your position, Mr. Evans. I

88

tried because Mary wanted me to. But it won't hurt her at all to learn a few dates. Thanks for your time, Mr. Evans."

Mrs. Frank left and Robert sat staring at her back and wondering why he should feel so weakly grateful.

There were other parents with problems, and there were students with problems, and Robert began to feel like a man made out of taffy or like a bull exposed to picadors or like Gulliver stretched out with the Lilliputians lassoing tiny vital areas and tugging. There wasn't anyone else with the attitude of Mrs. Frank. Everybody who came in said they wanted and expected something because Mr. Loomis had always done it so. Boys and girls wanted passes to go home for lunch. Mr. Loomis had always let them go home for lunch. It was not possible to examine the merits of each case. Robert said he would see no one else until specific rules could be considered.

He walked around the building with Perry. There were students in the halls, some in groups, talking, although classes were in session. There was no obvious start of guilt at the sight of the Principal. Robert asked some of them what they were doing. The answers varied according to the imagination of the student, but there was never a reason for any of them to be anywhere except attending class.

"I'll tell you about that," Perry said. "Loomis had a rule, nobody in the halls. Teachers were assigned to see that the halls were clear. But Loomis used to stop and chat with the kids and not bawl them out or anything, and after a while the teachers stopped questioning the kids, too. So there's always been a certain taken-for-granted traffic."

During the lunch period they went to the cafeteria to observe the flow of students. There were some who ate their sandwiches in the corridor as they talked to their friends.

Perry said, "When I first came, I was assigned to stop this eating anywhere except in the cafeteria. Then one day I walked into Loomis's office and saw a kid talking to him and eating an ice-cream cone. Mr. Loomis didn't seem to mind, so I stopped minding."

"His mind was on more important things."

"I'm sure he never noticed. Really. And if the kid had a problem, that was all Loomis was concerned with. And I do wish you wouldn't be bitter, Robert. You haven't even met him yet. You'll like him when you do, I'm sure of that."

"Talk about an image. The way his shines, no matter what. But what's going to happen to mine when I get done cleaning up after him?"

He noticed Porter Wilson sitting at a table talking to a plump girl wearing glasses.

"Who's the girl talking to our hag-ridden friend?"

"That's one of the Pringle girls. Alice, she's a senior. Mr. Pringle is a minister in town."

"Teachers have their own lunchrooms, haven't they?"

"Maybe he's on cafeteria duty. You want me to find out?"

"No. If that were a pretty girl, I might get worried."

"Not Wilson. He's more interested in factoring than—"

"Yes," Robert said.

They walked around the outside of the building. Across the highway from the entrance to the school parking area was a gas station, and next to it a small store with a sign saying "Sam's" and a smaller notice stating that sandwiches, coffee, soda, candy, and cigarettes could be purchased there. A number of boys and girls crossed the highway and went in and out of the store. Perry had to go back inside, but Robert waited until the lunch period was over; there were several youngsters still in the store. He went out at intervals during the rest of the day, and there seemed always to be some students there.

Robert Evans, Sneak, he thought. What have you done today about the level of instruction in the classrooms? What difference does it make if a couple of kids run across the street for a Coke?

It makes a difference, he answered himself, feeling his face go sullen at being questioned, just as one of the young students might. Didn't Eberly ask for a tight ship?

Just following instructions, then, is that it?

No, that's not it. What it is, is this. A school deserves a kind of respectful affection. It must not be considered the same as a clubhouse or a recreation hall. In my school nobody will spit on the floor and nobody will raise his voice in the library. If this is not understood, if I am no more than a dull conservative, and a tartar, and a man seemingly more interested in shining buttons than minds, then so be it.

Perry came in to report that Loomis was in the building.

"You spoke to him?"

"I didn't see him. One of the custodians told me."

"You know I never met him, Perry? Now he's visiting the school and he never came to see me first. I don't like that."

"Yes," Perry said.

"Yes?"

"I mean no. What I mean is, leave me out. I guess the fire horse smelled smoke. He'll drop in to see you. I'm sure."

"Perhaps. In any case, I don't want anyone visiting this school without reporting first to the office. Anyone, Perry."

"All right."

"If you should see Loomis, you don't have to tell him that, I'll do it with proper protocol, but you might indicate I would like to meet him."

"All right."

"I want an assembly tomorrow, Perry. The entire school. Will they all be able to fit into the auditorium?"

"Figuring the usual percentage of absentees, yes."

"And start working out a new schedule for teacher assignments during the lunch periods. I want teachers outside the building at all the exits. No student is going to leave this building during the school day for any reason unless they have express permission from me."

"Ouch."

"What hurts you?"

"Nothing, yet. This is what they call anticipation of pain. I yell as soon as I see the dentist pick up his sharp little instrument."

"I'm going to talk to Eberly. I want to cut down the lunch period."

"Robert—"

"Yes?"

"Are you sure you have to put changes into effect so quickly?"

"If a thing is wrong, why shouldn't it be corrected as soon as it's discovered?"

"Sure. Whatever you say, Robert."

"Now tell me what *you* would say."

"This lunchroom thing, leaving the building, kids in the halls —these aren't things that just happened. They've been going on for a long time. You see it, it's wrong, you change it. Fine. But broaden your vision for a moment. First—you're pointing the accusation of inefficiency at Loomis. Well, you don't care about that. Second, you're irritating the people who supported Loomis. Okay, you don't care about them either. Now, take Dr. Eberly. Our Superintendent is not a stupid man and he certainly knew about these things. So you're winding up, by inference, criticizing him, too."

"He said he wanted me to tighten things up. He said one of the problems I would have to meet would be kids running around where they shouldn't."

"Sure he told you that. And sure he wants the situation improved. He also wanted the situation improved when Loomis was here. Somehow I don't think he's going to like your moving so fast."

"I don't understand that."

"I don't *understand* it. I just feel it. There are so many subtle things going on in the administration of a school system—all these personalities, convictions, tenure, and lack of tenure. How is it everybody gets tenure except the Superintendent himself? All the brass gets it, all his assistants work into it after three years, but not the big fellow. He has to sweat out his contract renewals, and he walks a tight rope to do it. He can't support the best ideas because the best always represents the thinking of the few. And that goes for the worst ideas, too. So it's safe and proper that he stay in the middle, where most of the people are. In a sense he is forced to do this because otherwise he'd be out of a job. And he lives by rumor, by feeling, and never, never going out on a limb."

"So what if all of what you say is true? If I were superintendent and had a new principal, when the time for evaluation came, I'd say: Whom has he offended lately? Nobody? He must be a dud, let's get rid of him."

Bells rang, classes changed, the school day came to an end. Robert called Eberly and told him to be prepared for possible suspensions.

Eberly's voice was almost frightened. "What have you done, Robert?"

"Nothing, yet. But starting tomorrow I'm not going to let a single student off these grounds. The way it is now there's no control at all. Especially that store across the street. All we need is to have a kid bopped by a car on that highway during what is supposed to be school hours."

"I suppose that has to be done, Robert—"

"Suppose? Didn't we discuss this, Fenton? It was a priority thing, wasn't it?"

Eberly sounded tired. "It means we'll have Jennings on our neck."

"Jennings?"

"Sam Jennings, he owns that little store. This will put him out of business. He's sure to raise a fuss— You haven't done anything yet, Robert?"

"I'll set it up tomorrow at assembly."

"Maybe we can let it go for a while."

"I checked all day today, Fenton. There are students there at all hours, not just lunchtime."

There was no sound from the Superintendent's end of the line. "Fenton?"

"Yes. Well—all right, Robert."

"I also want to cut the lunch time to twenty-two minutes. It's a lot more economical use of the space to run four groups through instead of three and—"

"All right, Robert. It's your school, you're running it. But Robert—haven't you any popular ideas?"

"A good school, well run. That ought to be popular."

"We'll see, Robert. Let's hope so."

Robert hung up feeling unhappy. Nothing was simple. Tooth and claw was still the law of the world; all that civilization had done was substitute abstractions for flesh. Good will being throttled by the demands of ambition, and honesty rent by the ultimatums of security. The enemy had become shapeless; you fought water.

He called in Betty Turner. He had discovered that she could take shorthand, and he had been using her for dictation. Mrs. Farrow felt she was being supplanted. She was. He told Mrs. Farrow to come in early enough to arrange for the substitute pool so Betty Turner could take over her duties as principal's secretary. He had spoken to Eberly about a change in Miss Turner's classification. You were entitled to more money if you were a secretary rather than a clerk. Mrs. Farrow, he discovered, had never been classified as anything but a clerk, although she had assumed the responsibilities of school secretary. Mrs. Farrow never smiled. He wished that she would quit.

Betty Turner had graduated from Pine Hills High School and at once secured a job in the office. She was as thin as a pencil and wore her hair in spikes down her forehead. Once he had ventured some pleasantry and she had giggled for twenty minutes, so he was careful to be very formal and not set her off again. He dictated three letters and said they weren't important, he would sign them in the morning and she could go home.

He sat back in his swivel chair and swung it from side to side. Perry came in to say good night.

"Perry, get the art teacher to make a sign. I want it hung over the front door. To read: All visitors to the building must report to the office."

"That means Loomis never came in."

"Nope."

"That's a funny thing."

"It sure is. If a man hates you, he ought at least to take a look at what he's hating."

"Don't talk about hating. What's that got to do with anything?"

94

"All right, Perry. I'll just file this along with the long list I have of things I don't understand about people."

"It'll work out. Everything always works out. Longevity is the answer to everything. I've got to rush home to take Clare shopping. We have only one car. Around here that makes you either eccentric or dirt-poor. What a world."

"Good night, Perry."

He sat on. What else did he have to do? He enjoyed himself for a while in wry self-pity. No home, no family, and not, really, wedded to his work. Not, really, a dedicated type. Someday he would have to tell this to the Board of Education, otherwise he would be masquerading and he wouldn't want to do that. He didn't think the educating of children was the most important thing in the world. Sorry, men, if this makes me ineligible for the Selfless Educator's Medal, but facts are facts. I'm not even sure I like kids, as kids. I like some. I like most. On the other hand I hate others, and you're not supposed to hate a kid, you're supposed to subscribe to the theory that there are no bad children. Well, I don't believe that. I think there are nasty, vicious kids who are going to become nasty, vicious men and women.

This happens to be my day for questioning what I'm doing in this business. Backward, like I told Perry? Safety, escape? Not that there was anything else I wanted to be. Not actor, cowboy, head of the loan department in a bank. It's just that I'm not dedicated. When I leave here I don't want to think about it. When school's over let the parents worry about their own. Maybe one day I'll be white-haired, but I will never be kindly. I will never look over the tops of my glasses and say sage things that kids will remember all their lives. Gentlemen, I like a drink, and making love, and going to the movies. I get angry, very angry, and quite often; that's no way to be in a job like this. And every once in a while I am prone to heresy, like—I think a child's education finds its own level, like water, and this colossal, supercomplicated structure of ours is just so much nonsense.

He didn't mean all of that. But some. Definitely some.

Mrs. Farrow looked in to say there was a boy outside who

wanted permission to park his motor scooter in the parking lot.

"Motor scooter? That's a new one."

"We've never had one before, that's why I thought you ought to see him."

"Send him in."

An undersized boy came in. He had on thick glasses, chino pants with frayed cuffs, and a shirt too large for him, and he needed a haircut. He was nervous. Robert asked him his name.

"Joseph Maxwell."

"What's this about a motor scooter, Joseph?"

"Well, you see, I need transportation. I may get a job after school in a bakery in Newton—and that's about five miles from here—and I live north a ways from Pine Hills. So I need to drive to school, and if I get the job, I'll need transportation to the job and get myself home. I couldn't afford a car, so I had a chance to pick up this ve-hicle and I wanted to be able to park it here. So I came in for the slip."

"I don't think we can let you park a motor scooter here, Joseph."

Tears at once formed in the boy's eyes. "I just wouldn't know what to do, Mr. Evans. I have to have a place to leave it."

"Yes, but motor scooters—that's just one step away from a motorcycle. The one thing I won't let near this school is a motorcycle. That's all I need."

"But I just have to have a place to park it."

"Why the dickens did you buy it without checking first? What did you pay for it?"

"Three hundred dollars."

"Three—you bought it new?"

"Yes."

"You could have picked up a secondhand car—"

"Well, I just—"

"Why couldn't you leave it at the gas station across the street?"

"I'd have to pay for that, wouldn't I? And there's no way I could keep it safe. Somebody would be sure to come around fooling with it. It can't be closed off or anything. What would

96

be so wrong with my parking it in the school lot with the other cars? Lots of kids bring cars."

"I told you. This would be an opening. Next would be motorcycles and all the noise and horsing around that would go with it and somebody would get hurt—"

"You've got hotrods right here and they park all right."

"If they're hotrods, I don't know it. And if they do any racing, they certainly don't do it around here. The cars that park here all look like ordinary cars. If they're hopped up, I don't know it."

"What am I going to do, Mr. Evans?"

"Have you checked with some of the private homes around here?"

"No."

"You do that. Maybe they'll let you keep your scooter there during the day."

"Suppose I try and can't find a place? Won't you please let me use the school lot, Mr. Evans?"

"No. I can't let you bring a motor scooter onto the school grounds."

CHAPTER NINE

J oseph Maxwell, his eyes red, went out. Mr. Evans, his eyes clear, sat behind his big desk and swiveled left and right in his big chair. After a while he got up and went into the main office. No one was there. He went through the student files and looked up the information on Joseph Maxwell. He was a slightly below-average student; he had five brothers and three sisters, all younger than himself. His father was a laborer. This was Joseph's senior year. Robert put the file away and went back to his office.

How big, he thought, must a principal's feet be, the better to step on the aspirations of children. His decision, his no-saying, was correct. He thought of all the correct decisions he had made so far, in each case he had said no to someone. What had he done *for* anyone? Each person on this earth many times in his lifetime goes to someone to be told yes or no. The glory of yes and the profound depression of no. How many say no because they have had no said to them? Loomis would have said "Yes!" and fed the boy. Damn Loomis! Robert sat trying to ignore the ache that was centered in the V of his rib cage. The thing that bothered him most was the thought of Joseph Maxwell's shirt, the way it hung, too large for that skinny frame.

Carl Peters came in carrying a broom. He stopped at sight of Robert. "I'm sorry, sir. I didn't know you were still here."

"What is it, Peters?"

"I usually clean up at this time. If you don't mind, I'll start in the outer office."

"Carl, sit down for a minute."

Peters sat stiffly, holding the broom at his side like a lance.

"Will you put that damn thing away?" Robert said.

Peters laid the broom carefully on the floor.

"Carl, how old are you?"

"Forty-one."

"How about that. So am I."

Peters nodded in appreciation.

"Have you a family?"

"Just a little girl. She's ten."

"Where—"

"She stays with my mother down in Jersey. I bring her up with me on weekends."

"Are you a widower—like me?"

"I'm divorced."

Robert thought of the implications of a divorced man having custody of his child.

"We never had children," Robert said. "What's your daughter like?"

Peters grinned, and turned his battered face into a light beam. "Her biggest asset is she doesn't look like me at all. She's got long blond hair that's usually in two braids. She doesn't like dolls, loves all kinds of animals, stuffed and real. She says she's going to be a 'vetterarian' when she grows up. I like the way she says that, and I hate to correct her—what do you say about that as an educator?"

"Wrong, of course."

"Of course. She also says 'Aremn't I.' That sounds a lot better than 'Aren't I,' or 'Ain't I,' or 'Am I not.' That one I'm going to leave as long as I can."

"Sure."

"Besides," the custodian said, "with the trend of this new Webster's it'll probably find its way into the next edition."

"You bother me, Carl."

"Why?"

"The reason people cling to stereotypes is because they're comfortable. You know where you stand. But even without the snobbishness of status and all that. How about the money factor? Would I hurt your feelings if I pointed out that the skills required for your job are held by many people who never heard of the fuss kicked up by the new Webster's, or even that it was a dictionary?"

"That's kind of irrelevant, isn't it?"

"I don't know—it would depend on relevance to what, and I'm not sure what the point is."

"Nor am I. I have to get on with my work, Mr. Evans."

"Sure."

Robert sat and doodled in the manner of administrators: he made up directives; then he saw no need for them and tore them up. Then, on what he thought was impulse but which he at once recognized as premeditation, he went to the files again and looked up the boy, Joseph Maxwell. There was no phone listed; Robert noted down the address.

He went out to the hall and walked around. The school day was over, but this building could never be still. He came to the doors of the gymnasium. Two young ladies were peering through the glass triangle, and as Robert approached, one said, "I like the way that Harold handles himself. I sure do. Not like Jessup. Jessup is a clod." When they saw Robert, they froze and they giggled. The one who liked Harold said, "Good afternoon, Mr. Evans."

"Are you interested in basketball?" Robert asked.

"She's interested in Harold Smith," the other girl said.

"Really?" Robert looked through the glass. "Which one is Harold?"

"He's wearing the purple T-shirt."

"I think Harold handles himself very well," Robert said.

He nodded cheerfully and walked away, the back of his head sentient for reaction. "You think he's a nut?" he heard one of them whisper.

He locked his office and went out to the parking area. At the far end he saw Porter Wilson talking to the girl he had been with in the cafeteria, the minister's daughter. The girl was laughing. Wilson, one arm on the roof of a small foreign car, was talking easily and looked happy. There was nothing in their manner to warrant it, but Robert frowned. He'd have to talk to the man. In a society where a teacher could be cut up by tongues if he was seen patting the head of a little girl, this singled-out association was not a good idea.

Robert got into his car and drove to the exit, where a policeman was feeding the school buses into the highway. Robert asked where the Maxwell address was. Told how to find it, he drove off. He felt increasing anxiety. He had caused a thin little boy distress (why was it worse than if he had been big and fat?); and in this interval before correction could be made, any unhappiness the boy was feeling was particularly upsetting to Robert because it was unnecessary. It was like someone being killed because news of the peace had not yet reached his isolated place of combat. Robert drove south and west, and came to a section of dilapidated frame houses almost against the base of the mountain. He stopped the car and called out to a woman walking slowly, both arms in loving possession around a shopping bag. "Can you tell me where the Maxwells live?"

"Sure can, mister. Next house there, all those kids in the yard there are Maxwells."

They tumbled like members of a litter. There were five (he had overlooked one taking literally the crawlspace under the house), six, seven little ones between crawling and walking, and all dirty and none with clothes that seemed to fit. Sharing the yard with the children were a rusting hot-water heater and two automobile tires with holes in them and the useless guts of a television set. Robert looked up to see if there was an aerial on the roof. There was. Instead of a telephone. Perhaps they were right. He told himself, Just in case you thought all your students came from the upper middle. Variety. Meet America.

A shapeless woman in an orange dress came to the open door. "What you want?"

"Does Joseph Maxwell live here?"

"Joseph? What's he done?"

"Nothing. My name is Evans. I just wanted to see him for a minute."

"You police?"

"No. I'm from the school, Joseph's school."

"He's not here."

"Who you talking to, Rach?" A man came out of the house.

101

Next to the woman he had the stature of a child. His face was a walnut color; he had straight, very black Indian hair.

"He says he's from Joseph's school."

"That boy in trouble?"

"None at all," Robert said loudly. "If he's not at home, would you just tell him that Mr. Evans was here and said it's all right for him to use the school lot for his scooter. Would you tell him that?"

"What scooter?"

"Perhaps you can just tell him to come and see me in school tomorrow. Tell him everything's all right."

"Everything's all right," the woman repeated. "I'll tell him. Now maybe you can tell me—how come that boy didn't come home for supper?"

"I don't know."

"What about that scooter?" the man said. He came down the steps. The last ray of the sun caught his eyes, and he slitted them, drawing back his lips. He had teeth only on one side of his mouth.

"Are you Mr. Maxwell?"

"Mr. Maxwell. That's me."

"Joseph has a— Doesn't your Joseph have a motor scooter? Like a bicycle with a motor?"

"I figured you had the wrong place. What Joseph you want? There's Joe Sweeny, he has a bar over on Felcher Street. That the man you want?"

"Your son, doesn't he go to Pine Hills High School?"

"Sure. But he don't have no whatever you said. Joseph has to go somewhere, he walks. Like his father. I work over at the quarry loading the stone for crushing. You know how I get there? I walk. It's eight mile. How many times you think a man stops to give me a lift? How many times? In the rain, say, or the snow?"

The woman said from the door. "This man he come to see Joseph. Don't tell him your walking troubles."

"Well, good-by," Robert said.

He didn't know how to get back to his cottage. He drove

for a while before he found what looked like the main road. It was getting late, although with the gift of Daylight Saving, it was still light. Ahead at the corner of a secondary road was a building Norman-influenced, the sloping roofs and dull brown wood made to look like a country inn. It reminded Robert of hunger and he went in. It was more a country bar. There were booths against the wall. Sitting in one of them, a drink before him, was Carl Peters.

Robert went to him and said hello.

"Mr. Evans. You been looking for me?"

"Sheer accident. I came in looking for something to eat. May I join you?"

"Of course."

Sitting down, Robert said, "Is this a good place to eat? I was seeing a family and got lost and here I am."

"It isn't much of a place to eat, to tell you the truth. I come in here once in a while, most of the time I eat at home."

"So do I."

Peters gestured, and a tired man in a sport shirt came over.

"Drink, Mr. Evans?" Peters asked.

"I think I will. Bourbon over ice."

"What's good for dinner, Andy?" said Peters.

"Good? Are you kidding? There's *Sauerbraten* and there's liver and onions. I don't care for either, I had ham and eggs myself."

"I'll try the liver. Mr. Evans?"

"I always go along with professional advice. I'll have the ham and eggs."

Someone fed the jukebox and music blared. Robert winced. Peters said, "I like music with my meals. Especially this kind, brassy and with the kind of beat to drive you out of your mind. It's therapeutic."

"I'd have said ulcer-making. You don't believe in eating with calm and without tensions?"

"That's the point. You eat quietly and you find yourself chewing on yourself along with the victuals. This way introspection hasn't a chance."

"That's what I like, interesting new theories. Carl, how long have you been working for the school system?"

"About five years."

"Do you know this neighborhood pretty well?"

"I was brought up here."

"I just came from a family—" Robert told him where it was. "I come, myself, from a poor section upstate. But there weren't places as bad as this. I didn't go in, but from what I could see through the door, it looked as if the kids slept on the floor."

"Lots of hill people around there. Were they dark-skinned?"

"The man was. His son in school isn't, though."

"They're all mixed. Historians are mad for them."

"How is that?"

"They go back to the American Revolution. When the patriots took New York City, some of the Hessians took off and some of their women with them—that is, the women from the brothels that had been set up for the British troops. They came up here to these mountains. A number of racial strains came in—native Indian, and later Negro slaves who were escaping, and some Italians, and some of the original Dutch. The mountains became a refuge for anybody escaping from the law or just wanting to get away from the troubles below. They remained separate up there, inbreeding and unmolested. In recent years a number of them have come down. They come down without skills or education or money. They live poor because that's the way they are. You got an answer to their problem, Mr. Evans?"

"Carl, I'm so full of guilts right now that if you said the plight of these people was my fault, I couldn't deny it."

Peters looked at him with concern. "You in trouble, Mr. Evans?"

"Not trouble. Just the usual plagues of doubt, indecision, need for reassessment."

"You could use me if you want. I'm like Mallory's mountain. I'm here."

"Thanks," said Robert, smiling.

"It makes sense in a way, doesn't it? You and I the same age, you at the top of the school and I at the bottom. We've got the same number of eyes, heads, noses, and we bleed if we're cut, like Shylock. What would happen if we changed places—the prince and the pauper. Would I be able to solve your problems —would you be able to live with mine?"

"How did you get into this business, Carl?"

"Easy. Did you ever hear of a man who didn't have ambition the way a person is born without one of his senses operating? That's me. You don't say of a man, he has no ambition. You *accuse* him of it, right? As if it's a deadly crime. The truth is, I want to be just where I am. I want to be doing work so menial, there is no question of struggle for achievement or advancement or any of the other traps. I need very little money. Our society imposes so few working hours on a man today that there's more than enough time to use for that which pleasures him."

"You must have tried other things—"

"Everything. Both of us came out of high school into the depression. For you that was just a temporary difficulty—for me, excuse or not, it meant the end of formal education. The first thing I did was become a fighter. I mean for a living. Result— this face and something like fifteen so-called victories in around sixty fights. Then I got into the merchant marine. After the war I was plumber's helper, longshoreman, itinerant fruit picker—you name it. Then I got married to a woman was crazy about ugly men with muscles. She gave me my kid—for that I can never hate her the way you're supposed to hate a wife with the morals of a cat. I sued her for divorce, which is a dirty thing to do to a woman in New York State, but I wanted my daughter. So here I am."

"So you didn't take courses, then you must have read—"

"Just a habit I picked up when I was a kid. It could have been nail biting, or hair twisting. I'm real compulsive. Cereal-box labels, anything."

"A lot of readers make obvious mispronunciations. You don't."

"That's really for the kid's sake. Otherwise I wouldn't have

105

bothered. I use dictionaries and I listen. I listen like hell to radio announcers. And after all," Peters added slyly, "something has to rub off when you work in a school."

"You never feel a sense of waste?"

"No. Here I am with the Principal and he has problems that I don't have."

"Were you a custodian when you were married?"

"Hell, no. How could my wife admit she was married to a janitor? No, I did pretty well then. I ran a gym in the city—talk about the alchemists' dream of transmutation—I turned the sweat of fat women into money. My wife spent the money."

They ate and each had another drink. Robert said, "What you're saying, I think, is that this is your version of hermitism, but I think there has to be a fallacy—maybe it's how immune you are to social standards. You used the term 'janitor.' Given the fact that you're sensitive and thoughtful in other areas—wouldn't this ever bother you?"

"I don't have anyone around me to point out that my work is degrading to a man of my talents."

"Reason for being, how about that?"

"That's one of the traps I avoid. I went through a war, my ship was hit three times. I was fished out of the water three times. What I have now is sheer—and earned—gravy. Every day that I live, I'm one up on the fates. You see?"

"I'm not trying to shake your contentment. I just wanted to prove it to see if it's real. If it is, then for some reason I don't think I could explain, it's comforting to me."

"I know. I can't explain it either."

The bar began filling up, mostly with boys in their teens. They wore tight pants, and their hair was long and artfully combed. Their voices were loud, and they walked with shoulders slightly hunched and arms slightly crooked and fingers spread as if ready at any moment to engage in a gun battle.

Peters said, "About time to leave, I guess. At this hour the kids begin to take over. They come in from Jersey to drink here because in New York they can be served legally. They don't know how to drink and they cause trouble."

106

Outside, tires screeched and there was shouting and laughter.

"They get tanked and then they drive. With all this manhood they're all the time proving, their driving is risky enough, and with a few drinks it's murder. It's a damned disgrace. A number of them have been badly hurt, and a month ago—less —two of them were killed in a car smash down the road."

"I suppose age itself is no guarantee of responsibility."

"Maybe not. But if I were the boss, I'd be damned if I'd let kids play with loaded guns."

The youngsters crowded the bar demanding service, and when a drink was procured, they retained elbow space, holding the glass in the free hand and insolently surveying the room. There were some girls, not many, and their pants were tighter than the boys.' (Robert had overheard a student describing this style as so tight that if they had a dime in their back pocket, you could see if it was heads or tails.) They laughed overmuch and covertly appraised the boys who had not brought them.

Robert grew angry. It might not be reasonable to expect the young to be quiet and reserved among themselves. They needed, possibly, to test their approach to maturity; they needed the respect of their kind. But now the small liquor tolerance wagged the tongues and coarsened the language, and what was a good-natured shove a moment ago became serious affront.

Two of the boys suddenly began flailing at each other. An encouraging ring was at once formed. They began trying to hurt each other. Children by law, they were big and strong and dangerous in intent. Peters got up and, moving with deceptive slowness, pushed through the onlookers and grabbed one of the battlers by the arm, spinning him away in time to catch the wrist of the other and bring it straight down to his side.

The spectators yelled at Peters.

"You mind your own business, mister."

"More of that godamned grown-up stuff. Who the hell does he think he is?"

"I'll tell you," Peters said softly. "You two want to fight—go

107

outside, just the two of you, go somewhere without an audience and settle your problem if that's the only way you can do it. This is a public place and I paid for my own drink and I didn't see you listed anywhere as entertainment."

He turned and went back to the booth as if not for an instant in doubt that he had succeeded. The fight was not resumed. Robert looked at Peters in awe.

"I don't know how you stand it, the kind of job you have, Mr. Evans. Kids that age—" Peters dismissed them with the back of his hand. "For me they're a dead loss."

"You mentioned earlier exchanging roles. I have no doubt now that you could handle my job. I'm not so sure I could properly handle yours, though."

The voices at the bar were louder and sharper. One said, "Hey, I know that guy over there. Who do you think he is? He's a principal, a high-school principal, how do you like that? Pine Hills. I got a friend over there, and I saw this joker a couple of times."

"Which one?"

"The guy with the busted nose. Nah, they both— Well, he's the one with the tie. How do you like a principal getting a load on in a joint like this?"

"Then he goes back with all that advice to the kids. Clean living, Jack. Keep away from women, whisky, and hot crap games."

"Study hard, boys, study hard. Stand in line while I wipe your noses."

A girl said, "I don't believe he's a principal. Ask him, Teddy."

"Yeah, Teddy, go ask him."

A blond boy with square shoulders and heavy arms was pushed forward. He hesitated, was cut off from retreat, lurched toward the booth to stand uncertainly, lips thick with combined embarrassment and truculence.

"Ask him, Teddy!" the girl shouted, delighted.

"You—you a principal?"

"Yes," Robert said.

108

Teddy looked back to his inciters.

"What'd you say you'd do to old Simpson, our own buddy-boy principal, Teddy? What'd you say you'd do if you ever caught him outside the school, hey? So what's the difference, a principal's a principal."

"Let's go, Mr. Evans," Peters said. "Diminishing returns here."

He stood up and in so doing brushed against the boy, who gave ground and then, playing to the group, stepped forward saying, "Who you think you're shoving?" and pushed Peters hard on the chest.

Robert got between them. "That's enough," he said to the boy.

"That's enough, Teddy. You listen to that man. He's a *principal!*"

"Yeah, Teddy. Go back to your seat like a good boy. You don't want to have to bring your old lady to school now, do you?"

Peters secured Robert's elbow and began walking with him to the door. Robert, irritated at being protected, shook off Peters' hand. The boy, Teddy, danced around in front of them and began clowning, bowing low and making sweeping ushering motions to the exit. Robert stopped. He turned and faced the boys and girls at the bar. "Simpson, you said? Principal of which school? I'd like to know where you all come from."

"Oh, wrong," muttered Peters. "Oh, very wrong."

Now they began shouting, all the venom against authority, all the imagined enforced indignities, recalled. "You lousy fink," they said. And, "Listen to the bastard, he wants to know where we came from, let's show him where he can go." And, "Where the hell does he think he is, they're not so big when they're not behind their desk."

Robert, thinking he was controlled, as in a classroom situation, with a distant surprise heard himself yelling. "You're sick of being told what to do, are you? You're all grown up and experienced and capable, are you? Look at yourselves. Listen to yourselves. Have you anything to be proud of?"

109

A little voice said, "Oh, oh. The Principal ended a sentence with a preposition." And Robert had time unseen somewhere behind his anger to smile and like the one who had said it.

Then a bottle was broken, and a boy stepped forward holding it in front of him.

"You idiot!" said Robert in his normal voice. "Do you think this is a television program? Put that away."

A pale, sweated baby face on a tall, thick man's body. Eyes small and black and far away.

A girl shrieked with pleasure.

The boy moved forward slowly, placing each foot down with studied care like a stylized dancer, body rigid in the fantasy fashion of the bloodied awful self-hero of a thousand seminal dreams. Now Peters was in front of Robert, arms wide, shielding him. "Get away," said Robert to him irritably. The boy lunged. Peters flowed to one side and then his hand came out so fast as not to be seen and he had the wrist with the bottle twisting and the boy yelped and dropped it. Then Peters, who was half a head shorter, stood in front of the boy and took him by the upper arms and shook him. Peters shook him like a frantic mother with an incorrigible four-year-old, and the boy's head flapped as if the cords of his neck had parted. Then Peters let him go and took Robert's arm, and they left.

CHAPTER TEN

In the parking lot Peters said, "Well, these things happen."

"Not often, I hope."

"Damn kids. These are the ones from the decent families, these aren't the hoods. You see any difference? And they're supposed to grow through this period of rebellion to become normal adults. It's hard to believe."

"I don't know about the one with the bottle. I don't know about this just being a harmless phase for him. You were awfully good in there, Carl."

"It's nothing. I owe it all to a childhood diet of Frank Merriwell stories."

"Sure."

"Maybe that's their trouble. All this TV glorification of the hard guy instead of what we read. I guess you did, too, Mr. Evans?"

"I read Nick Carter. That was pretty hair-raising stuff, as I recall. Maybe the answer's not that simple."

"What's simple?"

"I suppose this should be reported," Robert said.

"Why? The only harm done was to that kid's pride."

And to mine, Robert thought.

"There's no point bringing in the police and getting involved," Peters said.

But if a boy like that wasn't stopped, wouldn't the same pressures in him make it happen again, and next time there wouldn't be a Carl Peters to get in the way.

"If the police come in," Peters said, "and there's all that red tape and time lost—you know how much time is spent with reports and making statements and all that? But frankly, Mr. Evans, it might be rough on me."

111

"Why?"

"Have you met Mr. Cartwright yet? He's Supervisor of Buildings and Grounds, and in charge of the custodial staff. He's very keen on his version of morality and behavior in public. Especially for custodians. Especially custodians who take a drink. So if he finds out about this—"

"But you haven't done anything to be worried about, Carl. Just the opposite. When I tell them—"

"Just being involved, Mr. Evans. That would be enough."

"If you feel that way, we won't do anything about it. See you tomorrow, Carl."

"Okay. Thanks, Mr. Evans."

Thanks? said Robert to himself, getting in his car and driving off. Who had done what for whom? He tried to ignore the fact that Peters had given him an excuse to shut his eyes in order to make an unpleasant thing disappear.

An hour later he was sitting in his living room with the radio playing softly; at his elbow was a glass of iced tea and open in his lap a copy of Charles Reade's *The Cloister and the Hearth,* which he had been rereading every couple of years since first discovering it when he was seventeen. He was convinced it was one of the greatest books in the world. He knew no one who had ever read it, and he did not wish to promote it or justify his opinion. It was as much a talisman to him now as a book. It was like sampling a special kind of drug. He would begin to read, and after a while stealing over him would come a sharpening of the senses, and he could feel his nostrils move in appreciation of the air and his shoulders lift as if relieved of a burden. Even the knocking at the door was not a distraction but something else to savor.

He got up and opened the door on Kathy Ballard. She said, "I hope I'm not disturbing you, Robert."

"Why, no. Of course not. I'm glad to see you, please come in."

Since her husband's visit to him, the potential familiarity with the Ballards had not come about. There had been several suggestions that he "drop in," but each time he had work to

112

do or someone to see. When they met greetings were cordial, but it was neighborliness and nothing more. On weekends when, through his window, Robert could see Kathy working in the garden, he resisted joining her. He could not forget Fred's "smell of failure" or what he had overheard from their bedroom. It had never happened again, that freak of sound current, unusual stillness in the air, the washing-machine bird that had awakened him. But under the circumstances you couldn't hang around an attractive woman dressed the way Kathy did for gardening unless her husband were convinced you were a eunuch. Fred Ballard, since that evening, spoke to him with restraint and the dignity of a man who obviously could not be called to account for confidences imparted while drinking. Robert realized this was the penalty one had to accept for listening. The confessor ear had to be concealed and anonymous. A man was entitled to resent the fact that it lived next door. The moral was obvious: if you want to be friends with somebody, don't let him tell you anything that, on reflection, he will find demeaning. But if you eliminated confidences, how do you form a friendship? It was very confusing.

The male urge, went the street saying, knew no conscience. There had been times after their first meeting when Robert had allowed himself the fantasy of his landlady and himself isolated from the world and its complications of fidelity. Sometimes they were on a desert island, and sometimes in a boat as the two sole survivors of a shipwreck, and sometimes they shared a space capsule. But Robert could recognize delayed adolescence when he saw it, and soon he was able to think of her with only a part of his mind, the part that identified her as the wife of someone else, a someone else who lived a house away.

"I didn't know whether you were busy," she said, coming in and looking around the room at the changes he had made. "Are you sure you're not busy, Robert?"

"I'm sure."

"You're not just saying that? You're sure I'm not disturbing you?"

"Well—" He saw the care she had taken—the fresh lipstick

113

and arranged hair, the crisp dress she would not have been wearing in her own home of an evening. "I wouldn't really be telling the truth if I said you weren't disturbing me a little."

She smiled, spinning around excitedly. "It's so *good* to have someone to talk to. You've done nice things to this place. Little things, nice. I was rattling around in the big house. Fred's away."

"Sit down, won't you? What can I get you?"

"Why is it, Robert, we've seen so little of each other? Tonight I decided I was just going to barge in."

"I'm glad you did."

"Sometimes people get stiff for no reason, and neither one wants to make the first move. You know how people read character from faces? I read rooms."

"This is your room."

"That's why I know exactly what you've done. Bringing that chair out—and the table there—very good, I never thought of that. You like to be comfortable, don't you?"

"I suppose."

"And a person like that—do you mind if I go on?"

"No."

"It shows sensitivity, especially in an emotional way."

"Oh, yes?"

"People who live in a Spartan way, they're not—sensual, you know?"

"I never thought of that."

"And you're so neat. Imagine walking into a bachelor's quarters and no overrunning ash trays, no empty bottles on the floor, no socks or shirts or anything about."

"Now, wait a minute. I have to defend myself. I emptied the ash tray a moment ago because there wasn't room for another cigarette in it. No empty bottles because the only thing I drink alone"—he gestured—"is tea."

"I withdraw your dismissal from the club. But there is one thing here I resent as a woman. The warm and contented feeling to this place. How can a man alone be that way?"

"I apologize."

114

"You should. May I have some tea?"

"Sure."

He brought in the teapot and a bowl of ice and a glass. "I'm fresh out of cookies or crackers or anything."

"Cigarette?"

He offered her one and lit it. She sat back and sighed. "I'm so glad I came. I was wondering about propriety and being a nuisance. It's nice here. I was beginning to hear the walls whispering."

"Fred working late?"

She poured herself some tea with concentration. "He had to go to Detroit, something with photographs, a new account. He won't be back until late tomorrow."

He felt a throb, and didn't know if it was joy or fright. He formed a picture of opening a tap and letting coolant flow into his veins. He looked up, startled, at the burst of laughter from her.

"Sorry, Robert. The look on your face when I said Fred wouldn't be back tonight."

"What look?"

"You looked scared to death."

"I did?"

"My goodness, Robert, that would be awfully obvious, wouldn't it, running over here at night and all with Fred out of the way? I admit to finding you attractive, I don't mind admitting that, you're not especially handsome, but you have a dry wit and I like that, but really—"

"If I looked worried, Kathy, it wasn't because of what you might have in mind. What I was worried about was myself."

"Not you," she said, sounding almost harsh. "I think you're the kind of man that's not really bothered by women. If you dream at night, it's probably about logarithms or parsing sentences or something."

"A while ago you said I was the sensual type. Now this canard. How am I supposed to defend myself?"

"How, indeed?" she said.

She was wearing a thin dress of mint green and her legs were

115

bare and tanned and she wore very simple Italian sandals and her toenails were red. She sat balancing the glass of tea in the cup of her hand with her fingers around it like a flower, and she was perfectly motionless and looked at him with a stillness around her mouth.

His mouth was dry, he sipped his drink, his fingers were not steady. We're talking about it, he thought. Balzac—somebody— said the first step is to talk about it.

"Is Fred doing well, then?" he said.

"Fred?"

For a moment he had the feeling she did not know who Fred was.

Then she said, "Something's come over him. He seems to take more pains with his clothes, and he walks with what you would think was confidence, and if you knew Fred—" She stopped and frowned. "I listen to myself describing the change in him. I'll be damned."

"You lost me."

"Robert, did it sound as if I were talking about a man who's found another woman?"

"Why, no," he said carefully. "Not at all."

"How do you think a husband would act if he were out fooling around?"

"I think he would make sure to act unchanged."

"You sound experienced. Were you always faithful, Robert?"

"There wasn't any reason not to be."

"I suppose there is with Fred. That night he was here—the big heroic act with the rent—I suppose he talked about me?"

"A little."

"Happily?"

"There were no—complaints. I mean no details or anything."

"Did he tell you it's quite a while since we lived together as man and wife?"

"No. He didn't tell me that."

"You want to hear about my married life, Robert?"

116

"Truthfully, no."

She didn't say anything. Nor did he. Then she said, "Perhaps I'd better go back."

"I'm sorry, Kathy. I'm a man with a lot of curiosity. I just didn't want you telling me anything that you'd be sorry for later and dislike me for."

"Of course, Robert." She smiled with no sign of strain or affectation. "How did we get on to this. Who came to cry?"

"Have a drink." He raised his glass. She clinked hers to it. "Cheers."

"You have a quality," she said. "You know what you are? A priest with pants, that's what."

"Now I've been called everything."

"A little philosophy about men and marriage. By Kathy Ballard, the Simone de Beauvoir of the suburban set. You take a man who shows qualities that make him less than a man. And suppose the wife caused them—or at least behaved in such a way that those qualities were intensified. Yet what counts is the product. If he were truly a man, should he not remain unaffected by the fact that his wife was failing him?"

"No. That is, if I understand you, and I doubt that. But if this wife understood her husband so well, how come she wasn't able to help him? There's supposed to be a *Gestalt* to marriage, isn't there? If it's just two people hanging around together, it sounds kind of pointless."

"Let me state it this way. Suppose the wife isn't the most understanding, sympathetic, loving, and tender woman in the world. Suppose she just isn't. And a man who needs those things as a result of not getting them becomes mealy and soft and unmanlike. How can he be lived with if he is something less than a man, regardless of who's to blame?"

"What's a *man,* Kathy?"

"Somebody strong."

"And a woman?"

"Oh," she said, her lips curving. "Don't you know, Robert?"

"You have a nice kitchen."

"What?"

"It's an old family joke. A subject changer."

"What's wrong with the subject?"

"Nothing. Except it's surrounded with barbed wire, a deep pit, lions and tigers, quicksand, and fiery dragons. I know what to stay away from."

"You're a challenge," she said. "That's what you are, a challenge."

He winced, since this was his word-to-be-eliminated for the month. "How's that?"

"I could explain it to another woman. You know how if you go outside of a winter's morning and there's a coating of ice over a pan of water, say, and you get this urge to poke your finger through?"

"Yes?"

"That's you. You're so pokable."

He laughed and, holding the pleasure in his cheeks, nodded at her and she nodded back, dimpling.

He said, "What you said before. About Fred. Whatever he is, is what attracted you to him in the beginning. So it seems that a woman gets attracted to certain things in a man for the pleasure of changing them. Right?"

"Sounds silly enough to be right."

"Why can't that first attraction last?"

"Who said anything has to last?"

"That's right. Who said that?"

"We don't take advantage," Kathy Ballard said. "That's the whole awful point. All this nice singing blood and how long is it going to feel that way? My God, you turn around and the gray is there and the wrinkles and it takes an effort to get out of a chair. Before you know it."

"Come on. There are certain things in a woman age will never bother, and you've got them."

"Have I, Robert? What are they?"

"I'm not an expert, like Benjamin Franklin was. He had his own favorite areas that he claimed lasted forever. But take the shape of the head. The length of leg. The mouth, the smile."

"Sounds like a song from *My Fair Lady*. Was your wife

beautiful? I know she was. Men with your funny kind of looks always have beautiful women. Faithful until death. That's forever enough. Why is it with some: faithful until and after besides?"

"That's a good word—'faithful.' "

"Is it? That's a quality we give to a horse, or a dog."

"You're a wild one, Kathy Ballard."

"Why won't you talk about your wife?"

"Yeah," he said, rubbing his chin.

"Let me analyze it. If you had resentments, just uprooting them might give you some pleasure. So you didn't dislike her. If you'd been awfully happy, you might want to talk about that a little. So I don't think you were. So what you were was something in the middle. Am I right?"

"Sounds like a description of everybody's marriage—something in the middle."

"I'd like to know about her. I'd like to know if you were happy together."

"Relatively."

"Did she give you less than you wanted?"

"Rather the other way round, I think. I did less for her than I should have."

"The whole notion of pairing doesn't make sense," Kathy said. "Do you think she'd have liked Fred?"

"I can't say."

"Oh, I'm sorry. No. It's your fault, or the fault of this damned tea. You want to get me a proper drink, please? You could come back to my place if you're out."

"I'll look. I may have something stashed away."

In the kitchen he told himself what kind of fool he was. He agreed. He told himself that all this maneuvering was pleasant to a lonely old man, and where was the harm?

He came back with the bottle and some more glasses, and she was standing looking at his books. "You've got a funny taste in books."

"Why is that?" he said, putting the bottle and the glasses down.

119

"It looks as if you went into a secondhand bookstore—a very old and unpopular bookstore—and scooped up an armload without looking. I mean, *Winnie-the-Pooh* and Wolf Solent and Sherlock Holmes (complete in two volumes) and Panait Istrati (who's he?) and M. P. Shiel and Plutarch's *Lives.* Well, Plutarch. I can understand a principal having a copy of that."

"Those are books I've had for a long time. Some of them go way, way back. If you have a certain background, and live at a certain time, and are a certain kind of person, then you fall in love with a certain kind of writer. Even though, you're right, no one of those is like the next. A contained omnivorousness is what it is."

"I used to read Zane Grey when I was a girl. That's strange, isn't it?"

"I don't know. I read *Little Women.*"

"Robert," she said, her voice very soft and solemn.

"What?"

"Robert," she said, pleading.

"What's the matter?"

"I'm lonely."

"I'm sorry," he said sincerely.

"I'll tell you what!" She put her arms out, suddenly gay. "Measure me."

"Measure—?"

"Didn't you ever play 'measure me'?"

"No."

"This is the way it goes. Come, stand in front of me."

"Yes?"

"Now we have to see who's bigger."

"I know who's bigger."

"Don't be silly, silly. You have to *measure.*"

"How do you do that?"

"Well, naturally, you have to get as close as you can if you want it to be accurate."

He stopped inches from her. He was swimming in color. Hairline golden over brown forehead, red of mouth, white of revealed tips of teeth, cool green of dress.

120

"That's no way to measure," she said, not moving.

"Why not?" He wondered at how difficult it was to speak.

"Closer."

Their bodies touched. Her arms went around him, hands pressing into the small of his back. His own hands he kept tentatively at her shoulders, as if proving he was not yet committed.

"Now," she said, her face raised to his. "Now I can tell that you're big."

She smelled like grass hot in the sun.

"You're getting bigger," she said.

He tried to move away; her arms were locked and strong.

"A bargain," she whispered. "Even exchange. My mouth for yours."

He started to speak, and she took the words from his tongue. There was pain in his back where her fingernails pressed. His hands went down her back, around the curve of hip, into the hollow.

Then up to her arms to push her away, having to use most of his strength.

She stood perfectly still. Then she laughed with complete engaging friendliness. "What I said. A challenge."

He went back to his chair and sat down.

"I'll have that drink now." Kathy sat across from him, and everything was different. She kept smiling. He put some ice cubes in a glass, and they tinkled because his hands were not controlled; she noticed it and was delighted. He poured bourbon over the ice and handed the glass to her. She was looking at him as if they had not stopped. Was so much and no more enough for this sudden breakthrough into intimacy? If it were so, then why his denial? He felt cheated, and resentful.

She brushed a loose strand of hair from her forehead. She raised her glass in salute and drank deeply.

"It wouldn't have been—smart," he said, feeling stupid, as if he had been pressed into explanation.

"Of course not," she agreed gaily. She drank some more. "And one has to be smart. Even us ignorant ones. But tell me,

Robert, how do you go about acting wise when you're not wise?"

She sat back, smiling, and looked all over him. He fidgeted. He wondered how it was that although he had ostensibly rebuffed her, she sat there smugly as if the situation were of her making.

He said, "You look as if you know things I don't know."

"I know one thing. I know the ice isn't all that thick."

"And now that you know?"

"Now that I know, I'll have another drink." She held out her empty glass.

Carefully he poured, and she held the bottle as he attempted to withdraw it and filled her glass halfway. "This is to wash down my inhibitions."

"I hadn't noticed—"

"Wait," she said, smiling.

She drank and set the glass down carefully, purposefully. She got up and came to him. He thought her action was like the rapist in Faulkner's *Sanctuary*, whose crushing out of cigarette was always preparatory to another attack. She was weightless on his lap. She put one hand in his hair and the other on his chin and brought his mouth up kissing him like a succubus, and he felt strength and wits and identity drain from him. She took his hands and slid to the floor drawing him down.

Then he stopped, braking, heels digging a furrow. She was too sure and he was stubborn. She had initiated it and he was jealous of his right to court. He could smell whisky instead of grass. She was importunate and he liked to be more than an instrument. He pulled her to her feet.

She straightened herself and brushed at herself. She looked at him with a weird kind of amusement. Without speaking to him she went out.

CHAPTER ELEVEN

He lay sleeplessly alone, thinking he need not have been alone, Kathy's desirability increasing with her absence; and he thought of the way she would look now alone in her bed, also awake, round and restless and inviting, and he was not proud of himself or congratulatory. He had not been spurred by any abstract morality. He could not, now in the night, understand why he had refused her and, the inclination full-blown and insistent, almost got up and went to her. But that was just dreaming.

He was up early, ready to leave by seven thirty. As he was finishing his coffee, there was a knock at the door and Kathy came in, as fresh as the morning, smiling, unbelievingly unaffected.

She said, "I hate, I absolutely hate to have breakfast alone. To me this is one of the main reasons for marriage, someone to look at over your coffee; he doesn't have to look at you, or even talk. I came over to invite you to join me, Robert."

"Have a cup with me."

"I was hoping you'd ask."

He marveled and was grateful for her cheerfulness, having created a bogey of a woman scorned for their first meeting. He got up to serve her, but she waved him back to his chair, filling a cup at the stove and sitting down at the small kitchen table with him. "I think I'm going to build something."

"What?"

"Haven't decided yet. But it's such a beautiful morning—just so long as it's out of doors. Maybe I'll make a birdhouse or I'll fix up the barbecue pit."

The man's things that she did. He could not remember having seen Fred working around the house.

123

"Kathy, about last night—"

"I knew it, I knew it." She looked at him in mock sadness. "You have to know *why* and *what* so you can make the proper notation for your records, is that it? As if it isn't the happening of itself that matters but what it means and what was the reason and are there any lessons. I just knew you'd want to talk about it. You're an example of everything I hate," she said calmly, sipping her coffee. "I don't know why I'm even bothering to drink your coffee, which, incidentally, is not very good—"

"All I started to say was—"

"Don't say it. You're talking about yesterday and that's the same as two thousand B.C., and if you want to discuss history, I am not your girl, I always found it boring. If you have anything to say about today or tomorrow, then speak up."

"I—"

"So what else is new?" she said.

"You mean you can take a thing and wish it away, and just like that it never was?"

"Silly things, unimportant things. Why not? What are you, a basket holder filled with trivia?"

"You're a wonder," he said.

"Someday the old lady will show her medals. Some of them look like scars. You'll be late for work, won't you?"

Robert stood with Perry Dickinson at the steps to the stage in the high-school auditorium, watching the students come into the assembly the Principal had decreed. There were the bright ones with the glasses and the clothes-conscious ones and the whispering uncertain ones. There were the stalking, insolent-moving boys with hair too well cared for over pimpled faces. There were girls already over the line to maturity proudly wiggling, and the board-front girls yet to catch up, envious and apprehensive; there were very plain girls and very pretty ones. Robert watched, very moved at the hundreds of scientists and congressmen and mothers and college presidents and poets and businessmen. Some of these boys one day would reach Mars, and some of these girls would help find a cure for cancer. Robert

124

felt very proud of what he was, and it was not a thing to be expressed to one who asked if he liked his work, and it was not a thing even to be expressed to himself.

When they came through the doors and down the inclined aisles, they stepped in molasses and took forever to select a seat, looking for friends and changing as they noticed more desirable companions in another place; they talked loudly and stood up and called out to their neighbors. The teachers in the aisles berated and gestured and accomplished nothing. Robert looked at his watch and waited.

Robert had a great failing as administrator, and he watched it begin to show itself. In the pit of his stomach somewhere a pilot light activated a burner, and the ever-ready pot sat there over the heat and the simmering started. The attributes required for his position were calmness, objectivity, the ability to see everyone else's point of view. You could never, never permit a neurotic reaction to a condition so impersonal that it was like an act of nature. You must never get *mad*.

When there was comparative quiet, Robert walked onto the stage and, facing the audience, said in a loud, clear voice, "I am unhappy about the manner in which you came to this assembly. This is the auditorium of your high school, and you are not to treat it like the bleachers of a ballpark or the spectator section in a circus tent. You are students. That is a proud thing, and I will not permit you to demean it, or behave in a manner so undignified that you are unworthy of it. You will all rise quickly and quietly, and go back to your rooms. You will wait there until you hear the bell, and then you will come back here, quickly and quietly, and take your seats. I want the back rows to leave first, and so on down toward the front, so that there will be no crowding. Now. You may leave now."

He stood on the stage, worried, and watched as they began, with infinite slowness, to move at his bidding. This could be a good thing or a bad thing, and there was nothing he could do now to influence the outcome. If they fought him as a group, it might take a little while, but sooner or later he would be forced out. He had taken the first, decisive, and as far as he was concerned, necessary step. Authority had to be established for its own sake before it could be used for good or bad.

As he came down the steps to rejoin Perry, he heard some of the comments he expected. They were not for his ears, but so often people speaking confidentially in a large group are unaware of the trickiness of sound. He heard a boy say: "Just what I was afraid of. We've got a Hitler here." He heard a girl: "Who does he think he is, pushing us around like a bunch of kindergartners?" He heard: "He tangles with me, and I push that nose of his back into shape." That one Robert wanted to identify, but it wasn't possible. And one lovely voice: "I think he's right. There's too much horsing around in this school."

Perry was smiling ruefully. "Go it, bear."

"Am I wrong, Perry?"

"No. It's just that every once in a while you convince me that I never want to be a principal."

Standing at one of the rear doors, clearing the students through, was Elizabeth Loomis. Robert reminded himself that he had to observe her teaching. That was part of the Principal's job. He also had to explain to her, in some fashion, what the reason was for his behavior during her interview. If she thought that brusqueness and authoritarianism were part of him, she would be confirmed after this morning. He would have to talk to her. As a teacher. Principal and teachers had to understand one another.

After the auditorium was cleared, he had Perry go back to the office and ring the bell. This time, Robert waited on the stage for the students to enter. They came in in good order and took seats with minimum commotion. He was relieved enough to feel his eyes smart for an instant. He stepped forward.

"I congratulate you. This is the way you will conduct yourselves in assemblies from now on, and not because you have to be coerced into decent behavior but because of the respect you owe your school.

"Enough of that. My name is Robert Evans, and I am the Principal here. I hope you all knew who I was before. I would hate to think you let some unauthorized stranger up here tell you what to do." He expected a small titter and got it. Oh, the pleasantries in public speaking. Some lightness would be appropriate now. A story. He couldn't think of one. He thought of what Rose Pink had said about his smile. Thinking of it was enough to make it impossible. Unless you were a model or a movie star.

"I would have wanted our first official meeting to be somewhat more agreeable, but it's just as well that you know some of my feelings about this school, and my part in it, and your part in it. I don't think it's possible for us to be opposed to one another, because we all want the same thing. A good school. That means it has to be run with some rules and some discipline. Otherwise it stops being a school and is just some chaotic meeting place. Once we establish the basic ground rules, I see no reason why our relationship should not be a pleasant one."

He looked over his audience. They were summing him up, each of them according to his own needs. On some of the faces were sneers and on some just the stoniness of the young toward any platform-speaking adult, but there were some quietly listening and suspending judgment.

"Soon we shall be starting an evaluation program at Pine Hills. This is going to take about a year, and will consist of committees of teachers in each department working on the examination of every phase of our school program. The aim of this, eventually, is to have our school accredited by the Middle States Association. I won't, now, go into the mechanics of this, but what it means is that we want Pine Hills to be recognized as a top-flight school by the member colleges of the association, and by extension to most of the other colleges in the country. Those of you who are juniors and seniors and are going through the miseries of college acceptance know how important this can be. I know you are all proud of this school. I am equally sure you would not object to our trying to make it even better."

He saw Elizabeth Loomis sitting near the far aisle. He could not read the expression on her face.

"I want to advise you of a few changes to take effect at once.

127

First—the halls of this school must be free of students at all times except for use as passageways between classes. Any student found in a corridor without an excellent reason for being there will be referred to me for disciplinary action.

"Second—lunch periods will be shortened to twenty-two minutes." He waited for the anticipated groans and got them. "You will find the new schedule posted in your homerooms. This does not mean that you will have less time in which to eat. From what I have observed the past week, by adding another lunch session so much less time will be wasted in waiting to be served in the cafeteria that you should find yourself with more rather than less time for the business of chewing." Now his smile came without effort. "And this will enable us to add thirty-five minutes to the school day."

He let the muffled ironic cheers die out rather than stifle them at once. Let there be less energy to protest the ruling he had been leading up to.

"I come now to what I regard as a serious problem. I have seen students leaving the building in droves at lunchtime. A number of you go across the highway to that little lunchroom, others go off up and down the road as if a holiday was declared. As of now, this situation is going to change. During the course of the school day I want no student to leave the grounds. If you have any doubts about the area that is so defined, from now on you will find a monitor or teacher at all the exits."

There was a great deal of buzzing as boys and girls leaned forward to comment to one another down the rows.

"I want no doubt of what I say, I want no one later to say he did not understand. After you report here in the morning, you may not leave this school without written permission from me until the school day is over. I will suspend any student who is found outside the school area without a pass. I am talking about immediate, automatic suspension.

"There are several excellent reasons why I feel this is necessary. With a student body this size it is difficult enough to know where each student is during the day. This becomes almost impossible when you are permitted to roam about as you

128

see fit. In the event of an emergency affecting the entire school, or a personal one affecting any one of you, I have to know where you are. During that part of the day in which you are supposed to get your schooling, I am responsible for you. I am responsible for the kind of education you should be absorbing, and within obvious limits, I am responsible for your physical well-being. Your parents entrust you to me for so many hours during the day, I'd like to return you to them in at least no worse condition than when I received you.

"That's all for now. As soon as I can think up some more unpopular regulations, I'll let you know."

They whispered and groaned and went back to their classes. On the way to the office Perry said, "You're going to need a police detail."

"For a while. Teachers outside lunchtime. I'll be there off and on. The first couple of days will be the hardest, until this thing sets and the kids are convinced I mean it."

"If a student missed his breakfast, Loomis would send him across the street for a doughnut and coffee."

"What a humanitarian that man was."

"This will drive Jennings out of business. He'll fight it."

"Why not? Everybody fights. Cowards, old ladies, ailing wives. Everybody, in his own way, fights like hell. No reason for Jennings to be different."

"I wish it could have been done some other way."

"Was there another way?"

"Maybe not. I agree you couldn't get the kind of student control you need now without this kind of restrictive measure. But it isn't fair to that man over there, it really isn't. When he set up his place, he was assured the kids would be able to come to him."

"That's not my fault. And before I start weeping for him, I think of a kid getting hit by a bus on that highway. Then I think of the kid's mother coming to me and wanting to know what the hell her kid was doing there when he should have been in school." Which didn't, quite, obliterate Robert's responsibility for hurt to a stranger. "At least I think I'll walk over and tell him myself. Better than his finding out from one of the kids."

The gas station was about a hundred feet from the lunchroom. A car was on the lift, and under it a man was operating a welding torch. Robert quivered at the marching ant army that began to move across his back. He had seen a man once welding in a grease pit suddenly become a torch himself. In the space between the store and the garage stood several automobiles. One had a for-sale sign on the windshield; on the dust of the body were scribbled a few words. Since mechanics and garage owners do not write these words over their cars, it had to be one of Robert's students. He was completely intolerant. I am not, he thought, really fit to handle adolescents. The well-adjusted principal who sees dirty words on a wall remembers all the psychological justification in all the scholarly papers he has read. I don't. I just get mad. He looked at the lunchroom and he looked at the gas station and he looked at the cars picking up speed on the highway as they passed the restrictive school signs. Robert went into the store somewhat less likely to be sympathetic than he had been.

There was a narrow counter with three round stools before it. In one corner was a soft-drink machine taking up a quarter of the floor space. Behind the counter was a coffee maker and a grill, at which a man stood frying a hamburger. He was a broad man with an interesting tonsure that looked almost orange. The back of his neck had a roll of fat that was neatly tucked over the white string of the man's apron. When he turned around, the color of his hair was matched by the freckles on his face. He had a nose so upturned as to present nostrils fully to the sight. His chin sloped in to join the continuation of neck down to breastbone in unbroken plane. "Yeah?" the man said.

"My name is Evans, I'm principal of the high school."

"Oh! Glad to know you, Mr. Evans." He put out a slab of hand that Robert took with some reluctance. "I'm Sam Jennings. I own this—" His hand gesture had the muted pride of designating a block of apartment buildings or a mansion on a hill.

"I'm sure glad you looked in, Mr. Evans. Can I get you something? Coffee's fresh—"

"I didn't—"

"You're looking out for your students, that's fine of you, Mr. Evans. Well, let me tell you, I give those kids prime beef, I want you to be sure of that, Mr. Evans. No sawdust, no junk. I don't skimp on the sandwiches, either. They get a fair deal from Sam Jennings. You haven't heard any complaints, have you?"

"No. I haven't heard any complaints."

"Good. Good. Can I get you a cup of coffee? On the house."

"No, thanks. What I came for, Mr. Jennings—"

"I'll tell you another thing. Mr. Loomis used to eat in here quite a lot. I guess that shows I give quality, right? And he used to say to me, if a kid was short to feed him anyway, and he would make it up. There was a man, right? The kids always came first with him. I'm glad to see you take an interest yourself, Mr. Evans, coming in like this to look the place over."

"Listen, Mr. Jennings, what I came in for has to do with something else, so let me come to the point at once. I came in to let you know that from now on the students will not be permitted in here during the school day."

Jennings looked at him with no comprehension.

"Did you understand what I said, Mr. Jennings?"

"I heard what you said. Not that it makes any sense to me. What do you mean, the school day? Lunchtime, is that in the school day?"

"Yes."

Color began to come into Jennings' face, the freckles pale islands. One eye blinked rapidly. Robert cautiously edged back a little, having a great respect for the explosive potential of strangers.

"What do you mean," Jennings said, "they won't be coming in here during the day?"

"School hours," Robert said.

"School hours. That's the whole day. I didn't set up here to serve those kids at night, you know."

"I'm sorry if this is going to affect your business, Mr. Jennings. But I can't have the students leaving the school grounds. I came over to tell you that myself in case there was anything about it I could explain—"

"Explain! I don't know what the hell you mean, explain. I think it's not explaining I need, it's explaining you need. I bought this little business, Mr. Evans, five years ago. Before I bought it, I talked it over with some of the School Board, and I talked to Mr. Loomis. I got their okay, especially Mr. Loomis, who thought it was a good idea having a place nearby where the kids could have a bite to eat or ice cream or a Coke or something. So I put up everything I had, Mr. Evans, and I've been making out pretty fair, I don't mind telling you that. You've been principal how long—a couple of months, maybe? Well, Mr. Evans, you want to make changes, you want to be a new broom, you go ahead. But not with my store, not with my living, you understand me, Mr. Evans?"

And Sam Jennings took his orange-freckled face and stub nose and that backward-flowing chin and shoved them across the counter top at Robert, and Robert wished that he felt more secure about what he was doing so he could be more righteously unfeeling about Mr. Jennings' problem. The trouble was that Mr. Jennings, for all the unloveliness of his disposition, had a point on his side.

A mechanic from next door came in and helped himself to a bottle of pop from the vending machine. Jennings called, "Hey, Al, you know the Principal?"

All the automobile mechanics Robert had known were either happy-seeming, as if pleased in this difficult world to have found a haven of grease and cogs and engine noises in which they could function importantly as friend, adviser, physician, to trusting women and hypochondrial men; or they were distant and sullen individuals whose addiction to their craft precluded explanation and resented the unknowing. Al was one of the happy ones. Grinning, he said, "You Mr. Evans? Pleased to meet you. Whyn't you bring your car in, Mr. Evans. Buy your gas here and you get a break. Professional discount."

132

"Al, he's going to keep the kids away from here, what do you think about that?"

"Huh?" Al said. Then he laughed. "That's always been the trouble with Sam here, Mr. Evans. Never could take a rib. Well, I hope to be seeing you, Mr. Evans." Al tilted the bottle to his mouth and walked out that way, like a performing bear.

Jennings said, "See that, Mr. Evans? That's what I mean. Nobody can even take it seriously." He frowned. "Maybe you *have* been kidding me, Mr. Evans?"

"No. I haven't been kidding you. But I wish you could realize that there's nothing personal here. After all, I didn't know anything about you. I wish you well. It's just that I can't permit my students to wander off—"

Uncomfortably, Robert knew he was protesting too much.

Jennings clutched at the top of his head, forgetful of the loss of hair there. "With all respect, Mr. Evans, I don't think you understand the situation here. I mean, you just don't understand the situation. I *depend* on those kids coming in. That's why I bought this store, you understand?"

"I'm sorry about that, Mr. Jennings."

"Sorry. Sure. I have to ask you to change your mind about that new rule of yours, Mr. Evans."

"I couldn't do that."

Jennings' hand went up again in a claw to his head and, both the loss of hair and the need for calm remembered, straightened out and rubbed the baldness. "It's not as if we were peddling narcotics or dirty pictures or any of the things you read in the papers takes place near a school. This is a clean place. So I don't understand what's in your mind."

"I have to get back now," Robert said.

"You have to get back! Five years I put in building up this place, and you haven't got five minutes to tell me why you're tearing it down. What kind of man are you, Mr. Evans? Don't you care about other people?"

"It's necessary," Robert said.

"We'll see about that." Jennings reached for the wall phone and dialed a number with a vicious finger. "Sal? This is your colleague. Yeah, the other fellow you know's in the feed business. Sure, Sam. How are you, Sal?"

Robert started to leave and stopped at Jennings' holding gesture. "Sal, something's come up I wanted to talk to you about. Mr. Evans is here. Yes, from the school. He just came in and said something that I think you ought to know about. He came in and told me he's keeping the kids away from my place. Yeah, how about that, Sal? I don't know why, he just came in and told me that."

Jennings listened for a while, then said, "Well, he's still here if you want to talk to him. Yeah, I'll be there. Monday night. You bet I'll be there. Thanks, Sal." To Robert, "Mr. Casella wants to talk to you."

Irritated, Robert reached across the counter for the phone. He said hello. Casella's voice, crisp and businesslike from his office, said, "Evans? Robert?"

"Yes."

"What is it, Robert? Anything I can do?"

"I don't think so, Sal."

"That's an excitable man, Sam Jennings. What's that about your keeping kids out of his store?"

"I don't want to go into that now. This is hardly the time and certainly not the place. I have to go now."

"From what he told me, he's got a real problem. I told him to come to the Board meeting, that's Monday night. Will you be there, Robert?"

"Are you saying you think I should be?"

"Well, yes. Whenever a member of the community comes up with a gripe, it's a good idea that the person responsible is able to defend himself. That's democracy, isn't it?"

"I don't like that word, 'defend.' "

"I didn't mean it that way. Everything else all right, Robert?"

"Everything is fine."

He hung up and went out as Jennings said, "This isn't the end of it, Mr. Evans. Not by a long shot it isn't."

134

Back in his office, Robert was informed by Mrs. Farrow that Dr. Eberly had been trying to reach him for the past hour. Her face and voice were so empty of expression that she had to be blanking them consciously not to seem smug or snide because he had been missing all the time the Superintendent was so urgently looking for him.

"On the other hand," Robert said, "if I just stayed at my desk waiting for the phone to ring, how could I get anything done?"

"What's that, Mr. Evans?"

"Nothing. Sometimes I just say things. I want Joseph Maxwell to come in and see me. Twelfth grade, I don't know the class."

"Yes, Mr. Evans."

He called Eberly, who said there were a few things he wanted to take up with Robert and could he come over later that afternoon.

"Anything I have to know of in advance?"

"A couple of parent complaints. Not serious, but we ought to have a talk."

"All right. Is anything the matter? I mean, with you?"

"No. Why?"

"I don't know, you just don't sound your usual—" He almost said, babbling, "vital self."

"Just one of those days, Robert. Do you ever feel sorry for God, the way he has to please everybody, or at least have the right reasons for not pleasing everybody? You know what I mean? I don't want to sound irreligious—"

"I understand, Fenton. Who's been in today? The head of

135

the PTA? How many irate parents? How many bee-bonneted Board members?"

The Superintendent sighed. "While I think of it, Robert, there's a Board meeting Monday night. They expect some preliminary presentation from you concerning first steps toward an evaluation program."

"I'll prepare something. I was going to attend anyway. There will be a protesting citizen."

"Who?" Eberly said, a man with no trouble believing the bell was always tolling for him. "What's up?"

"Sam Jennings. Very high up."

"Robert—"

And Robert was sorry for him, for the sound of distress in the voice; not personally sorry as you would be for someone you wanted to help, but just sorry the way you would understand the problems of a man whose duty it was to execute people.

"Robert—you went through with that lunchroom thing and Jennings knows—"

Robert refused again to remind the Superintendent that he had been in agreement. "Yes." He thought of what Perry had said about changes that were approved and even suggested by leaders who wanted no more than talk about change.

"Robert?"

"Yes?"

"How far did you go? Maybe—"

"I announced it to the students this morning. And then I went over to tell Jennings myself. While I was there, he called Casella and complained. He also complained to me. It was Casella who suggested both Jennings and I appear at the meeting."

"A thing like this can look terrible. You know how a thing like this can be stirred up? The touchiest thing is a man's business, the way he makes his living. Any Board member has to be sympathetic to a thing like that. They're most of them businessmen."

136

"They're supposed to be concerned about school problems, isn't that why they ran for the Board?"

"Yes," said Eberly, irritation evident in his voice, and Robert thought of the bearer of bad tidings who was usually executed by the king for his news. "I'll see you later, then, Robert."

"Yes."

He went out to prod Mrs. Farrow about Joseph Maxwell. She said he wasn't in school.

"You sure?"

"He's marked absent."

"Oh."

"You suspect truancy there, Mr. Evans? You want me to notify the attendance supervisor?"

"Who said anything about truancy? Can't a boy be sick? Just make a note, in case I forget. Check him tomorrow. I want to see that boy."

The door to Perry's office opened, and a man came out; Robert knew he was a teacher but had never met him. He was a young man with a plumpness almost womanish because he carried more weight on the hips than a man should. He wore the intellectually popular black heavy glasses. His face was full, with a small pouting mouth. Perry came out behind him, saying he was sure everything would work out. The teacher said he hoped so. He nodded as he saw Robert, and left. Robert stared after him.

"Gilbert Gist," Perry said. "He was one of our catches last year, Eberly grabbed him as he came out of Oberlin before he settled down to graduate work somewhere. Social studies."

"I didn't know Eberly was so anxious to bring in the brilliant set."

"It was one of those unbalanced years. We had applicants for everything, but not social studies. Happens that way sometimes."

"Always."

"Gist lives with his mother in the city. I doubt that we'll keep him long enough for his tenure. I doubt that he considers Pine

Hills the apogee of his career. Anyway, he just came to me with a problem."

"Lives with his mother and travels up here every day. That's at least two problems right there. How come I overlooked him?"

"He was late getting back from vacation."

"So?"

"He came to see me as discipline officer. There's a boy in his class giving him a hard time. Boy named Foster. He says this kid's been making cracks. The mother's boy kind of thing. Under-breath allegations about manhood and all that. Gist says the boy always stops short of being open enough to send him in on a specific charge, but the situation is getting less and less bearable."

"This is Gist's first teaching job?"

"Yes."

"Good experience, wouldn't you say? You know the Foster boy?"

"He's a rough one. Overgrown wise-guy type. He'd be a hood with just a little encouragement."

"What did you suggest?"

"I thought Gist ought to stand up to him. But that's a kind of personal thing. There really is no blueprint. I said if it got too tough for him, I would handle it."

"Let me know what happens."

A man came in, and Mrs. Farrow went to see what he wanted. Robert was pleased to notice that she no longer kept anyone waiting. The man asked to see the Principal. Mrs. Farrow said he would have to make an appointment. Better and better, Robert thought. Then he spoiled her progress by going over and introducing himself to the man.

"I'm Angus Palmer, Mr. Evans. I wonder if I could have a minute with you. I don't have much time, I just took a chance that you might be able to talk to me for a bit."

"Come in." Robert led the way to his office.

Palmer was a thin man with the dark intensity (crew cut, narrow-shoulder suit) of the maligned Madison Avenue worker

138

who, Robert found out, was a research chemist at a local vitamin plant.

"I'm going to sound like a nut," Palmer said, "but from your chair I suppose you're used to it. My son is stuck this year with a teacher I had myself when I went through Pine Hills High. It's a damned tragedy that this teacher is still here, still teaching. I don't know if anything can be done about it, but I wanted to get it off my chest."

"Who's the teacher?"

"Alice Cresswell."

"Ah, yes," Robert said.

"Can you give me one good reason why that woman is still permitted to teach?"

"There's one excellent reason," said Robert, smiling. "Tenure."

Mr. Palmer was not amused. "Do you know her? Have you observed her work?"

"Yes," Robert said. "Yes to both."

Miss Cresswell was about fifty-five years old and looked like a woman who reported to work after the business offices were closed for the day. She always wore her version of the Hawaiian one-piece dress, under which her heavy unsupported breasts hung somewhere near her waist. She wore on her feet what looked like carpet slippers. Her hair was gray and stringy, and she was always poking in hairpins that did little to keep the strands in place. Her subject was mathematics. Robert had visited her class when she was demonstrating the proper approach to the solution of a problem involving rods and acres and, for all Robert knew, hectometers, since this was a subject in which he had been deficient since the third grade. The fact that he had become a principal despite abysmal arithmetical ignorance meant a professional lifetime of inspired concealment. Nevertheless, he had never seen such an example of droning incompetence. Although "droning" was not the word to describe the flat nasal irritant that was Miss Cresswell's voice. The class was very well behaved, and this, Robert at once realized, had nothing to do with his visit but was an obvious pattern. The students were quiet and industrious because they paid no attention at all to the teacher, who, in turn, paid no attention at all to the class. She spent the entire period at the blackboard, making obscure notations and more obscure comments, while the boys and girls caught up with their homework in other subjects or quietly read. Miss Cresswell's evaluation card had been consistently marked satisfactory by Mr. Loomis, with particular credit for class discipline.

"Well?" said Mr. Palmer.

Robert had talked to Perry about her. Perry had pointed out that nothing really could be done. Miss Cresswell's pattern of instruction had been fixed for many, many years.

Robert had tried. He had visited a few more times to make sure it always went that way, and he had called Miss Cresswell into his office and pointed out that she was less than inspiring. Miss Cresswell, in that grating voice, had pointed out that she had been in the school system much, much longer than Mr. Evans, and so far as she was concerned, she was doing a fine job.

At Robert's insistence, Eberly had spoken to her, and came away from the interview flushed and unhappy-looking.

Through some miracle of youthful resilience or just plain luck, a percentage of Miss Cresswell's students met the minimum requirements.

After Robert's expression of dissatisfaction with her, and after the Superintendent's mild plea for improvement, Miss Cresswell was granted a salary increase of close to a thousand dollars.

This was based on an accumulation of in-service credits. The teacher, like his professional counterparts, must not permit his skills to become dulled but must continually strive to increase and broaden his intellectual grasp. (From *The Teacher's Manual*.) This was the first school Robert had been in that increased salaries proportionately with the number of these excursions into professional improvement. Robert had thought this a fine idea until discovering that any course could be considered for in-service credit at the discretion of the Superintendent.

And any economic-minded teacher would have been an idiot not to take advantage of the unrelated garbage available that required nothing more than so many hours of sitting through the classes.

The record of Alice Cresswell, teacher of mathematics, showed that she had satisfactorily completed improvement courses in "The Slow Child," "The Gifted Child," "The Average Child," "Historical Sites in the State of New York" (lectures plus photographs), "How to Improve Reading Skills in the Foreign-born," "The Place of Humor in the Classroom," and a special series sponsored by the Teachers' Association that consisted of invited speakers from representative local industry. Miss Cresswell had been exposed to the background and contributions to society of a well-known cosmetics firm, and a business that destroyed mountains for the manufacture of gravel. And there was more, much more. Had a course been accredited in "Fly Casting for the Left-handed," Robert could see Miss Cresswell loyally in the first row, muumuu and carpet slippers, blissfully accumulating credits.

But what did you say to a parent? Mr. Palmer was waiting.

"If you have a specific complaint, why we could have Miss Cresswell in and perhaps come to some solution—"

"My complaint is specific enough. I want to know what she's doing teaching here at all."

"She's not the best teacher we have. Granted, Mr. Palmer. But she has met the requirements for her position, her students achieve as well as those of the rest of the staff—their regents grades show—"

"Forgive me, Mr. Evans, but can't we dispense with this principal-parent picture, just for a minute, and be honest? I know you have your professional manner to maintain and all that, but I'm getting tired. I spoke to Dr. Eberly last week. He's a master of meaningless phrases. All I want is to have someone in authority admit to me this teacher is a dud."

"And that will satisfy you?"

"No. But at least I will have the illusion of talking to candid people."

"Why illusion?"

"This nonsense about regents. Most of the kids who do even fairly well have had to be privately tutored, don't you know that? You think old lady Cresswell can teach a kid enough to pass an objective examination? I know you haven't been here very long, Mr. Evans, but certain things—well—in my business you don't have to have a graduate degree to know H_2S stinks."

Robert listened and wondered how a man who at first seemed such a decent fellow could have become so objectionable. Although what he said was perfectly correct, this did not restore his likableness. "Miss Cresswell," said Robert, "will probably be retiring soon."

"How convenient. How many hundreds of students has she ruined, and how many more will have to suffer before nature takes its course? Is that what it means to administer a school system, doing nothing about people like that?"

"Are you opposed to teacher tenure, Mr. Palmer?"

"Ah, ha. Sure. Tell a jingoist you like Tchaikovsky, and right away you're in favor of the Communists taking over the world. I'm in favor of job security for everybody. I'm not in favor of anything strangling the educative process."

"I vote yes and no along with you. Short of immorality or gross incompetence—and how do you prove either?—a teacher under the present tenure law goes on teaching. If they're old enough, they're encouraged to retire."

"That's lousy."

"The Principal visits the classroom, and makes suggestions for improvement if he thinks they are in order. Some progress is made. I will grant you, Mr. Palmer, not enough."

"I think something ought to be done. I think the PTA ought to take this up. At least I can quote you as saying this is an incapable teacher and your hands are tied, the law says she has to be retained."

"You certainly may not quote me as saying that, Mr. Palmer. You see, that's the trouble, and now I will speak frankly. There are problems within the school system that have to be handled by professional people. I might be interested in the effects of vitamins on my children, but I don't come into your laboratory and suggest what you should do. Yet you do not grant the same professional status to educators, do you? As a parent, member of the community, PTA, what have you, you want information, you want to complain, all certainly your privilege as a citizen. Then you ask for expression of interdepartmental difficulty, you ask for honesty, and at once you're off quoting the Principal to have the laws changed. So I will say I never saw you before. I care as much about this problem as you do, and possibly I care a good deal more because you're concerned about your son, but he's only one, and I'm concerned about hundreds. This is a live problem, a not uncommon problem, and everybody from the Superintendent down is aware of it and involved in it. Alerting the PTA into a witch hunt against one old lady isn't going to solve anything or prove anything."

"I never suggested any such thing."

"I'm glad you didn't." And now Robert switched rapidly enough to make it bewildering, even to himself. But he was getting sick of people who thought any problem involving a human being could be simple. "Alice Cresswell may not be the greatest teacher in the world, but she has devoted her life to it. Never got married, never raised a family. You know what the greatest loss in teaching is, it's the same in other fields, the girls put in just enough time to begin to repay their training period and then they're off getting married. Of course, when things are rough, they go on teaching, but when times are good we lose them. But an Alice Cresswell goes on, year after year, and maybe she doesn't dress as well as Elizabeth Taylor and maybe in her profession she would not be invited to lecture to the Institute at Princeton and maybe over the years exposure to immature minds dragged down her own mental level, but remember this, Mr. Palmer, this woman has put in a lifetime here. You just don't throw people out because a father has problems with a son who might not really be studying"—Robert put up his hand against the protest—"I didn't say that was the case with you, but it is with others, lots of others. The easiest thing in the world is to blame the teacher. And you certainly don't address a PTA meeting saying you have the word of the Principal that this is a dreadful situation but his hands are tied and why don't they get up a petition to the State Education Department."

"You're getting excited, Mr. Evans."

"I don't know whether that's a caution or a compliment. Let me sum it up. She's not the best of teachers, Alice Cresswell, but she meets state minimum standards. Under the tenure regulations there is nothing to warrant dismissal action. On the contrary, with all the in-service courses she takes, she would seem to be commended. Now I want better teachers than Miss Cresswell in this school. I want better teachers than a number who are teaching here now and about whom, for some reason, there are rarely complaints. The screening of the new ones, and especially the decision whether to grant tenure after the probationary period—that's where something can be done."

Palmer stood up, saying, "Well, thanks for your time."

"I know I haven't said anything to make you feel better. But just try and remember that an awful lot of babies are out there with the discarded bath water."

"Sure. And a lot of kids graduate from this noble place of learning lacking fundamental knowledge."

"I regret that, if that is so. I'll do everything I can to make it less likely."

After Palmer had gone, Robert said aloud, "I know. What kind of way is that to talk to a parent?" Then he marveled at his defense of Miss Cresswell. What he had been driven to defend, of course, was the professional versus the amateur. He hated amateurs. Almost as much as he hated incompetent professionals.

It was nearly lunchtime. His phone rang. Mrs. Bruno, the school nurse, said, "Mr. Evans? I think you ought to come to the infirmary right away."

"What happened?"

"There's a boy here who has been badly beaten."

Like the newsman says on television, Robert said to himself, what kind of day has this *been?* "I'll be right there, Mrs. Bruno."

144

Robert stopped long enough to pick up Perry. In the infirmary (it was really just the nurse's room, because no real treatment was permitted), Mrs. Bruno, a stout competent woman, took them behind a screen. A boy sat there. His face was a raw mess. One eye had closed and the other was on its way.

Perry said, "Foster? Dan—what happened?"

"Hi, Mr. Dickinson. I wish I could say you oughta see the other guy, only I didn't lay a glove on him."

"Who did this?" Robert said.

"Mr. Gist."

"Wow," said Perry under his breath. "I told him to stand up to the boy but—"

"How did it happen?" Robert said.

"The class was leaving for lunch—I said something, I don't remember what it was, but it couldn't have been that bad—anyway, all of a sudden he was sailing into me. I didn't even get my hands up. Then that crazy bastard—" Dan Foster looked up startled, as if he had heard someone else use the word. "I'm sorry. Mr. Gist tells me to go up to the nurse as if I was picking up a cold or I got something in my eye."

"Looks as if you did get something in your eye. I want a doctor to look you over."

"I called my father, he's coming."

Robert looked at Mrs. Bruno, who said, "I thought he ought to be notified."

"Yes. Dan—what was it you said to Mr. Gist?"

"Who can remember a thing like that?"

"I want you to think about it, it's important that you remember."

"I don't know, I was just kidding."

Mrs. Bruno dabbed at Dan Foster's cuts, while Robert and Perry went into the anteroom. Robert said, "Thank goodness he's a big one. As big as Gist, isn't he?"

"At least. What I can't understand is why Gilbert isn't up here with a busted jaw."

"The boy says he didn't strike back. I wish he had. Somehow it wouldn't look as bad."

"I wonder if Foster provoked him and then took his beating just to make it look especially lousy for Gilbert."

"He'd have to be pretty sly for that, and very tough," Robert said.

"He's got an abundance of both characteristics."

A man came to the door, looked in inquiringly. His lack of stature exaggerated his breadth. He had a fleshy red nose, with fine red and purple lines across his nostrils like the tracing in a currency bill.

"My name's Foster." His voice was a rasp. "My kid here? What happened?"

"I'm Mr. Evans. Your son was in a fight, Mr. Foster."

"Again?" said Foster proudly. "Damned kid, he's been fighting since he was four years old. He's even offered to take me on a coupla times. I tell him he's too big for me." Mr. Foster chuckled, a phlegmy sound in the back of his throat. "So, what hospital's the other kid in?"

"Other kid?" Robert said.

"Takes two to tangle." Foster laughed. "Heard that on a TV show. You know, two to tango? Get it?"

"I get it," Robert said.

"The only thing I worry about is that the kid doesn't really hurt somebody sometime. He's pretty good with his hands, you know?" Foster made a few rolling motions with hands in parallel. "Seventeen and he's built like a horse. I always raised him not to take no crap—" He bobbed his head at Robert. "Excuse the French. I just didn't want him to get pushed around, you know what I mean?"

"I know what you mean."

"So where's the battler?" Foster went in to his son. Robert heard him laugh. "Hey! You walk into a meat grinder? How many of them were there?"

"It wasn't a fair fight, Pop. It wasn't one of the kids."

Robert and Perry, outside, exchanged glances. Robert said, "Get Gist into my office right away."

Foster said, "Who was it?"

"A teacher."

146

Robert went in in time to meet Foster's glare. The short man seemed to take a deep breath and hold it. His face swelled and turned a dark red. Mrs. Bruno held up her swab of Merthiolate-tinged cotton and looked alarmed.

"A teacher?"

"That's right, Pop. A teacher slugged me."

"What do you know about this, Mr. Evans?"

"Very little, yet, Mr. Foster."

"Danny says a *teacher* hit him!"

"Yes. Well, we'll get at the truth."

"I'm taking him to the hospital right away. This kid could be *hurt*."

"Yes. You have him examined, Mr. Foster."

"Come on, Danny." Mr. Foster helped his son to his feet. On unspoken cue, Dan Foster leaned on his father as if both legs had been injured.

"You'll hear from me," Foster promised.

Robert went back to his office and waited for Gilbert Gist. He picked up a pencil and rolled it in his fingers. He jabbed it viciously back into the holder. Perry and Gist came in. Robert told Perry to close the door.

Gist said at once, "I was telling Mr. Dickinson just this morning. That boy has been tormenting me since last year. But I don't know what came over me, I really don't."

He sat down, hooking heel on instep, knees apart. His heavy thighs strained the tight trousers. He mopped his face with a crumpled handkerchief. His small full lips trembled.

"Exactly what happened?" Robert said.

"Well—the background. He's always—looked at me. A sneer. A remark. Dirty and shameful—innuendos."

"Why didn't you ever turn him over to Perry?"

"Well, it's never been—specific. I mean, an attitude, but—it's as if the boy knew just how far he could safely go without inviting disciplinary action—"

"What did he say this time?"

"Well—it was lunchtime. The students left, Daniel lingered. I was busy at my desk getting some papers together. I looked up and asked what he wanted. He said he wanted to talk to me. He said he wanted to know why I was picking on him."

"Were you?"

"Well—his attitude. I resented it. I took the opportunity once in a while to mention his lack of manners, his vulgarity."

"Go on."

"I think I told him he was heading for a bad end. That it was inevitable, given his—social pattern."

"And he objected to that?"

"He laughed. Then—"

"Yes?"

"He wanted to know why I had not married. He wanted to know whether I intended to live with my mother for the rest of my life. Imagine—bringing my mother into it!"

"What else?"

"He asked me—"

"Get on with it, Gist."

"He asked me—crudely—whether I had ever known a woman."

"And?"

"I hit him. I just hit him."

"You sure did. Well, put this in writing. Make a detailed report, you'd better make a couple of carbons."

"Yes, I'll do that. I'm sorry I lost control, Mr. Evans. But I suppose nothing will happen, will it?"

"Why shouldn't anything happen, Mr. Gist?"

"Corporal punishment—that's permitted in the school system in this state, isn't it? I mean, it's not against the law."

"Is that what you were doing—meting out punishment?"

Gist shrugged, and mopped his face.

"Let's take a look," Robert said. He looked through his papers and found the one marked "Standards of Conduct" and under that, "Discipline." "Here it is. *The teacher's report should include name, grade, date of incident, nature of punishment—* What would you put under that, Mr. Gist? Battering with the fists? Also witnesses, if any, and basis for use of this type of discipline. Then—" Robert turned the sheet. "Inside is an ex-

148

cerpt from the penal law. It says the use of force or violence, by
—teacher—not unlawful—if reasonable in manner and moderate in degree. Reasonable and moderate. I saw that boy's face.
What about that, Mr. Gist?"

Gist pursed his mouth. "He asked for it. Yes. I am convinced
now that I should not be held responsible for a situation into
which I was so obviously forced. That boy wanted trouble right
from the beginning. But he got more than he bargained for,
didn't he?"

Gist smiled.

Robert resisted an impulse to hit him.

"For your information, Mr. Gist. Down here at the bottom of
the page. An excerpt from a school law letter of some years
ago. He talks about corporal punishment, the legality of its use
and so on. Let me quote a little:

"*A teacher who suffers such poverty of imagination, ingenu-
ity, and patience that he must resort to corporal punishment is
unworthy of his profession. Furthermore the law indicates
clearly that any such punishment, however slight or legally jus-
tifiable, is the material of which lawsuits are made—*

"There's more. No sense in going into it. But if I were you,
Mr. Gist, I would feel neither satisfaction nor a sense of
security."

"You think that—"

"Do you know a good lawyer, Mr. Gist?"

Robert stood up to encourage the teacher to do the same.
Gist said, "That report—"

"Yes. Right away."

Gist went out, mopping his forehead. Robert said, "From the
look of Foster's face, this one used his fists, wouldn't you say?"

"I would," Perry said.

"You'd have expected fingernail marks, wouldn't you?"

"There you go again, Mr. Evans, Principal, sir, if I may.
You're intolerant. You don't give people a chance to be de-
fended by all the subconscious pressures that formed them."

"I'll tell you what bothers me about this incident, Perry. Who's
the *hero?*"

CHAPTER THIRTEEN

How about some food?" Perry said.

"That's all it is, the middle of the day? I feel as if I've gone through a bad week or two since this morning."

"Man cannot live on bread alone. He needs problems, too."

"Thanks, sage. I don't feel like bucking that chow line or eating with teachers right now. There's a time for snobbery. Snobbishness. Which is it, Perry?"

"I regret—"

"Sure. Assistants."

"If you're trying to make me feel guilty enough to bring you a sandwich—"

"And, as our English friends say, a cuppa. And one for you. Join me."

"You take advantage," Perry said, "of my natural wish to be liked."

After a while he came back with two sandwiches wrapped in wax paper and two cups of coffee on a tray.

"Thanks," Robert said sincerely. He unwrapped one of the sandwiches. It was wet tuna-fish salad, which had penetrated the spongy white bread.

"Eat it," Perry said, taking a bite out of his. "Maybe the coffee's dry."

"Joseph Maxwell," Robert said. "You know him? A senior."

Perry looked down as Robert imagined all the cogs and levers and flashing lights and relays. "Yes," Perry said.

"You're a wonder. There's a rumor you were built by IBM. Perry, what worries me is someday I'll have to give you up. Sooner or later you're going to get your own school."

"I don't know if I want that."

"Serious?"

"It's the only way to get extra money, and if it were offered me, there'd be a struggle. But I really don't know if I want a school. I put in for your job, that's true. But I don't know if it's worth it."

"Worth it?"

"Look at you. One routine morning and you're eating your liver."

"A damn sight better than this sandwich, I can tell you."

"It's not the responsibility that worries me," Perry said. "It's hurting kids. Loomis had the answer, but obviously at the expense of discipline, efficiency, scholarship, and so on. I'd like to know if it's possible in this world never to hurt anyone, no matter what."

"What would become of the phrases we live by? For your own good. Somebody's got to do it. Honesty pays."

"Those poor simple patriotic volunteers in the war. Excuse me, maybe you were one— Somebody's got to do it. Suppose nobody ever did it, what would happen? And as the man says, honesty never paid very much. You know, Robert, there's a thought here so profound it scares me. Suppose we just threw out every stock phrase. What would happen? Complete collapse?"

"Don't go testing out your subversion on me. Tell me about this Maxwell boy."

"Kind of a nice kid. Not very bright, at least measurably, but he'll probably get a non-regents diploma."

"Would you say that he was a liar?"

"N-no."

Robert told him about Maxwell's request for a parking place for his scooter.

"I turned soft, and I went to his house. Those people are *poor,* Perry. Three hundred bucks for a motor scooter. It doesn't make sense."

"So what happened?"

"Now the boy hasn't shown up in school."

"One day? What are you worried about?"

"Ask me tomorrow."

"You and me, Robert. Let's get a job doing research. Working with fish. That's the answer, some line of research involving fish."

After they ate, Robert went outside. The sun was bright, the morning haze had burned off, the air had the quality of autumn on its way. He walked around the building, making himself aware of distance. This was a special thing he was able to do only once in a while; it had the effect of drawing the load off, of taking concentrated personal concern and diffusing it.

Standing near the exit, across from Sam's lunchroom, was Elizabeth Loomis. Her back was to him. He walked toward her. She had a cardigan drawn across her shoulders cape-fashion. He tried to analyze the appeal of this. The classic casual air, the femininity. He called hello before coming up on her. She turned and smiled.

"You're beautiful, Miss Loomis."

"That's a trick," she said. "That's disarming."

"Does it work?"

"Yes."

"Otherwise you'd be stiff to me, a little antagonistic?"

"Perhaps. But not for the reasons you think. I wish we could talk about that, Mr. Evans."

"Yes. But first—you *are* beautiful. Is there a law against using the truth as a trick? The reason I said it was I was walking around looking off at those mountains, the line of trees where the sun catches them. You see that? And over there, the sky, the pure blue. Then I saw you, with that sweater, and the back of your head and neck. There's something about that, the hair. You turned around then and smiled and you *were* beautiful, so I told you so. At nearly all such times the person is not told. So I thought I would."

"You don't talk like a principal."

"I'm probably not as good a principal as your father."

"That's it, that's what I must settle with you. And then I'll come back to that other thing, that silly thing. I walked into your office, and there you were, waiting, with that awful chip on your shoulder marked: Knock it off, Loomis, I dare you. You couldn't see me at all for the name I bore."

"I saw you. I saw you fine."

"You played a game, and you took all sides."

"You look like a person making up her mind to get angry."

"It's you. Looking hard enough for a bad thing and finding it, looking so hard you were *making* it."

"From the moment I was interviewed for this job, I was compared unfavorably with your father, after I was hired people felt sorry for me because of the inevitable comparison, and now I can't stretch out my arms without something tottering that he set up. How about that, Elizabeth Loomis?"

"It would be nice to have an answer, Mr. Evans. I don't."

"You see?"

"I don't worry about being compared to Horace Mann. I think I'm a pretty good teacher."

"Is that the sort of comparison—"

"Now you're doing what my husband— I can't really refer to him that way, a marriage that's annulled means it never happened."

"What did he do that I do?"

"I don't mean exactly. But he couldn't talk to me for very long, about anything, without getting angry. I reminded him of something very horrible. I reminded him of being married."

"And what has that to do with me?"

"Are you ever going to be able to look at me without suffering from that awful Loomis syndrome?"

"Give me a chance to try. Now, without sarcasm, how is your father?"

"Fine."

"How is he taking retirement?"

"Wonderfully."

"Isn't he bored? Doesn't he miss running a school?"

"My father is a man with lots of resources. He's studying now, he's actually thinking of getting his Master's. When he came out of college, nobody ever did that."

153

"Why did he never come in to see me? You would think—It becomes ridiculous, our never having met."

"I suppose the two of you are a bad combination. You for whatever series of grudges you're nursing, and my father for being probably the shyest man in the world."

Robert looked off at the hills and tried to recapture his enjoyment of the day, but he couldn't stretch out any more. He found himself studying her left ear. There was just enough lobe. It wasn't, really, a place you'd expect to find attractive. He realized, feeling oddly concerned about it, how interested he was becoming in Elizabeth Loomis.

"Once and for all," he said roughly, "I have to know. You said I didn't see you because of your father, and I want to know if you can't see me because of the same reason."

"Am I supposed to understand that?"

"Yes."

"Well, I do."

"And?"

"I see you," Elizabeth said.

"Will you have dinner with me tonight?"

"Yes."

"You're not the kind of girl who shillies and shallies, are you?"

"Do you want me to be?"

"No."

"You yell a lot," she said.

"Nervousness. Are you out here on business? Are you checking the kids?"

"I'm supposed to be. But if I saw a boy sneaking out, I would probably not tell you. I'm no squealer."

"Taking you to dinner is one thing, school business is another. Did you see any students leave?"

"No."

"You heard me make a big point of this, you heard me say there would be automatic suspensions."

"I heard you. You were convincing."

"This school was a mess," he said truculently.

154

"So my father tells me."

"What?"

"Fooled you, didn't I? That's what you get for being so self-righteous. My father knows a lot of things were wrong. He also knows he wasn't the man to change them. To my father each student was a person in himself. He didn't believe that there could be workable rules for everyone. He always found so many exceptions that rather than prove the rules they abolished them. He says what you are attempting is correct, but he could never do it."

"When he used the word 'correct,' that isn't the same as approval, is it."

"No. It's like a general deciding that a platoon of men has to be sacrificed so that a regiment can be saved. My father would say that might be correct, but he couldn't approve of it, and if he were the general he could never give the order."

"Somewhere along the line of this reasoning I come off as an awful heel."

"That's your problem. Tough disciplinarians never worry, they just *know* they're right."

Two boys came out of Sam's place and walked across toward the school. Robert watched them. Elizabeth said, "Well, Mr. Evans, isn't it about time for us to go back?"

"You can go back, Miss Loomis."

"Are we still having dinner together, Mr. Evans?"

"What?" Robert said, his eye on the boys.

"Good-by, Mr. Evans."

They had crossed the highway before seeing him, and then it was too late. One was a skinny boy in a sickening lemon-green and scarlet shiny-surfaced windbreaker. The other was a pleasant-looking boy in white shirt and sleeveless sweater. They both wore chino trousers and sneakers. They stopped for a hurried consultation, then both came up to Robert. The skinny one was visibly trembling, the other seemed unmoved.

"Don't stop, boys. Right into my office."

"Mr. Evans—" the sweatered one began.

"In my office."

Robert walked behind them like an MP shepherding in some AWOL's. In the corridor they were stared at and whispered about. I lack the gun, the whip, the dog on leash, Robert thought. Someday I think I'll do things right, in costume.

In his office he decided to take the thin boy first, and had the other wait outside.

His name, he told Robert, was Philip Otis, and he was in the eleventh grade.

"You knew what you were doing? You knew what would happen? Wouldn't it have been a lot simpler just to obey a regulation? Why did you *have* to leave the school area?"

"It wasn't my fault, Mr. Evans." The boy was near tears. Robert thought that the kids in this school cried easily. Why, at New Canniston, he hadn't seen a weeper more than once or twice. "I don't want to be suspended, I don't want to get in trouble."

"Then why?"

"He said it would be all right." Philip gestured toward the outer office.

"He?"

"Angelo. He said there wasn't anything to worry about, and he said he was going to buy, he wanted company." The thin shoulders moved up and down. "Somebody offers to buy you a lunch, and seeing as how he gives you a guarantee that nothing would happen—"

"You believe it when another student says you need not obey a rule?"

"Not just anybody. But Angelo ought to know—"

"Why? What's so special about Angelo?"

"His father is on the Board of Education. So I figured it would be all right."

"Angelo what?"

"Casella."

Robert nodded. Philip Otis brightened. Robert said, "All right, Philip. You're going to be suspended because I said it would be automatic if anyone left the grounds without a pass. It will be a temporary suspension for three days, and will be

156

lifted after your mother and father come in to see me. Is that clear?"

"I'm sorry I did it, Mr. Evans. Can't you just let it go?"

"No. You're probably learning an expensive lesson at a cheap price. Or I hope you're learning it. Keep away from the operators, Philip. The sucker leads a miserable life."

He called in Mrs. Farrow to prepare a suspension form. He told her to send in Angelo Casella. She and Philip Otis, his face set in a tragic mask (did Mr. Otis use a strap?), went out.

Angelo Casella. The boy, when young, of whom his father had spoken with such joyous pride. Salvatore Casella, member of the Board. What happens when you suspend the son of a Board member, especially the one member who has been solidly behind you? Get out of this one, Evans.

Angelo Casella came in quietly. No sullen, sneering hoodlum, this. The all-American boy, clear eyes, firm mouth, politely interested in Robert's problem.

Robert's problem.

"You're being suspended from school for three days. I must see both of your parents before you may resume classes."

"You can't do that," Angelo said.

"Why not?" Robert asked in a quiet, interested manner.

"My father's on the Board of Education. It would be very embarrassing for him if you suspended me."

"Are you concerned about your father being embarrassed?"

"You mean, if I were, then why did I get into this in the first place?"

"Something like that."

"I don't know if I really care about him. The only reason I mentioned his being embarrassed was so you wouldn't do anything to me."

"What do you mean you don't care about your father?"

"Oh, I'll probably get over it. I'm just going through a period, I guess. This business of being an adolescent isn't easy."

Robert reached across the desk and hit the boy hard across his cheek with the back of two fingers. "I'm going through a period myself. It's even worse than adolescence."

157

Angelo's eyes turned darker and small and mean and his lower lip hung loosely and he did not look like the all-American boy any longer. He said, "You bastard."

Robert hit him again in the same way, so swiftly the boy had no time to dodge.

"You use your tongue on me," Robert said, "and I'll break your little adolescent neck, and won't your father be embarrassed about that."

"You can't rough me up like this. I'll have the law on you." Angelo got up.

Robert said, "Sit down."

Angelo made for the door.

"Last chance. Sit down."

The boy hesitated, came back. In the chair, he said, "My father is going to know exactly what happened here."

Robert said nothing.

"I'll have him file a complaint against you."

Robert looked at him.

"The one thing you can't get away with is beating up kids. I know that."

Robert kept silent.

"What's going on? Why the silent treatment? All I did was go out for a burger. Where's the crime?"

Robert said, "Are you enrolled in this school? Officially?"

"What do you mean?"

"Do you really belong here?"

"Of course I do. What—"

"What was your grade average last year?"

Angelo shrugged. "Around a seventy-five, I guess."

Robert nodded.

"What are you trying to show, I'm retarded or something?"

"Why did you leave the area when I said you couldn't?"

"I wasn't going to get poisoned with that swill they feed us in cafeteria—"

"I eat there every day."

"So? You like it. That's your business."

"That's twice. Third time and out."

158

"I have certain rights if my father is on the Board of Educa tion."

"You certainly do. The most important is that you set an example of scholarship and ethical behavior. You're suspended, Angelo."

The boy shook his head. "You don't understand, Mr. Evans—"

"I understand this much. As far as I can see, you're worthless. It's a shame. Your father was telling me what a great kid you used to be."

"A teen-ager has certain problems. I'm surprised at you, a principal, not seeing that, Mr. Evans. How do you expect us to get through this period if there isn't the understanding—"

"Angelo."

The boy shut up.

"If you ever talk to me again about the pangs of puberty, the aches of adolescence, the trials of teen-agering—I'm going to throw you right through that wall. Is that clear?"

"Yes, sir," Angelo Casella said.

"If, on the other hand, you ever want to have a talk about life, books, education, girls, college, fathers, automobiles, or any other likely subject, you come in and see me. Do you understand?"

"Yes."

"Now go out to Mrs. Farrow, who will make out a suspension form for you, and go home with the glad tidings."

Angelo went out.

Robert whispered, "You got a sense of humor, Mr. Casella, member of the Board? You tolerant?"

He began to whistle a theme through his teeth. After a while he recognized it as the same melody hummed by Rose Pink the day he had walked into her office. That fat, stable woman had said he would get himself into trouble.

Who was there left for him to offend?

At half past one Robert left the school in Perry Dickinson's hands and drove to the offices of the Board of Education. In the parking lot he saw Superintendent Eberly getting out of a car as old as Robert's. At twenty-one thousand dollars a year Robert decided this was an affectation.

Eberly greeted him with a hand wave. There was a small autumnal breeze and Eberly's trouser legs flapped, the superintendent wearing clothes somewhat fuller in cut than the ordained fashion. They walked up the hill together.

Eberly said, "I just came from East End elementary." He pronounced it elemen-*tary*. "A kid was hit by a car while he was crossing the street. Right in front of the school, special patrolman on duty and everything. Little boy of seven."

"Hurt bad?"

"Possible fracture. The car was driven by a woman who just plowed on through the patrolman's signal. She got out, saw the youngster lying in the street, and fainted dead away."

"I'd like to see the fellow who gave her her license faint dead away."

"It could have been car failure."

"Of course. It just makes it easier if you have someone's stupidity to blame."

"Kids," Eberly said. In his voice all the implicits that they be cherished, guarded, educated, admonished, trained, loved, disciplined, blamed, and rewarded.

Robert had not seen this before. Eberly, he had thought, was a man with a job, performing it cannily and securely.

I am, Robert thought, a profound misjudger of people.

"I'm sorry I haven't had you to the house yet," Eberly said. "To tell the truth, Mrs. Eberly's on my back about it, but it gets so damned involved, all this staff. I'd like to have you in for social, not professional reasons, Robert, you know what I mean? One of these evenings—"

"Sure," Robert said.

When they climbed the stairs and were walking down the hall to the Superintendent's office, Eberly looked into one of the smaller rooms and said hello to someone. To Robert: "You haven't met Harry Cartwright yet, have you, Robert?"

"No."

A man came to the door with hand outstretched.

160

"Harry's supervisor of buildings and grounds."

They shook hands. Cartwright was a big man, taller than either Robert or Eberly, with a face in proportion—heavy nose, mouth, prognathous chin.

He said to Robert, "I'm getting another cleaner into your school. You think getting competent teachers is a problem? These drifters. Here, I got an application right here I was going through. You want to see a mess?"

Robert took the form because it was handed to him. Being the docile type, he thought, he would have accepted a grenade with the pin out. He glanced at some of the headings. One question was: Do you use alcohol, and if so, to what extent?

"This item," Robert said. "Is this a standard question?"

"Hell, no," said Cartwright proudly. "I had these forms made up myself."

"I wouldn't care to answer a question like that."

"Of course not! Neither would I. I like to hang one on myself, once in a while, I don't mind telling you—"

"I didn't mean that. What I meant was, it's kind of an invasion of privacy, wouldn't you say?"

If you're going to say this kind of thing to somebody, you're supposed to say it smiling. There was something about this overfleshed man that Robert found objectionable, and he didn't smile.

Cartwright lifted his heavy shoulders and let them fall. "You know the kind of people come in for a custodian's job—"

"No. I don't know what kind you mean."

"Well—" Cartwright included Robert in a look directed at Eberly, the equal, comfortable, superior look. "They like to drink. I mean, not the way any of us might, with some sense, some propriety. These fellows get a jag on in a corner gin-mill, they might be wearing the uniform, no telling what they might do to the detriment of the community and to bring the district into disrepute."

"Harry's been here only a couple of months, but he's really taken hold," Eberly said.

"Thank you, Fenton," Cartwright said. "But as I was saying,

161

you should see the home life of some of these cleaners. We call them custodians—that gives them a little status. On every level people like to have a little status, right?"

"Right." Like Supervisor of Buildings and Grounds.

"It's my experience that you take your chances when you hire for the menial jobs, you have to be careful."

"That question about drinking. Besides the fact that it's demeaning, if a man was an alcoholic, would he put that down?"

"Of course not. But it makes them know we're aware, that we know the score. And if they're careless—" Cartwright made the umpire's sign of Out!

Eberly took Robert around and introduced him to the Assistant Superintendent for Business Affairs, the Assistant Superintendent for Curriculum and Instruction, the Director of Elementary Education, the Co-ordinator of Pupil Personnel Services, the Supervisor of Physical Education, Health, and Recreation, and the Supervisor of Plant Operation and Reconditioning.

In Eberly's office, Robert murmured, "Custodian. I like that. That's a good term."

"What's that, Robert?"

"Nothing. I was thinking of something Cartwright said."

Eberly put his hands together, examined them, and somewhat reluctantly left their scrutiny for the less inviting sight of the Principal's face. "Well, Robert?"

CHAPTER FOURTEEN

Well, Fenton?"

The Superintendent popped his fingertips together. "You remember, Robert, I said you had a free hand, you make the decisions concerning the high school—"

"Yes?"

"When I said that, Robert, I had no doubt that you knew the importance of things going smoothly—I'm referring to the community to which we *do* have a responsibility, do we not?"

"I'm very conscious of that responsibility."

"So. But a little flexibility is good for the soul. I'm talking about a very minute deviation from the strict letter of the law —if by so doing, we are able to soothe ruffled feelings, make a parent feel we really care about his problem—"

"Which one got onto you?" Robert said.

"Mrs. Chullin came in to see me. She wanted her son put in a different class. She said you were absolutely unsympathetic."

"I don't know about my being unsympathetic. It's just that there was no justification for making a horizontal change. You know what could happen, Fenton, you let this kind of thing start and the parents begin to do all the scheduling. The popular teacher—he could be a real dud, but maybe the mothers like his smile—will have seventy kids wanting to get into his class, and somebody else'll have six."

"I couldn't agree with you more, Robert. I never said you were *wrong*. But we were talking about flexibility. Please understand this, Robert, I gave some assurance to Mrs. Chullin that I would look into the matter—"

Robert said coldly, "Did you tell her that you would arrange the change for her?"

"I simply assured her that I would talk to you about it, that you were a reasonable man and—"

"That's the trouble, Fenton. I am not a reasonable man."

Eberly, looking up at the ceiling, said softly, "I would like you to change that boy's class, Robert."

Which put an end to all this silliness about independence. You could make noises like a free man, but there was always somebody in a position to tell you what to do. Robert, trying not to sound sullen, said, "It would be wrong."

The Superintendent's eyes grew tired of the ceiling and fastened on the top of Robert's head. "Casella said you were a hardhead, that was the word he used, and he said that was what he liked, because, although you might be difficult to get along with, in the long run your stubbornness might make for a better school. He also said we weren't taking that much of a chance, since until you got tenure, you were on a year-to-year contract—"

"I thought, when you hired me, that we were in agreement. It isn't a question of classifying my personality. I thought you realized I was comparatively sincere in my desire to improve Pine Hills High School. I think it has a long way to go. I'm a little shocked and unhappy that you're giving me a vote of no confidence so early."

"Come, Robert, it's not that way at all. I think you're doing a fine job. But you must understand my position. You are simply not exposed to the same pressures, certainly not to the same degree. You may think that my relationship with the community has nothing to do with your educational motives. But everything is interconnected. The Chullins have been a part of this town for fifty, maybe seventy-five years. A grandfather of Mrs. Chullin built the first library and donated it to the village. Mrs. Chullin's husband is a village trustee, and vice-commander of the American Legion post. Mrs. Chullin is active in a half-dozen civic organizations. You must admit, Robert, that it is an extremely unpolitic thing to antagonize people like that."

"Yes, Fenton, you're right."

In surprise Eberly's eyes dropped to Robert's.

"I won't even bother," Robert said, "to extrapolate from what you've just said. I mean, I won't go into the kind of school situation you could get into that would involve a lot more important concessions than changing a Chullin from one class to another. Because if you want to play that kind of game, then I guess you know the rules yourself. I turned Mrs. Chullin down. She said she would see you about it. She gets what she wants, and her son is in a special category. How many categories are there room for in the high school? You tell me to do this, Fenton, and I will do it, I was in the army and I know about rank. I just would be happier if you did not tell me to do it."

"But I do have to tell you, is that it, Robert?"

Eberly leaned back and played another tune with his wide fingertips and smiled. True, the smile did not go very deep and there was a flushed area under his eyes, but it was a smile. Robert admired him for it as he admired anyone who could do things he could not. Sword swallowers, channel swimmers, singers of operatic arias.

"There is always a way," Eberly said, "to work things out without hurting anyone's feelings. We don't have to lock horns over anything as trivial as this, do we, Robert?"

"I hope not, Fenton."

"Suppose, then, I *asked* you, as a favor to me, to make that change."

Feeling revulsion against this word game, Robert said, "All right."

Thinking of the portfolio he had brought, under his fingers now on the desk. Thinking of the matters still to come.

"Are you sure it's all right, Robert?" Eberly asked with real consideration in his voice, like the fellow who has just won the prize fight and is terribly solicitous about his fallen opponent's cuts and bruises. "I doubt that anything could be worth any real schism between us, like if you felt you had been forced into this and then you held a grudge. You see, Robert, just as I see the necessity for working smoothly with the people

165

of this school district—and quite often it results in a situation like this that could be unpleasant were it not for your understanding, and I do appreciate that—you must grant me the same sincerity about wanting to work smoothly with you."

"I do, Fenton, I do." And he did. He thought he understood Eberly. This was a decent man who had been a teacher and a principal and had advanced in his profession. He was not bright in any intellectual sense, but few members of his profession were. He had literally no time to be concerned about the quality of education in his school district. His concerns were budget, and bond issues, and having new schools open in time, and placating parents and addressing organizations. The man had only one real failing: in wanting the most amicable public relations, the most co-operative staff relations, he achieved mediocrity. Which meant that the people on his administrative staff had indifferent talents, and so did most of his school principals, and so did most of the teachers he interviewed and recommended for employment.

Robert was a problem.

Robert opened his portfolio and took out the material he had brought. He handed Eberly the records of the two pupil suspensions and the account of the Gilbert Gist incident.

"What's this?"

"Just the results of a routine morning. I had to suspend two students and a teacher beat up a kid."

"I see," Eberly said, smiling.

He picked up one of the suspension forms. He looked up at Robert and said, "Oh." He read on and said, "Otis. That's the boy—his father's a salesman who's home only half a year. We've had some difficulty with this student before. There's no question about it, look into the home and you find the reason for antisocial behavior."

"Right," Robert said.

Eberly was reading the nature of the offense. "Went across to Jennings' place?"

"Yes. An open flouting of my ruling."

"All right," Eberly said firmly. "You've gone along with me,

Robert, and I'll go along with you. Once you lay down the law, you have to stick with it."

"Exactly what I feel."

"What else have you got?" Eberly looked at the other form. He looked at Robert, who kept his face perfectly blank, and back to the paper. "You rigged this. You're a practical joker, aren't you, Robert?"

"No."

"Casella?"

"He was the one who persuaded the Otis boy to go along. He thought he had immunity because of his father."

"It was a nice job while it lasted. I think I'll go back into the shoe business. You know I used to be in the shoe business when I was going to college? It nearly ruined my sex life. I grew to hate the sight of a woman's knees. What business you going into, Robert?"

Eberly was disturbed. Eberly was not the kind of man who made sex references.

"I kept my reserve commission. I could always get back in the army."

"Casella will murder us."

"I didn't have a choice, Fenton. But I would have done it anyway. This is a bad kid. Casella knows it. I don't see why he should resent our trying to do something about his son."

"That isn't it. The point is that this becomes an open thing. It's juicy. The papers might like it. Here's a man serving the community on the Board of Education whose son gets suspended from the high school. Robert—why didn't you stay in New Canniston?"

It was a little heavy for humor, and Eberly's smile barely reached his lips. "The point," said Robert, "is that I didn't."

"Loomis—"

Robert thought of a block of ice, thought of himself in the middle of it. He thought of a lake quiet between mountains. He thought of green grass, serenity. His voice had barely any tremor when he said, "Don't say it, Fenton. Whatever you were going to say about Loomis, don't say it."

Eberly took a deep breath, let it all out. "We'll get Casella in. We'll talk this thing out. It'll be all right."

Eberly's litany. Anything could be talked out and made all right.

The Superintendent went on with commendable lightness, "At least you keep things from getting dull around here. What else have you got?"

Robert pointed out Gist's report. Eberly began to read it. Robert lit a cigarette.

Eberly said, "Gist? He could no more hit anybody than he could fly."

"He's been flying pretty good."

"Robert, do you *make* these things happen?" Eberly's voice was plaintive.

Robert felt ashamed, like a catalyst with a conscience. He was making Eberly miserable. In the years the Superintendent had worked with Loomis, how many suspensions, how many serious teacher problems had there been? Had there been any? When a man has too many accidents, he is called a prone and is presumed to be unconsciously seeking them out. Was Robert a trouble-prone because he did not want to stay in Pine Hills, and was he making it inevitable that his contract not be renewed?

It can't be, Robert thought. I like it here.

They discussed the Gist affair from the standpoint of school responsibility and probabilities of parental legal action. Given this kind of specific problem, Eberly was incisive, informed, efficient. You could mock his occasional vagueness, or criticize his everybody-love-me approach to his employer, the public, but he knew his job.

"How about Gist? Would you want to keep him on?"

"No," Robert said. "He's a hysterical personality, for my money, and I don't think he ought to be teaching."

"Well, we'll wait and see what the Fosters come up with."

It was a quarter after five and Robert went back to the school. Only as he parked the car did he think of Elizabeth Loomis. For a moment he felt almost relieved, as if this lapse proved that he was not dangerously involved. He thought himself too old and too memoried for the mechanics of courtship. Having loved and lived with a woman, how did you begin again with someone else? But how fast this speculation, and on what grounds? That the girl had agreed to have dinner with him? And how easily the Principal had overtaken the man.

He couldn't call her. Not and have the phone picked up by Loomis, to introduce himself and say he was taking Loomis's daughter to dinner. He was suddenly overwhelmed by his aloneness, a porcupine man who had never learned the secret of retracting his quills. The right to irascibility, like a man's beard, has to be earned; otherwise it is nothing more than a petty expression of unsureness. Even the absorption in his school role he saw now as a false thing, a declaration of incompleteness, an escape into a safely regulated private haven.

Perry had gone; the offices were empty. Robert went through the building with the instinct of a ship's captain. He looked in Elizabeth Loomis's room, and she was sitting at her desk. He felt a slashing joy. She looked up and said coolly, "Hello, Mr. Evans."

"Overtime?"

"I had test papers to correct and preferred to do them at once rather than take them home."

"I see."

She went back to her work, then stopped and looked up inquiringly.

He said, "Weren't we supposed to have dinner together?"

"Were we?"

"Would you hold it against a man that he doesn't know how to apologize for behavior he neither understands nor seems able to control?"

She didn't answer.

He said, "I did ask you to have dinner with me, you did accept—"

"It seemed to me that either you had not intended the invitation seriously, or you had regretted it as soon as it was made."

"Why did it seem so to you?"

"I stopped existing for you as soon as you saw those two boys."

"That's true."

She shrugged, meaning, That's all right with me, Jack.

He said, "If it's possible, I would like to go back to wherever we were before."

"I suppose that would be all right, since we were never anywhere in particular."

"Miss Loomis, I would be very pleased and grateful if you would have dinner with me this evening."

"Certainly," she said.

He laughed. "Taking the wind out. Could you wash your face here so that you don't have to go home first?"

"If you like. Although my father was not going to be home this evening anyway."

"I didn't say anything about your father."

"I know you didn't."

"Suppose we meet in the parking area in ten minutes."

"Fifteen," Elizabeth said.

Robert went back to his office and sat in his chair with his feet up on the desk. He looked at his watch and gave himself ten minutes for private satisfactions. He had a date. The girl was lovely. He forgot that he was no longer a boy, that he had been concerned about outgrown patterns, that he was a man who liked to define things. He felt a mild, pleasurable anticipation that did not require images. It was just a fine thing for this evening that he did not have to eat alone.

The phone rang. Robert picked it up and identified himself.

"This is Chief Allen, Pine Hills Police Department."

"Yes?"

"We've got a report of someone missing. I thought I'd better check it out with you."

"Yes?"

"A boy named Joseph Maxwell."

"Oh."

"Could you tell me if you know of anything wrong, his

schoolwork, anything like that? His father says you were at their house looking for the boy."

"Yes."

"Was he in any kind of trouble?"

"Not that I know of."

"Any reason why he might want to run off?"

"Is that what he did?"

"We don't know what happened. All we know is he's been reported missing."

"Poor kid. I hope he's all right. He didn't come home last night, then, is that it?"

"That's it. Why did you go to his house, Mr. Evans?"

"They have no telephone. The boy had asked me for something, permission for something. I wanted to tell him it was all right."

"When you spoke to him last, was he upset?"

"Not upset enough to do anything foolish."

What a stupid thing to say. How upset was upset enough? Who knew what went on in the mind of a boy?

The Chief said, "He comes from those hill people. This kind of thing happens often enough. Could be his old man beat him up, and he's out sulking, or he's trying on some woman for size, he's old enough, or could be he's out somewhere sleeping off a jag. What some of those people do, it's weird."

"None of those possibilities sounds like Joseph," Robert said.

"Well, if you find out anything, please let us know."

"Of course. And I'd appreciate your letting me know when he turns up."

Robert hung up, pinched his nose, and looked at the wall. There was nothing in the cinderblocks to provide an answer. Robert thought of that thin, anxious face.

Elizabeth came in saying, "I was waiting—" Then she said quietly, "What's the matter?"

"That was the police, they just called, seems one of our students is missing."

"How long?"

"Since sometime yesterday, it looks like." Robert stood up. "Shall we go?"

In his car he asked her for restaurant recommendations because she knew the neighborhood and he didn't, and not because, he pointed out, he was the kind of man who wanted the girl's opinion in an area that called for the man's decision.

"The student," Elizabeth said. "A boy?"

"Yes."

"Isn't there anything that should be done?"

"I suppose the police are doing what should be done. About that restaurant. I'm an early eater. Is this going to be too early for you?"

"This is hardly a fashionable hour for dining out, I must admit. I must also admit that I'm kind of hungry. There are one or two nice places quite close, but perhaps the Principal should not be seen locally taking out a lady teacher."

"You think that's something to consider?"

"I do."

"We're both available. It's licit."

"That sounds terrible."

"Perfectly good word."

"I can just see a man leering at me and suggesting a licit relationship."

"I'll tell you. I've been eating my own cooking, and for a change I would like something fit to eat. I'll suggest the type of restaurant, and if a good one is nearby, that's where we'll go, and if not then we'll go traveling. All right?"

"Name it."

"Italian."

"Five minutes away."

The restaurant was called Il Duomo, a pleasant, white-painted country house. Inside, in a small room with white tablecloths, the name was explained by photographs of Florentine churches blown up into a wall mural. They ordered Martinis, which came chilled and deadly and marvelous, and Robert said, "Il Duomo. A place to remember."

After that they both ate seriously, with just enough conversation for companionship but not enough to distract from the food.

Robert said, "You're a pretty good eater."

"A freak of metabolism that has lost me every weight-conscious female friend I've ever had."

"I like the *way* you eat. With attention and respect. I don't think you're going to be very happy when they synthesize all this stuff."

"By then it won't matter. They'll have synthesized teachers and ideas and affection."

"I didn't mean the conversation to get so serious so soon."

"You've been serious," Elizabeth said. "You've been serious right along."

"I hadn't noticed."

"You've been thinking about that boy."

"Joseph Maxwell. A senior."

"A boy sleeps at a friend's house, forgets to phone, or maybe he had a disagreement at home. It wouldn't be serious."

"The family hasn't got a phone. They can't afford a phone. But Joseph has a motor scooter for which he paid three hundred dollars. He asked me for permission to park it in the school lot. I said he couldn't. I'm worried about that kid, Elizabeth."

"The first time," she said.

"For what?"

"You've used my first name for the first time. I watch for that. Do you ever watch for that?"

"Yes. And you haven't."

"Haven't what, Robert?"

"Thank you. It's the only thing we have that's anywhere near the second person singular of the other languages. Where the shift occurs."

"The boy."

"He's what they call—hill folk? I was told they go back to the Revolution."

"Jackson Whites. Actually, Jackson's Whites."

"I heard something about them."

"A man named Jackson, supposedly, was commissioned to

bring several boatloads of women in for the British troops at so much a head for them. He was supposed to get recruits from the brothels in London and Liverpool and so on, but any young woman careless enough to be alone on the streets at night was more than likely to be taken. On the way over, a ship was lost and Jackson wanted a replacement. It wasn't feasible to return to England, so he put in at Barbados and filled a boat with Negro women. They were among those who came up to these mountains along with the Hessians and Indians and Dutch and so on."

"Joseph begged me for a place to park that scooter. I was scared about leaving an opening for kids with motorcycles. Then I got real softhearted, or headed, and I went to his house yesterday."

"You did that?"

"Was that wrong? As I said, they didn't have a phone. I went looking for the boy and he wasn't there, he never came home at all."

"If you're blaming yourself, that's the silliest thing I ever heard of. How can this possibly have anything to do with you?"

"How do I know? And who said it did?"

"He'll show up tomorrow with a plausible story about studying late at a friend's house and then deciding to go to a movie in New York."

"Sure," Robert said. "That's the way it will turn out."

"But you don't believe it."

"No."

"Is there anything you think you ought to do?"

"No."

"Is there anything you think you might want to do?"

"Yes."

"What's that?"

"I might want to go to this kid's house just to see what's going on there and where they're looking for him, if they're looking."

"What are we waiting for?" said Elizabeth, getting up.

CHAPTER FIFTEEN

W here do you think you're going?"

"With you, to Joseph Maxwell's house."

Robert got up uncertainly and looked for the waiter, who came with the check. He followed Elizabeth to the door, saying to her back, "What are you, some kind of creature of impulse? What kind of a date is this?"

"It wasn't a date, it was dinner, and we've had that."

"Then I'll take you home."

"Why can't I go with you to that boy's house?"

Robert started to tell her why, then he didn't know why and he said nothing.

Elizabeth said, "I'm concerned, too, don't forget that."

"You don't even know the boy."

"You don't really mind if I go with you?"

"I don't mind."

In the car, he looked at her beside him, mysterious in the dim reflection of the restaurant neon sign. "Put your sweater on, it's getting chilly."

He helped her, fingers on the collar adjusting it, the softness of wool and smoothness of neck, the scent so distant it seemed almost imagined. She sitting straight and proper allowing the service like a model, he with arm extended and that distance away.

She said, "Thank you."

He did not take his hand away. He touched her neck, the hair bristly to soft, the concave part made for a thumb.

She said, "If you don't stop—"

"Yes?"

"I'll—"

"Yes?"

175

And it was so easy, had required no forethought, happened the way the best things happen: of themselves, of need, of rightness. His fingers had moved just a little up and around toward the line of her jaw and she had moved just a little toward the crook of his arm and they were together: close, safe, completed.

He moved just enough and she moved just enough so that their lips could meet. It was a kiss of greeting, that first one.

Robert said, "Did you know about this? That it was coming? Do you think it was all arranged somewhere?"

"I think everything you do is a preparation, and you never know for what until you are there, and you see the use of it all, nothing really wasted, all the thinking and studying and being. The hurt, too, and the miserable business of getting up in the morning when there isn't anyone you want to see or talk to."

"I know about that. But you're going to complicate things."

"What things?" Elizabeth said comfortably, and he saw that she had settled in with the really important matters confirmed, and troubles from now on could be only minor.

"Things."

"A man struggles. For no reason, really, except that somewhere back in the ooze or coming out of the trees, some male idiot set a standard for these things, and racial memory or something keeps it going. It's really very silly. A woman doesn't feel surprised, just grateful."

"I saw a very good movie once, it was from a Sinclair Lewis novel, and Walter Huston played the middle-aged man who falls in love. I was younger then, and impressed with the fact that older people knew about that sort of thing. However, the girl wasn't as young as you."

"Nor are you as old as he was supposed to be then. I know about that movie, too. And anyway, my school record lies. It says twenty-nine, but I'm really thirty."

"I'll have to report that."

"Do that," she said.

"There are certain things I have to know about you. I have to know your attitude toward Mahler and if you sneer at people who read detective stories and if you're a bather or a showerer.

These are really vital things. The only thing I know about you so far is you like to eat."

"Uh-huh," she said, under his chin.

"How come you're so *sure*."

"Because I am."

"That doesn't sound very scientific to me."

"The first step in your reconstruction," she said, "is that you have to stop getting irritated at people. This comes from not being very happy. You haven't been very happy, it occurs to me."

"You're doing it," he said, amazed. "This universal female craziness. You look for a fellow you like, and then you want to change him."

"A girl doesn't look for somebody perfect. She looks for somebody with potential. Anyway, what's the matter? Are you against happiness?"

"Just watch it," Robert said. "I heard a psychological theory the other day that a number of people commit suicide not out of desperation and misery but at the peak of accomplishment, when you'd think they had everything to live for. So I'm not so sure I want you making me any happier."

"Are we going to Joseph Maxwell's house or are we going to sit here forever?" She made little movements to indicate that she intended to sit there forever.

"We're going to Joseph Maxwell's house, the man said, disengaging his arm and engaging the clutch."

"Disengaging the clutch, you mean."

"Clutching at the disengage. That means grabbing the woman who just gave the ring back."

"It's true there are a number of things about you I will have to work on."

"How easily a girl gets possessive. One kiss and you're so sure I'm sewed up."

"Have you ever wondered why there aren't any women tailors?"

"The same reason there are no male seamstresses."

"If there were, they would have to be seamsters."

Robert started the car and turned onto the main road. "I'm not sure exactly how to find that Maxwell house. There's a turnoff somewhere beyond a bar. I was there only in daylight, and I've got a lousy sense of direction."

"Robert, we didn't use any of the words, did we?"

"Seems to me I heard a couple."

"I mean the words people use when— I don't think I want to use those words, Robert."

"Don't fall into the trap, Elizabeth. Words aren't things. It's important to remember that. Because this fellow of yours— never mind, I don't need to know his name. Just because he said the words doesn't make the thing for which the words stand better or worse, real or false. You understand that?"

"Yes."

"Like blasphemy. How can a word be a sin? I've often wondered about that. I say 'holy' but I am not, or I say 'depraved' and I am not that either. When I asked why you're sure and you said because you are, that's closer to truth than anything."

"Yes, Robert."

"I think it's here." Robert turned into a secondary road. The headlights cut a path through blackness. "You know what dark is?"

"What?"

"Look." Robert pulled to the side of the road and cut the lights.

"It's scary," Elizabeth said.

"Of course, after a while your eye would get used to this and be able to make out shapes and so on. Once I was in a cavern someplace sightseeing, and the guide cut the lights to show what absolute darkness was, we were down a couple of hundred feet. Or maybe it was the absence of sound he was demonstrating. The point is, we never experience any kind of absolute as far as the senses are concerned."

"Please put the lights on."

"Sure." He drove on. "What was I trying to prove? Oh. Brainwashing. The first thing they did was take the victim, and through various uncomplicated means they disoriented him.

178

After a while, from not knowing where he was or when it was, he wasn't so sure *who* he was. And then they could build him up to be somebody else. Or at least make him behave like somebody else. The damned elusiveness of the *I*, spelled *I*. So how is it we found each other, and more important, what is it you think you found, and for how long, and through what kind of stresses?"

"Oh," she said, "you're an analyzer, and that's a terrible thing to be. Take the phrase, 'as good as new.' You know that's impossible? Because once anything is tampered with, it's no longer the same. Just what you said about brainwashing. Especially feelings must never be examined or explained, because in order to do that you have to hold them still, and when you do that they shrivel. You said the word was not the thing. But you can change the thing by prodding it with the wrong word. You know what I'm talking about?"

"Heavens, no," he said, reaching over to press her hand. "You know it was backward? I kissed you before ever holding your hand."

They came to the house.

"This is it, I could never have found it myself. I just gave the old bus her head. Whoa, Dobbin."

He parked and went around to help Elizabeth out. The house was mostly dark, a dim light upstairs and a flickering blue light through a window downstairs. It was not inviting, the way a lighted house can be inviting from a dark street.

He said, "Perhaps you'd better wait in the car."

"I'd be frightened to sit out here in the car alone."

"All right." They went up the front steps, which underfoot had the rigidity of a rope ladder. Robert knocked on the door.

From within came the blast of a medical problem. Kildare, or Malone, or somebody was in trouble. There was a lot of loud, ominous music that either indicated or added to the doctor's dilemma. Robert knocked on the door again. "They'll think it's the patient's heart," he said to Elizabeth.

"Maybe you'd better wait for the commercial."

"That'll be even louder than the operation."

He raised his hand again, but the door was open and he held back just in time. Mrs. Maxwell loomed in the doorway. He heard Elizabeth gasp. The woman said, "What you want?"

"I'm Mr. Evans. I was here yesterday—?"

So that's where it comes from, he thought. That irritating rising inflection at the end of statements that had been impossible to erase from the students' speech patterns at New Canniston. It came from talking to people who you felt didn't seem to understand what you were talking about.

"Evans. The Principal of Pine Hills High School."

"So?"

Elizabeth said, "Mrs. Maxwell—Joseph, is he home yet?"

"No."

"Do you know—have they found out anything yet?"

Mrs. Maxwell said, "You are the Principal? Then you tell me, where is Joseph?"

Inside, the doctor had decided that the only way to save the patient was by resorting to some terribly risky procedure that could not possibly work. The patient said he was willing to undergo it because he felt the doctor was a good man.

"I came to find out what is going on," Robert said. "What are the police doing?"

"Police? I don't know about police."

A little desperately, Robert said, "Could I talk to Mr. Maxwell?"

"What for?"

Elizabeth stepped forward, lost against the woman's bulk. "Let us in for a moment, Mrs. Maxwell. We came to help."

"Help?"

"Yes," said Elizabeth firmly, and for some reason the woman stepped back.

Robert followed Elizabeth inside, Mrs. Maxwell having left just enough room for him to pass. Her dress rustled and smelled of dust. The blue crackle of the television set came from a room on the left that was bare and unlighted except for the old small screen that sat on a chair. Children lay around on the floor watching.

180

"You come in here." Mrs. Maxwell led them down the hall into the kitchen. Two men sat at a table under a small unshaded overhead light. They were drinking beer from cans. One of them was Maxwell. He waved his hand. "The Principal." He looked at Elizabeth with a flicker of interest that at once was extinguished. The other man got to his feet. He was slender and Indian-looking like Maxwell, of indeterminate age. "I am Groat, James Groat."

"How do you do," said Robert, feeling somehow foolish at the amenity. "My name is Evans and this is Miss Loomis."

"Joseph's principal," Maxwell said.

"Ah," said James Groat. He smiled and bobbed his head and went out.

"You want a beer?" Maxwell asked.

"No, thanks. Any word of Joseph?"

"Police was here this afternoon, after I went to the station and told them. They know nothing. They say he is not in hospital."

"Did he ever do this before?" asked Elizabeth.

"Never."

Groat came back and said, "It is a fine thing, a principal comes to find out about a missing boy." He smiled, and sat down. He picked up his can of beer.

Mrs. Maxwell said, "I go to the kids." She went out.

Robert and Elizabeth standing, the men sitting, the poor light, the bareness, the smell of age and neglect and sourness in the house—all combined for Robert into a feeling of infinite sadness. Misery and comfort were too close to each other; there should be more separation between laughter and tears, between the good life and animal scrabbling. It was as if all it would take was one slip, a misstep, a miscalculation—and one was dirty and poor and sat in a drab room under a dim bulb drinking beer out of a can.

Elizabeth said, "Mr. Maxwell, is there anything more that can be done? Isn't there anyplace you can look for Joseph?"

The television volume rose as a former beauty queen sold a soap powder to antiseptic America. Mr. Groat smiled. He had two gold teeth in front. "Maybe Joseph went to Hollywood to be in the movies. Maybe he went to ride in the rocket around the world. Who knows where is Joseph?"

"Don't you care?" Elizabeth said almost fiercely, including both Groat and Maxwell. "Aren't you worried?"

Groat said, smiling, "Is it you who are worried about our little Joseph? Mr. Principal, you are here because you are worried? Why? Joseph is not a friend, not a cousin, like I am a cousin to him. Why are you here, Mr. Principal?"

Maxwell laughed, showing the gap in his mouth. He held up the beer can. "Hey, Jimmy, why you didn't buy enough beer?"

Robert touched Elizabeth's arm. "We'd better go."

Maxwell belatedly gave attention to Elizabeth's question, as if his synapses had first to be cleared of prior messages. He leaned across the table toward Elizabeth. He suddenly seemed pointed and ugly. "What do you mean, I don't care? I am not a father? You think my feelings not so good as your feelings? Who went to the police and told them? You? What you mean, I don't care?"

He made to rise. Robert stepped in front of Elizabeth. Groat got up easily and pushed Maxwell down. Smiling to Robert, "You did not say why you are here."

"There is a chance," Robert said slowly, "that Joseph might not have to grow up and live in a house like this. At least he will have the same chance as anybody else. I care about Joseph."

"Good!" Groat shouted. He shook Maxwell by the shoulder. "You hear? You hear how the Principal says he cares about Joseph?"

Robert took Elizabeth's arm and made for the door.

Groat said, "I know where Joseph is."

Robert stopped, knowing the statement had been made to stop him. He looked at Maxwell, who appeared unconcerned. "Where?"

"When I say I know, that is perhaps not true. But I think. I think there is no other place for him to be."

Robert waited for Maxwell to ask where the place was. Silence forced him to ask, "Where?"

"In the hills we are all the same. Or if one is better, it is because he is bigger or stronger or braver or more cunning. But down here we are not the same as everybody. For us this is bad but—" He shrugged. "You live with things as they are. For Joseph, a boy who goes to school with everybody else, this is worse than for us. You know what I am saying?"

"Yes," Robert said.

"Now, something happens to Joseph, something makes him unhappy. I don't know what, but he is unhappy. So he wants to run away. Where? It has to be a place where he can feel the same as everybody."

"Joseph has been in school here for eight years. This is not a case of some newly uprooted foreign—"

"Foreign?"

"That's enough," said Robert irritably. "Don't start proving to me how American you are. It doesn't make any difference and I don't care. If you think you know where Joseph is, you tell me."

Groat smiled and drank some beer.

Maxwell nodded at some inner voice, and lifted his own beer can.

Elizabeth said in a voice in which Robert thought he alone could hear the loathing, "If you have an idea where the boy might be, how is it you've said nothing, why haven't you told his father?"

"Oh, you are worried, too," Groat said politely. "You are his teacher, perhaps?"

"I am a teacher."

"Enough," Robert said. He took Elizabeth's arm again.

"Wait," Groat said. "Joseph—I think he went up to the hills to stay with his grandfather."

Maxwell, who had been dully contemplating the label on the beer can, raised his head. "He used to go back there when he was little."

"Why didn't you say something to the police?"

Groat smiled. "If he is there, he is where he wants to be,

yes? But to run away from school, that is against the law, yes? So I am to take my little cousin and put him in jail?"

"He is seventeen. There is no question of jail, it is no crime for him to stay out of school. Except the crime he does to himself."

Groat looked vaguely disappointed.

"Where is this place?"

"If I told you, would you want to go and get him? Is that why you want to know?"

"I would want to go and get him."

"All right," Groat said. "I will take you." He got up, smiling. Robert looked at Maxwell.

Groat said, "He is a hard-working man, he does not climb the mountain. I work at small things, this and that, I do not need to save my strength as my cousin does for hauling the rock."

"Yes, Jimmy," said Maxwell, smiling slyly. "You go. You and the Principal."

"Now?" Robert said. "At night? The mountains?"

"You don't want. All right." Groat sat down. His smile was a knife to Robert, raking across his chest.

"In the morning," Robert said.

"Sure." Groat's smile questioned Robert's integrity, his manhood, his motives, his honesty.

"How far is it?"

"Who knows? Who measures?"

"How long would it take?"

"In the morning? An hour, maybe. At night, a little longer."

Elizabeth said, "Tomorrow." This time she took Robert by the hand and tugged him from the room. As they passed the television set, they saw Mrs. Maxwell sitting on the floor in the midst of her brood. On the screen was a commercial of a man and his wife visiting Europe as a result of their foresight in having used a certain savings bank. The children were asleep in little mounds on the bare wood floor. Elizabeth said good night to Mrs. Maxwell, who did not turn from the set or say anything.

184

Outside, Robert stopped and looked behind the house. The mountain was a slightly darker mass in the overcast sky.

"Ridiculous, the notion of going into that in the dark," said Elizabeth, shivering.

"Ridiculous."

"That man, that Groat. Did you feel what I did? He's a hater. When you meet a man like that, the best thing is to keep as far away as you can."

"I wonder if he was right about Joseph."

"Somebody can go up and see in the morning."

"What if the boy is hurt, or hungry? What if the morning is too late?"

"There's something wrong about the whole thing, Robert. If that man really thinks Joseph is up in that mountain someplace, why is it he hasn't convinced the boy's mother and father? How is it Mr. Maxwell went to the police but didn't say anything about that? It doesn't make sense."

"You're right."

The two men had come out of the house and were standing on the steps. Groat called, "I'm ready to go right now, Principal. Like everybody, you talk but you don't want to do anything."

"Mr. Maxwell, do you believe Joseph is up there?"

"Jimmy knows things."

"Then all you have to do is get word to Joseph that he must come back to school and everything will be all right."

"Joseph won't listen to me," said Maxwell.

"Joseph will listen to his principal," Groat said. "Imagine a principal who cares what happens to a boy from the hills. I guess this never happened before, eh?"

"Robert—" said Elizabeth.

"Yes?"

"Is there a reason why you have to listen to that man?"

"Yes."

"I can get the police, something can be organized."

"No. This isn't for the police. Not now. Tomorrow, maybe, if anything goes wrong." Robert grinned to remove the melodrama. He took a step toward the house. "Groat!"

"Yes, Principal?"

"I am going with you."

"Good!"

"I am going to take Miss Loomis home, and then I want to change clothes. I will meet you here in thirty, forty minutes."

"That is fine. Time for a couple more beers."

In the car Robert said, "I don't know where you live."

Elizabeth directed him. They drove without speaking. Finally Robert said, "Is that disapproval I hear in your silence?"

"No. Worry."

"Why? Even though they're called mountains, they're really just hills. Nothing is going to happen."

"Bad things have happened up there, Robert. If I knew how to stop you now, I would."

"Nothing will happen to me," he said with conviction.

At her house Elizabeth looked at him for a long moment, her face very solemn; then she smiled and squeezed his hand and ran inside.

CHAPTER SIXTEEN

The Loomis house had been built before Pine Hills was incorporated; it stood in a quiet street just beyond the village center. Robert's cottage was closer to the mountains. He drove home and went in, shut the door, put on a light, and let himself fall into a chair. What the devil had he got himself into? He was neither hero nor mountain climber, and he was just as afraid of the dark as anybody.

Then he must be doing this to impress Elizabeth. He laughed aloud. Elizabeth. The last refuge of magic in a pragmatic world —this trick of seeing what happened sometimes suddenly with a girl, this marvel of uncoating; one moment she is just a person like any other with communication limited to speech and glance, and then quick as revelation a marvel of uniqueness.

He stripped his outer clothes and found a pair of heavy corduroy pants, his old army shoes, a sweater. In the car he checked the flashlight and drove to the Maxwell house.

The proper thing to have done was to notify the police, at least have some experienced people along. But Groat wanted Robert alone, wanted valley authority to be shown how dependent it could be. Knowing this, why go along with him? Even Isaac had not been told what his father had in mind.

The word might not be the thing, but a man needed guideposts and symbols. Joseph Maxwell was Robert's *charge*. That meant trust, and responsibility. It also meant burden, trouble, inconvenience, liability. It also meant injunction and mandate. And it also meant advance on the enemy.

In Robert's desk at school, along with the innumerable mimeographed sheets that flowed endlessly from the offices of the Board of Education, was a two-page stapled pamphlet entitled *The Building Principal.* It was divided into "Areas of

187

Major Responsibility" (the Principal should represent line authority, the Principal should be a consultant in curriculum research, the Principal should specialize in co-operative policy development) and "Representative Duties" (internal organization, supervision of instruction, curriculum offerings, school plant). Under "Pupil Relations, Guidance, and Activities" were the subheadings: "Developing proper student attitudes"; "Guidance program"; "Extracurricular activities"; "Faculty participation in activities."

There it was, clear as anything, available for reference whenever the nature of his duties was in doubt. So now he was preparing to climb a mountain in the dark with a guide of doubtful motives in order to look for a student who for one reason or another was hiding away from school. Would this come under "Developing proper student attitudes"? Or possibly "Faculty participation in activities"?

Oh, wryness is great when you're scared. But why, Robert, really why?

I don't have to know why, he answered himself, Elizabeth is right. It's just that this Joseph Maxwell does not have to grow up to be an extension of his father, or of his cousin, James Groat. James Groat made a lot of fun of caring. It was a thing to make fun of when the most popular of phrases is "Who cares?" Who, especially from this world, cared about anything in his? Maybe that was the point, if there had to be one.

When he reached the house, it was completely dark, and Robert did not try to hide from himself his honest and flooding relief. It had never been intended seriously, then. He was willing to be the butt of the joke rather than go through with the climb, and now that he seemed out of it, he was able to face the extent of his release. What Robert most of the time tried to forget was his own aversion to all crawling and buzzing and slithering things. Especially in the dark. During the war he had been interested in the interrogation of prisoners, having heard of the inhumane methods of the Nazis. He had never been impressed with their modern versions of thumbscrew and rack. How simple it would be instead if one were to determine individuals' phobias. As in his case. What secret could he possibly have retained if his astute questioner had approached with a snake in one hand, a hairy-legged spider dangling on a string from the other?

Robert was about to drive off, thinking of getting Elizabeth back to share the remainder of the evening, when James Groat stepped out of a shadow at the side of the building. Almost with a groan, Robert turned off the ignition.

Groat said, "I am ready."

Robert said, "I am ready."

He got out of the car and slipped the flashlight into his hip pocket. Groat began to walk, and Robert followed. They went behind the house and beyond the cleared section, Groat walking with a careless sure-footedness, and Robert unwilling yet to reveal dependence on his light. Groat said, "Off there is a path." He pointed. "It goes into the woods, and then the climb starts. It is not a wide path, I will go first. Stay close to me, Mr. Principal. In five seconds you can get so lost you will never be found."

"Never be found?"

"Are you a man that knows the woods?"

"No."

"I was born up there. I know it like you know streets in the village."

"I'm glad of that."

"Without me," Groat said, "you could die up there."

They were in the woods now and climbing. Robert could see nothing of the path in front of him, if there was a path, but Groat went on surely and Robert went behind. Groat moved with a swinging ease, and Robert tried to emulate this, having read about the woodsman and the mountain man, and knowing theoretically all about the way it was done, the bent knee and long stride. Robert found to his surprise that he was enjoying this—the excitement, the sense of small gain, the assurance of fitness in yet unaching legs and untroubled breathing.

"How's it going, Mr. Principal?"

"Well."

"You keeping up pretty good?"

"I'm trying."

"Then I go a little faster, okay?"

They walked for a long time. Through a flat open area where fire had leveled the brush, and over a stony place where Robert stumbled and fell and was up again before Groat could say anything, up at once at the expense of a twisted thumb, which he gingerly investigated with the other hand but could not stop to look at it. Then Groat was two yards in front of him, and three, and then he was around a tree and was gone.

"Groat?"

No answer and Robert called again, and louder, and shouted, "Groat! Where are you?"

There was silence and he thought, The damned trickster, and reached for his flashlight. It was in his right rear pocket and it was his right thumb that had been hurt, so he had to reach behind and awkwardly across his body with his left hand. Then, of course, the side of the light caught in the lining of his pocket and he tried to release it using the back of his right hand and his hand slipped and he grunted at the pain as his thumb scraped down.

"Groat?"

Easy, he told himself, and don't panic, and take a deep breath and relax, you're a big boy now. The flashlight fought him stubbornly and the night pressed in. There was a book of matches, he remembered, in his side pocket on the left, and he took it out and managed to strike one. He held the flame up, confirming his isolation, trees and whispering growing things and coiled waiting things, and the light burned his fingers and he dropped it.

"Groat!"

How damned silly can a man be? He wasn't more than a quarter of a mile from the town. You could get this feeling of being lost in the night in somebody's back yard. He looked up at the sky, but there were no stars to guide him. Even if there had been, he doubted that he remembered enough boy-scout lore to locate the North Star and find his way back.

Back was down. All he had to do was walk downhill. For a

moment this was so obvious and so reassuring that he smiled. But all the senses were interrelated, and without being able to see clearly the contrast between up and down, how was he to feel it? The slope at this point was so gradual that he could spend hours walking around and around. Didn't the lost man in the forest always walk in a circle? Something brushed the back of his neck and he struck at it in panic.

"Where are you, you damned—"

Calling out made it worse. As if instead of advertising himself he should be keeping his presence secret. He was an intruder.

The thing to do was sit down and wait for dawn. The night would pass. All nights passed. He examined that for comfort. It was true. Since the beginning there was no such thing as a night that did not in the blessed order of things give way to the light. He let his breath out, only then discovering he had been holding it, that he had tensed himself so tightly from neck to knees that his muscles were beginning to hurt.

He sat down with his knees drawn up and rested his forehead against them. He heard a sound and was on his feet, shaking, hand out holding off assault. He saw the figure of himself: shoulders hunched against mysterious deadly attack, helpless and craven. He forced himself to jeer. Bookman, music listener, civilized viewer of foreign films. Wordplayer, lover, drinker of dry Martinis, smoker. Alone in the wood—like the poet. He reminded himself that the two things he feared with unreasoning reaction, spiders and snakes, made no sound, so how could he be dismayed by the noises around him?

He sat again and nursed his thumb, blowing on it, warming it with the other hand, almost glad the hurt was there for his attention. A little while ago (the elasticity of time) he had talked to Elizabeth of this, the disorienting of darkness and fear. Not me, he thought. Not old Evans, with all those inner resources. Let's have a concert. The Budapest String Quartet, playing the Beethoven Opus 131. The music began. He held himself to it, his hands on either side of his head like horses' blinkers to help him focus. He managed part of the first movement. Then there was a squeal, a rustle, a sighing, and he scrabbled to his feet again, standing like a boxer, chilled, very scared.

Elizabeth, he thought. He tasted her kiss again, he remembered holding her.

He looked up at the sky for signs of light. Hours had passed, surely hours had passed.

Groat said, "Principal? Where are you?"

"Here! Here! Where are you?"

"I thought you were right behind me," Groat said.

"What kind of a game—"

"Principal! Everybody is good at something, right? So what makes a man better than another man? Why do I have to work in people's toilets? Why can't I be in an office and wear a white shirt?"

"Take me up to the boy or take me back, Groat."

"I see you now. I can see in the dark like a cat. Who is better, Principal, you or me?"

"You. I cannot see in the dark. I don't know where I am. You are better, Groat."

"Ah, good."

"You have proved it. Now show me where you are and let's get out of here."

"You are a fool, Principal, to come into the mountains. A man came up here last year to hunt. He was killed. His body lay here for two days before they found it. The man who killed him, he was never found. That was in the papers, you didn't read about it?"

"I wasn't here last year."

"You know what I want? I want to live as good as anybody."

"That's fine. I don't object."

"If I leave you, Principal, you will never find your way back. Never. You will rot here. Because a man like you knows nothing. Do you understand? You know nothing."

"I admit it. You are the master here."

"You mean that? Or are you laughing at me?"

"I am not laughing."

A shadow, a form, Groat was standing before him.

192

"Was it a lie, about Joseph?" Robert said.

"Follow me."

Robert went after him, driving his legs like pistons, stumbling but not falling, never allowing himself to fall, clinging to the shape in front of him as if to life. It went on and on, over rocky upthrusts and sudden unexpected clearings, and suddenly again woods as thick as jungles. Robert began to sob with the effort of keeping the breath in him. The pain in his thumb extended now to the entire hand. He kept it inside the sweater, his little finger hooked in the waistband of his trousers. And after a while, as Groat did not outdistance him, Robert began to feel a silly pride whose existence made him smile. Like basic training in the army and having to keep up with candidates years younger. It was silly because it mattered not at all to the younger ones whether you kept up or not. What you were competing with was yourself at that age, so who was it who won or lost?

Toward James Groat Robert had first felt a distant sympathy based on what seemed social injustice or maybe guilt for having been born luckier, and then irritation turning to active hatred when Groat had left Robert alone; now Robert felt admiration for the figure before him to whom he was presumably tied forever in this night-rock-forest world. Robert had never been able to hate anyone for long when the object of his hatred was *good* at something. Groat went on like Henry Fonda in the opening scenes of that movie about the Indians. He was built for this, this tireless loping through the dark that was daylight to him, and having been formed with these talents, what was he supposed to do with them? There were very few openings down in that valley world for night-seeing runners.

Groat stopped and Robert almost crashed into him. Groat pointed. Robert could see nothing. Then he made out a flicker of light.

"That's the cabin."

"Groat."

"What, Mr. Principal?"

"There is no grudge."

"All right, then."

"Tell me now, you think Joseph is really here?"

"I know Joseph is here. I brought him."

"His father and mother don't know?"

"Sure they know."

"Then why did Mr. Maxwell go to the police?"

"Because he thought it was against the law to do this. So if he told them, then he is not to blame. He knew they would never look for Joseph here, they never come up here."

"Then why did you tell me?"

"You said you cared for Joseph. I thought it was another lie. Now, what will you do?"

"I think Joseph will decide what it is he wants to do."

There were more obstacles to the foot around the cabin than during the climb up to it. Bits of plumbing and cans of all sizes and bedframes and lumber. The house was small and seemed fashioned of odds and ends. Groat pushed in at the door and Robert followed.

The light came from a kerosene lamp hanging from a rafter by a wire. There was a table and some open shelves, a dry sink, a wood stove, a trunk, an army cot, some wood chairs and crates. The floor was packed earth. A man sat at the table. He was as dark of complexion as a Negro, with white hair that was straight and long. On his snub nose sat a pair of steel-framed spectacles. He was holding at arm's length a page from a Sears catalogue. He looked up incuriously. "Ah," he said. "James Groat."

On the bed lay Joseph Maxwell. He was dressed as he had been when Robert had seen him last. On his feet were socks with holes in the toes. He lay on his back with his arm across his eyes.

"Jared," Groat said. "I brought up the Principal of Joseph's school. The head man. To talk to Joseph."

The old man said in a thin sweet voice, "You are welcome to my house, sir. Will you sit and have some refreshment?"

"Thank you," Robert said.

Jared got a jug down from the shelf. He wore one-piece overalls, and his feet were bare. He put the jug on the table and

194

added two cracked mugs and an empty jelly glass. He poured out a generous helping of colorless fluid. He picked up his and said, "To the damnation of the enemy."

Groat saluted with his cup and drank. Robert took a cautious sip from the glass, trying to ignore the fact that it was not clean. It was raw fire. The old man was watching him. Robert drank, remembering to close his lips tightly around the drink to keep air from being swallowed with it. He did not cough. Jared nodded in approval.

"You are the headmaster in Joseph's school?"

Robert nodded.

"What is taught there, sir?"

"English, history, mathematics—"

"My grandson learns the same as the others?"

"Yes."

"You must excuse my ignorance. I have never been out of these mountains."

"You speak like an educated man."

"Many kinds have come into these hills. Once there was a schoolmaster who lived here. I bartered bed and board for his knowledge. He had killed a man in a place called West Virginia. Do you know it?"

"Yes."

Jared waved his hand. "He had some books, they are gone. My eyes—I cannot read anyway. Tell me, what will you say to Joseph, who ran away from school for a reason he does not speak of?"

"I will tell him to come back to school."

"Then tell him." Jared went to the cot and shook Joseph by the shoulder. "Joseph! There is someone here for you."

The boy woke up fumbling with hands and mind. He blinked and remembered and reached under the bed for his glasses. He sat up on the edge of the cot, the sleeves of his shirt down over his knuckles. He sat blinking.

"Joseph," said his grandfather, "do you know this man, come all the way up here at night to see you?"

Joseph peered at Robert. Robert smiled. Joseph shook his head unbelievingly.

"Hello, Joseph."

"Mr. Evans?"

"Yes."

"But—"

"The Principal," said Groat, "cares about you."

Joseph reached down quickly for his sneakers, getting his toes in to conceal the holes in his socks.

Robert said, "Is there a way I can talk to Joseph alone for a few minutes?"

Jared said, "James and I will take the air. I always take the air before retiring."

Alone with the boy, Robert said, "Where is your motor scooter, Joseph?"

"What?"

"You came to me for permission to park it, remember?"

"Yes."

"The one you paid three hundred dollars for."

"That one," Joseph said.

"Yes. That's the one I'm asking about."

Joseph sat on the edge of the cot with his toes hidden in his sneakers and his wrists hidden in his sleeves, his hand bracing him. He shook his head slowly like an old, tired man. "There never was no scooter, Mr. Evans."

"Then why did you come to me for permission to park it?"

I went up a mountain in the dark with a bitter guide, Robert said to himself, who was playing with the idea of leaving me lost there, to talk to a student of mine who came to ask permission to park his motor scooter, which he never had.

"I do things, Mr. Evans—sometimes I don't know why, and that's the truth. You ever hear—no, I guess nobody ever acted this way."

"I guess you're wrong, Joseph. I'm sure a number of students —especially seniors—have done dopier things. There was one I had who decided he was afraid of the finals, and he went to

196

Florida. Just disappeared and went to Florida. Gave his family a terrible time. When they found him, they brought him back and—"

"What happened to him?"

"Nothing. He passed his exams and he graduated. But tell me about that scooter."

"Well, if you'd said yes, if you said I could park it in the school, why, then I was thinking of buying one."

"Three hundred dollars?"

"That's what it said in the catalogue."

"You have that much money?"

"I could save it up, I guess."

"Yet, if I remember, I wanted to know why you hadn't come to me first to find out about the parking situation before you bought it."

It was becoming twistier and twistier, Robert thought.

"I'm not the smartest kid in the school, Mr. Evans, and I don't have much of a home to bring a friend to. You take the way the family lived up here in the hills—" Joseph looked around the room. "You'd think it'd be different down there. Anyway, I was thinking—what could I have that would be different, something none of the other kids had, something real fine. And I hit on the scooter. Nobody had anything like that. And the more I thought about getting one, the closer it got. It just didn't seem such a crazy idea. And then I figured I better go ask you about parking it."

"And I said you couldn't."

"That's right. And then—I don't know how to put it, but it was like everything fell in on me, you know? I just had to get away."

"But if I had said you could park it—?"

"That would have been all right," said Joseph softly. "That would have made me like anybody. Like—lucky, you know?"

Robert nodded, found himself reaching unconsciously for the drink and shuddered. There were chinks in the walls in which rags had been stuffed. The lamp swayed and guttered.

"How does your grandfather live up here?"

"He hunts a little, snares rabbits, grows a little vegetables."

"I see."

Four black ants, larger than any Robert had ever seen, marched sedately across the floor and disappeared. Something howled outside, a long keening protest. The wind produced a hurried colloquy in the trees.

"Tell me, Joseph, why do you think I came up here?"

"I guess there's a law—I'm in trouble, Mr. Evans?"

"No. You're in no trouble."

"Gee, I don't know then, Mr. Evans."

"I came up to tell you that you may park your motor scooter in the school lot any time you want, Joseph."

"I just told you I never had—"

"I know, Joseph."

The boy looked blank and then he smiled. It was a wide, sunny, healthy smile, and Robert had difficulty keeping solemn in the face of it.

Joseph said, "If I can say something without getting you mad, Mr. Evans, you sound like just as big a nut as I am."

"I'm afraid I can't give you much of an argument there, Joseph." Robert smiled. "So how about coming back to school? This is your senior year, I'd hate to think of anything going wrong with your graduation."

"You're not mad at me, causing you all this trouble?"

"I'm not mad, Joseph."

"Well, I would like to go back, Mr. Evans, I really would."

"Fine. Let's go, Joseph."

CHAPTER SEVENTEEN

That was Thursday night and the next morning Elizabeth was in school before him, standing at the entrance talking with Carl Peters. Robert approached with eyes all for her but with the decorum of the man in charge. He said good morning and they said good morning. Carl said something and Robert answered, but the point of view was Elizabeth's, he heard his voice as it sounded to her. He didn't look at her, concentrating on what Peters was saying, alert and smiling, as if the custodian's remarks about the need for better supervision of the boys' room was terribly important and also fascinating.

Carl Peters, a man of sensibility, looked at Robert and then glanced down, although another man would have included Elizabeth. Carl said, "Well, good luck," which Robert thought a perfectly natural expression, although neither of them was going anywhere or engaged upon anything. Peters unlocked the door and went in.

The morning after the discovery of the night before is always critical. So without making it obvious, they were examining each other, or perhaps they were examining themselves with the eyes of the other. You could combine need and propinquity and come up with something that for the moment seems awfully good and even permanent. But the next morning you notice the down along the side of her face and you have never been able to abide facial hair in a woman, and she sees the way you carry your shoulders and reminds herself that she could never like a man who was careless about his posture.

They were both worried about this.

She said, "What happened last night? Did you go with that man?"

Robert told her about it.

199

"That's very good," she said. "That's *very* good."

Then suddenly everything was all right, there had been no mistake, everything that had happened was real. So they stood without touching one another, and it was as if they embraced.

"Tonight, Elizabeth? And tomorrow? Well?"

"My father and I have to visit relatives. We won't be back until late Sunday night."

"You'll just have to do something about that."

"I can't. And anyway, it's better this way."

"How could it be better?"

"If I were here, I would be with you every minute I could. That's how I feel, and I'm sure it would be wrong. It's like over-cultivating a new plant when it ought to be left alone for a while."

"These botanical references leave me cold. When Burns said his love was like a red, red rose, he must have been out of his mind."

The rest of the staff began arriving. They went inside.

At nine o'clock the phone rang and Casella said, "I tried to reach you yesterday."

"I usually say hello myself," Robert said.

"How are you?" Casella said grudgingly.

"Fine. You coming in to see me?"

"This is kind of ticklish, Robert. Did you make a mistake, is that it, you didn't know who the boy was?"

"Oh, thanks. Thanks, Sal Casella, for teaching me the damn thing all over again. That nobody, *nobody* acts out of pattern. I always appreciated Hitler's honesty—he was a man who screamed. The soft-spoken tyrants with the long words who read poetry—oh, boy."

"I'm not sure I understand you, Robert."

"Are you Sal Casella, Board Member, or Mr. Casella, father of Angelo, that's what I mean."

"There's no call for you to get so hot. I just called up to—"

"Sure, Sal. To what?"

"About Angelo—"

200

"He's suspended. You want to come in with Mrs. Casella and talk about it?"

"Mrs. Casella?"

"That's the procedure."

"Dammit, Robert, are you trying to prove that a man can get along without friends?"

"I'm not trying to prove anything, Sal. Would you and Mrs. Casella like to come in this morning?"

"Yes," Casella said evenly. "We'll be in within the hour, if that's all right with you."

"I'll keep the time open."

And as if on cue, when he hung up Mrs. Otis called. She at once began to rant about her husband who was never home, and how could you raise a boy properly whose father was always on the road? Mr. Otis was not due home until December. Robert said he would accept Mrs. Otis alone for an interview if he could have an assurance of seeing Mr. Otis in December. He asked Mrs. Otis to come in after lunchtime.

He waited for Casella. On the surface he was busy with several things, but what he was really doing was waiting for Casella.

He liked Pine Hills. It made the New Canniston years seem spent in purgatory. There was money here, the community was education-conscious, and this was a good combination. It meant you could teach more and better. The evaluation phase of the accreditation program could be used to uncover the soft spots, to shore up, to clean out and start over. Pine Hills could be made into a fine school. The students were as bright as he had found, they wanted more than they were getting. And he liked this part of the state. Close enough to the city and still with a few mountains left to stare at. And Elizabeth Loomis lived here and taught here. This was not a job he cared to throw away.

Therefore, face the necessity for certain practical behavior, and do not sneer or be ashamed. There wasn't a president the United States ever had, no matter how revered, who had not understood and practiced the art of politics. Politics was the art of friends and favors. If your friends cared about you, they did

201

not ask for dirty favors, so there didn't have to be problems of conscience.

A principal does not go out of his way to offend a member of the Board. Axiom number one, two, and three. Probably four also.

Mr. and Mrs. Casella came in, and Robert stood up and was gracious. Mrs. Casella was not, at sight, the kind of woman he liked. She was a product of the beauty parlor. The beauty parlor implemented the suggestions of the fashion magazines, whose purpose seemed to be to make every woman the duplicate of her neighbor. Mrs. Casella's hair was a tremendous pile on top of her head. Around her eyes were intricate shadowings and line accents, and it was, for Robert's taste, much too early in the day for this, like having a Sunday dinner for breakfast. Her hands were so well cared for that there was obviously someone at home to spare them exposure to dishwater. Behind all this was a woman into her forties who couldn't possibly eat anything at all in order to keep her figure from its evident urge toward self-improvement. Her voice was deep, pleasant, and uncultured.

Having an inborn contempt for this kind of woman, who willfully fled from individuality for the sake of a spurious sexuality, Robert then discovered after a few minutes of conversation that he liked her. This process he continually went through of having unfair preconceptions explode in his face had no permanent chastening effect.

Casella was sullen and wary, as if he suspected Robert of concealing a source of strength.

Robert said, "The immediate issue is simple and probably not the most important. Angelo deliberately disobeyed a regulation, involved another boy, presumably because he felt, because of his father's status, that he had immunity. For Angelo's sake, for my sake, for the sake of the rest of the school, and for your sake, Sal, he just can't get away with it."

"My position—"

"What would you have me do?"

"You might have spoken to me first."

"I couldn't. I told the school assembly, I stressed this, that there would be immediate suspension of any student who left the school grounds. I said immediate and automatic. That doesn't mean until after I speak to his father."

Mrs. Casella said, "The boy is a big problem. I am in favor of finding out if there is something we can do."

"He's just mixed up," Casella said.

Robert said, "All his testing says he's bright, and all his grades say he's mediocre. What does he care about?"

"Girls and clothes," said Casella. "The hell with him. You think I came in to talk about him? I'll tell you, I crossed him off already. I'll support him till he's eighteen, and then I'll throw him out."

"You won't," said his wife comfortably. "How silly can you get, talking that way about your own son?"

"I'll let the army get him. What I care about is that this could make me look like a fool. I'm surprised at you, Robert. I'm really surprised you could do a thing like this to me."

"I wasn't doing it to you."

"I want you to call this thing off. There's time for the boy to get back in school today, I told him to stay in the house and wait for a phone call. That will take care of it. All right, Robert? We can work out Angelo's problem later, I would certainly appreciate your help on that, but the important thing right now is to make this suspension like it never was. There's this Board meeting Monday night, we're better off concentrating on this lunchroom business."

"I guess we would be."

"I saw an article," said Mrs. Casella with engaging irrelevance. "I forget the magazine, I was under the dryer. You know, Mr. Evans, how much women read in the beauty parlor? You ever thought of that? You think maybe beauty parlors and education go together?"

"That never occurred to me."

"Sure. Everybody's reading there all the time. It isn't as if women go in and waste the whole day. Sure, there's talking and so on, I don't mean to say it's a library. Anyway, I saw this ar-

ticle about teen-agers. And it said that they have so many problems and strains, the best thing is to leave them alone, that
too much discipline could be bad for them because when a person is under a lot of tensions, you ought to keep them calm instead of getting them excited."

"Is that what you think would be good for Angelo, letting him
do as he pleases?"

"Who knows? Who knows these kids today? My father—"
She made a chopping motion with her hand. "Boy, my father,
he took out the strap whether we needed it or not— We never
had any of this wildness you read about. The trouble is Sal
would never touch the boy."

"I can clear it with Eberly," Casella said. "So you can feel
justified in dropping it."

"Justified?"

"Why don't we have any trouble with the girls?" asked Mrs.
Casella serenely.

"Come on," said her husband. "They're teen-agers?"

"Maybe the first thing we ought to do," said Robert, "is eliminate that expression. We put them in this special category, and
then we're surprised when they act special."

"So what if the girls are little?" Mrs. Casella demanded. "It's
the pattern you set right in the beginning, right, Mr. Evans?"

"I suppose. But I'm afraid I don't understand your position,
Mrs. Casella. Did you say you believed in discipline or you did
not?"

"Well, that's it. Here's my husband on the Board of Education, he was elected by the district, and that's a proud thing,
wouldn't you say? And here's yourself, and you're what you
would call a professional in the field, right? And it isn't only
my Angelo, it's all over the country—not that Angelo's a
bad boy, I mean he's no gangster or anything. So wouldn't you
say it's up to you, Mr. Evans? I mean, I don't want to be crude or
anything, but what are we paying you for?"

"*Mea culpa,*" Robert said.

"Look, Sal, he speaks Italian."

"If it's settled," said Casella, "I have to get back to the office."

204

"I don't know if it's settled," Robert said.

"One thing I don't like to do is push my weight around. I never liked it done to me, and certainly I never want to do it to anyone else."

"I'm glad of that."

"So why can't we understand each other and come to terms with this thing?"

"I think I understand you," Robert said, "but I'm not so sure you understand me. I can't just unsuspend Angelo, pretend it never happened, just because you are in the position you are. Do you really want me to do that, Sal? I mean, in the open, explicitly, is that the kind of man you are?"

"I'll tell you, Robert, you're getting me mad, and that's going to make it easier for me. I liked you right from the start, we hit it off well, I thought. So why change that?"

"Sal—what if this were some other Board member's son? Farmer, or Vincent. What would you think of his putting pressure on me?"

"Are you kidding me? You were in the army, you certainly heard of RHIP. You were an officer, you want to tell me you never took advantage of your rank? Rank has its privileges in private life, too. What do I get from serving on the Board? Pay? Not a dime. You know how many evenings, how many days I put in?"

"Mrs. Casella said it, it's a proud thing."

"Yeah. Now I come to you for a lousy little favor, just a little consideration, and you want to put it on some high moral level? Cut it out, Robert. You trying to tell me you're a girl scout or something?"

"That's what it comes down to in the end, is it? Who's pure? How do you dare take an ethical position, anybody? Everybody's got his hand out, right? Then tell me this, Sal. You were awfully interested in the education of the young when we were talking in that restaurant a month or so ago. So what kind of education would you like me to see that your son gets? What's the next step—using your so-called influence to improve his marks?"

"Nobody talks to me like that," Casella said.

He stood up. Robert stood up. Mrs. Casella said, "Easy, Sal, he's bigger'n you."

It was silly enough to stop the idiocy.

Casella said, "All right. He stays suspended?"

"That's right. Three days."

"I came to you and you turned me down. Now I'm telling you, don't come to me."

"If that's the way you want it," Robert said.

Mrs. Casella said, "Awfully glad to have made your acquaintance, Mr. Evans." And behind her hand, as Casella went speechlessly and red of face out of the office. "He's excitable. Doesn't mean anything."

Robert saw her courteously to the door. He went back and sat down and broke a pencil. It was satisfying and he broke a few more. In order for the bile in him to settle he had to sort himself out in relation to the world. It seemed to be something he was forever doing.

He was disappointed in Casella, whom he had liked. He was disgusted with Robert Evans, for had he not determined in advance to be circumspect, aware that his future might depend on Casella's good will?

What bothered him especially was the imputation of his own freedom from taint. He resented this bitterly. He reserved the human right to behave erratically, with venom, through self-interest, and with selfish disregard of truth and the feelings of others when he thought it necessary. The fact that he found himself in holier-than-thou situations had to do more with stubbornness and a fierce compulsion to prick ethical pretensions than his own standards of behavior.

Why couldn't people just admit that moral codes were something for the Sabbath, and then only when the preacher's eye was on you. And so far as the man of the cloth was concerned, how come he accepted a car at wholesale from the dealer who wanted to have his insignia displayed by the representative of God? Why didn't the clergy insist on no favors for fear they might have to intercede spiritually with a little more fervor for the sins of those to whom they were economically or socially indebted? Why was the Justice of the Peace secure from parking tickets? Why did principals deliver commencement exercises that distorted the truth? What right had a member of the Board of Education, elected to serve the interests of the community, to demand special consideration for his son?

A day that started that way was usually a total loss, and sometime he would have enough conviction to follow this kind of reasoning by at once going home and getting into bed and starting again twenty-four hours later. The trouble was, in this uncertain world, you couldn't be sure even of bad luck.

Robert spent the rest of the morning with Perry Dickinson, going over the preliminary assignments to the committees that were to begin the evaluation of the school. Robert had to depend heavily upon Perry for the choices of teachers. At lunch Robert got involved in discussion with Altman, the art teacher. He was a man who wore woolly shirts that were not designed for ties, nor were the patterns and colors of the shirts ever designed for the patterns and colors of the ties.

Altman had a square face that required shaving twice a day and rarely got it. With the heavy shirts, he wore Harris tweed jackets, and Robert itched and felt warm just looking at him. Altman looked as if he were just about to need a haircut, and he had his hair cut just enough to continue to look that way. He carried a pipe and sometimes stuck it between his teeth, but mainly it was used for emphasis. Once Robert had seen him fill and light it, but he had permitted it to go out after a few puffs. He had rigged up a hi-fi set in the art room and it went all day. Some of the teachers in the adjoining rooms complained, but Robert wouldn't do anything about it. The thing that bothered Robert was that he had no idea if Altman was a good painter or a good teacher. Robert knew nothing about art, which did not interfere at all with his arguing about it.

He said to Altman, "I'm bothered that most of your students are doing nonobjective things. This can't be natural to children. So you must be influencing them."

"Of course. I'm an art teacher."

"I thought your job was to assist them with techniques, but not to interfere with their normal expression."

"That is nonsense." Altman was born in Brooklyn and had never been away from the Eastern seaboard, but he sometimes spoke English with the exaggerated care of the foreigner. Robert thought this might have been an early home influence, but Perry had told him that both Altman's parents were native-born and well educated. "Children know nothing. There is an exhibition of children's art, and everybody oohs and ahs and says, How sweet, How expressive, these lovely unspoiled primitives. Nonsense, Mr. Evans. A primitive is a highly skilled artist who has spent a lifetime perfecting his technical prowess—"

"Grandma Moses—"

"Everybody—excuse me—who knows nothing about art always says Grandma Moses."

"Does that mean you think she's good or bad?"

"You were talking about children?"

"I thought I would see more representational things."

"Out. Gone. Painting has to come from inside. Before the development of the camera—"

"I think I remember reading recently that all this abstract stuff is going off the scene. Another ten years—"

"Reading who, Mr. Evans? A fortuneteller? Because to see a tree and paint a tree is nothing. To see a tree and paint the turmoil that takes place in the artist when he sees it—"

"It hurts to watch a tree?"

"You must paint from here," touching his diaphragm with two fingers on which, Robert was pained to notice, the nails needed cleaning.

"Communication?"

"So?"

"What other purpose can there be to painting? To any of the arts? Sharing an experience—?"

"When I paint, I'm sharing. Who said I'm not sharing?"

"But if I don't understand?"

"That is my fault?"

"Well—yes."

"For the first time in the history of painting we are revealing the soul. Better than trees, isn't it?"

"What you're saying is that the viewer now needs as much preparation and experience as the artist. If you're painting the psyche, the only qualified viewer can be a psychiatrist. You're wiping out everybody else. Instead of museums you want your work hung over couches?"

"Ha."

Elizabeth, carrying a cup of coffee, came to join them. She said demurely, "Mr. Altman, Mr. Evans."

"Miss Loomis," Robert said.

Altman said, "And you, Miss Loomis? What do you think?"

"Is this 'pick your category'? Movies, politics, poetry?"

"Art. Mr. Evans thinks the artist should do what the camera can do better."

"That's not really what I said."

"I like what I know," Elizabeth said.

"What painter do you like, Miss Loomis?"

"Burchfield."

"Sure," Altman said, waving his pipe. "And you have in your home, perhaps, a print of 'Ice Glare'?"

"Yes. How did you know?"

"It takes brains? The steps of the house. You can feel them, sit on them, run your hand over them and get a splinter?"

"Yes."

"And that you call art?"

Altman grunted and went off to get himself another cup of coffee, which he drank black and with a lot of sugar. Elizabeth held her cup and talked calmly to Robert. They looked like two people who meet casually between groups at a cocktail party. Actually they were two people in the middle of a crowded room desperately making love.

She said, "Your tie isn't straight."

"Dying to get your fingers on it, aren't you."

"Yes."

"How frustrating it must be. I'm looking at your mouth. I'm talking to you and looking only at your mouth."

"Stop it."

"Weekend with your father, will you."

"Robert—after Sunday—"

"Yes?"

"Is Monday—"

"I'll hold you to that," he said.

CHAPTER EIGHTEEN

Monday evening, on his way to the Board of Education meeting, Robert, driving down Main Street, saw a light in Rose Pink's real-estate office. He parked his car and went in to say hello. She was eating a sandwich and drinking tea from a cardboard container. "Why, Robert, I'm glad you dropped in." She put the container down, wiped her lips delicately, and extended her left hand to him.

"How have you been, Rose?"

"Getting rich. They're buying houses as fast as the builders can put them up. I suspect they're offering bonuses, like free ice cream for a year or scholarships to Yale. I don't know. I think some of these frantic people have never *seen* a house. They go wild over the built-ins in the kitchen, and they think cellars are *supposed* to have wet walls. I tell you, Robert, it bothers me. As soon as I make enough money, I'm going to quit."

"That's noble enough."

"And how are things with you, Principal?"

"I thought I'd drop in and have you tell me."

"Well, you didn't exactly rate with Mr. Oniotny."

"Mr. Oniotny?"

"Just First Vice President of the Savings and Loan, that's all."

"What did I ever do to him?"

"He has a daughter named Veronica."

"And that's my fault? Veronica Oniotny? Really, Rose—"

"That's her name. Moreover, she's been in the Honor Society for the last two years."

"Well?"

"But not this year. Or maybe ever again, and she's only a junior. So Mr. Oniotny is peeved."

"I think I understand. Miss Oniotny will not have a ninety-or-better average."

"That is correct, or at least likely, since she has never done better than eighty-two."

"What a farce that was, Rose. National Honor Society. The best students, a real honor. Technically they were supposed to be selected on the basis of scholarship, service, willingness, decency, and what have you. All on teachers' recommendations. What I found was that some teachers were selecting friends of friends, or the good-looking ones, or the best pencil sharpeners, I don't know. So all I did was tighten it up a bit. And now nobody gets in the Honor Society who doesn't hit a ninety."

"That's what I said. Mr. Oniotny doesn't care for you."

"I'll tell you a secret, Rose. I suspect that Mr. Oniotny has lots of company."

"Could be. But before you go off to lick your wounded pride—"

"Would I do that, Rose?"

She smiled. "No. You'd spit in their eye. So before you start spittin', let me tell you that the odds aren't so bad. Most of the teachers like what you're doing, they have a feeling of being part of something worthwhile. And most of the kids, too. The bright ones, no question. You're doing all right, Robert."

"Sure?"

"Sure."

"I hate to tell you how relieved that makes me. I was beginning to feel the stones I was throwing set up no ripples, just sinking without a trace. What is this quality of yours, Rose, that makes strong men bare their souls to you?"

"Compensation. I get the souls." She laughed to take it away from self-pity. "What the hell, Robert. Someday I'll sit you down to listen to my troubles."

"Anytime," he said, meaning it.

He found Eberly leaning against his desk in his office, the door to the board room open, but with no one yet there.

"Hello, Robert."

"Fenton."

212

"Hello, Robert," said a feminine voice. He looked into the room to see Lobrige in one of the deep plastic chairs, feet crossed at ankles stretched out straight. She was smoking a cigarette in a long holder. Her glasses, because of her position, were for once in place.

"Hello, Sally."

That was the way it was when you were not a petitioner.

Then the rest of the Board members came along, and they went into the board room. Same place, same cast. Robert thought back to remember how he had felt then, and decided he felt the same way now: a little nervous, and consequently tending to be a little touchy and a little self-protective. He said "Hello Bill," and "Hello Vince," and was introduced to the two members he had not met: Arnie Miller and Ralph Lund. And then it was Arnie and Ralph and Robert.

He thought of Elizabeth using his first name, and his using hers.

Casella came in late. He said hello to Robert without embarrassment and without warmth. Robert wondered what kind of antagonist he was going to make, for there was no doubt in Robert at all that Casella had become an enemy. The man he had liked, who, according to Eberly, had swung the Board around to Robert in the beginning, would for that very reason be unassuagedly bitter toward him now. Biting the hand that feeds you is, to some, the one sin that can never be overlooked, and Robert was sure Casella was such a man.

Robert looked around. Who, then, was left to be for him? If I am not for myself—

And they called him Robert, all these strangers. He could remember, as a boy, fighting with a friend. And since the friend had become a foe, he could no longer be addressed by first name, which meant intimacy, so Robert had used the boy's surname. He had been eight, or nine. "Listen, Logan—" And that had sounded so ridiculous to them both that they had broken up in laughter and the fight was forgotten.

What ought he to do now, call the man Casella? If only now, too, that would bring on laughter and wipe off resentment.

213

Sam Jennings came in and used everybody's first names except Lobrige and Eberly, both of whom nevertheless called him Sam. Jennings looked uncertain when he came to Robert. Robert said solemnly, "Hello, Sam."

A man took a seat without saying hello to anyone. He was dressed neatly with a shirt collar too tight, which kept his neck red, which accentuated the pallor of his face. He didn't wear glasses but had the pinch marks on either side of his nose.

They began the meeting with a discussion of the choice of an architectural firm for some proposed new school buildings. They discussed the type of form for the architects to fill out prior to their coming before the Board with a presentation. Robert, listening inattentively, was impressed with the thoroughness of the information they required of the applying firm, the exhaustive examination of background, experience, familiarity with school structures. Robert was also impressed with the lack of anything that questioned the architect's concept of what a school building should be. Nothing about whether a school should look different from a factory or a movie theater. Nothing about whether any of them had the courage to get away from the damned cinderblock.

They talked and he had difficulty staying awake.

A long and—outside of the moment or two he had spent with Elizabeth—joyless Friday, and Saturday, and Sunday.

Mrs. Otis, Friday afternoon. Weeping. She told him about her marriage. Why him, he wondered without pleasure.

She was a woman without charm: bony, voice too high, a bad-color print dress. What could he—Robert—expect of a boy with a father like that?

"You think nothing can be done with your son?"

"Ever since he was a baby—no father! He could have gotten an assignment to the home office—New York—but he wouldn't take it. He'd rather go off around the country with a cushy expense account. Why not? Lives in the best hotels, eats of the best, better'n he gets at home, plenty of parties with women in his room, don't think I don't know about that!"

"About Philip."

"His father just doesn't care about him!"

"I want to know whether you care about him."

"What do you mean, Mr. Evans?"

"Do you work?"

"No."

"Does the boy have breakfast?"

"You jump around, Mr. Evans, I just can't follow you."

"I asked whether your son has breakfast before coming to school."

"Really, I just don't know what kind of a question that is, Mr. Evans."

"I'm pursuing a theory of mine. I find that often kids who get into trouble never seem to have breakfast at home. Silly, isn't it?"

"It sounds silly to me. Philip certainly has breakfast. I mean he does when he wants it."

"Do you prepare it for him?"

"Well, honestly, I sleep late in the mornings. I have to, you see I'm not a very good sleeper and I watch the late movies—that's a godsend, that television, you know, Mr. Evans? So naturally I'm not up when Philip goes to school, the bus comes so early."

"Do you know what his program is this year?"

"What do you mean? What's he taking? I guess I do—a language and—"

"What language?"

"I don't see why you're questioning me this way. You'd think *I* was suspended." Nervous giggle. "French, I guess. Or—"

"Do you know just how and why he got into trouble this time, Mrs. Otis?"

"He broke a rule, didn't he? He just hasn't any regard for the proper way to behave. He's rude to me often, his own mother. And without a father to step in and take over—well, what can you expect, Mr. Evans?"

"So you think he's just a bad boy, is that it?"

"Maybe if his father—"

Robert said slowly, "If Philip got into trouble often enough, and badly enough, so his future was affected, perhaps even not graduating with all that might mean—I guess that would show Mr. Otis what a rotten husband and father he was, wouldn't it?"

"It sure would," said Mrs. Otis with pleasurable emphasis.

"In that case, Mrs. Otis, why should you care about trying to keep Philip behaving properly?"

"What do you mean? I'm his mother—"

"One of the reasons for suspending a boy is to make his parents realize the seriousness of an offense, and perhaps by consultation guarantee that it doesn't happen again. Can you give me such an assurance, Mrs. Otis?"

"You see, you've hit it on the head, Mr. Evans. Now if Mr. Otis could be made to see how necessary it is for him to be home—"

"Is that all Philip is, a lever to influence Mr. Otis?"

"I'm sure I don't know what you mean—"

It was true. Mrs. Otis did not know what he meant. Robert felt old and tired again. If he kept this up, one of these days he was going to *be* old and tired, and what will have happened to his prime of life? Whittled away by all the absent Mr. Otises, whom he couldn't blame for staying as far and as long away from the Mrs. Otises as possible.

"Maybe you could write a letter to Mr. Otis, Mr. Evans? Do you think that might help? Something stern and official to make the man see he has to stay home if he wants to keep his son from turning into a gangster?"

"I'm going to lift Philip's suspension temporarily. You said you expected your husband in December? He must come in to see me then."

"I must say, you've been very understanding, Mr. Evans."

Arnie Miller was making a point to the Board about certain legal procedures to be followed when a contractor was behind schedule. He had been a practicing lawyer for several years and looked young enough to be entering law school. He had a high, somewhat bulging forehead that seemed to have pushed out the

216

hair above it. What was left he wore combed across his scalp. His face was so young that this looked like a teen-age style rather than the masking effort of age.

Robert felt it was safe to go back to the reverie that was on the border of sleep.

The weekend. He had always known what to do with his weekends and looked forward to them. Now, one dinner and some conversation with Elizabeth, and without her he no longer knew what to do. He stayed close to the cottage, read a great deal, the radio on constantly. He lay on his bed and read messages on the ceiling. He slept. It was the army again, the pain-killing sack time.

On Sunday morning as he went out for a change of air, he met Fred Ballard on his way to the store for breakfast requirements. Fred insisted he come along. They rode in Fred's old Mercedes and discussed cars. Fred said that no American car could ever suit him because Detroit did not dare put out a car with a hard suspension, and with their interest in the soft, cushioned ride they sacrificed road holding and there was nothing they could do about the mushy sway on corners. "You can't have it both ways, Robert. You want to be insulated from the road, you have to give up stability."

"What I'm against is all this pressure to have you buy a new car every year or so, else you're a traitor to America because our economy depends on the automotive industry. Someday America's definition of a good citizen might be someone constantly in debt because he's loading up on all the new appliances and cars and gadgets, because otherwise what happens to our industrial complex?"

"You've got a point," Fred said. "I don't think it's *that* original, but it's a point."

"The only thing I want in a car is to have it last. My old Plymouth has a personality, it's a friend of mine. If she sways going around a bend, I forgive her, just as she forgives me if I shift badly."

"I've heard of the car being a sex symbol, this is the first time I ever heard of it being a mother."

They parked and went into the store that sold smoked fishes and cheeses and rolls and breads. Robert sniffed. Fred said, "All these magnificent smells getting you?"

"They are, but I was thinking of that story you told me."

"Yes. That story. The smell of failure, right? Well, those people are long gone. This isn't that store. And, for that matter, I'm no longer the man who told you that story. Do you know that, Robert? Can you tell the difference in me?"

"Yes."

Fred purchased with the abandon of a man filling a larder after a famine. "I hope you like this stuff, you're having breakfast with us, Robert. You haven't eaten yet?"

"I had some coffee."

"Join us, then."

Refusing required a reason, and Robert couldn't think of one he could readily express. He had been trying to avoid Kathy.

Fred was a confident man, he sat with his head high. A man has to be sure of himself to invite someone to breakfast without consulting his wife. Robert helped carry the paper bags into the kitchen. Fred called out, "Wear something, Kathy, we have a guest."

She came in without a smile, although she managed a faint one as she said hello.

"I bought whitefish, smoked carp, salmon, swiss cheese, muenster, bagels and seeded rolls, and some thin-sliced pumpernickel," Fred said proudly.

"It's conspicuous consumption, but all right. Coffee's ready."

The carnival symbols for marriage, Robert thought. The merry-go-round. This was a seesaw. Maybe with practice it was possible to balance, but it would not be easy. Kathy had been the higher, and now Fred had managed to lose weight or had learned how to slide forward. It was undoubtedly good for Fred, but the change in Kathy was marked. She had managed, regarding her husband as a failure, in some fashion to achieve gaiety apart from him. It was even possible that she had been feeding

218

on his lack, becoming the more as he showed himself the less. You could keep a snake happy by feeding it mice, but the mice wouldn't think this a good arrangement. Kathy did not bubble with that inward laughter any more. It was possible that Fred was getting his own back. His tone was assured now, and he told Kathy what he wanted, and she did it for him. Fred might also have achieved dominance in bed. Perhaps not to Kathy's contentment but probably to Fred's.

"Marvelous coffee," Robert said.

"I seem to remember your not being able to make the best coffee in the world," she said, sucking at her lower lip and staring at him.

"You been entertaining my wife?" Fred said, mouth full.

For a shocking moment Robert thought Fred's new confidence ran to hindsight.

"Hardly," Kathy said. "I just tried some of his coffee once."

Robert, speaking too quickly, said, "Single fellows shouldn't be trying all of this modern stuff. Percolators are for families. Hunter style, coffee in an open pot. *Fendel* coffee. You ever try that, Fred, dropping the grounds right in the boiling water?"

"I was never a hunter," Fred said.

"Oh, well, neither was I. But just to be sitting near a mountain stream, say, after a night in the open, and the smell of that coffee—"

"I remember that when I was a girl scout," Kathy said, "except we didn't have coffee, and the camp was on a second-class pond."

"I wonder what happened to it?" Robert said.

"What?" said Kathy.

"The point."

"I think you'd be interested in knowing what happened to me, Robert," Fred Ballard said. "As a kind of psychological exercise, perhaps."

"Oh, Fred," Kathy said.

"I'm sure Robert would be interested."

"Sure," Robert said.

"I haven't been a success," Fred said. "I can face that with

219

perfect calmness, you know, I lived with it, and that's the way it was. Kathy suffered—well, if that's too strong, let's say she wasn't very proud of her husband, and a wife has to have pride in her husband. I think that might be a prime requirement for marriage, wouldn't you say, Robert?"

"Sounds reasonable."

"Anyway, not a very good life, not for either one of us. And you know what the trouble was? It was so damned simple after I had figured it out. I was hanging on to this dead dream, and believe me, Robert, a dead dream decays just as fast as anything else that ought to be buried. There I was, an unsuccessful artist, and it never occurred to me I might be a successful something else, that it might be possible to live an enjoyable life even without painting."

"Lots of people seem to."

"That's just how I saw it. Suddenly. And then it was so easy, it was funny. I just started being good at this job, which up to then I'd been holding onto just for bread, you know? And when you find out you're good at something, you begin to like it— how about that for an interesting reversal, Robert?"

"Yes."

Fred left for a while, and Kathy, unasked, poured Robert some more coffee. She said, "If things are so good, then tell me, Robert, why am I so damn *depressed?*"

"I don't know. Do you hate that fellow?"

"No."

"You can't adjust to success, that's your trouble."

"Robert, I won't refer to this again. But just this once. That night. It wasn't because I'm that kind of woman, and it wasn't because I fell in love with you either."

"I know that."

"Why don't I know what I want, Robert?"

"Why doesn't anyone?"

Back at the board room they were still talking about architects, equalization rates, a proposed bill before the legislature that, if passed, would provide considerably less state aid than the district had received in the past. Ralph Lund thought that the school budget could go no higher without losing community support. He was an apple grower, and Robert decided he looked like one of his products. He was broad at the temples, his face tapered to a rounded chin with a cleft in the middle, and his cheeks were red and polished. But he spoke more like a banana, Robert thought, a man whose tongue seemed too big.

Farmer said, "My own feeling is that we don't have to run scared about budgets. Not in this community. Look what happened last time. We came up with a budget over six million. Six million! It scared the hell out of us, and Fenton here worked like a Trojan trying to pare the thing, and managed to lop off nearly three hundred thousand—"

Eberly smiled like a soldier modestly receiving praise after a battle.

"And then what happened at the budget hearing? Not a single complaint, you would think they never even looked at the figures. All they worried about was the services we tried to curtail."

"I'd like to see us begin to level off," Lund said. "I don't like the feeling of sitting in the middle of a spiral."

"How the hell can there be an end to it," Vincent said, "when they keep moving up with housefuls of kids?"

"I'll tell you how it'll level off," said Casella. "Inflation carries a built-in solution. Things will get so high, the tax dollar so large, nobody will be able to afford to live here, they'll move off to less expensive communities, and we'll be stuck with a billion dollars worth of new, empty school buildings."

Farmer said, "I think—if there's no more old business—we ought to get to Robert's presentation about the evaluation program in the high school."

Robert tried to clear his throat silently, suffering at the beginning of any public address until he could hear the reassuring sound of his own voice.

"I'll go over the general area briefly," he said, "and then you can ask for particular qualification if you like. You know the history of the program in the school system, how it was established and so on. The first phase is self-evaluation, which we are beginning. The bible is this big red book, *Evaluative Criteria*. I brought a copy for you to look at, and I've ordered copies for each of you. Using this as our guide, we're setting up committees for major section and subject matter, with teachers assigned to two committees each. I serve on the Steering Committee and the one on Philosophy and Objectives. You can see the breakdowns—program of studies, school plant, instructional materials, and so on. This self-evaluation should take us about a year. Regardless of what happens afterward, we're bound to come up with a better school. Around next November we should be ready for a committee of twenty-five educators from the Middle States area who will spend three intensive days here. They will analyze our own evaluation, and will make recommendations. The chairman will give us a tentative oral appraisal, which is not official. After that we wait for a written report from their headquarters in Washington, which will be a notice of accreditation or not."

Lobrige said, "We've functioned here for a long time with a fine school system. Why do we need this accreditation? Seems to me a lot of work is going into something that I fail to see the necessity for."

"I'm not trying to sell this," Robert said. "I understood this was a decision you had reached before I came—that you wanted it. I think it's a good thing."

"Forgive me, Sally," said Eberly, "but we've gone through this before. Accreditation—my heavens, Sally, we'll be the first in the county! That's a great feather in our cap!"

"Sure," Vincent said. "You be on the school board that got our high school accredited and it's something to be proud of."

"I don't know," Lobrige said. "I'm not talking about credit for it, I want to know how much it counts, really. You take this committee. They come in for three days, and right away they know if we have a good school? We take a year and they take three days?"

"I understand," Robert said, "from those who have served on such committees, that they can really get the feel of a school."
222

"So can I. And John Loomis ran a fine school, and he didn't need accreditation or evaluation or anything else."

"It's not a reflection on Johnny," Eberly said.

"It better not be."

"What I wonder about," said Lund, "is how do you really judge a school. Seems to me only the kids, where they go and how well they do afterward—that's the only test."

"All we can do," Robert said, "is go along with the kind of yardstick that is normally accepted. Just as a doctor's diagnosis is based on taking a pulse or using a stethoscope and so on."

"If we get it, how long's it good for?"

"Ten years. Then we go through the whole thing again," Robert said cheerfully.

Casella said, "This evaluation. All phases of the school operation, right? Subject matter, instruction?"

"Yes."

"Administration? The Principal?"

"Yes," said Robert, feeling a coldness creep into his stomach.

Casella looked at him with an even, calculating displeasure.

CHAPTER NINETEEN

T he man with the tight shirt collar turned out to be a lawyer named Amboy who said he was representing the Foster family. Eberly looked visibly annoyed that Amboy had come to the Board meeting.

Farmer said, "This is not an executive session, and certainly anyone is welcome to sit in. Mr. Amboy notified me that he would like to make a statement, although over the phone I tried to indicate to him that I thought this a little premature. I spoke to Superintendent Eberly, who assured me that the situation was being looked into, that there would shortly be a hearing of the involved parties—"

"I spoke to Dr. Eberly, too," said Amboy. In acquiring his law degree he had bypassed any exposure to the smoothing out of speech patterns. He spoke with a strong dentalized *t* and a tendency to begin a new word before the prior one was well on its way. He sounded, Robert thought, a great deal like Foster himself. "I didn't get any satisfaction from Dr. Eberly. I mean action, something to go on, some indication that we're all not just going to sit on our behinds and let time pass. We've got a boy here's been beat up. That's clear enough. I've got the doctor's certification right here. By God, gentlemen, this is the middle of the twentieth century, and a schoolboy is entitled to some protection. I want all of you to know I'm going to push this thing all the way."

"Somebody better tell me what this is all about," Lobrige said testily.

Farmer nodded to Eberly, who told her briefly about Gilbert Gist. "I hadn't thought of bringing this before the Board. Not yet. I told Bill about it, and I guess he spoke to some of the others—"

"I just can't get you on the phone, Sally," Farmer said. "Aren't you *ever* at home?"

"There are *so* many things to do."

Eberly went on, "This incident just occurred, and I was waiting for the boy to be well enough to have him in the office with Gist to get at the truth of it. Mr. Amboy insisted on coming here this evening—"

Lobrige said, "Robert. One of *your* teachers?"

He thought, The way to treat her needling is to pretend to be unaware of it. A bull could drive the picadors crazy by not reacting to their pricks.

"I go to the top," Amboy said. "Always have, that's my nature, that's the way I get things done. I would think nothing of taking this to Albany, the Commissioner of Education, why not? We've got to protect our young people, I say, against the abuses of a system that permits a child to be assaulted right in the classroom by some hooligan of a teacher who never should have been hired in the first place."

"I promise you a complete investigation, Mr. Amboy," Farmer said. "And we would not need your reminder to do it, I may say. But I have to tell you that if you're here legally to represent a client, you are welcome. But your allegation about the quality and competence of this body and this school district are not welcome, sir, and I must ask you to desist."

"Sure, I didn't think I would get any co-operation. I know how you fellows work, a closed corporation, one protecting the other." He prepared to leave. "All right. This is a country of law and human rights, and by God I'm going to see that this boy gets what's owing him." He went out.

Lobrige said, "What have you done about that teacher, Robert?"

"Well, I—"

"He's not still teaching?"

"He is. Pending the hearing Dr. Eberly referred to."

"Well, I think that's a disgrace. How do we know the man hasn't gone completely berserk, how do we know he won't be attacking another student tomorrow?"

Casella said, "Fenton, that sounds like a good point. Shouldn't that teacher be relieved of his duties until the matter is cleared up? Suspensions seem to be in order around the high school, why is this man exempt?"

"Not exempt," said Eberly uncomfortably. "Robert, perhaps—"

"Sure," said Robert. "We can suspend him. I'm not sure I want to keep him on, maybe after this is examined, we might want to ask for his resignation. But right now this is all somewhat excitable and untimely, I think. I don't condone what the man did, but he had a lot of provocation from the boy."

"I've never *heard* of this sort of thing happening at Pine Hills," Lobrige said.

"A man like Amboy is just the kind to run to the papers," Vincent said.

Robert caught Sam Jennings' eye, speculative and faintly gloating.

"What about it, Robert?" Farmer said.

"What about what?" said Robert with open irritation.

"I just wondered if you thought everything had been done in this affair that should have been done."

"Yes. Yes! May I ask how I managed to get on the hot seat?"

Eberly said, "Certainly Robert handled the situation without any reproach being in order—"

"I didn't mean anything like that," Farmer said.

"I just want to know," said Lobrige, "how it could have happened in the first place."

You hired him, I didn't, Robert thought. You're supposed to check teachers before they're taken on, except that you don't bother. The power of people like Sally Lobrige, he realized, was that they never seemed to be accountable for what they said. They sat in seats of decision and ignored the obvious, and crazily facts were altered.

He almost missed Arnie Miller, who was saying, "In law it seems that the man who yells the loudest is always the least sure of his legal position. I wouldn't worry too much about this man Amboy, and I think particularly we shouldn't let ourselves

226

feel blackmailed into making more of the situation than exists. Pending Fenton's hearing, I think we should let this matter drop now. What do you think, Bill?"

"Fair enough," Farmer said. "And certainly we've kept our friend, Sam Jennings, waiting long enough."

Jennings stood up. "I'll tell you right now, I wish I had somebody like that lawyer to speak out for me—"

"You can feel free," Farmer said. "You're among friends."

"Friends. Sure. Then how come you're taking away my store? How come you're putting me out of business?"

Lobrige said, "Why is it, won't somebody please tell me, that I never seem informed of what is going on? I received my copy of the agenda this morning, Sam wasn't on it, I don't know why he is here, yet the rest of you seem to know."

Farmer said, "As I told you, Sally, you're never home. I tried to reach you at least half a dozen times. When Sal spoke to me, I checked with everybody."

"Well, if you tried to reach me today, I was in the library most of the time on a research project for the Historical Society. Early American ironware. We're going to have an exhibit on the first of December, and I expect all of you to attend."

"Why sure, Sally, we'll be there," Farmer said.

"Cooking utensils, mostly, although we've gotten hold of some of that marvelous hingework that you see imitated all over now. What *is* your problem, Sam?"

With great satisfaction, detail, and controlled pathos, Jennings proceeded to tell her. Robert had to listen to himself described as heartless, a tyrannical destroyer of the free-enterprise system and the God-given American right to earn a living.

She glared at Robert. "I've never heard of anything so—"

Eberly stepped in nervously. "You remember, Sally, how we discussed this in the past. This has always been a chronic area of difficulty. You remember our discussing the obstacles to school discipline in the students wandering off—"

"I don't see what that has to do with Sam's lunchroom. From what he says, this could put him out of business. Well, I for one will not be a party to anything like that."

227

"It's not that I am in favor of a man being deprived of his livelihood," Eberly made sure to record.

"Then the solution is simple enough."

"What would that be?" Robert asked.

"Why, simply retract that ruling. It was an arbitrary thing to start with, and doesn't need a two-thirds vote or anything, does it?"

Jennings said, "I'm glad you see it that way, Mrs. Lobrige. I'm sure glad a man can come to a meeting like this and get his rights."

Lobrige smiled graciously.

Robert waited, but it looked as if no one was going to say anything else about it; it actually looked as if no one was going to say anything. He glanced at Eberly. The Superintendent's face was studiously blank.

Farmer said, "Yes. Well. Where were we."

"I'd just as soon vote to adjourn," said Lobrige, "if there's nothing else to discuss this evening."

Robert choked. He had to leave his seat and stumble out to the water bubbler in the hall. When he came back, the meeting had turned informal. Some of the members were standing. Jennings was telling a story to Vincent, something involving broad gestures and grimaces, and Vincent was nodding and smiling.

Robert went over to Eberly and said, "What about this?"

"Patience, Robert."

"Patience! Am I really supposed to rescind that ruling? Because Sally Lobrige says it's arbitrary? Do we just let the damned thing go?"

"Tread softly, Robert. All the Board members are here. If none of them wish to do anything—"

"But it's up to us, isn't it?"

Eberly shook his head.

Robert looked around the room. He caught the edge of Casella's glance. Casella was waiting for Robert to hang himself.

Robert said, "Mr. Farmer."

228

"Yes, Robert?" The implied rebuke that he was not addressed as Bill.

"I'd like to make a statement about this. Surely there is more to be said than I've heard so far."

"Why, go ahead, Robert."

"I just don't understand this apathy, or at least this unwillingness to discuss or consider this matter. I've been made out to be an ogre, and I just don't feel like an ogre. A decision concerning the school has managed, inadvertently, to involve a businessman. Because he has come here to complain about it—justly, I think—I am merely, according to Sally Lobrige, but by your silence you all seem to concur, to reverse myself, and that's the end of it. Well, it isn't the end of it."

Lobrige said, wide-eyed and silken and dangerous, "I don't know what you mean, Robert, when you say it isn't the end of it."

"I mean that when I was hired, it was established clearly enough, I think, that the Principal of the high school was the one who was going to run the high school."

"That's your responsibility," Farmer agreed. "In all matters referring to the school. But we on the Board have a double responsibility: to the schools in our district, but also to the community. When one is in conflict with the other, we have to consider very carefully the best course to take."

"I don't disagree with that. But I haven't noticed your considering—"

Then he felt like a fool as the obvious occurred to him.

There was no discussion because a decision had been reached in advance.

"Oh," Robert said. Now he understood the reason for the sounds that accompany acute frustration. They came from recognizing that articulate expression was dead, and all that was left was the relieving whimper.

Sam Jennings had had the entire weekend. Prominent business people, local politicians. How the phones must have crackled as Robert lay in suspended animation studying the ceiling in his bedroom.

People like Mr. Oniotny, already aggrieved, to Farmer: "Hello, Bill. How's everything? Those investments we spoke of coming along all right? Sure, the missis is fine. Bill—what's this I hear about Sam Jennings' little store being closed down by that new principal of yours? Bad relations, Bill, bad relations."

Oniotny to Vincent: "Vince? How've you been? Say, what's the renewal date on those policies you sold me? Slipped my mind. And Vince, since when are you against small businessmen?"

Oniotny to Lund: "Ralph, I'm glad to say that your request for that loan looks good to us. By the way, Ralph, I was talking to Sam Jennings. I hope you're not for that move to close him down. That would be a rotten thing, wouldn't you say?"

And Robert Evans to the Board of Education: "All of a sudden this has been made to look like an effort on my part to eliminate Sam Jennings' store. But this has to do only with the situation at the high school. This has to do with the discipline and safety of the students. You are ignoring these essential matters, while the only thing that seems important to you is whether Sam's business is going to suffer. I must keep those students within the school area. There is a completely chaotic situation at the school, and I must correct this, and the fact that Jennings is involved is just an unfortunate happenstance."

Then Farmer said mildly, "I might be on a highway in an awful hurry, going somewhere in my car for an awfully good reason, but I just don't run over somebody in the way. I have to figure out that he has a right the same as me."

"Then give me an answer to this: in order to keep Sam Jennings in business are you prepared to jeopardize the well-being and safety of the students?"

"Aren't you exaggerating?" Casella said. His tone was maddening, adult to willful child. "I mean, Robert, let's not get melodramatic about this thing. It's not all that complicated. I think it might be a good thing for you to learn that everything isn't all black or all white. Now, you have a problem with your students. Seems to me you're looking for an easy way out, and because you haven't put enough effort in, Sam here's been hurt. I don't, myself, want the kids to feel that school's a jail. They're entitled, it seems to me, to a little freedom when it comes to the lunch hour."

"It's twenty-two minutes."

"I've heard some comment about that, too. Making the kids gulp their food."

"I think you're suggesting a return to the permissiveness that resulted in the situation as I found it."

Lobrige said, "I don't think you have a call to say that, Robert. It certainly sounds to me as if you're overly critical of the way John Loomis ran that school. I never thought you were this kind of personality, if you want my opinion. The children in this district have been accustomed to decent treatment, and I personally am against this kind of dictatorial attitude."

Fighting against water again. Robert breathed in deeply, held it, let the breath out slowly with lots of control. He said calmly, "I wonder if we can get back to the issue. I wonder if we can't consider why I had to make the decision I did and, for the moment, leave Jennings out of it. This was never directed at him."

"Maybe the answer is you ought to have considered him," Casella said. "It's all very well to operate as if you're in a world of your own, but we're here to safeguard community needs."

"I thought you were here to safeguard educational needs."

"You don't have to get sarcastic. Maybe you never learned that the schools and the community are interrelated, then it's about time you did. I myself would consider it part of the education of the students that they learn to recognize the rights of the other fellow."

Verging on desperation, Robert said, "That just isn't the point. Are you doing this willfully, is there any reason you don't want to understand what I'm talking about?"

"There's a legal angle here," Arnie Miller said. "Maybe not the kind to stand up in the courts, but certainly there is an ethical responsibility. As I understand it—I wasn't a member of the Board then—Jennings was given some kind of verbal assurance that the students would be permitted to patronize his store during their lunch period, and on the basis of that he went ahead and built his place. Isn't that so, Sam?"

Jennings, who had been following events with a sharp, teeth-baring delight, said, "Why, sure, Arnie, that's the way it was."

Robert looked at Eberly. The Superintendent was not participating. He had withdrawn to eye the ceiling, to tap his fingers. Robert said, "When I assumed the principalship, I was informed that there were certain areas that required urgent attention. One of the most important was the laxity of pupil supervision, particularly their wandering off the grounds. I did something about that, it was my duty to do something about that. I consider the action of this Board in not upholding me detrimental to the discipline of the school."

Casella, with an infuriating mask of sympathy, a show of not allowing himself to be angered by Robert's intemperateness, said, "You've been here just a short time, Robert. Nobody expects you to fit into every phase of this particular community right in the beginning. Maybe where you came from, they didn't have the kind of co-operative relationship we're proud of having here. We don't believe in unnecessarily antagonizing anyone or separating ourselves, we believe we run the schools the way the people want us to, and once we stop doing that, we become ex-Board members. And that condition of being *ex* applies right down the line." He smiled pleasantly.

It was all hideously wrong. It was like running up to the backs of old friends to say hello and having them turn around to reveal the faces of animals. He should have been automatically supported. Eberly should have spoken out. There would have been expressions of sympathy toward Jennings, and maybe an effort at some kind of compromise, but that they were unanimously against him was unbelievable.

It was time for a man of independence to quit. Robert tasted the words of resignation in his mouth. They were bitter.

Eberly said, "Just a word, if I may. I can't go along completely in your assumption that Robert took an arbitrary or unilateral position in this. I was aware of what he was proposing to do, and for the most part I was in favor. I was disturbed, of course, by the possible damage to Sam's business, and I hoped we could work something out about that. I think you must all recognize the excellence of the job that Robert has been doing. This presentation we have just heard concerning evaluation—the benefits to the district to be derived from his efforts—"

Farmer said, "Heavens, Fenton—Robert—there was no implication here of dissatisfaction with Robert's handling of the job."

"Heavens, no," said Casella, smiling.

Vincent said, "I hope you won't regard any of this as criticism, Robert."

"Heavens, no," Robert said.

"I think," Farmer said, "that we can safely leave the working out of this problem to Fenton and Robert. Between them I'm sure they can come up with something to keep the students in line without forbidding them—if they want—to patronize Sam's place—"

"I never said they couldn't do that," Robert said weakly, ashamed of himself, yet unable to still the sudden pounding of the relief in him.

"We'll manage something," Eberly promised.

The meeting was adjourned.

Jennings came to Robert and said, "No hard feelings, Mr. Evans. I know you were just trying to do your job, just as I was trying to hold on to my business—"

"Sure," Robert said.

Eberly asked Robert to stay after the others left. With the breaking up of the meeting they had become individuals, with no more power than anyone else, pleasant and friendly. Lobrige said, "Good night, Robert," and Robert said good night to her, and the same to Farmer and Lund and Vincent and Miller. Casella said good night and waited for Robert to do the same.

Robert did with no sign of rancor. Casella said, "Nobody stands alone, you know what I mean, Robert? You have to have friends."

"Sure," Robert said.

"A friend is somebody you do something for, and he does something for you, right?"

"Right."

When Eberly and Robert were left alone, the Superintendent showed Robert into his office and dropped into his desk chair like a sack of meal. Everything sank down, his jowls, even his eyes, as if they had been kept at everyone's level only by some tremendous effort.

"Robert, I'm going to show you something that no one else in this world but me knows about." He selected a key from a chain, opened a bottom drawer, and took out a bottle and a couple of paper cups. "For supreme emergencies of state." He poured two drinks.

"Thanks," said Robert gratefully. They toasted each other silently.

"I guess you're pretty peeved at me," Eberly said.

"No. What for?"

"For not standing up to them?"

"I thought you did."

Eberly shook his head. "What I said was for you, because I thought you were about to do something foolish. Christ, I'm bushed. This job. Three, four nights out every week. Only Monday and I'm beat."

Robert nodded.

"That new budget. Impossible. The costs go up so that one of these days—boom! Everything will stop. Frozen. I tell you, Robert, I'm scared stiff at the thought of bringing these new figures to the people of this district. And still they keep yelling for more new schools and higher teacher salaries and special courses and transportation. Transportation. The state minimum of a mile is not good enough for them. Almost every family around here has two cars, and you'd think if we didn't supply

234

the buses, there'd be no way for their kids to get to school. And what about walking, what happened to that? And bicycles? Values. Everything distorted."

"What about values? What about a principal running his school?"

"Don't be bitter, Robert. It's a luxury in our business, no room for it. I don't know what you worked with in New Canniston. They just left you alone?"

"I had a feeling I was respected, and trusted to do my job. What happened here tonight—"

"Sure." The Superintendent filled their cups again.

"What about the students leaving the grounds, Fenton?"

"You'll have to let them."

"The way it was?"

"Same framework, maybe different reins. Is that what they call mixing something or other? I'm not a well-educated man, Robert. All my degrees—state schools and teacher colleges. Another drink and I get maudlin. Do you believe I'm a man who cares about the way children get educated?"

"Yes, I do."

"It's too big. The whole damn thing's too big. What I wanted to tell you—you have to accept what you have to work with. You know? You couldn't be a principal without all the background, schooling, experience. But all you have to do to be a Board member is be elected. Then they run you. And they run me. You know, Robert?"

"Yes."

"You have to learn how to give. Then the trick is to learn when to stop giving, or there's nothing of yourself left. You follow me, Robert?"

"I think I do."

"Things will work out. Don't worry. Let's close up shop, now."

They went out together and down to the parking lot, where each got into his own car. Eberly drove off. Robert sat staring down at the ignition key. After a while he recognized its function, and he turned it on and drove away.

He was ashamed and depressed, but more than that he was worried. He didn't know if he had been a coward or not.

All his toughness, the stubborn way he had been able to stand up for what he regarded as important principles. Bravado, without bravery. What had he risked? He had some money saved and no one dependent, and with his qualifications could always find a job.

Now, at the first sign of danger, he had buckled.

Because this was where Elizabeth was, and this was the place in which he wanted to remain.

CHAPTER TWENTY

The edges of newness were abraded away, and what was left was a circle with no sign of the joint of its fashioning. Robert was locked inside; the wheel spun away the days and months. His clock was a school bell, and when the students left he stayed on, and unless Perry took him home or Elizabeth made him take her to dinner, he ate sandwiches without taste or forgot to eat entirely.

Gilbert Gist was persuaded to resign. At first he resisted, but Robert pointed out that, lacking tenure, he could be dismissed by the Board, and they were in a temper to do it without concealing the reason that would have made a school career for him almost impossible. He left, and would find a job in another school district to perpetuate his incapacity for teaching. The Foster case against the Board was happily dropped when the boy considerately left school and enlisted in the navy.

Robert had good days in which everything was sharp and clear; he felt the bite of correct decisions and heard around him the hum of a thousand minds, and he knew he was building a school. He had days when he saw the ineptness of teaching and the sloth of learning, and he saw it all as folly and façade, with the children who were bright taking care of themselves and the others being pushed along to a meaningless diploma. When it was bad, he felt there was nothing he could do to counter the influence of the giant machinery pouring a river of directives from Albany, the stream of mimeographed orders from Eberly's office, all neat and correct and part of the *record;* each department, each clerk, and each secretary able to show she was doing her job well, everything classified according to the books and the pamphlets and the periodicals. Everybody knew what he had to do to hold onto his job, everything fit, the organization

237

functioned splendidly. So how was it, he thought grimly, a student could graduate from high school and know so little?

At first the teachers assigned to the evaluation committees resented the extra time they had to give. Twice a week they had to stay in meeting until five o'clock or later. Robert visited each group and, after the mechanics of the task was explained, had this to say:

"This is your chance to do something about all those educational gripes you've been saving. I don't know how many of you regard your work as just another somewhat tedious job, more or less well paid, ample fringe benefits, minimum effort, and the tenure system enough to keep you paying your bills for the rest of your life. I know there must be some of you who feel that way. To the others, to the frustrated others who want to teach and like to teach, who sometimes find themselves part of a system they hate and haven't been able to do anything about, to those I want to say this—this is what you've been waiting for. We're going to dig into every phase of this school. We're going to turn over the rocks and lift the rugs. Each of you has found something to criticize, maybe many things. Now let us bring the complaints out in the open, and if they're justified we'll make changes, and if they're not justified you'll know it."

In one group Robert heard part of a sentence. He said, "Speak up." No one did. "Come on, let me prove what I said, that this is wide open and anything can be stated."

A teacher of physics, a burly man with hair winglike over his ears in the Einstein tradition, said, "I'll repeat it. I said this evaluation has to be a whitewash, like anything else. No school system is going to stand for an honest overhaul."

"It's Mr. Somers, right?"

"Yes."

"I'm glad you mentioned what a number of you might have been thinking. All I can say is—try me. Remember, the results of our findings, of our self-recommendations, are going to be examined by a group of educators from a number of different schools and positions. If they can come in and smell a weakness and find we have overlooked or ignored it, it's going to make us look silly. No whitewash, Mr. Somers. My word on that."

Robert found that at first, with an officially sanctioned forum, the tendency was to unburden the accumulation of personal and professional thwarting that had little to do with the area for which the individual committee was formed. Robert thought this a healthy preclearing and instructed the chairman to permit it, at least in the beginning. So the teachers sat around and bitched. And mostly the target was the education courses they had been forced to take, which had given them little except facility in the jargon and an accumulation of in-service credits for salary increases. There were idiots among them—what field is exempt?—and with Perry's help Robert had tried to scatter them sufficiently to minimize their obstruction. There were good teachers among them, and Robert was convinced that progress would be made.

He was impressed with men like Porter Wilson, whom he had once derided for lack of forcefulness. Unobtrusive, shy, with the professional stoop in his thin shoulders as if his models had all been elderly men, Wilson had a love for his subject, and said that this feeling, translated into classroom terms, was what students should be exposed to.

"This is what the math teacher is up against," he said. "There's no problem with the kids who are good. And equally, there's no real problem with the ones who are below average—there's a special course of treatment for those. The ones who bother me are the kids who are bright in other subjects, the A and B students in English, languages, social studies, etc., who come into a math class and fall apart. They come with a built-in rationale—and very often they get it from their so-called intellectual parents. It's considered natural for the good English student to have a hard time in a math course. Natural, and even something to be a little proud of. As if it's taken for granted that proficiency in the one means inevitable lack of comprehension in the other. It's absolutely fantastic the blocks they set up—these verified bright ones—it's the biggest waste I ever heard of."

"What do you do about that?" Robert asked.

"We talk about numbers, for example. The excitement of them, to me, and then I try to figure out why I'm excited, and tell the kids, and hope this is a feeling they can share. I have to break down all the misconceptions about math being dry and mechanical, and how only a certain kind of mind can cope with it, and if you get pleasure from Dickens and Tolstoi, or mystery stories or poetry, then you can't possibly like mathematics. I try to show the students that mental excitement and emotional excitement can tie together."

"Does it work?"

"Not always, and certainly not with everybody. I've been lucky on a fundamental level, I get these kids who are worried about college acceptance with screaming nightmares about math bringing down their average, and I show them how to look at the subject so they can handle it. I don't get them all to love it, but I can get most of them to learn to live with it." Wilson smiled faintly. "Maybe I'm doing my bit to prepare them for marriage, I don't know."

Robert left and went on to another meeting, but something about Wilson was nagging at him, so he went back and asked the math teacher to come into his office.

Robert felt a dry embarrassment, but he was convinced he had to do this. For a while they talked about Robert's admiration for Wilson's approach, and Robert told him how glad he was to have the teacher in the school.

"Thank you," said Wilson with honest pleasure.

"I wonder why you stay in secondary education?"

"Well, I was going to teach in college at first, as a matter of fact, I began there as an instructor. But the attitude of the college teacher—if a student who comes in is top-notch, the student gets the credit, but if he's not so well informed, the tendency is to blame the teacher who had him in high school. You fall into this, there's so damn much snobbishness around. Anyway, it seemed to me I'd be doing a lot more good if I could get to the students earlier. Their minds seem to set so fast, often they get to college and it's too late. So for me, anyway, high school is the place with the most rewards."

"You've four children?"

"Yes."

"How the hell do you manage on your salary, Porter? And how do you keep out of industry? I'm sure you could double your income—"

"Excuse me, Mr. Evans, but now you sound like my wife."

"I bet."

"I'm doing the work I like, where I want to be, wouldn't you say that was quite important?"

"More important than anything."

"I'm glad to hear you say that, Mr. Evans. Most of the time I feel I'm being selfish about it. Anyway, I do some moonlighting, like most of us. I teach three nights a week and I do campwork in the summers. We get along."

"I'm glad you do and I repeat, I'm glad you're here, Porter. So may I say something—be frank?"

"Why, of course."

"A school teacher's in a funny position. Anybody working with young people is, I suppose. I—" Robert grinned. "At this point I don't know how to say what I want without sounding the way I don't want. I'm not even talking to you as a principal so much as—well, somebody else working here along with you. It's advice I'm talking about. We're in a business where you're dead if somebody says you were seen patting a little girl on the head. You know? Not that anybody said anything to me. I just want to caution you—"

"What do you mean, Mr. Evans?"

"Are you going to help or hinder?" Robert said, becoming irritable. "Don't get touchy, for the love of Pete. It's just that you see a girl student once in a while outside of the classroom, don't you?"

"I never—"

"Please. Understand me. This is no inquisition. You've been teaching long enough, Porter, to know all the harm dirty tongues can do."

"Yes," Wilson said, suddenly thoughtful.

"So that's that."

"Mr. Evans, I wonder—"

"What?"

"I *have* been wanting to talk to somebody—"

Oh, no, thought Robert, not a confidence.

"What is it?" he said. "Is she pregnant?"

"*Mister* Evans!"

"Good. At least that's out of the way. So what is it, then?"

"I have been seeing a student, Mr. Evans. It's kind of a relief to talk about it. I'm married, four children—it sounds pretty stupid, I know."

"How far's it gone?"

"It hasn't really gone anywhere. We take a walk, sometimes go in for a cup of coffee. And that's all. We talk. She's a happy person. Being with her is good for me. My wife—well, my wife is not a happy person. There's never any talk at home that isn't—sour."

"I understand. And believe me, your private life is none of my concern. It's just that—well, it really isn't a very good idea, is it?"

"I give you my word, Mr. Evans. It's the most innocent thing in the world."

"Sure, Porter. But it's a bluenose world. I'd hate to lose you, innocently or otherwise."

Somewhat reluctantly, but not feeling strongly enough to fight against it, Robert found himself expected to attend all the home football games. Some of the teachers attended, and sometimes Elizabeth came. Sometimes, rarely, they sat together. Neither wanted their attachment to become obvious. As the unmarried head of the school, he was under almost constant surveillance to see where his interests lay, and neither of them liked holding hands in a fishbowl.

Even her one visit to his cottage had been brief and unsatisfying. Robert felt that he was exposing her to the sharp eyes of a sleepless and starved-for-gossip small town.

"It's so wrong," Elizabeth said, "to feel guilty when you've done nothing to be ashamed of."

"I can think of nothing more irrelevant than whether we're guilty of anything or not."

"Nevertheless," said Elizabeth, "you can't keep me away from your natural habitat any longer. Before it's too late, I have to know whether you sleep on a shelf or squeeze toothpaste from the top or if you have closets full of pancakes. A girl has to see these things for herself. It's not what you *say*, Robert."

She came and looked and sighed. She studied his books approvingly. She opened the door of his kitchen cabinet and shook her head sadly at sight of a jar of instant coffee.

"It was just a moment's madness," he said. "I only used it once."

He could not enjoy her being there. He was nervous. He thought that the door might open and Kathy Ballard come in. Who, then, had to be explained to whom?

She said, "You're jumpy as a cat, and you can take me home."

In the car he asked if she was angry.

"I can't say you acted as if I were welcome."

"You weren't. I've got a special place for you. I'm building it. When the time comes, I'll take you there."

One Saturday afternoon close to Thanksgiving, Robert sat in the stands with Perry Dickinson, who, for purposes of adroit cover, had brought Clare along to sit with Elizabeth in the row in front of them. The band played, the teams ran out, the cheerleaders went through their skilled little dance, and the students yelled happily.

"Of course, Perry," said Robert, "you find all this shameful."

"Indeed I do."

Clare Dickinson turned her head and said, "Perry, you just watch what you say to that man."

"Sport," Perry said. "Just take a good look at that word. It hasn't a single connotation that— Take your pick. It stands for amorous dalliance. Is that what we're in favor of? I mean, for kids? Then it means killing animals as a pastime—and I'm not for that."

"Be no stopping him now, Robert. When he's against something, he studies all about it."

Perry went on unmoved, "Then it means a joke, right? Well, it's no joke when a kid can get his leg broken. Then it has to do with some abnormal form of something, right? A mutation. You certainly can't be for any of those, Robert. So what are we doing here?"

"You were cheating. You left out recreation. Re-create. I'm interested in that. Good for the player and good for the spectator."

Elizabeth said, turning and by no accident grazing Robert's knee with her shoulder, "All I can see is those poor kids on the bench. This idea of 'Now, Coach?' is a terrible thing."

He bent forward to get the smell of her hair. "You, too, Miss Loomis? Where were you brought up? South America? No, they play ball. Japan? Just as bad. Mexico? Bullfights. Where *did* you and Dickinson come from? Is there any place in the world where these things don't go on?"

"It's a sad world," Perry said. "Pine Hills is just part of it."

The game began. One team, grotesque in padded armor, hurled itself at the other team. The little girls in short skirts ran out and whirled and jumped. Students and parents cheered. A whistle blew. The clock stopped.

"There's an idea we might use in the classroom, Perry. Timeout clocks when a student is being chided or pencils are being sharpened. How about that?"

Undiverted, Perry said dolefully, "Rome. The arena. What difference if we've cleaned it up, when the symbolism is still there? Thumbs up, thumbs down. I worry about the loser."

"Look at the banners. Look at the faces. Pride in their school. How can that be bad?"

"We handed it to them, this *way* of feeling pride. We're holding up the same signs our teachers were given and passed on to us. Nobody stops and worries whether the messages on the signs are good or not."

A boy broke loose and ran down the field, clutching the ball.

"Hooray!" yelled Robert with the rest of the stands. "Come on, Perry, you don't think that's exciting?"

Four tacklers reached the runner and smeared him. Perry said, "If that was my kid, I'd tell him, give them back their ball, you don't need it that bad."

In front of him Elizabeth's hair shone in the sun. The back of her neck was slender and sweet. Robert wanted to show his gratitude. You could burst with the joy of being alive. What you wanted to do was run out there on the field and grab that ball. The hell with your symbolism, Perry. Kids get charged up on a golden day like this and want to run. The trouble with getting old was that you might still feel like running but you weren't able. If we dress it up into teams and winning, that's just to keep the thing organized.

At half time Robert had to go down to officiate at a ceremony to dedicate the new bleachers. Perry was against that, too. "Everything's a ceremony. So when a truly important occasion comes along, it's washed away in the spate of nonsense. They built some new seats. Fine. Now they have to be *dedicated?*"

Evidently they did. Eberly was there, talking to the minister whose turn it was. In recognition of democracy and the absence of a state religion, each faith was given representation at official functions. There was always an invocation, and a benediction, and you had separate clergymen for those, and the rotation system was carefully followed. Today it was the Reverend Arthur Pringle. Eberly introduced them. They chatted. Not Pringle with Evans, but the Minister with the Principal. They smiled and moved their lips in unhearing conversation, aware of the flashgun in the hand of the local newspaper photographer.

Pringle was a very cheerful man, a red-lipped, white-teethed, clear-complexioned cheerful man. He was short and carried himself as if he didn't know it. He told Robert how much he liked children, football, the weather, the way Robert was running the high school.

Robert was willing to have that last thing amplified, especially before Eberly, who was adding his own mouth and gestures to the conversation. "Yes?" Robert said invitingly.

"Discipline and purpose," Pringle said. "When children know what it is they have to do and what it is they may not do, then they're safe, they're happy. Wouldn't you say, Dr. Eberly?"

"Why, certainly I would," said Eberly.

"I have two daughters," Pringle said, with pride at once tempered by modesty. "Alice, of course, is a senior here."

"Of course," Robert said.

"Sweet child," Eberly said.

"I imagine it's not easy to grow up with a minister for a father," Pringle said with engaging frankness.

"I guess it's not easy to grow up with anybody for a father," Robert said.

The band played a piece, there was a fanfare, and Robert went to the microphone to begin the proceedings. He said that this wouldn't take long, they didn't want the teams to cool off. The students cheered. He said that one thing that seemed to last in this world was seats, and he cited Greek and Roman ruins, and how you could still sit in some of the seats after a couple of thousand years. He said the only thing that lasted longer than seats was ideas. He didn't know how long these new bleachers were going to last, but when they finally crumbled, the world might still be benefiting from the mind of someone sitting here with them today. While the spectators were examining each other for signs of immortality, Robert introduced the Reverend Pringle. Pringle said that these bleachers represented America and God. In this country we settled our differences by battling them out on the playing field with rules and in the sight of our fellows to cheer us on. The greatest thing in our democratic way of life was the quality of sportsmanship, and when you sit in those bleachers to cheer the team of your choice, remember you're part of the American pattern, a country endowed by its creator with the love of fair play.

When the game was resumed, Robert could not get back to the stands because he felt obligated to remain with Pringle, who wanted to watch some of the game from the sidelines. Eberly had excused himself, saying he had promised to make an appearance at a boy-scout picnic. Pringle, glowing, said to Robert, "Isn't it just wonderful, our whole way of life, Mr. Evans, where in the world can you find this enthusiasm, this sweet health?"

"You mean this football game?"

"Yes, I mean all of it." Pringle's wave took in the faces in the crowd, the cheerleaders, the hot-dog stand run by the GO, the bright sun-filled air.

"It is a good thing to see." Then, infected by some of the dark thoughts of Perry Dickinson, he said, "Sportsmanship and fair play. You believe in those things, Mr. Pringle?"

Pringle kept his smile ready until he was sure Robert was serious.

"I want to know," Robert said, "if it's really possible to go along without being vicious, or hurting anyone, or taking advantage of the weaknesses of others."

"We have a number of examples of those who have done it, haven't we?"

"I never knew those people, so I couldn't say. Once in a while I'm not sure of these things, and I wonder if being a minister makes you more certain."

"Are you talking about religion, Mr. Evans?"

"Well—religious ideals, American ideals—they're pretty close. If we had a machine to screen every spectator here not to let him in if he had an unsportsmanlike attitude in his heart, would we have an audience?"

"By and large, Mr. Evans, wouldn't you say we live in a fairly moral community in a fairly moral country?"

"We don't seem to read the same papers."

Pringle sighed. "Being mortal, we have our limitations. Being men, we're given the strength to fight against them."

"In your church you can instruct in morality without having to justify it, in school we have to make these things reasonable. Some of those kids out on that field are not above using their knees in a pile-up. They're heroes so long as they're not found out."

"Mr. Evans," Pringle said, shaking his head with the comfortable superiority of the untroubled toward the doubter. "I hope this questionable attitude of yours does not get through to the students—"

"Questionable? Answerable is what I want it to be." Then Robert smiled and patted the minister on the arm. "We'll have to have a talk sometime."

"I wish you'd come and see me," Pringle said. "After all, we're more or less in the same field, aren't we?"

"More or less," Robert said.

After the game Robert and Elizabeth went to Perry's house. Elizabeth and Clare found a lot to do together in the kitchen. Perry said, "It's the alliance. Be careful, Robert, the hooks are out."

"In," Robert said. "Do you like her, Perry?"

"Very much. Outside of Clare, she's the only girl I've ever seen who doesn't play at it. It's a set, serious thing, isn't it."

"It's being sure. To an old waverer like me—" He made a gesture of impossibility. "She's real, Perry."

"That's what I meant."

They talked shop. Perry was skeptical about the permanent value of the evaluation. "The absolute rarity of the really good teacher. Nothing is more fundamental. What do we do about that?"

"That's society's problem, isn't it? We have to use what we have. The lousy ones we will just have to make better, the impossible ones we'll have to find jobs for in the library, or as curriculum consultants drawing up revisions we will never use. Who the hell is looking for perfection, Perry? If that were our aim, we would have to scrap ourselves along with the other deadwood. *I'm* a principal? *You're* an assistant?"

"Sorry I brought it up."

"Pessimism and you, Perry, don't seem to go together."

"It's bigness. It scares me. In everything. Women, corporations, labor unions, mountains, government. The state ed department is too big. This school is too big. To tell the truth I
248

don't know what I'm doing here. Some cozy little private school somewhere, that's my speed."

"Mark on a log, eh?"

"Who said I'm a teacher? The other day Martin asked me why elephants are gray. I went into a long thing about camouflage, pigmentation, light absorption, and whatever else I could think of to conceal my ignorance. So when I got all done, the little devil, who had been listening very patiently, said no, that wasn't it. The reason elephants are gray, he said, is in order to tell them from bluebirds."

"Sell your television set, that's your solution. Or sell your child."

"Robert—how is it you've managed still not to meet Elizabeth's father? Seems to me you're dodging like a lopsided ball."

"He's dodging pretty good himself, if you want to know. Elizabeth says she's tried to have me in for dinner with him, but he always has an excuse. You know he's now in demand as a speaker? Our only living ex-principal. Also, he spends a lot of time with relatives in Connecticut. I don't know, Perry, do I have to force a meeting? It gets harder, and less believable. He never comes to the school, not since I insisted that all visitors report to the office."

"Doesn't Elizabeth mind?"

"Mind what?" Elizabeth said, coming in with a tray of canapés as Clare brought in glasses and ice.

CHAPTER TWENTY-ONE

H er own business," Robert said. "And maybe you'd better stop fraternizing with the enemy. I suppose Clare was in there teaching you how to make a chocolate cream pie that drives men mad."

Clare said, "This girl needs no help from me."

"Mind what?" Elizabeth said, offering some salami wedges to Perry.

"One thing I hate," Robert said, "is a repetitious female."

"We saw that new Italian film at the Mall," Clare announced. "Like it?"

"I did, very much. I'd even want to see it again. Not my husband, though."

"I don't like foreign movies," Perry said. "Subtitles irritate me, and so does dubbing. The only foreign language I understand like a native they don't make pictures in."

"What's that?" Elizabeth asked.

"Eskimo."

"Eskimo?"

"The ones I really like," said Perry, "are those British murder stories where the Inspector is an intellectual and everything is underplayed, and they have a lot of those incidental types, each of which is a gem; they work at that."

"I like Westerns," Robert said.

"You?" said Elizabeth. "I'm glad I found out in time."

Elizabeth. Perry. And Carl Peters. The custodian came in to clean the offices every day at five, and Robert usually got him to sit and talk. Robert admired and resented him. The admiration came from the man's physical strength and quickness, the incongruity of hi speech and cultural interests, but above all

250

from his stability. He was a rock in his steadiness, contained, sane. Robert was resentful that Peters held the kind of job he did, and the resentment was all the sharper for Peters' apparent contentment.

One afternoon Peters came in with his mop and pail, and Robert said, "You play chess, Carl?"

"I do a problem once in a while."

"You doing anything tonight?"

Peters hesitated. Robert wondered irritably why it was so difficult in democratic America to cross a caste barrier.

"No," Peters said.

"Have a sandwich with me and then come along to my place for a game, all right?"

"Well—"

"Look, if you'd rather not, all right, but if your nose is up, then that's not all right."

"I wasn't—"

"You don't patronize me and I won't patronize you."

Peters laughed. "If you want to mix with a custodian socially—"

"As long as you don't have anything against principals."

"I'll accept the sandwich part of the offer. But then how about coming back to my room? I've got a bottle of slivovitz I clipped from a Romanian wedding where I tended bar."

"You just threw the big persuader."

Peters lived in a two-story frame house converted into apartments. In his room was a divan covered by a bright bedspread, a soft chair and reading lamp, a small rug that looked like a Sarouk. The rest of the floor was bare. The wood had been scrubbed down to the grain and waxed. On the wall were two long shelves of pine on metal-strip holders. Robert blinked at the books. At least half, in paperback editions, were poetry. There was a doorway, from which the door had been removed, to a tiny cooking area with stove, sink, small refrigerator. Everything was shining, and Robert thought ruefully of his own slapdash housekeeping.

"There was a lot of stuff in here, but I had the landlady take it out."

Peters went to a closet and pulled out a folding bridge table and two matching chairs. Robert helped set them up. Peters brought out a chess set and board, put it down, and went to a cabinet for a couple of glasses and a bottle. "You like this stuff fixed any special way? Ice, or anything?"

"I haven't had it more than once or twice in my life. Is there a technique to drinking it?"

"All you do is swallow and hold your hand over your mouth to keep your teeth in."

Peters took a cardboard packet from the shelf and extracted a thin twisted black cigar. He offered one to Robert, who took it curiously. "Italian cigars?"

"That's what they call them because Italians smoke them, but actually they're historically American. This is the famous stogie, originally 'stoga' after the Conestoga wagon, after the name of the town."

"You're a mine of information."

"It's nothing," Peters said modestly. "You want to know how these are made?"

"I can't help myself."

"They take these long leaves and soak them in water until fermentation occurs. Then they roll the cigar and let it dry. In New York I sometimes buy them in long lengths and cut them down."

"They look so vicious I've always been afraid to try them."

"I like them. They have a kind of sweet taste, but don't ever make the mistake of inhaling them. I hear they stink, but that's the advantage of living alone."

Robert lit his, holding it awkwardly between his fingers. He took a swallow of the slivovitz, which exploded in his stomach but at once cured the hurt with a pervading glow.

"I'm really a cigarette smoker who's at home with a glass of beer. Now with this stogie and this drink I feel as if I'm acting the part of somebody else."

"They say you can build a personality from the outside in."

252

"I always had the notion that the cigar man was the confident type, the kind to make decisions without fooling around. I'm talking about the standard, fat cigar, of course. I don't know what personality goes with these little stinkers."

"The man of action, controlling his destiny. Snapping that long bull whip over a six-horse team, or calling Black Bart's bluff in that big game at the Last Chance saloon."

"You know it's getting to me? I feel daring. I think I'll open with queen's pawn."

They played silently for a while, between moves pouring a little more of the scalding liquor, relighting the cigars. Robert said, "Strange combination. I feel I could move a mountain with my bare hands, and at the same time I have a little trouble telling a bishop from a rook."

"I don't know what's worse, a drunken principal or a plastered custodian."

"You said it."

Robert wasn't going to win. Peters played with a careless-seeming skill against which Robert found himself helpless. Robert grew angry. It was like wrestling with someone who couldn't be bothered using more than one arm. Robert resigned. "You could have mated me three moves ago."

Peters grinned.

"You bother the hell out of me," Robert said.

"Why is that?"

"You're a waste."

"Look, Mr. Evans," Peters said pleasantly, "you want to show me your Salvation Army card?"

"Sorry," Robert said.

"You want another game?"

"Another lesson, you mean. No, thanks. Carl, how's your daughter?"

Peters' battered face creased in vast contentment. "What a joy that child is."

"Isn't it tough, just seeing her weekends?"

"It had to work out that way. My mother takes care of her. I could hardly bring her up here. This way, I go home Friday night, we spend all of Saturday and Sunday together. I guess if you figure it out in hours, we're together as much as the seven-day-a-week father whose kid is sleeping when he gets home and has time only for a good-morning kiss before the old man leaves for work in the morning. She saves things up for me. The week's activity, questions, stories."

"How old is your mother?"

"Sixty-three. She's strong and active."

"You ever think of marrying again, Carl?"

"No. I tried it once."

"Have you?"

"She gave me this kid, I'll always be grateful."

"Do you know anything about her, what she's doing?"

"I know she was in some show in Chicago. Once in a while she drops me a card. I tell her how the kid's getting on. Sometimes she cares and sometimes she doesn't. Like now, I haven't heard from her for months."

"Shame."

"No. If I never heard from her again, that'd be perfect."

Most people, Robert thought, had a piece of happiness. Peters had his daughter. Himself, Elizabeth. As if it were up for grabs in the market place, and at the signal off you went, tearing. Some were able to snatch more than others. The truth was there never was enough to go around, so you hoarded what you had.

Just before the Christmas vacation Mrs. Norton, one of the guidance people, came in to Robert with a request. "This boy failed English eleven, and we doubled him up in English twelve. He's been sitting in on some eleven classes, and I would like to see him take an examination."

"He would have to in order to graduate."

"I mean I think he ought to take the exam now, if possible, I think this would be his best chance of passing."

"Who is his English-twelve teacher?"

"Miss Pomeroy."

"Did you speak to her?"

"Yes. She says she will wait until the end of the year."

"And then have the student take both together? I agree, if he could do the make-up now, that would be preferable. What's his name?"

"Joseph Maxwell."

"Ah, yes. All right, Mrs. Norton, thanks for bringing this to my attention."

He had her come to his office. She came at the close of the day, majestic and condescending. She had never forgiven him for the way he had attacked her curriculum. Her attitude was not hostile; she merely refused to recognize that Robert had anything to do with the school. She was wearing a pale-blue dress that seemed made of crepe paper, and her hair hung down, as the song went, in ring-a-lets.

"Yes, Mr. Evans?" she said, as if he had come to an audience with her.

"Joseph Maxwell's examination for English-eleven credit. Can you give it to him tomorrow morning, here in my office?"

"Mrs. Norton mentioned that. Why, no, Mr. Evans, that will not be convenient."

"Why not, Miss Pomeroy?"

She smiled frostily, willing to overlook his *gaffe* in questioning her. He pretended not to notice, and waited for an answer.

She said, finally, "If there is one thing I cannot countenance, it is in any manner to show favoritism or give any student preferential treatment. One simply does not give an examination of this type before the end of the school year, Mr. Evans."

"The boy failed last year's English. Unless he makes that up, he cannot graduate. I thought, if he passed this exam now and got it out of the way, it might make it easier for him to concentrate on his twelfth-year work."

"Really, Mr. Evans, I assume you taught before becoming an administrator, you know that one does not make up an examination for the convenience of a single student—"

"It doesn't have to be very extensive. Just enough to indicate whether he ought to have a passing grade on record. Is he doing satisfactory work this year?"

"Just barely. He is not really a very intelligent boy."

"But he is willing, and decent, and I would like to see him get his diploma, Miss Pomeroy. I think giving him the eleven exam now might be easier for him than taking two together. So please see to it, will you?"

"I don't really—"

Robert said, chilling every syllable and enjoying it, "Please see to it, Miss Pomeroy. First thing in the morning."

This was the first time in his life that Robert heard anyone actually say "Humpf!" Miss Pomeroy did, and left the room.

Robert examined himself for signs of shriveling. He was pleased to find he remained the way he was. He said to the vapid scent she had left behind: I'll have you know, ma'am, that I am the *Principal!* "So there," he said aloud. And sat down and laughed.

Mrs. Farrow found him laughing. She looked cautiously pleased. Not because she liked the thought of Robert being happy, but because, he said to himself, she could add this to the dossier he was positive she was compiling. "And then I found him laughing, all by himself, and this is obviously a sign of mental deterioration—"

"*Hel*-lo, Mrs. Farrow," Robert said brightly. "What can I do for you?"

"Mr. Otis is here."

"Otis? Appointment?"

"He said you had requested him to come in when—"

"Oh. Yes. He's home, is he. All right, ask him to come in, please."

Mr. Otis did not look the way Robert had pictured him. He thought that very few people did. Instead of an effusive, back-slapping, drummer-type, in walked a small, serious man with a nervous mouth who took Robert's hand with the tips of his fingers and pressed once and let go. What can he possibly sell, Robert wondered.

"Sit down, Mr. Otis. Glad you came."

"Philip. I had no idea—"

256

"Doesn't Mrs. Otis write?"

"I send cards home to show where I am and that everything is all right. Mrs. Otis writes long letters. I am afraid that I—"

"You don't read them?"

"Well, not thoroughly."

If she writes the way she speaks, Robert thought. Interminable, whining letters. This man had evidently solved his particular marital problem. Robert cared not at all for either of them. People made their own hell.

"What would you like me to do, Mr. Evans?"

"I would like some assurance from you that you will keep your son out of trouble."

"As you know, Mr. Evans, I am away from home so often—"

Robert shrugged. He wanted to say that he was not running a private school in Switzerland or someplace to which one sent his youngsters for complete afamilial upbringing. "All we can do with your son here is try to supply him with a high-school education. This is being jeopardized for Philip because of certain traits he possesses. I will accept some of the responsibility, Mr. Otis, but frankly, I expect you to accept the major portion."

Mr. Otis took out an excellent linen handkerchief and blew his nose daintily.

"You don't smoke, do you, Mr. Otis?"

"Why, no—"

"Drink?"

"Rarely."

"Women?"

Mr. Otis's eyes widened a trifle, but he answered at once, "I consider myself a moral man, Mr. Evans."

Robert had no right to ask these questions, and he was prepared to have Mr. Otis tell him so. But there were some people, and he was sure Otis was one, who sat in this office as if in the presence of the district attorney, or their religious leader, or a member of the FBI. It would never occur to them that the Principal was exceeding the scope of his office. They didn't know

257

how to tell a figurehead to mind his own business. So Robert was able to go on with his amateur probing.

"Have you always been away for the most part, even when Philip was a child?"

"I took this job when Philip was three."

"When you are at home, do you see much of your son? Do you talk much together?"

"I am not one of those fathers who takes his son fishing, or to ballgames, if that's what you mean. I don't like those things myself."

"I don't think that that makes you a bad father. But is it true that you know little about your son? I mean, could you describe his tastes and desires and leanings and ambitions?"

"Well—I know that he is not a stupid boy. He does things —I don't approve, but the other boys I hear about seem to act in the same way. I never thought he was behaving abnormally or anything."

"Do you love your wife?" Robert asked, ready to be slapped down.

"No," Mr. Otis said.

"Do you love your son?"

"Yes. But Mrs. Otis said to me that it is your opinion that I must stay at home, take a job in the main office. Mrs. Otis said that you said that is the only way to save Philip's future. If I don't do that, she said, the boy is going to be expelled from school. I am concerned about my son, Mr. Evans, but I can't stay permanently with his mother."

"I did not say what Mrs. Otis says I said."

Mr. Otis nodded without expression.

"How is it, feeling the way you do, you never got divorced?" Robert asked companionably.

"I consider divorce ethically wrong," said Mr. Otis, sitting very straight.

"Well, about Philip. His school record is not that bad. He passes his subjects, if not brilliantly not at the bottom of his class, either. He has been in trouble once or twice before, and it always seems he is a follower, he never seems to get in

258

trouble alone. May I venture a lay psychological opinion, Mr. Otis?"

"Yes?"

"Philip seems to have a need for fatherly authority. Not getting it from you, he accepts it from any youngster shrewd enough to recognize a dupe. Philip wants to be told what to do."

"In that case," said Otis, "he should be a model student. How is it the discipline of the school does not keep him in line?"

"It could be that most of his teachers have been female." Robert smiled. "This is pretty theoretical. But for his senior year I'll try to schedule him for male teachers, if I have a choice. I will also have Philip in to speak to me when I can. Will you do what you can?"

"What do you think that should be?"

"Sit him down, now that you're here, and tell him what you feel he ought to do. And when you leave, write to him, to him personally, have you ever done that?"

"No."

"I think Philip has missed having a father around. In that sense, Mrs. Otis is probably right."

"Is that all, Mr. Evans?"

"Yes, unless there is anything else you want to discuss."

"No."

Mr. Otis stood up. Robert did also. He would have put out his hand, but he didn't want another grasp of those limp fingers.

Mr. Otis said, "You're guessing about why Philip gets into trouble, aren't you, Mr. Evans?"

"Of course. How can anybody tell what goes on in the mind of a boy?"

"If I may use the image of a scale, Mr. Evans, one side goes up because it's lighter, or it goes up because the other side is heavier."

"Yes?" Robert said, trying to figure that out.

"In other words, Philip could be missing the father, or he could be having too much of the mother."

When Otis left, Robert worried about that last statement. It sounded ominous. Robert didn't know anything about the man, and he had an awesome respect for violence-spewing aberration. Would a man who was "ethically" against divorce go home and do in his wife? Robert saw the little man going about it in some uncharacteristically messy fashion, with a baseball bat or something.

Robert called in Perry. "I need a friendly kick in the rump."

"At your service," Perry said.

"The Otis man was here. You know how his old lady's only interest in Philip's problems seemed to be to use them to keep her husband home?"

"Having had the pleasure of talking with Mrs. Otis, if I were he I'd—"

"That's what has suddenly begun to bother me. I told him I thought his son was running around looking for a father substitute and finding these young hoods to tell him what to do. The last thing Otis said was, maybe the boy wasn't suffering from too little father but too much mother."

"That could be. So now you figure he's on his way home to bash her head in?"

"How do you know I thought that?"

"Look, son," said Perry, offering Robert a cigarette and taking one himself. "Father Dickinson has seen this happen before. The geniuses who made up the state education law were guilty of some pretty moldy notions, but about one thing they were very sound. The need, in academic life, for vacations. To get away from the kids. Christmas is coming. Robert, go away."

"You think the head is getting soft?"

"Yes. An occupational hazard. There's no cure except open spaces and the absence of anything resembling a student. Believe me, Robert."

"I believe you."

"Once," said Perry, "when I was teaching on the Island, I got it into my mind that two kids were going to blow up the gymnasium. It was shortly after the war, and there were all these movies about the French resistance and the partisans in Italy, and so on, and once in class I talked about it, and the no-
260

tion that those kids were going to experiment just wouldn't leave my head."

"So what did you do then, take a vacation?"

"We all had one. The silly kids used too much soup, and the whole school went up."

Perry grinned and ducked out.

CHAPTER TWENTY-TWO

Joseph Maxwell came into Robert's office the next morning. He was wearing a clean shirt that was just as big on him as the others he wore. Robert wondered who was handing them down. It couldn't be the father—Mr. Maxwell was barely taller than his son.

Joseph said worriedly, "Miss Pomeroy said I had to come in here and take an examination."

"Good morning, Joseph. That's right. English eleven that you were careless enough not to pass last year. It shouldn't give you any trouble."

"I don't know about that, Mr. Evans. Any examination gives me trouble."

When he smiled, as he did now, Joseph's mouth seemed to stretch to twice its width. It was the kind of smile only a statue, or a Miss Pomeroy, could fail to respond to.

"You'll lick this one," Robert promised. "Everything all right at home?"

"Sure, Mr. Evans. My folks talk about you. They're still trying to figure out your angle. Especially my cousin, Jim. He said to me he figured that you were just some kind of nut, and I told him off."

"Did you," Robert said, very pleased.

He drew over a chair and cleared a space at the end of the desk. "This ought to do it. This all right, Joseph?"

"That's fine, Mr. Evans."

"Just relax now until Miss Pomeroy gets here."

Robert began to go through his correspondence. Miss Pomeroy came in with the examination. Robert said good morning to her and went back to his work. Miss Pomeroy put the sheet in front of Joseph and handed him some ruled paper. "You have forty-five minutes," she said, looking at her watch.

Robert was aware, with delayed reaction, that she had not returned his greeting. He looked up. Miss Pomeroy had an expression on her face as if she had seen a cockroach walk across the desk. Robert said, "Was there anything—?"

"No." She went out.

Joseph said, "I guess she don't like me."

"Why do you say that?"

"She told me I wasn't going to pass."

"When?" Robert asked sharply.

"This morning, when she told me to come in here."

"Did she say anything else, Joseph?"

"She said I didn't have to think I was going to graduate just because folks were sorry for me."

"*Sorry* for you? Now why the—why should anybody feel *sorry* for you?"

"Don't know," Joseph said, letting go with his big smile. "Got two good hands and feet and a mouthful of teeth to chew with."

"Get going, Joseph. Go on now."

Joseph took out a ballpoint pen and began to read through the questions. Robert went out to have some letters taken down by Betty Turner rather than have her come in and disturb the boy. When he finished with the correspondence, he took his customary walk around the school. He said good morning twenty-three times. Underwood, the head custodian, was wrestling a length of plastic tread that was intended for wet-weather use at the entrances. Underwood had the unwieldy roll clutched to his substantial belly and his arms were just a trifle too short. Robert insisted on helping him. They carried it into Underwood's shop, where the custodian was going to cut it into appropriate lengths. It was about a half hour later when Robert returned to his office. Joseph was sitting and staring at the paper. Looking over his shoulder, Robert saw that the boy had written no more than a few lines.

"You've got only about ten more minutes. What's the trouble, Joseph?"

"I just don't know this, Mr. Evans."

"Try, Joseph."

"I guess Miss Pomeroy knew what she was talking about, all right."

Robert picked up the examination and began to look through it.

Miss Pomeroy came in and took Joseph's paper. She glanced at it. "You might at least have made some effort. You may go back to your class now, Joseph."

The boy went out, the flopping shirt somehow accentuating the hopelessness of his walk. Miss Pomeroy put her hand out for the examination paper.

Robert said, "This seems very difficult."

"It's a standard examination based on the curriculum for the year."

"I wonder how well I'd do on it myself."

"I have a class waiting for me, Mr. Evans."

"Just a minute, please." Robert read through the rest of it.

Miss Pomeroy patted peevishly at the piece of black velvet she had around her throat. She straightened the two rings she wore on her left hand, the third finger pointedly bare.

"I do not consider this a fair examination. Really, Miss Pomeroy, I know you consider *A Tale of Two Cities* the greatest book in the world, but to ask, as you do, for a description of the hero's clothes in the third chapter—"

"That was discussed in class."

"And these words you want defined—"

"Part of the year's reading."

" 'Jejune.' I've never been quite sure about that word myself. What does it mean, Miss Pomeroy?"

"I—"

Robert's eyebrows went up. "I'll be damned."

"I will not remain here and be exposed to offensive language."

264

"Do you know what the word 'jejune' means, Miss Pomeroy?"

She did not answer, haughtily studying a spot over his head.

"All right," Robert said softly. "You tried to scuttle that boy, didn't you, Miss Pomeroy. Perhaps it was also designed as a lesson for me, was it not, Miss Pomeroy? Now suppose, just suppose, it gets around this school that the head of the English department cannot define one of the words she includes in an eleventh-grade examination?"

"Of course I know what the word means."

"What?"

"I will not be examined by you. This is not within your province."

"The determination of the competence of a teacher is very much my concern, Miss Pomeroy."

"How dare you. I have taught here for—"

"A long time, I know. That does not prevent you from allowing personal pique to influence your professional judgment. This examination was prepared for the purpose of failing that boy, was it not, Miss Pomeroy?"

"You are exceeding your authority, and I will not—"

"How is this for authority, Miss Pomeroy? Listen carefully. I want you to prepare another examination. And it will not contain words you cannot define yourself. Is that clear, Miss Pomeroy?"

"Mr. Evans, I have had a long and honorable career in this school. Yours is not the final say in this district. We have a superintendent of schools and we have a school board. And it is my belief, Mr. Evans, that you may not be with us much longer."

"Is that your belief, Miss Pomeroy. Now add this to your belief. If a new and reasonable examination is not prepared and given to Joseph Maxwell before this day is out, I will have you before that superintendent and that school board to explain what I consider gross and willful dereliction of duty."

Her face turned pink under the dead-white powder she had affected that morning. She swept out of the room in awful majesty. Heads, Robert thought, will roll. Mine, if I'm not careful. He ran his hand reassuringly around his neck and reached for a dictionary. "Jejune, jejune," he said to himself, thumbing the pages.

The school prepared for the Christmas vacation. Although Robert felt the professed good will of the season had no bearing on the relationship of man to man except for the boozy cheer of office parties, the thought of the time off to come relaxed the tensions of the battle between teacher and student. It was a time when parents stopped yelling at their children. Whether this had any effect on Miss Pomeroy could not be ascertained, but by the end of the day she had come up with an examination that Joseph Maxwell was able to pass. When Joseph told Robert of this—it was a shift in classes and they met in the hall—the look on the boy's face was more than enough to counterbalance the professional guilt Robert felt at his interference with school procedures.

Robert sent word to Miss Loomis that the Principal wanted to see her in his office when her class was over. She came in carrying books in the crook of her arm like a college student. After the ante-bellum frowziness of Miss Pomeroy she was delightfully clean and young and beautiful.

"Yes, Mr. Evans?"

He sat back in his chair. "Don't rush me, Miss Loomis. Let me sit and look at you and feel grateful."

He got up and dusted off a chair and held it for her. She sat and he kissed the top of her head.

She bent her head back and looked up at him. He leaned over and kissed the tip of her nose.

"I can hardly regard your manner as professional, Mr. Evans."

"Why do you say that, Miss Loomis?"

"Suppose somebody walked in just now."

"They would see an example of the best in staff relations."

266

"Well, what's on your mind, Mr. Evans? I mean, outside of staff relations?"

Robert went back to his chair. "I wanted to ask—what are you doing for the vacation, Elizabeth?"

"Father's going up to Hartford to be with his brother and family. He goes there every Christmastime. I had been half thinking of going with him."

"Could you half think of not going?"

"Why?"

"Couldn't we— Elizabeth, let's go away someplace together."

"Mr. Evans, what could you be thinking of?"

"I'm thinking of you and me without students, without people—"

"You need that," she said seriously. "Perry is right."

"Been talking to you, has he," he said, holding up his hand and making it shake.

"I have been thinking of going away with you."

"You—" He smiled like Joseph Maxwell, all joy.

"I've been wondering what I would do if you hadn't mentioned it first. I mean, how unladylike—"

"That's the first thing that attracted me. I remember looking at you and thinking, She's no lady—"

"Are you prepared to take the chance, Robert?"

"What do you mean?"

"An hour or two—how long have we been together? All we've been getting is the saved-up best. This way—suppose you found out that I bored you to death?"

"Or me, you."

"That's right, Robert."

They stared solemnly at each other. Then, together, they said, "It couldn't—"

They laughed.

Elizabeth said, "Did I ever mention my cousin, Sarah Maury? She's a buyer for Bloomingdale's, she has three children and she's divorced. She's a funny person, I mean she's genuinely happy and laughing. Imagine being divorced, with three children, and finding life amusing."

Elizabeth shook her head in wonder. Robert shook his head because he wondered what Elizabeth was talking about.

"The one thing she wanted to hold on to—she didn't ask for alimony or support for the children, she has always made more money than her husband anyway—the one thing she kept was a little beach house in Westhampton."

"Oh?"

"This time of year—"

"Is it just a summer place?"

"There's a gas heater, if that's what's bothering you."

"It sounds marvelous."

"I'll call her," Elizabeth said.

The richness began in the car as they drove, the two of them encased. Robert wore a heavy hunting jacket because, as he had warned her, the car heater worked poorly, and Elizabeth had on a black turtleneck sweater and bandanna, so that she looked, he told her, like a character in one of the Italian movies they had argued about. One of the real sexy ones, he said.

"But not just sexy. Appealing, too, right?"

"Yes."

"And understanding, and intelligent."

"Oh, yes."

The sound of the engine, the tires on the macadam of the parkway, the dry, bright look of the countryside in the sun as it sped past, combined with the quietness of their talk, the occasional outrageous remark and laughter, the periodic need for a cigarette, which Elizabeth lit for him while he glanced at her mouth to think of as she put the cigarette between his lips.

"There are people," he said, "who go through life alone. Some of them say they like it."

"That's not the worst thing. You can be so afraid of loneliness that you rush into something much, much worse. Too many of the married people I know are unhappy."

"Clare and Perry Dickinson. What's the secret of that?"

"Luck."

"What did you bring to read?"

268

"Just some Housman that I want to memorize. What we're going to do mainly is walk on the beach and collect stones and look for driftwood."

"What kind of stones?"

"On the beach, glistening in the water, they look like jewels. When I was a child, I used to collect them and varnish them. They're beautiful."

"We're going to collect stones. So that's what we're going to do."

"I told my father where I was going, and with whom."

"Ouch."

"He's a wise man, my father. You know he left a day ahead so when you came to get me there wouldn't be embarrassment?"

"Because I was hauling his daughter off on a sinful excursion?"

"Sinful? Sarah's going to be there to chaperone us, didn't I tell you?"

"No," said Robert. "You didn't tell me."

The road wound ahead like the mother serpent who encircles the earth. They drove through little towns where Main Street was a general store and a gas station. They were out in the flatlands and could smell the sea. Robert listened with a practiced ear for signs of his old car's being unhappy, but she was purring soundly.

Elizabeth said, "My father is very fond of me. More than that, he thinks I'm kind of a special person."

"We weren't, of course, talking about him. I mean, not lately. But that's all right, you just bring out statements without antecedents and I'll nod my head. I'll say, 'Indeed?' "

"Don't be obtuse. People who are close don't find anything the other says unconnected."

"Sure. I agree with your father. About you. You know how I hated him when I started this job?"

"Do you still feel the same way?"

"How can I dislike anybody who's related to you?"

"He said he couldn't very well talk to me now as he might

269

have when I was younger, and before I got mixed up in that silly marriage of mine. He said he wasn't even going to offer me advice, because he thought that in this particular area I knew more than he, but he said he was never a believer in the theories of Judge Ben Lindsey."

"That was before your time. His book raised a big fuss when it came out. It was called *The Companionate Marriage*, and some people thought it advocated free love but it didn't. I met the man who did the writing with the Judge. His name is Wainwright Evans, and he lives in New Mexico. A very good man."

"My father said the trouble with a free-wheeling relationship is that you can feel able to get out of it whenever you want. Maybe for trivial or sudden reasons. In marriage, because it's tougher to dissolve, you might be forced to work a little harder at getting along."

"I don't know why he bothered telling you this. Didn't he know we were going to be chaperoned?"

"We were just talking generally."

"How does a man get up enough courage to speak candidly to a daughter?"

"I can just see you—say seventeen years or so from now."

"Seventeen years—damned if I'll add it up."

"Would you want children, Robert?"

"Yes. I've always been envious of every father in the world. Are you the mother type, Elizabeth?"

"I want two or three boys. Tough, experimental, knee-skinning boys."

The sign said "Westhampton Beach." Robert followed the arrow around a curve and down a broad street with houses hidden behind high hedges. At Elizabeth's direction he drove over a small bridge and turned right at the T, the crossbar of which was called the "Surf Club, Members Only." He drove on a stretch of road that paralleled the ocean, although the water could not be seen because of the dunes. They passed several co-operative apartment buildings with long two-tiered verandas. Along the beach were houses no two of which looked alike. Some were functional boxes and others nautical in design, and

270

some looked the work of weekend amateurs and others from the drawing boards of mad architects. One was a circle and one two diamonds connected by wood struts, and there was one on long stilts that looked as if it belonged in a rice paddy. Nowhere was there sign of life.

"That's the one, the pink one."

Robert drove off the road and stopped the car on the sand in back of the house, which stood on pilings; high wood stairs went up to a small porch. Robert followed Elizabeth up. "Doesn't seem to be anyone here," he said.

He opened the outer door; there was a note pinned to the inner one. He handed it to Elizabeth, who read it and shyly gave it back. The note said: "Sweet Elizabeth—everything works—gas, electricity, water. The icebox is stocked, I recommend the steaks in the freezer. Have fun, you mad cousin. Sarah."

Robert said, "This doesn't sound as if she intended to stay here with us."

"It doesn't?"

"No. And if she had changed her mind, wouldn't she have said something about that?"

"I'll get my bag."

"You knew all the time she wouldn't be here."

"I don't know what you're talking about."

"How are we supposed to get in?"

Elizabeth bent down and fumbled around under a fiber mat and came up with a key. Averting her eyes from Robert, she opened the door.

Immediately before them was a kitchen, with a wall divider of white-painted brick. There was a large dining table of old pine with captains' chairs around it. Robert walked around the brick wall. He stopped and made sounds of wonder.

The far wall was of glass and framed in it was the ocean. The water was the blue of the sky and sparkling in the sun, and it lashed playfully at the beach as if, sated now, it yet tested its claws. Elizabeth came to stand beside him. He put his arm around her.

271

"The movement," he said. "The never-ceasing, like birth and destruction."

"Don't be grim."

"If you lived here all the time, you could get used to this being in your front yard. That bothers me, that you could get used to this."

"You set them up and you knock them down. The Robert and Robert debating society."

It took an effort to look away from the water. The room was high, with the exposed timbers painted a dark brown. Two Mexican rugs were on the floor. There was a day bed and two Danish-type chairs and a coffee table that had once been a bass drum. On the wall hung some crude seascapes. "Sarah's. In there is the kids' room." A double-decker bed on either side, walls hung with children's paintings in crayon and water color.

"It's ten years since I was here. Something I want to show you." Elizabeth slid the window open and led Robert out to the small railed balcony. Leaning against the wall, he felt the sun and the salt, but the wind was gentle. Elizabeth put both arms around his waist, her head against him. "I wanted you here. I used to stand out here when I was growing up, and I used to think of who would come for me. What he would say, and how he would look, and what he would be able to do. I used to talk to the ocean about him."

"The Mother," Robert said.

"I used to think I would bring him here for her inspection."

"Did you? The fellow you married?"

"No. We never went anywhere, he got carsick."

Robert felt his lips begin to quiver, and then he was shouting with laughter. She looked up at him without taking her arms away, at first in puzzlement, and then it swept over her, too, and they laughed together.

After a while, quieted, she said, "I don't really know why that's so funny."

"You don't have to know why. It just is."

A gull flew down surprisingly close, its mean beak chattering disapproval, and soared away.

"We've been inspected."

"Everybody wants to know everybody else's business."

Robert said, "I feel all this magic and excitement and wonder and gratitude—and at the same time I'm off to the side watching myself feel these things, saying to myself I'm not a boy any more. The worst part of growing older is this damnable tendency to examine things that aren't meant to be examined."

"Shaw—was it he?—said youth was wasted on the young. Maybe that's true for love, too."

She turned to face him, and he kissed her for a long time. There was a surprising eloquence to her mouth.

Later, she said to him, "I didn't know about the sadness. I thought it was all sunshine."

"Who said sadness is bad? What else do you feel when you listen to music?"

A wave came in, broke, threw up spume to the wind, which bore the spray to them. Robert bowed his head. It was like a baptism.

CHAPTER TWENTY-THREE

They stayed there for a week and they found each other without flaw. To Robert, she was a continuing delight. She had strength and fire, sweetness, a quick understanding, as if she had studied him for years, a sense of humor to match his: sometimes mad and riotous, sometimes quiet. And she was lovely. That she was beautiful he had known before, but he had not suspected the depth of it, the soundness, the unalterable core that made being with her at once balm and elation.

They talked. Each opened himself to the hunger of the other's need to share all the wasted years between birth and now.

Robert said, "Why did I stay on at New Canniston when it was such a torture to her? You don't torment someone you love. And when she died, I came here. Why didn't I make the change when she wanted it?"

"Does it bother you, not knowing why?"

"I want to believe in a reasonable universe, with my part in it equally reasonable. I don't have to understand it, but I want to believe that things make sense."

"That you and I are together makes sense, doesn't it?"

"Yes."

They had been walking and were sitting now in a sheltered spot between two dunes, Elizabeth with feet drawn up and arms around them, Robert stretched out, leaning on one elbow. She had a smudge on one cheek from some charred wood on the beach she had touched and transferred there, and he would not tell her about it, liking the gamin look it gave her. Robert was smoking a pipe, which tasted just right, and as always when this happened, he wondered crossly at the hold cigarettes had on him.

274

Elizabeth said, looking out at the ocean, "I'm very jealous of her."

"Why?"

"She was your wife."

"So shall you be."

They had decided to marry in the spring of the year, when Robert would be assured of contract renewal. This had become important. At first he had thought of delaying until tenure, but he knew he could not wait that long. He wanted to hold on to what he had found in Pine Hills. He thought of a place with a view of the mountains where they might have a house built for them. He thought of the mistakes in human relations he had made, the offenses of careless speech, and he thought that none of it was irreparable; he would smile as Rose Pink had told him to, and be forgiven.

He used the smile now. "Like the pregnant woman said, she was eating for two."

"Which means?"

"Like me. I was thinking. Working for two. I have to be liked now. The most popular man in town."

"Like my father?"

"I may have to ask him for some pointers."

"You change," she said, "you become somebody else, and I'll kill you."

"I already am somebody else: I'm me plus you. When I was me minus you, I was a shell of a man. A husk."

"That's what I fell in love with, a husk?"

He pushed her off balance and was over her like a tiger. "Husk no more, lady."

"My head's in the sand."

"Ostrich." He kissed her. She grabbed him and rolled over, reversing their positions.

"Now who's the ostrich?"

He lay on his back, exulting. Above him her face was all the enchantment in the world. He said, "Listen."

"To what?"

"The plangent waves."

"Shelley?"

"Evans. 'Plangent' is a word I always wanted to use. Now I have. Because of you I fulfill my ambitions."

He kissed her, pulled her close. He turned without releasing her, and they lay side by side. He said to her mouth, "A moment ago I thought I couldn't love you more. And now I do. Is there no limit?"

"We'll bust. The two of us. And they'll put up a stone saying, 'Elizabeth and Robert, they busted for love.'"

"The answer to the problems of the world. If you're in love, you can't hate anybody."

"Nobody?"

"Nope."

"Eberly?"

"A prince."

"The School Board?"

"Gentlemen all, and a lady."

"The teachers?"

"I love them all."

"Everyone? Lucretia Pomeroy?"

"Now you're not being fair."

"Make your point or withdraw it."

He sighed. "Even Pomeroy. You've turned me into jelly."

And it was true. He went back to Pine Hills mild and smiling. It was the New Year. He was not going to get embroiled again. It did not mean he had to alter his notions of right, he did not have to compromise with the things that were bad. It was all a question of method. Loving your enemy did not mean you had to stop recognizing him as your enemy.

When he saw Lucretia Pomeroy, he greeted her warmly, asked about her health and whether she had enjoyed her vacation. She responded, if somewhat warily. Of course it is true, Robert said to himself, that you catch more flies with honey than vinegar. The problem was, what do you do with all those flies?

276

Perry congratulated him. "All over the school is sweetness and light. See you in the cafeteria, Robert."

"What for?"

"You'll be dishing out the soup, won't you?"

"Under the surface amity," Robert warned, "the mailed fist still hides."

"Very good. You been seeing an English teacher?"

"Careful. You want to start a rumor?"

"Clare says you're going to make it legal. Nobody tells me anything. In the spring?"

"When I get one of those evaluation requests. That's tantamount to renewal, isn't it?"

"Yes. All the principals are asked to write out formally what they have accomplished. You never saw such a bunch of lies. They come through around April. I've never heard of anybody being asked to fill one out who was not renewed."

"That's it, then. I get the paper, and we take out the papers."

"I'm glad of two things," Perry said. "I'm glad you and Elizabeth are getting married. And I'm glad you decided to stay here. For a long time you had me worried."

"Why?"

"It looked as if you didn't care whether they renewed your contract or not."

"All that's over. I love everybody."

And that was the way it went, because month after month Robert grew happier, and it wasn't until the end of March that he began to hate people again.

Carl Peters was coming to work drunk. Robert found out about it one afternoon when Peters came in without greeting and began to clear the floor preparatory to mopping it. Robert said, "Carl?"

Peters looked up.

"Whyn't you sit down for a bit?"

"My job," said Peters precisely, "is to clean this office. That is what I intend to do."

"Is that ambition or lack of friendliness?"

"Whatever it is," Peters said, "it has nothing to do with you."

Hurt, and trying not to feel reactive annoyance, Robert went over to him. Smiling, he put out his hand to Peters' shoulder. Peters jumped back with mop handle across his body like a rifle. "Lay off."

"I didn't—"

"Just lay off."

In curiosity and concern Robert looked carefully at the custodian's face. His upper lip was tight and clammy-looking with beads of sweat. His eyes were narrowed and red-rimmed.

"Are you all right, Carl?"

"I'm fine. Now would you mind getting out of my way?"

Frowning, Robert left him alone.

The next day Underwood sought out Robert and said, "Mr. Evans, I wanted to talk to you about Peters. On account of you seem to be a little friendly with him—"

"He seemed ill last night. Do you know what's the matter?"

"I sure do. He's stinkin'. When I said to him this morning he oughtn't to come to work in that condition, he grabbed me." Underwood opened the top button of his shirt to show Robert a red welt across his neck. "I don't know what to do, Mr. Evans. Peters was always a decent kind of guy, I don't want to get him in trouble."

"Where is he now?"

"I don't know. I don't even know if he's in the building or not."

"Well, if he's been drinking, we can't have him in the school."

"That's right. The reason I came to you is I thought, if we could find him, he'd listen to you. If Mr. Cartwright hears about this, Peters is out of a job. No questions, nothing. Cartwright won't fool around."

"Yes, I know. All right, let's look for Peters."

They found Carl Peters in the closet where the brooms were kept. The door was partially open. Carl was facing the wall and hitting it with the flat of his hands. He was doing it in a

278

purposeful, vicious manner, one hand at a time, and the smacking sounds were very loud.

"Carl," Robert said.

Peters whirled about, hands out and crooked. He crouched a little, and he looked very dangerous.

"Carl, don't you know me?"

"I know you, all right. I know all you bastards."

Underwood whispered in back of Robert, "We could shut the door on him and get some help."

"It'll be all right," Robert said. He took a step forward. "Carl, it's Robert Evans, let's go back to your place, all right? We could have a talk—"

In the windowless closet the smell of whisky from Peters was overpowering. Robert was relieved to be able to point to it as a reason, glad that he did not have to deal with a Peters out of his mind, even if the result was the same.

Peters said, "Take one more step, brother, and I'll split your head."

He made fists, and Robert was fascinated with the slow tensing of the muscles in Peters' shoulders, clearly visible through the clinging shirt. Robert was also afraid. And because of this, ashamed of weakness, he did a foolhardy thing. He rushed at Peters and stopped suddenly and grabbed him at the knees. They crashed down together. Then Underwood piled on, too, and between them they were able to get Peters up and hustle him through the hall, luckily free of students. They might not have been enough for Peters had he fought, but he had turned suddenly flaccid. They got him out to the parking area and into Robert's car, Underwood sliding in next to him as Robert went around to the driver's seat.

"I don't know if he's just drunk or sick or what?" Robert said to Underwood, meaning should they take Peters home or to a hospital.

Peters was sitting very still, and it seemed to Robert there were tears in his eyes.

"Carl?"

Peters seemed oblivious of everything except his own misery.

279

"Maybe all he needs is to sleep it off," Underwood said.

They drove to Peters' house and led him upstairs. He went between them without resistance. Before his door he reached in his pocket for the door key but could not manipulate the lock. Robert took the key and opened the door. Inside, they put him on the divan. By the time Robert got Peters' shoes off, he was snoring. It seemed safe to leave him.

Going back to the school, Robert said, "Has this ever happened before?"

"No. I mean, just yesterday. If it had, I guess I wouldn't have cared, a man comes in drunk on the job I figure he deserves to be canned. But I never saw Carl like this."

"Let's hope he's all right by tomorrow."

The next day Robert thought of checking on Peters, but the day was a full one and one of the committees had a problem and it stretched on. Besides, in Robert sympathy combined with irritation. Why should Peters be that stupid?

Almost every evening he spent with Elizabeth. Her father had been away for a month, and would remain away for as long again. His brother in Hartford had begun some kind of new business, and Loomis was advising him.

"Imagine," said Robert to Elizabeth, "being introduced to your prospective father-in-law at the wedding. That is, if he'll be there."

Carl Peters did not come to work the next day or the next. Underwood said he was carrying him on the sick roll, although he had not heard from him.

Robert went to the custodian's home as soon as the day was over. He knocked and there was no answer and he tried the door. It was open and he went in. Peters was sitting at the folding table on which they had played chess. On the table was a bottle, a glass, an ash tray that had reached its capacity ten cigarettes ago. Peters, unshaven, sat quietly fondling the glass, watching the swirl of liquid with a child's absorption.

"Carl? Carl!"

Peters looked up with no recognition. Nor, Robert was pleased to see, with hostility.

Robert pulled over a chair and sat down beside him. "What do you say, Carl?"

Peters said mildly, "What's all the fuss, Mr. Evans?"

"Thank goodness. I thought you were off your rocker."

"No, I'm on it. Back and forth. Sometimes I'm here and sometimes I'm not. I see you now, friend. You got a problem?"

"What happened to you?"

"Happened? Nothing much. They all make fun of Chicken Little, but he knows when the sky is falling, all right. You know that's my daughter's favorite story? The sky is falling—"

"Has something happened to your daughter?"

"No."

"What, then, Carl. Come on, tell me."

"You want a drink, Mr. Evans?"

"No, I don't want a drink. When did you eat last?"

"Eat?"

"Look," Robert said. "I'm your friend. Not your doctor or your nurse, and I'll be damned if I'll play games with you. You got some soup around, bread?"

"Why, sure," Peters said, as if humoring him.

"I'll make something to eat if you'll take a shower and shave. You stink."

"All right," said Peters with the same half-amused indulgence. He got up and went into the bathroom.

Robert emptied the ash tray, and found a rag and cleaned off the table. He opened a window. There was no sign that Peters had used the bed or been in the kitchen. Robert found a can of tomato soup in a cupboard, but he couldn't find a can opener. He yelled at Peters, but the shower was going full blast. In one of the drawers Robert found a screw driver and used it to punch holes in the can. He poured the contents into a saucepan and lit the burner. He put some slices of bread in the toaster.

Peters came out with a towel around his middle. He had shaved himself raw, and wore strips of toilet tissue to stanch the cuts. He was smiling. "Hey, that soup smells good."

"You look better. Not good, but better."

"Wait till I stop bleeding."

"That's just what I'm waiting for," Robert said.

"Sure. Sure, Mr. Evans, you're right."

Peters put on shorts and a pair of trousers and a clean shirt. He went to set the table. "Will you join me for dinner, Mr. Evans?"

"Why not?" Robert said.

They faced each other over their bowls of soup. Peters ate with delicacy.

"Are you surprised," he said, "are you surprised, Mr. Evans, that a grown man, a supposedly intelligent creature (what a relative term that is, whoever heard of a cockroach behaving this way?), are you surprised to see me this way?"

"No. All my friends get drunk and violent and act stupidly."

"You sound a little prissy, Mr. Evans. You never ran away from something was too lousy to look at?"

"I'd have to have the same thing happen to me before I could be a judge. Are you going to tell me?"

"It's no big thing. You could hear me out and say, is that the big deal? I thought he lost an eye, or he just murdered somebody. At least. Those college courses—comparative religions, comparative this and that. They ought to have a course—comparative tragedy. You know?"

"Sure."

"My wife. I tell you about my wife?"

"What did she do?"

Peters shrugged, his mouth stretched down in mock mask of tragedy. "She got married again."

"I didn't think she meant that much to you."

"Meant? I've been reading the obituary columns for years hoping to see her name."

"Then?"

"So now she's married, some guy made her respectable again —and she decides she wants my daughter."

"Oh," said Robert.

"Yeah. Oh."

"Well, I don't see that—she can't really have much of a chance, can she? You were given custody—"

282

"Sure. So when I heard from her lawyer—yes, she has a lawyer, this isn't just a passing fancy of hers—so I went out to get a lawyer, too. And I told him the same thing you just said. What is she, out of her mind, thinking she has a chance to get that kid? After the courts ruled she was an unfit mother—"

"So?"

"So I find out the law never gives up, it's always the mother, the mother. All they have to do is show she's a proper person. She's reformed. Here she is married to some joker who's earning a living, and he wants the kid, too. What looks bad for me is the fact I haven't made a home for my child, according to law we do not share the same roof. So my lawyer (that's a laugh, isn't it, *my* lawyer) says we'll give her a fight, but I don't have to feel that optimistic."

"And that's why you've been swimming in booze?"

"You got a better reason?"

"You need your job, especially now, don't you? What the hell will you be using for money? Don't you know Cartwright will hang you if he suspects you've been drinking? You can thank Underwood for covering for you up to now."

"Yes, I'll thank him. And I thank you, too."

Robert used a word not usually said by principals. "Sure it's rotten. But I don't understand how you expect to fight this by staying drunk."

"Oh, I like the straight way you think, Mr. Evans."

"I can leave if I'm bothering you."

"I'm sorry."

"The thing that gets me," Robert said, "is I've always admired your strength. Not like me, I get doubts, I'm unsure of myself often—"

"*You?*"

"Yes."

Peters laughed. "You know, to me you were always the kind of guy people lean on. Somebody to have with you in a tight spot. What I liked about you, Mr. Evans, was that you were so *steady*."

"That's what I thought you were."

"What a face we show the world."

Robert said, "Maybe it's easy to be aware of your weaknesses, and maybe you can't see your own strengths. Maybe the face isn't all that wrong. Finish your soup."

"It's no use, Mr. Evans. Not any real use. I can eat this soup and talk to you, but as soon as you go—" Peters shook his head despairingly. "I'll be back in the middle of it. I can't lose that daughter of mine."

"You've convinced yourself it's going to be that way. The chances are it won't happen—"

"You can be reasonable. Not me. Even a little chance that I'd lose the kid, and I can't stand up to it. Listen, Mr. Evans. Let me tell you about me. I didn't just learn to be a drunk. I'm an old hand. I've been drunk most of my life. Twice I stopped. When I got married—until I found out what a tramp she was. And then when my daughter was mine—mine to keep—then I stopped again."

"What kind of a story is that? An alcoholic can't turn it off and on. You haven't been on the wagon that I could see. And you certainly stopped in plenty of time."

"I was all right just as long as I didn't need to blank things out."

"You don't now. I'll help. First let's find out how good a lawyer you picked. Maybe we'll get a better one. What's his name?"

"Carpenter."

"Hell of a name for a lawyer."

"You used to ask me what I was a cleaner for, a clever guy like me. And I told you I had done a lot of things in my life, right? I was born a healthy citizen of the United States of America. That put me at the top of the ladder, didn't it? Only it was a damned slippery ladder for me, Mr. Evans, and I didn't grow up on it, I grew down. No matter how hard I squeezed to hold on, down I went, a rung at a time, and sometimes two or three. Death wish, eh? Who knows. I never had a *reason*." Peters clenched his fists, squeezing out the word. "A productive, happy life. Great words. You go to bed at night and ask yourself, what did you accomplish that day that was of any value? Did you

284

gain something or did you lose something? Did you grow a little or did you shrink a little? Mr. Evans, I was a shrinker. Every day I got a little smaller. What the hell did I go into the ring for if it wasn't for a chance to hurt somebody else?"

"But you stopped that, Carl."

"Only because I wasn't good enough, because I was getting my own brains beat out. Maybe I couldn't learn how to stop dying, but I wasn't stupid, I didn't want it to happen all at once. Or maybe I did, maybe the fight business was too slow. Because I did everything I could think of that was dangerous. You ever drive a dynamite truck, Mr. Evans?"

"No."

"I got medals in the drawer there from the navy. You want to see them, Mr. Evans?"

"No."

"What the hell am I talking to you for, Mr. Evans?"

"Because you're about to come to the good part of the story. How I Became a Decent Man, by Carl Peters, Father."

"Are you making fun of me?"

"I'm just envying you," Robert said quietly.

"*You?*"

"There we go with the face again."

"Sure," Peters said. "Sure I leveled off. I never knew what it meant to love somebody, a warm, skinny, long-haired—" Peters pressed his lips together.

"She's still yours, isn't she?"

"Yeah, but what do I do when I think of her being taken away from me, what do I do then, Mr. Evans?"

That night, after Robert left, Carl Peters went into a bar and drank steadily. When the police came, he was out on the sidewalk swinging at three truck drivers from a construction company. In the bar two men were moaning on the floor. There was a lot of broken glass. Luckily, this happened on a Tuesday night, so there was just time for the paper to use the item for a front-page box they had been saving for something of local interest. Prominent in the story was the place of employment of the chief culprit.

CHAPTER TWENTY-FOUR

Robert received a request from Superintendent Eberly for the Principal's recommendations concerning Carl Peters, since when a man was discharged his folder was neatly stacked with statements from those involved. Robert called in Betty Turner and dictated a long report of Carl Peters' faithful service, the lack of incidents of this kind, a plea for consideration of the unusual personal motivations behind the custodian's behavior. Robert sent the report to Eberly's office.

Meanwhile, Peters, having paid a fine for disorderly conduct but otherwise in no further trouble with the police or the bar owner or the patrons with whom he had fought, came in to work. He came in smiling and looked for Robert, to whom he said, "Mr. Evans, I didn't want you to feel that the help you offered me was ignored. I mean, I listened to you, I profited by your visit."

"And then you went out and got stoned."

"You know how there's a brief touch of light left in a bulb after you turn off the juice? I was just tying things off."

"Looked as if you were tying things on."

"Well—it's out of my system. And things look much better."

"Better?"

"My lawyer talked to her lawyer, and my lawyer got the impression that if we fight it hard she'll withdraw. Her character hasn't changed. Everything has to be quick and easy. And also she would not like it to come out how she lost the child in the first place."

"And so everything's all right."

"Everything's going to be, Mr. Evans. And please believe how sorry I am for the trouble I caused you and how much I appreciate your interest. Maybe I needed to slide off that way

286

to know what I have and take care of it. I'm due for an increase in July, and maybe I'll find a new apartment and take Mom and the kid in with me."

"Carl—Carl, don't you know Cartwright wants you fired?"

Peters' face was empty and careful because some people learn at an early age that it's a mistake to show you're being hurt.

Robert shook his head in frustration. "Carl, did you think Cartwright would just forget about it?"

"Why do you think I came in here so bright and babbling, Mr. Evans? Of course I didn't think Cartwright would let it go. I was just whistling in the dark."

"I'll try—"

"Mr. Evans, I'm sure there's quite a bit you could do? They'll certainly listen to you. All of a sudden this lousy job has become important to me."

"I'll do what I can, Carl, of course. But it isn't my department, you're not working for me."

"They'll listen to you."

Later in the day Eberly called. "Robert, I just looked through your report on Peters."

"Yes?"

"We'd better talk about this, Robert. Can you get away?"

"Now?"

"If you can."

Which meant now. Robert told Perry where he was going and drove to Eberly's office. His secretary told Robert to go right in, and he found Cartwright and Eberly, each with a cigar, laughing at something the Supervisor of Buildings and Grounds had been saying. They greeted Robert as if he were a friend who had turned up at the club. Cartwright said, "I was telling Fenton, Bob—"

"Robert," said Robert, smiling.

"Sure. I was telling Fenton about this fat little cleaner over at the Parkside school, comes in the other day and says from now on he's not going to clean toilets. The little kids over there make a mess, that's the truth. Anyway, this guy says he saw a movie about the Nazis, how they made this concert violinist scrub out the latrines, and this cleaner made up his mind, no more of that for him."

"What did you do?"

"Booted him out, what do you think? What gets me is they take on a job like that, no skills or education required, and then because we give them a clean uniform and they get the notion they're working for the government, they get the idea they're as good as anybody else."

Eberly said, "We've got some good family men working in the custodial department, Harry."

"Oh, sure! There are a lot of decent people who just didn't have an education, I never said not. My point is you get a few here and there think they're too good for the job, and the thing to do is weed them out."

"I've found," Robert said, "that, no matter on what level, there are some people who do their job well and some people who should be in some other line of work."

"You can say that again," Cartwright agreed vigorously.

I would if I thought you'd listen, Robert said silently.

"About this fellow," Eberly said. "Peters. I read the report you sent over, Robert. It wasn't quite the sort of thing I was looking for."

"What do you mean?"

"It isn't a question of deciding whether to keep him on or not, that's already been decided. But we have to keep up his file and I thought it would be a good idea if we had some consistency there."

"What you wanted me to do was recommend dismissal?"

"You couldn't very well look at it any other way, could you, Robert?"

"You read my report, you know how I feel."

"What this Peters did," Cartwright said, "is the sort of thing I'm always on the lookout for. I try to stop it before it happens, that's why I check on their drinking habits. This boy must have been going out of town for his benders. Anyway, it's a good thing we nailed him now."

"I don't understand," Robert said. "Peters has been an employee for five years and has never got into trouble and has done his job in a satisfactory manner. I don't know any other classification of employee in this school system who isn't allowed a single mistake."

"Mistake!" Cartwright said. He looked at Robert with ostensibly kindly but really very insulting appraisal.

Robert thought, With a big man like that, if you could get in close fast and pound him just over that beltline—

"Where the major harm was done," Eberly said, "was it getting in the paper. Harry would be down on any employee for drinking in public, and certainly I would back him on that, but I'm not saying we might not look into the matter more deeply, background and the personal troubles you say the man had, if it were just that. But do you know Johnson, the man puts out the Pine Hills *Weekly*?"

"I never met him."

"Anything about this school district and the man goes off raving. I really think he ought to be committed."

"It sure is bad when you provide ammunition for an antischool character like that," Cartwright said.

"Ever since I came here," Eberly said. "The man editorializes even in his news items against every bond issue, he's against every item of the school budget, line by line—"

"Salaries," Cartwright said. "Did he take a blast at the salary schedules up here."

"Yes," said Eberly hastily. "What I'm getting at, Robert, is this man is dangerous. He's dangerous to everything we try to do to improve the quality of this school system. He's a backwater, small-town reactionary of the worst sort. So just give him a chance to snipe at us and he goes all out. Let's say—for the sake of argument—that we decided not to take a strong stand on this Peters business, let's say we regarded it, as you said, as just a forgivable mistake—"

"Murder," Cartwright said.

"Johnson'd use it as a club to beat down and discredit us. He'd steam up this community—"

"It can't be," Robert said, "that you would throw a man out of his job just to pacify some local publisher. You wouldn't do that, Fenton."

"Of course not! I was just using him to make a point."

"Maybe I can clear this up," Cartwright said, smiling at Robert like a big brother, or like a provably sane man in the face of mental wandering. "I'm all for loyalty. I don't mind saying, Robert, that I admire your stand, sticking up for somebody works in your school. Of course, he's in my department, and just assigned to your school, right? Isn't as if we're talking about somebody on the teaching staff—then, of course, I wouldn't have a thing to say, would I? So, as one of *my* men, I believe in sticking up for him, too. I said to Fenton—didn't I, Fenton?— that this is a matter we had to investigate, we shouldn't just take the paper's word—and didn't we check with the police?"

"You didn't check with Peters," Robert said.

"That would be beclouding the issue, wouldn't it, Robert? I mean, seriously? Because what happened here was the man was *drinking,* and we've got those kids to consider."

"I wonder," said Eberly, "if I could talk to Robert alone for a bit, Harry."

"Sure thing!" Cartwright jumped to his feet, slapped Robert on the shoulder, hesitated at the door. "I forgot, you like one of these cigars, Bob?"

"No, thanks."

Eberly sat back and joined his fingertips and looked at the ceiling. He said, "Robert, do you think I have no feeling about dismissing a man?"

"I'm sure you have."

"And do you think my only motivation would be concern over what a newspaper publisher would say?"

"I can't believe that."

"Robert, by now you must have some realization of what my position here is. How delicate, how calculated, everything has to be. If it were just a question of administering the school district— It's the human side, the relations with the public.

Peters has to be let go because he got drunk and was mixed up in a public brawl. That's what he did, and that's more than sufficient reason for firing him. Without looking into it any further, you understand?"

"Yes, but—"

"So it isn't a question of bending facts or distorting anything. Were I, against my better judgment, to keep the man on, it would mean nastiness in the press, parents telling me off, and so on. That's beside the point, although I'm just as happy I can take a clear stand without incurring any of that. You understand?"

"Of course I do, Fenton."

"So all I'm asking you to do now is give me a short statement for Peters' folder. You can say he's been a good worker, that's all right, but something like—you feel he has given grounds for dismissal by his behavior, just a short statement like that."

Robert thought of the time Eberly had revealed his feeling for the children in his care when one of them had been run down by a car. He said, "I haven't told you what I know about Peters' reason for behaving as he did."

"I'm listening."

Robert told him about Peters' desperation. "I just think it would not be fair to fire him."

After a while Eberly said, "Fair? I don't think we would recognize the world we live in if things were done because they were fair."

He drummed his fingers and looked up.

Robert sat forward, aware of tenseness, thinking how much he wanted Eberly to reconsider.

Eberly brought his eyes down to Robert's. "I'm sorry you feel so strongly, Robert. I cannot let the man continue working for us."

He held Robert's eyes, and waited.

Carl, Robert thought. My brother. He thought of Peters in the bar with the teen-agers, his courage and quickness. He thought of that bruised and maltreated face softening as he

291

spoke of his child. How could you, calmly removed from the man's anguish, agree that, having broken a rule of deportment, he had to be fired.

"Really, Robert," said Eberly, shrewdly stepping in to forestall rashness, "this isn't your area, is it?"

"It isn't right, Fenton."

"On the other hand, Robert, is it worth making an issue of?"

"I don't see why this man cannot be given a decent chance. What harm would be done by being generous?"

"I've gone into that already." Watching Robert closely, Eberly went on, "There are some things I've been meaning to talk to you about."

"Yes?" Robert said.

"I think, on the whole, you've done a good job here, and I'm pleased."

"Oh?" Robert said, surprised.

"Yes. I think you're a capable man. I had hoped that you would also have turned out to be a little easier to get along with."

"In what way?"

"You've done a certain amount of bristling, right from the beginning. You've bucked me, for example, on certain—admittedly minor—matters."

"I have?"

"You've succeeded in alienating some people whom it would have been quite politic to be friendly with. You haven't always looked out for your own best interests, Robert."

"I haven't gone out of my way to be nasty. I was concerned—"

"In doing a good job. I know that. But you know as well as I that good will is important, that the opinion of others, even if not so valuable as your own, still needs to be considered. I shouldn't have to go into this again, you know what it means to function in our profession. Democracy means that amateurs have a right to tell professionals what to do. And that's not all bad, Robert. Checks and balances. They still haven't

292

found any education or training that equips a man always to be right."

"I'm sure I never thought I was always right."

"Are you interested in staying on here, Robert? Be honest with me. Would you like to make this your home? Do you like this town, this school district? I imagine one of these days you'll be thinking of marrying again—"

"I would like to stay on here."

"Good. Then listen to me. After all, I am a little older than you, Robert. Some of the Board members seem to feel that you've been a little big for your britches. You could soften up just a little, that doesn't mean you have to compromise your standards, does it now? I'd like to have you work with me, Robert, I really would—"

Robert felt his eyes smart at the warmth engendered. It was like being offered membership in an exclusive society in which you would be guaranteed all the good things.

"I think I can manage to build up your image a little, Robert. You can leave that to me. That is, if you'll promise to work along, and stop being so godamned stubborn and hotheaded—"

"Peters—"

"Has to be fired. Let's face it, suppose he worked in some other school and you never knew the man. So then you happened to pick up the paper, and you read about this custodian getting drunk and fighting in the street. What would be your reaction? You mean to say you wouldn't think it a damned shame that people like that were employed in the school system?"

"I might think that."

"Sure. So there's no point in getting sentimental just because it's your office the man happens to clean."

Robert found himself on his feet because the Superintendent was standing, and Eberly put his big hand on Robert's shoulder. "We're going to build one of the best schools in the state, right, Robert?"

Robert frowned a little.

"Take my word for it, Robert, you have a lot of potential,

a lot of potential, and all that you need is to acquire just a little bit of mildness, you know? Everybody's got to get along with everybody else, right? It's not bad, you can live with the notion of buttering a piece of my bread if I butter a piece of yours—"

"Self-interest," said Robert, smiling.

"Right! And why the hell not? In the long run it's just the same as altruism, because you cast your bread out and it comes back."

"And, as you say, buttered." Robert smiled again and said good-by. Outside he felt a strange spinning sensation in his head, and he pushed up and down at the loose skin over his eyes. He knew what Eberly meant, but it was odd the words he used to get there. It could have sounded like an argument to help Peters, except that Peters wasn't able to do anything in return. It was like a new commandment, prepared especially for the twentieth century. Be helpful and considerate of everybody, just so long as they have the power to be helpful to you.

Robert thought of not going back to the school. But he did, and Carl Peters came in, as Robert knew he would.

Robert said quickly, the way you shuck a coat that has been fouled, "It was no good, Carl. You'd better be looking for another job."

"I see." Peters stood straight, his face composed.

"I was able to exercise no influence at all."

"That's all right, Mr. Evans. I don't want you to be feeling guilty. I had it coming."

"What are we going to do now?" Robert said.

"We?"

"Did I say 'we'?"

"It's not that tragic. You look as if you were the one who got fired."

"The face we wear, the one we were talking about. Actually, I couldn't care less. You always mopped a lousy floor, Carl."

"Sure. Secret resentments and all that. Delusions of being better than my station in life."

"You know what I hate, Carl? I hate a man who's had some

bad luck acting unmoved about it. I'd rather you looked grim and cursed. You might start by telling me off, your friend, who didn't do a damn thing to help you."

"I believe you did what you could. Anyway, it doesn't matter now. One thing that's always in demand in this automated world is a floor washer and wastebasket emptier. It's not as if I lost some prize of a job. I could always work in a supermarket, I could drive a cab. I wouldn't care to have you feeling sorry for me, Mr. Evans."

"Will I see you?"

"Why not? I'll keep in touch. Maybe you'll get a chance to meet my daughter someday."

"I'd like that."

"I don't care for these long, weepy farewells. So long, Mr. Evans."

Peters left. Robert swiveled his chair so his back was to the door, so he could let his face go.

That evening Elizabeth and Robert ate at the Duomo again, having made it a regular thing, once or twice a month, because it was the first place they had gone to together. Having until now lived in ignorance of the other's existence, they had to begin acquiring places and memories belonging to both. So this had become "their" restaurant. The waiter was always anxious to see them because Robert conscientiously overtipped him. Elizabeth objected on grounds of taste, social standards, and economics, but Robert refused to listen to her. "I hate tipping," he explained. "It demeans, like Shakespeare said, him who gives and him who takes. It saves the restaurateur from paying his employees a decent wage. It teaches subservience to the means of exchange, which is false and against nature. It means to take a girl out leaves a pretty big hole in a man's pocket. I'm against it."

"Why?" Elizabeth said. "I mean, why are you against it?"

"Argh," he said.

"All right, but why do you tip more than you should?"

"That's the point. If I had nerve, I wouldn't tip at all. So this is the only way I can show my disapproval of a detestable practice."

"By overtipping?"

"It shows my refusal to conform."

The food was too rich and heavy for him; he drank a lot of coffee and smoked a number of cigarettes.

Elizabeth said, "What's the matter?"

"I was wondering when you were going to get around to asking."

"Is it anything serious?"

"I've done something I'm ashamed of. This bothers me, and there is a need for self-justification, but that's difficult and not really satisfactory, so the best thing is to have someone whose opinion I value justify my behavior to me. The one person I know who can do this for me is you. But the problem is, if I tell you what I've done, you might love me less, and how could I stand that?"

"Looks like we'll have to preface this confession of yours with a definition of love. My love. It might have started with some analysis, it might have been tickled into growth by considerations of the way you look, your habits, personal and social and so on. And before it got really rooted, it could have been altered by your being nasty to me or kicking old ladies or things like that. But now it has set. Symbiosis has taken effect. I'm stuck on you, friend, and stuck with you."

"Thanks."

"What happened?"

"I saw Eberly today. He told me he was pleased with my work, he said he would like to see me stay here."

"That's what I want."

"He said that I have annoyed some people with the lovable nature of my disposition, but if I would try to act like a nicer guy, he'd be willing to smoothe some of the feathers, and the future should be bright and shining."

"That does sound like trouble."

296

"The reason I was there in the first place," Robert said, "was because of the difficulty Carl Peters was in."

"Yes. I saw it in the papers."

"I was a friend of Carl's. I liked him. He had some lousy things happen and that was why he went out to get potted." Robert told her about it.

"The poor man."

"So I went to Eberly to use my influence. And what Eberly wanted was my recommendation for Carl's dismissal because his folder has to be neat and unanimous. I tried to speak up for Carl, but Eberly and Cartwright—that's the bastard who's in charge of the buildings, that means the custodians—they felt they had to fire him mainly because it had reached the papers and Johnson—the newspaper owner who hates Eberly's guts and every change the district makes—Johnson would fry the lot of them if Carl were kept on."

"So you spoke up for Carl and they felt he had to be fired and you were overridden."

"Yes."

"Where were you at fault?"

"I could have put my own job on the line. I could have said, You fire Peters, by God, and I quit."

"Oh, that would have been brave. And suppose you did that and suppose they said, Okay, we'll get a new custodian and we'll get a new principal."

"They wouldn't've—"

"Why not? Didn't you say Eberly said you'd caused a few people of influence to dislike you?"

"At least I might have felt like a man. What I did was not only back down, but I soaked up everything Eberly told me about my luscious future and I loved it."

"All right, husband-to-be. You want me to justify what happened and I will. Your future is now my future, and I know what you were thinking, you were thinking of me, and I do not feel you were less of a man for not making what would have been a really useless gesture. Nor was the principle that impor-

297

tant. Carl Peters did a thing for which any custodian would have been fired, with or without Carl Peters' reasons. And not only custodians, but teachers, too, and principals. You were not wrong, Robert, and you were not weak, and I love you."

He looked at her and blinked and sighed.

"Come on, Lugubrious Louie, I want a B and B."

"That's expensive!"

"Consultations come high," Elizabeth said.

CHAPTER TWENTY-FIVE

There had been times, in Robert's growing up, when he had lived on very little money. So little that most members of our middle-class America could not, even theoretically, understand what happens, during this condition, to the soul. The body, having had a long history of adaptation, in and out of the trees, to wars, famines, catastrophes man and God-made, had little difficulty in shrinking the stomach, toughening the sole of the foot, and so on, and was just as warm under patched garments as new clothing. But the spirit cannot so easily bear shriveling, because the harm persists long after the cause has been ameliorated. So when conditions improved for Robert, and he all but forgot there had been a time when a nickel bus ride was out of his reach and you made a hot dog stretch for two meals, he had acquired as part of his personality a distrust for euphoria, in the way that Moses took the roundabout route to the promised land knowing that born slaves could never achieve freedom, that a new generation had to be born into it.

So Robert was giving a remarkably good imitation of a man ecstatic with happiness. Elizabeth, by now knowing him so well that she added to her love a therapeutic factor based on wry destruction of defenses, said that she had had an uncle who all his life waited for something tragic to happen to him. He propitiated contentment by speculation about the myriad opportunities for illness, accident, misfortune in this uncertain life, and he read the paper trembling, from the obituary news to accounts of being waylaid by hoodlum gangs in the city parks. He lived a long life, free from serious ailments and dangerous occurrences, and Elizabeth said that on his deathbed he had a look on his face of either terror or sly triumph, she had never been able to decide. Robert said that if she wanted him on the couch that was a pretty tricky way to go about it when all she had to do was hold out her arms.

If you wanted to judge events by results alone, then he had no reason to question the rightness of things. Once, at the time of Sam Jennings' victory, he had been forced to back down, and again at the time of Carl Peters' dismissal. But it had become possible to keep Jennings in business and still control the student body by a system of monitoring; the co-operation of the township, which supplied a policeman at the point of crossing the highway; and the incorporation of a point system for latenesses, which resulted in privilege losses that the students were anxious to avoid. Robert had to admit that a steady diet of the state-administered cafeteria menus was no match for the sizzling appeal of Sam's hamburgers, and he went to Jennings' place once in a while himself. Jennings, as he had said, bore no grudge.

Carl Peters got a job driving a truck in the construction company the drivers of which he had fought with that night—this proving, according to Perry Dickinson, that things are either ordered or they are not. Elizabeth and Robert were invited to Peters' new apartment, where they met his daughter, who was sweet and doting on her father and who, Robert said later to Elizabeth, he found a little bland. "Our kids," he told her, "better have some spice to them." Peters' mother was a thin, busy woman with a loud voice, and the new apartment was nothing like the spare cell in which Peters had lived before. However, he seemed happy, even while apologizing for not being able to offer his guests a drink. His mother served cookies and a thick, indigestible cocoa.

And then, to provide final proof that Robert had entered an era of absolute harmony with his surroundings, Angelo Casella became a serious student. Robert had touched something, whether of fear or shame, and the boy sought opportunities to put himself before Robert's eye, rushing to volunteer information if Robert was visiting one of his classes, coming to Robert for advice in programming even though the guidance department was established for that purpose. Robert never

300

succeeded in liking the Casella boy, feeling that there was a streak of opportunism in him; but on the surface this was a victory.

In due course Robert received the request for his estimate of his accomplishments, and he returned a paper devoted largely to the progress made by the school committees on evaluation. He projected certain new courses he intended to introduce, especially one that had been a pet of his—a combined course in English literature and the history of the period. He knew who the English teacher would be (unless she was pregnant by then), but had not yet selected the social-studies man. He thought of what Peters had said about going to bed at night. What kind of day did you have, did you grow a little or shrink a little. Robert made his paper look as if he had grown, but he was not sure whether or not he had shrunk.

"Consistency," Perry assured him, "just for its own sake is hardly a virtue. When Job accused God of lack of consistency, he was told to shut his mouth, he didn't know what the score was."

Robert was silent.

"I hate to present you with an unpleasant fact, Robert, but he who travels fastest—you know. Marriage doesn't make a man accomplish that much quicker all the dreams he started out with. Marriage makes a man satisfied with less, with the woman taking up the slack in performance."

"Worth it?"

"Damn right. It keeps you alive, it stops a man from trying to hold back locomotives with his hands."

The valedictorian and the salutatorian were selected, as usual no more than a quarter of a point between them. Robert disliked them both, skinny, tight-eyed intellectuals who already read books Robert could not understand and would go on to become physicists and astronomers. The kind of valedictorian Robert would have wanted to see was someone like Joseph Maxwell. Instead of whither are we going, he could have made a speech about the symbolism of motor scooters and never, once, having worn a shirt that fit him.

By now the colleges had decided whom they wanted, and the pressures were off for another year. Robert hated the period of waiting for acceptance when the seniors went around with glazed eyes and nervous fingers, and it was impossible, the final quarter, to get anything done in class. In desperation some of the students applied to ten schools or more, and mothers came in for advice and special letters of recommendation and in general behaved as if it were Robert's fault that too many students wanted to go to too few schools. He suggested applying to schools in the Midwest, and they talked about Amherst and Princeton and Yale as if the Eastern seaboard had a monopoly on college education and Robert was forced to recognize that in Pine Hills it looked as if they had.

Then, when the rejections arrived, he was responsible, personally; the visits were not as bad as the phone calls, some of which were terribly insulting. Robert also had the pleasant task of calling up the parents of the fifteen students or so who were not going to graduate, and please would they not show up at the ceremonies. These students had been spotted at the beginning of the year and their parents notified many times, but now there was screaming and charges of inefficiency and discrimination.

And then there were the bribes, some of the offers barely breathed but some arrant, not only for the diploma but for the slight increase in grade to build up the horribly important average, since unless the student were in the top ten per cent, or fifteen, or twenty-five of the graduating class, he stood not a chance. Here Robert forgot his image and ranted and grew abusive, because he had read of a boy whose grades had been paid for through medical school, which then gave him the legal right to kill patients.

Still, although down at the bottom there was a lot of mud, the rest of the pool was clear; this was a good graduating class.

Elizabeth and Robert had decided to get married by the Justice of the Peace, the informal wedding to be attended by Perry and Clare, Superintendent Eberly, and Elizabeth's father. But Loomis was still in Hartford, where his brother was in trouble. He had invested too much money in a business he did not understand, and John Loomis, who knew no more about it, had been consulted because he was the older brother.

"It's always been a weird family," said Elizabeth without concern. "Uncle Dick is the only one who ever made any money, and he claims he did so only because of Dad's advice. So now he won't let him come home."

"I don't care to have my wedding plans depend on a family whim of your uncle's," Robert said stuffily.

"Dad would come home today if I wired him—"

"Never mind. The way things are going I can't take more than ten minutes off anyway."

But he found he had to because Eberly, on the phone, sounded frantic. It was ten o'clock in the morning. The Superintendent would give no details, as if he were speaking for someone else's ears besides Robert's. Robert told Perry and asked, "What could be the worst thing you could think of?"

"A bomb in the school."

Robert ran out and drove too fast. In the office of the Superintendent was the Reverend Arthur Pringle. He stood up and put out his hand, smiling with his white teeth. "Mr. Evans. A pleasure to see you again, sir."

"Hello, Mr. Pringle." Robert glanced at Eberly.

The Superintendent was not patting his fingertips or studying the ceiling. His face was grim. He was a big man, with a big face, and for the first time Robert realized how formidable he could look.

"Mr. Pringle, would you be good enough to repeat to Mr. Evans what you said to me?"

"Certainly. I came here, Mr. Evans, to lodge a complaint against one of your teachers. Mr. Wilson. He teaches mathematics, I believe."

"What's he done?"

"I don't know how to say this, quite, Mr. Evans. Embarrassing to be the father of two growing daughters, a minister—shall they or shall they not be permitted to do that Twist dance and so on. And of course people are aware of their behavior. Well,

303

your Mr. Wilson has been seen with my daughter Alice. I mean on the streets of the village in circumstances that did not suggest a teacher-student relationship. Once he was actually holding her hand. And just yesterday in his automobile. Believe me, Mr. Evans, I should hesitate to damage a man's reputation, I understand he is married and has four or five children— It's a terrible thing."

"Yes, it is," Eberly said.

"You can understand the infatuation of a young girl—their heads are so easily turned—but that a grown responsible man should take advantage of this. Surely, sir, this must be considered a crime."

"Did anything happen?" Robert asked.

"Robert!" Eberly said.

"It's something we have to know, Fenton, whether we like it or not. Wilson is being accused of a crime, and we have to know what that crime is."

"I'm afraid I don't know what your question suggests," said Mr. Pringle. "Surely the facts that I have given you are sufficient—"

"Was there more to their relationship than walking together or—what was that you said—holding her hand? That's what my question is, Mr. Pringle."

"Robert—" Eberly said softly and warningly.

"I haven't really talked to Alice about this. All I did was bring up the subject and she broke into tears. But if you are alleging any sort of improper behavior on the part of my daughter, Mr. Evans—"

"*I* am not alleging anything, Mr. Pringle."

"I am glad of that. In any case, Mr. Evans, there might be better supervision—" Pringle stood up. "You'll take care of this matter at once, then, Mr. Eberly?"

"Immediately."

"Good. And remember," Pringle added pleasantly, "that man has to be separated from the school system."

"What?" Robert said, but Mr. Pringle had left the office.

The Superintendent and the Principal looked at each other.

"This is all we need," said Eberly.

"Porter Wilson, that poor idiot. I told him—"

"You knew about this, Robert?"

"Oh, months ago, I noticed Wilson talking to the Pringle girl, and I thought it was worth cautioning him. He said that was all he did, talk to her once in a while. It seemed innocent enough."

"When a male teacher even raises an eyebrow at a female student, that's not innocent. What do you mean, 'innocent'?"

"I know. I told him."

Eberly picked up the phone and got the high school and said he wanted Porter Wilson in his office right away.

"What kind of a teacher is Wilson?"

"Very good."

"We may have to ask him to resign."

"Fenton! We don't even know if anything—"

"I'm not so sure it matters."

"I don't follow you."

"It's a case where the allegation of itself is almost enough. It's like a doctor being sued for malpractice."

"Has Pringle that much power? Suppose his target were you, or me?"

"If there were grounds, no matter how slight, it would be a tough fight. And even if we won we'd lose. As soon as you deal with children, it doesn't matter much what the field is, you've got to be so far beyond reproach that you come off your cloud only for a faculty conference. But what am I telling you this for? You know about it as well as I."

"I know, Fenton. But let's move slowly."

They sat in silence broken by the arrival of Porter Wilson. He came in, curious and a little worried. With hat in hand and topcoat still buttoned, there was something old-fashioned about him, distant in time. This was the anxious clerk in a Dickens novel, this was the minor government official in a story by Chekhov. His glasses were rimmed in metal instead of the omnipresent heavy plastic frames. His thin hair was flattened on his skull. Had he worn a high celluloid collar it would have seemed perfectly in place.

"Sit down, Wilson," Eberly said. "And take your coat off, for heaven's sake. It's warm enough in here, isn't it?"

"Yes, sir," said Wilson, nodding to Robert, taking his coat off awkwardly and hesitating before setting it down in a heap on a chair.

"Mr. Pringle was just in here. Alice Pringle's father." Eberly watched for reaction.

"Ah, yes," Wilson said. "About that last examination? It's true there was one question on work that may not have been adequately covered in class, but I upgraded every paper to account for that. Actually, Alice is an excellent student."

"Mr. Pringle was not concerned about her grades. He was concerned about your having an interest in his daughter that was not completely scholastic."

"Ah, yes," Wilson said. "Mr. Evans—had spoken to me about that. There was really nothing to cause anyone any uneasiness, Dr. Eberly."

"Just what was there?"

"I was interested in Alice, and somewhat stupidly, I'm afraid, I saw her once or twice outside of school. A walk and, yes, I did once buy her a cup of coffee. I also drove her home yesterday, Mr. Pringle could have been referring to that. It certainly was not by prearrangement, I assure you, because after Mr. Evans made me aware of how this might look to someone else, I've actually been avoiding Alice."

"Mr. Pringle thinks you should be dismissed from the school."

Wilson's face turned a muddy gray; Robert was not sure but he thought he saw the teacher sway. Robert reached out for him, then took his hand back as the teacher seemed all right.

"I don't think there are grounds for that," Wilson said. "That is, unless you're questioning my professional ability."

"No," Robert said. "Certainly not."

"I may have acted unintelligently," Wilson said. "Consider-

306

ing what has developed here, I am convinced I did. But certainly there can be no suspicion of—impropriety."

"All right, Mr. Wilson," Eberly said. "You may go back to your duties now."

"I hope I have convinced you that—"

"I'll be in touch with you," Eberly said.

Wilson left, his color barely restored.

Robert said, "You've given that young man a sleepless night or two."

"I hope that's all he suffers from this."

"What now?"

Eberly shrugged. "I'll speak to Pringle again after he has a chance to calm down. And if I can't get anywhere with him—I'll just buck this to the Board."

When Robert arrived at the parking lot, he saw Porter Wilson leaning against his car and looking off at the pond in the middle of the park. Robert went to him.

Wilson had a look on his face of a man beyond pain, having reached the serenity of a suicidal decision.

"Porter!" Robert said sharply.

"Mr. Evans. Hello."

"Would you like to sit in my car for a moment?"

"Certainly, Mr. Evans."

They got in and Robert said, "I'm glad I caught up with you, Porter, I wanted to go into this thing a little more—"

"It's shocking. I don't quite know how to tell my wife—"

"Why tell her anything? Nothing has happened yet."

"There's been no resolution," Wilson corrected him mildly. "A lot has happened."

"I don't think anything drastic will come of this," said Robert, lying.

"But the accusation was made. I'm afraid it's difficult for me to cope with a thing like this, Mr. Evans. You know why mathematics appeals to me so? It's so coolly removed from the stresses of social living—I don't seem able to handle these problems—"

"Take it easy. I need to know something from you. Please

307

tell me the truth. Was there—anything between you and Alice? I mean—anything?"

"Sexual. Is that what you mean, Mr. Evans? Well, there might have been. Alice is nearly eighteen years old. And she made me feel very much a man. So different from my relationship with my wife. Do you know my wife, Mr. Evans?"

"No."

"She has the strength in the family. She chews me up—" Wilson's eyes went vague for an instant, and Robert took him by the shoulder and pressed hard. "You asked about Alice. No, Mr. Evans. Call it lack of opportunity, prudence, maybe even lack of desire. No, Mr. Evans, there was nothing like that."

"Then I don't think we have anything to worry about," Robert said firmly.

"I haven't?" Porter Wilson said.

Robert grinned. "Principals make stupid remarks like everybody else. But this will pass."

"Thanks, Mr. Evans."

Wilson got out of the car, and Robert drove off quickly because he did not want to look again at the man's ineffectuality.

The rage began. It was like an ulcer in his stomach that had lain quiescent under the anodyne of Elizabeth's love, and now it had been prodded and provoked and was flaring mad.

He said to Elizabeth that evening, "It's as if I work for some damned academic Moloch, and I stand helplessly by and watch the sacrifices fed in. Everybody's afraid. Eberly looks like a piece of mountain, and yet the minister comes in and says calmly he wants a teacher fired—"

"He's worried about his daughter. You think a man should worry about his daughter?"

"Yes."

"You think a teacher ought to go around with a young girl?"

"No."

"What you're against," Elizabeth said, "is punishment."

"Maybe. Maybe I am. No. What am I saying? It's the manner of it I'm against. And I hate the self-protective, slimy, sadistic—"

308

"Sen-sen?"

"What's that?"

"Just some more alliteration."

"Don't kid," Robert said.

"I'm just trying to quiet you down a little."

"I don't want to be quieted down."

"Then fight them."

"Sure."

"You do what you think you should, Robert."

"Anything?"

"Look, a teacher is supposed, theoretically, to be able to support a family, right? And I'm a teacher, right?"

"I love you," he said.

"How neatly I elicited that."

At the Board meeting Farmer, Lund, and Miller were absent. Although this was an executive meeting, a man was present, sitting unobtrusively at the far side of the room, whom Robert did not know. Evidently he was known to the others, for his presence was unquestioned. The Board decided unanimously to ask for Wilson's resignation.

"No," Robert said, getting up.

Vincent said, "We've listened to all the facts, Robert. Fenton told us where Mr. Pringle stands, and you told us what Wilson said, and under the circumstances I don't see that there is anything more to discuss."

"It's not a question of anything more to discuss. I agree you heard all the facts. But there certainly is a large question about your decision to let this teacher go. He's a fine teacher. We don't have many. As a matter of fact, we have damned few. He may have committed a social error, but it certainly went no further than that. You can't just throw people out this way. This business of backing down at any sign of pressure has to stop or we'll wind up with nothing and nobody. I absolutely insist that you reconsider this."

"Insist?" Casella said.

"Yes. Insist. I am the best judge here of Porter Wilson's

competence and worth, and I want him in the school. I do not believe there is any reason to ask for his resignation."

"We've already reached that decision."

"Then take it back," said Robert, his voice, unfortunately, rising.

"Let's be calm about this," said Vincent uneasily.

"No," Robert said. "Let's not be calm about it. Let's get excited over injustice and cowardice."

Lobrige said, "I resent what Robert is saying. Vince, you're chairman. I'm not going to listen to another word."

"You're out of order," Vincent said.

"That's correct," Robert said. "I'm against your order of things. I was hired to administer a high school, and you sit here and sabotage my purpose. Why doesn't this ever happen to all the deadwood I'm forced to carry? Why does it have to happen to one of the few really good teachers we have? Why do you ignore everything this man has to give and think only of the threat implied in displeasing Mr. Pringle? I listened to that man talk about fair play and sportsmanship to the students. Isn't it about time we came out from behind all this hypocrisy and began to function like decent people with a trust?"

Casella said, "This Board hired you, Robert—"

It was surprisingly physically pleasurable, the fury churned up with the honest fear. Now, he thought wildly. You didn't have enough guts to do it for Carl Peters.

The man he didn't know was standing and asking Vincent to be heard.

"Why, sure, Johnny," Vincent said.

"Tell him off, Johnny," Lobrige said. "Let's hear from the kind of principal we've always admired."

"Loomis?" Robert said.

Loomis smiled. He was a short man with the kind of white hair that looks as soft as the hair of an infant. He had a small, bitter-sweet mouth. His voice was at once gentle and strong.

"Perspective," Loomis said. "I suppose the only way to really have any is to die. This almost happened to me when I retired. (You know, I never met your new principal?) Some idiot once said that retired people had to die. I just realized I had to break this foolish notion. Nineteen twenty-two—that's when I started as a teacher. May I ramble for a bit? I won't take much of your time, I promise. We had the junior and senior high in the same building, and maybe two hundred, two hundred and fifty students. We didn't have any money, we couldn't afford small classes, for example, none of the marvelous things you have today. What we did do—we decided that a student was more important than the subject matter. And we followed that as a rule, I did till the day I left. We tried to hire teachers who believed that. Sure, we had the same percentage of duds then, Mr. Principal. That's what you'll always have to work with. After a while I had in my classes some of the children of students, and even some of the grandchildren. I was proud of the fact that I knew each student. I felt you had to be close to them. I did scout work, Sunday school, I tried to be interested in the things children were doing. I was proud that a parent could come to me and say 'you know more about my son than I do.' My office was always open. There was no guidance department, the Principal did it all. Now—how does a principal function with a thousand students? Why, not even all the teachers know one another—imagine, *two* teachers' rooms. It was too much for me, and I was glad to retire.

"Now you've got Mr. Evans. He is not me, Sally Lobrige, and if he were, he could not handle his job any more than I could. But I know what he's done. He's making a fine school out of Pine Hills, and let's face it—Sally, Vince, Fenton—I was letting it run down. I couldn't hold it, my hands weren't big enough. The hands of Mr. Evans are. Now he wants to hold on to a good teacher. Isn't that what a principal is for? I listened to him and I was proud. I've heard enough here to know that Art Pringle is trying to tell you what to do. I've known Art since he was a boy. He's a good person, and a good man of the church, but he likes to stretch himself out a little too much. Well, don't let him. Don't let anybody stop you from doing the job you're supposed to do. And don't let yourself take a chance of losing a good teacher—or a good principal."

311

After that the Board saved face with a little more discussion, but there wasn't much to discuss.

Robert and Loomis walked out together.

Loomis said, "I understand we're about to become related."

"Yes."

"Elizabeth doesn't know I'm back yet, why don't we both go to the house and surprise her?"

"All right."

"You don't talk much, do you."

"Give me a minute. I have to get used to the idea that I like you."

"Come on," Loomis said. "Can't you walk a little faster?"